Sing Sweet Nightingale

A Snowberry Novel

Rebecca Rennick

Copyright © 2024 by Rennick Rennick

ISBN: 979-8-218-45837-9

All rights reserved.

No part of this book may be reproduced or transmitted in any form or by any means, electronic or mechanical, including mechanical photocopying, recording, or by any information storage and retrieval system, without permission in writing.

This book is a work of fiction and any resemblance to persons, living or dead, or places, events or locales is purely coincidental. The characters are productions of the author's imagination and used fictionally.

Cover by BloodWrit
Map by Pinapali
Formatting by Rebecca Rennick

For anyone who always wanted a giant furry werewolf to cuddle ... and knot.

Content Warning

This is a paranormal romance novel that includes explicit sexual content, some including non-human beings. It is not completely a monster romance but monster adjacent. If that's not your jam then read at your own risk. This book also includes cute cuddly wolves, werewolf shifters, mates, biting, knotting, and a small amount of primal chasing, as well as mention of emotional abuse from a relative.

Prologue

Lottie

My black Prada boot cracks the glass windowpane and splinters into a spider web pattern across the surface. *Good. That'll irritate my mother when she has to get it fixed.* You'd think being a twenty-five-year-old adult would deter me from throwing a tantrum. You'd be wrong. It's the only way to vent my frustration at the woman who's taken control of my life like a blonde Hitler in stilettos.

Cracking a window so that she has to deal with it as my overlord is the least I can do to pay her back for the atrocity that is my life. Okay, maybe not an atrocity, but definitely indentured servitude.

This is not what I expected when I signed that stupid contract. I thought hiring my mom as my manager would be great. It would be easy. She knows me, knows my style, my music, my voice. She'll look out for me; I am her daughter, after all. Silly me, forgetting she doesn't see me as her daughter and never spent time getting to know who I am or asking what I want.

All she wanted was a cash cow, a golden goose, Midas's golden touch. She wanted someone to support her and give her the life *she* always wanted. Not the life I wanted.

And now I'm stuck with her. At least until the contract expires. Which couldn't come soon enough. I know she'll try to get me to sign a new one, but no way that's going to happen. I already gave her the last ten years of my life. I wrote and recorded music the label wanted, touring and performing according to their schedule. Bending over fucking backward to fulfill my "duties" according to the contract I signed.

"I hate her! I hate him! I fucking hate them all!" I scream, ripping my other boot off my foot and throwing it towards a second window creating a matching spiderweb crack.

"What did she do this time?" Luna, my ever-present bodyguard and only real friend, asks.

Standing at attention at the entrance to the sitting room attached to my private quarters, Luna watches on in amused concern as I pace back and forth, stomping around like a petulant child. It's well warranted this time. It is every time. The things she does are cruel and selfish. But from the outside, people don't see that. They see a loving, doting mother who helped create a world-famous pop star. Barf.

Picking up a throw pillow from the couch, I swing it like a baseball bat against the cushions, screaming out my frustrations. When I feel a bit of my anger dying out, I stand straight and face Luna breathing heavily.

"You remember my *boyfriend*?" I spit out the word like acid.

"The pretty boy who didn't know when to quit flirting with me until I almost broke his fingers? Yeah. What about him?" she replies snarkily. She never liked him as much as I did.

"Well, you were right about him. Not only was he a

relentless flirt, but it turns out he didn't even like me."

"Explain." Luna's voice turns harsh and feral, as I've noticed it does whenever there's a threat to me. She really is the best bodyguard.

"My oh-so-benevolent mother and manager *hired* him to be my boyfriend. She paid him in publicity and cash to play the part. Our chance meeting? Arranged. He knew who I was, thought I was hot, but had no real feelings for me."

I continue my angry pacing. Not only mad at my mother but also mad at the ass face I thought cared for me.

"You want to know how I found out? Cause it's a doozy." I don't wait for Luna to reply. I know she's listening *very* intently. "I found him with his pants around his ankles and balls deep, pounding away into one of my backup dancers. Yeah, that's right. *My* backup dancer. The one who's supposed to be loyal to me. Like he was supposed to be loyal to me. Apparently, he's gone through most of them while I was on tour. Because apparently fucking a pop star to ride her coattails to fame wasn't enough. He needed to bang his way through the other wannabes, too. Promising them their fifteen minutes of fame because he's my boyfriend and can do that sort of thing. What a complete douche canoe. I knew he was a horndog, but I at least thought he was a monogamous horndog. I mean, for fuck's sake, we did it like twice a day when he was traveling with me on tour."

I growl out a loud exhale and plop down onto the couch, exhausted from the emotional rollercoaster I just rode.

This is not how I planned to spend my first day home after months away on the international leg of my tour. I just returned home to Los Angeles for a short break before starting the six-month-long American leg of the tour. The last leg of the tour, thank fuck. Tours are exhausting. They used to be fun back in the beginning. Now I feel like a robot doing as I'm told. Rehearsal, fittings, hair, makeup, perform, sleep, travel, repeat. No more fun. Only the money-making machine they've turned me into. For once, I wish my music wouldn't sell so well. Then maybe I could take a vacation. A little time to myself.

"Where is he now?"

I tilt my head back to glance over at Luna, who is still standing where she normally is, when she watches over me. Luna's been my bodyguard for about five years now. My mother was skeptical about hiring a female to guard me, but I made sure she knew Luna was more than capable of doing the job and doing it better than a man. If I were going to be with this person, nearly twenty-four-seven, having a female instead of a male would have made me far more comfortable being myself in private.

Luna is tall and stunning, with a muscular physique I envy. I may be fit, thanks to the forced workout regime and custom-tailored meal plan, but she's ripped—six-pack and all. She could probably hold me over her head and snap me in half without breaking a sweat, which is why I trust her to keep the weirdos away.

Her dark brown hair is pulled back in a tight ponytail, revealing rows of gold earrings lining the entirety of the shell of her ear. She wears a tiny earpiece that's nearly invisible when communicating with other members of my security team. But in private, only Luna is present. Striking gold eyes stare back at me from tawny bronze skin, lids lowered in a menacing glare.

"Why? Are you going to kill him?" I ask seriously. Shit like that happens all the time. It wouldn't surprise me if she did.

"Not personally," she states flatly.

"Okay then. I have no idea. After he chastised me for interrupting him and not letting him 'express himself sexually,'" I say in a mocking tone using air quotes, because, yes, he actually said that. "Then, telling me he was tired of playing the part of loving boyfriend, which my mother had *hired* him to do, I left. So, he's either still fucking my now ex-back-up dancer on his kitchen island or who the fuck knows where."

Normally, Luna would have been with me as my primary guard, but occasionally, she does rotate with others. She has a life, too; I can't take up all of it. I have no doubt in my mind that if she were with me, she would have beat the crap out of Asshat, as I'm now referring to him.

She nods and lifts her wrist to speak into the microphone there. "Remove Mr. Lewis from the approved list of guests for Alexandria."

I really wish I didn't have to go by that name in private as well as public. But it's not like my security staff knows my real name. Not that Alexandria isn't my real name. It's just my middle name. My mother and the record label thought Charlotte was too sweet and too southern, and that's not the image they were going for. They wanted mainstream, sparkly, fashionable "it" pop girl. So, Charlotte was out, and Alexandria was in. I think they wanted me to be like Cher or Madonna with just one name, and they succeeded.

There are always people out there who are so obsessed with me that they try to discover my real name. Thankfully my team has suppressed that info like the plague. The public world only knows me as Alexandria the singing sensation, not Charlotte Pickle the little girl with a guitar and a voice too big for her body.

Once upon a time, I wanted to be a star, to write my music and sing it for the world to hear. But that was when it was mine when I was me, not this thing they've made me into. Singing is still in my blood—I know it is, I can feel it—but performing has become my nightmare fuel.

"Don't worry about him, Lottie. He won't be getting near you again." Luna switches back to calling me by the nickname my father gave me when I was a toddler. The one that is more me than Alexandria. It's what I would prefer to have gone by if I were singing and recording what I wanted and not what the label wanted. Now, I'm secretly happy my mother forced me to go by Alexandria because if I produce any of my real music in the future, I'm going by Lottie, and I don't want it to be connected to Alexandria in the least.

This career and life may have given me anything and everything materialistic I could ever want, but they lack the substantially important stuff, like happiness and love.

"Thanks, Luna. Although I don't think that's an issue. He didn't seem to want to be anywhere near me anymore. I think he's more than done with me and I him."

"His loss."

"Agreed."

A semblance of a smirk pulls at one side of her lips. Her version of a smile.

"What would I do without you, Luna?"

"Probably murder your mother in her sleep."

I turn an open-mouthed gawk at her. "Was that a joke?"

"Oh, please. You know I'm hilarious."

She kind of is in her own dark and cynical way. At least she always knows how to make me laugh. What does that say about me then?

I turn to look out my now cracked windows. Outside, it's dark; small lights line the walkways of the expansive yard and pool area below. My rooms are on the second floor of the mansion I call home. It's never felt like a real home, more like a prison. Since I can't ever leave without permission or guards. With gilded walls and marbled floors. High-end electronics and state-of-the-art appliances. Filled with art by people I've never heard of but are apparently worth twenty-five thousand dollars for a few splashes of paint on a canvas.

There are rooms for just about everything you could ever want in this house, and I hate it all. That is why I stay in my quarters, mostly allowing my mother and team free range over the rest of the mansion. Only venturing out to the kitchen or gym, sometimes the pool, when I have a free afternoon.

But if I want to go anywhere? Tsh. Forget about it.

"You know I never wanted any of this." My statement surprises Luna. I can tell because her brow furrows.

Sensing an impending breakdown, she rounds the oversized couch and sits on the armchair nearby. None of my other security would dare be so casual around me, but Luna's different. She's like an overprotective big sister and the concerned mother I never had.

"I just wanted to write music and play my guitar. Sing my songs. I suppose it's my own fault for allowing her to take control of everything. I'm sick of playing the music they want me to. Wearing the clothes they pick out, styling my hair the way they want."

I finger the long blonde locks that they told me I couldn't cut because it's "part of my look." If I want to go out for any reason, it always has to be approved by my mother. Then the glam squad has to pick an appropriate outfit, and hair and makeup must be perfectly paired. All those photos you see of celebrities in sweats with messy hair and big sunglasses? You'll never find one of me like that. My mother won't allow it. My photos are always immaculate.

I fucking hate it.

Since when did everything have to be so perfect? Sometimes I just want to spill coffee down the front of my white silk blouse just to fuck up their plans for my scheduled paparazzi shots.

"All I want is to go grocery shopping by myself, wearing jeans and a slouchy t-shirt with my hair in a messy top knot. But nooooo. The glam squad won't allow it without three hours of prep time and an outfit that costs more than a car. And I could never go alone. That's preposterous," I mock.

I can't do anything like a normal person anymore. Sometimes, I just want to go for a walk or out for a coffee without an entire security team or swarms of fans mobbing me. Fame was something I had never really considered in my dreams of being a musician. I only thought of the music, not the effect it would have on my private life.

"Do you know I can't even pick out my own underwear? Once, I tried to buy a pair of cotton bikinis; you know, for those days when you just want to lounge around and be comfortable in pajamas and eat ice cream, and she wouldn't let me. I love a thong as much as the next girl, but sometimes you just want to be comfortable in a pair of granny panties. Why can't I just have a pair of granny panties like a normal twenty-five-year-old girl?"

I'm whining and I really don't care. I've come to the end of my rope. My limits have been reached and I'm ready to jump off that cliff.

"I'm done, Luna. I can't do this anymore," I say softly.

She's quiet for a minute, watching me slowly sink and melt into the couch, hoping it will swallow me whole and that I can disappear without a trace.

Wait.

I sit straight up in my seat, a new wave of energy revitalizing my worn-out nerves.

"That's it."

"What's it?"

"I'm going to run away. Disappear. They can't force me to be their singing puppet if they can't find me. I can take the cash I have stashed away and just leave."

Why didn't I think of this earlier? I've imagined running away many times before but always gave up. The guilt well bred into me from my mother. But now? Now I have zero fucks left to give. I'm older, and I have the cash squirreled away because when you're the breadwinner and are put on a monthly allowance, you tend to hoard it like a chipmunk preparing for winter.

"What about the rest of your tour? And breaking the contract?"

"I don't care anymore if I break the contract. They can have all the money, properties, cars, fashion lines, merchandise, and royalties. I don't fucking care anymore. They can have it all. As long as they leave me out of it."

"And the fans?" Luna adds quietly.

I may despise what I've become professionally, but the fans still love it, and I respect them. It's not their fault my life is the way it is. They don't deserve to feel the backlash of my rash decision.

This tour has been sold out for months, and thousands of people are waiting to see me perform. Not all my songs are forced hits. Some I like; they were from before when I was writing for the love of it and are some of my top-grossing singles. I can manage six more months to finish the tour.

"You're right. The fans don't deserve it. I'll finish out the tour. But after that, I'm running away. I'm through with all of this."

"Fine by me."

Luna cocks her head at me and looks me over quizzically.

"What?" I ask.

She's looked at me this way a few times before but always brushed it off and changed the subject when I asked. Maybe this time she'll actually tell me what she's thinking.

"There's always been something about you, Lottie. Something extra that I've never been able to put my finger on."

"Is it my winning personality? The witty comebacks and perfectly timed puns?"

She doesn't laugh at my joke and just keeps eying me in a way that makes me think she's seeing more than what's on the surface.

"It's not that. It's something more."

"More?"

She doesn't respond to my question but changes the subject. "If you're so set on running away, I might have a place you can run to. Somewhere safe, secluded, and quiet. There are people there I know. That I trust."

"And where is this magical place that you speak of where no one could possibly recognize me and immediately post a photo of me on social media tagging the location?"

If such a place exists, I'll move there in a heartbeat.

"It's a small town in Montana not on any maps. They like their anonymity and seclusion. They like that no one knows where their town is. They're not into social media and gossip sites. Half of them probably don't even know who you are, let alone what you look like. If we cut your hair and give you a more average look, get you a few pairs of jeans and slouchy t-shirts, and you'll fit right in."

I perk up a bit. This place sounds like a dream. There has to be a catch.

"What's the catch?" I ask suspiciously.

"No catch. People there like to keep to themselves. So, if you do the same and respect their right to privacy, they'll respect yours. Now, that doesn't mean they don't like to be in each other's business; like any small town, there is gossip, but it's all word of mouth. Nothing online. They're friendly and although mostly wary of newcomers, I'll ensure you have a local guide to help you fit in."

I stare at her in disbelief, far too hopeful what she says is true and a little peeved she never mentioned it earlier.

"Why are you telling me about this now? Why not years ago?"

"You weren't ready to leave years ago. You couldn't. Now that your contract is ending, you can leave and not worry about what might follow you legally. You can start over if you want, or just take a break and return and do your next record differently. It's up to you."

It's up to me.

Words I never thought I would hear. Nothing has been up to me for the past ten years. But now, here it is. My future freedom dangles in front of me like a carrot on a string. Should I reach out and grab it? Or, like so many times in the past, will it pull just out of my reach?

"I choose?"

"You choose."

"Okay. I choose to leave. But it has to be secret. No one but you can know. I can't trust anyone else."

Luna smiles, actually smiles, *with teeth*, flashing her extra-pointy canines. It's beautiful and scary, and she could probably keep all the weirdos away from me without ever lifting a finger if she smiled wickedly like that at them. And I knew right then that Luna would do anything to help me achieve my goal, to keep me safe.

In a matter of months, I'll be free. There will be no glam squad, no record label forcing me to record only upbeat, poppy songs, and no demanding momager telling me what I can't wear, eat, or go. I'll be free, making all the decisions myself, and I can't wait.

Chapter 1
Lottie

If I had to choose a city to abscond from my life, Las Vegas would be it. Thankfully, that happens to be where the last show of my tour takes place. It worked out perfectly.

Trying to plan an escape from the mansion or a less populated city would be more difficult. There wouldn't be an ever-present flowing crowd of people to conceal one inconspicuous girl like there is here. Night or day, thousands of people are ever-changing on the streets and in the casinos. Even with the most cameras in one place in the world, a person can still disappear amongst the crowds. And that's exactly what I want.

Luna helped me plan the whole thing. Contacting her surprisingly confidential people. One was a girl named Ginger who got me set up in a cabin in Snowberry, Montana. Even the name sounds perfect. I'm so excited to be leaving that my final performance has a little extra pep to it that my team misinterprets as a performance high.

Really, I'm just nervous my mother will interfere or catch me. That something will go wrong, or one of the few people who know what's going on will spill the beans and rat me out for a hefty payday. I'll just have to keep my fingers crossed and stay optimistic that things will go my way for once.

My personal assistant Sabrina and my extensive security team meet me the moment I step out of my dressing room backstage at the Sphere, where I just finished my last song. I'm still wearing my closing outfit: thigh-high silver boots with sparkling Swarovski crystals, metallic high-waisted booty shorts, and matching crop top. I feel a little like a walking disco ball. I think my stylist wanted me to be seen from space. Which is a shame, considering it was an indoor venue.

Not changing out of my stage outfit and taking a visible route back to my hotel suite is all part of the plan. Draw attention to myself, show off for a bit, make sure I'm seen and adored so my mother will be more likely to leave me alone for long enough to escape.

My security team today consists of no less than six large men dressed in black with matching earpieces, Luna at their lead. Ever since the inception of our plan, she's stuck closer to me than she had been before. Taking less time away and being my silent cheerleader. Every time I looked at her, she would give me a secretive smile, saying, "Keep going, you're almost there." Even now I can't help but smirk in her direction.

Keeping this secret from Sabrina has been difficult. As my personal assistant, it's literally her job to be my shadow and get me what I need. Wedging time out to discuss the specifics with Luna felt like I was part of the CIA, but we did it. Late-night rendezvous and whispered conversations in the back of limos have all led to this—here and now.

Hours, I am hours away from freedom. I've contractually

fulfilled all my obligations. The tour is over, and I can leave with no guilt weighing me down.

My circle of black-clad muscle guides Sabrina and me backstage and, under Luna's direction, towards the area where fans are known to wait to see the musicians and performers up close and personal on their way out. Since my mother is off "managing" whatever it is she manages at the end of a show—probably the paycheck to make sure they pay as much as she can squeeze out of them—Sabrina is the only one I have left to deal with.

We step out into the dry Nevada heat that never seems to dissipate. Thankfully, the sun is far beyond the horizon, and the strip is lit by its ever-present flashing neon lights.

A crowd of over a hundred waits for me, and I smile, for once not having to fake it. I'm actually happy right now.

"Is this the way you're supposed to be going? I'm sure I heard your Miss Susan mention something about avoiding signing autographs after the show. I don't think she would approve of this change."

Poor Sabrina. She's a nice girl but far too concerned about losing her job because she didn't follow every minute instruction from my mother, who asked to call her Miss Susan like a kindergarten teacher. Allowing them to just call her Susan was too informal for "the help," and calling her Ms. Anderson made her feel old. Sadly, Sabrina wouldn't be the first PA to be fired over such a thing, and it pains me to see the panic and fear in her pretty brown eyes.

She pushes her thick-rimmed glasses up her nose, magnifying her dark green eyes, which shift back and forth from me to the crowd behind me. Shifting her weight from foot to foot, she can't help but fiddle with the tablet in her hand. I grab her free hand, forcing her to stop twitching and look at me.

"It's okay Sabrina, I talked to her about it earlier. I wanted to do something special for the fans at my last stop on the tour. As a matter of fact, I plan on taking a bit of time to myself to recover and relax. Why don't you take the next few days off as I won't need you? Okay?"

I squeeze her hand and give her a reassuring smile hoping she won't freak the fuck out, and run right to my mother to clear it with her. From the concerned pinch to her mouth, I have a feeling that might be exactly what she's thinking.

"Don't worry about my mother. You're not going to get in trouble with her. I'll even throw in a bonus for all your hard work. Thank you so much for everything you do for me. Take this time to go see your family or visit a spa."

Sabrina blows out a breath that deflates her entire posture.

"You sure? I don't want to leave you if you need me."

"I am absolutely sure. I'll let you know if I need you, but don't bother worrying about me. Focus on yourself for once."

She nods, and I hug her before having one of the security team lead her back to her hotel room. Like most of the crew and team, I'm hoping she leaves tomorrow as planned. We craftily arranged for almost everyone to leave the day after the end of the tour, while I had decided to "hide out" in my penthouse suite in Vegas for a few days to decompress and have a little me time.

It took a while to convince my mother of it, but after months of wearing her down, we got her to agree to it. But I won't stay in Vegas and get spa treatments and room service. If all goes well, no one will even notice I'm gone for multiple days.

I walk out through the barricaded walkway and stop to sign autographs and pose for selfies, knowing these fans will most likely never have the opportunity again if I decide to remain in hiding.

After a good half hour, we finally reach the limo, and I get in, followed closely by Luna. I flop back into the seat and relax every muscle in my body, releasing every ounce of tension and anxiety I can.

My head lulls back onto the leather seat, and my long blonde ponytail pokes at the back of my head. I growl and shift my head from side to side until I'm comfortable enough not to rip my hair out of my skull.

"We'll be back to the hotel in twenty and back in your suite in no more than thirty. By tomorrow morning you'll be well on your way."

She doesn't say to where , just in case someone is listening. They wouldn't know what specifically we're talking about or where I'm on my way to. Could be to vacation, home, relaxing, whatever.

I smile up at the limo ceiling, imagining being in nature, in the forest with the trees and open sky, with absolutely no one around, especially no momager.

The daydream puts me at ease as it has over the past six months, and the last bits of anxiety drift away on the heated Nevada breeze.

"Almost there," I whisper to myself. Luna's keen hearing picks up on it; she always hears no matter how softly I whisper.

"Don't worry, Lottie. I've got you. Everything's set and nothing will get in the way. I have everything in line to ensure no one will even consider bothering you for the next twenty-four to forty-eight hours."

"I think I may have gone insane without you, Luna. What can I ever do to repay you?" I ask, swiveling to look at her sitting at my side. She turns to me and gives me a serious look.

"Nothing. I want nothing from you other than for you to

be happy and live your life as you see fit. No one should have another controlling their life. You deserve so much more, and I just hope you find it." She speaks in low, hushed words. Her voice laced with hopeful determination.

"Thank you."

"You're welcome."

As promised, I'm back at the door to my suite in the Bellagio in no more than thirty minutes. My anxiety and nerves all but replaced with relief and anticipation for tomorrow. It can't come any sooner.

Opening the door to the penthouse suite, I feel like I'm walking on air, that is until I notice a shock of platinum blonde hair sitting at the bar, sipping a glass of amber liquid. My light-as-air high becomes a rapid freefall without a parachute.

Fuck.

I took so long signing autographs and being seen by the fans that my mother had time to sneak into my room. I was hoping she wouldn't do this, considering everything we did to make sure she stayed far away from my room and me after the show.

"Mom. What are you doing here?" I can't keep the shock of surprise out of my voice, and I don't try.

"Alexandria. What took you so long? I thought you were heading right back to start your *weekend of relaxation*?" Utter derision drips from her tone.

She doesn't approve of me taking time off. She doesn't like when the workhorse needs a break. In her mind, I should be working nonstop to create more award-winning records and bring in more money. That's all she's cared about for the last decade. Money and how much of it I can make for her.

"I thought I would give the fans a little something special to end the tour with. What's it to you? I thought you would be at the tables by now. Or on your way to wherever the hell it is, you go when you're not micromanaging every second of my life."

I can't help but be snarky with her. I have to get one last dig in because after tomorrow, I hope not to speak with her for many moons.

"Oh, don't be so dramatic, Alexandria."

I'd argue with her about calling me Alexandria and instead Lottie like Dad used to when I was younger before he died, but there's no point. I think that's why she doesn't call me by the nickname; It reminds her too much of our lives before his death and before all the fame and fortune. She doesn't want to remember the before. Not like I do. If she could, she would permanently wipe the memories from her mind, whereas I just want to return to those times. Playing guitar with my dad while singing along and dancing around the living room, enjoying the music. Enjoying life.

That's where my love of music came from, my father. It's because of him that I was drawn to music. He nurtured my natural talent, showing me what music can do and how much happiness it can create. How music can affect others and allow them to feel what I'm feeling through my words.

After he died, I made sure to continue playing, writing, and singing because I knew that's what he would have wanted me to do.

Unfortunately, after he died, something in my mom changed. The free, fun spirit she used to be with my father disappeared, and the stress of being a single parent and supporting us got to her. That's when she became the money-hungry, greedy, controlling, unfeeling person she is today.

I sigh and clench my teeth, biting back all the cruel things I want to say to her. They would only make things worse, and even though I despise her at this moment, she is still my mother, and I don't want to say something I can't take back.

"Why are you here, mother?" I ask again, hoping to get whatever the hell this is over with so she'll leave and I can prepare for tomorrow.

"I just don't understand why you need to stay here and take a few days off. Why can't we go home, and you can relax there?"

She stands and flips her long platinum hair over her shoulder. I think she makes me keep mine long so we can match, and people can easily associate her with me. Since she has no talent, the most fame she's ever going to get is being known as my mother and manager.

"Because I'm always in that house. I just want to be somewhere different and just have some time away from everything and everyone."

She scoffs, and I scowl. The fact that I have to beg my mother for a few days of alone time to do as I please is ridiculous. But I'm so close to the finish line that I'm not going to trip now by arguing with her and losing my window of opportunity. Once I'm away and out of her clutches, I'll be able to breathe and make all the decisions for myself without her breathing fire down my neck.

"Look, Mom, it's only a few days, and we already agreed to it. I have massage therapists, cosmetologists, dermatologists, and estheticians all booked and ready. Just let me have this. I've been going nonstop for the past six months since the American leg of the tour started, and I need this in order to keep going."

I don't often try to sweet talk her or use begging to get what I want; normally, I argue and strong-arm her to get anything out of her.

I give her my most dejected and pleading look without

looking too hopeful.

"Fine," she concedes in a clipped tone.

I want to scream, but instead, I drop my shoulders and soften my expression to hopefully make her think this was all her doing, that I'm so grateful she gave me such a gift. She loves feeling like the powerful one in our dynamic.

"Thank you, Mom."

"Just be ready to get back to work when it's over. We have a meeting scheduled with the label about your next album and some legal things we need to go over."

She grabs her sparkly clutch, and the echoing click of her stilettos on the tile floor as she crosses the space makes me want to cringe. That sound is the equivalent of the Jaws theme song in my mind.

I also notice how she glosses over "legal things," like I don't know my contract is ending, and she wants to try and trap me in another one without my knowledge. She has no idea what I know. She likes to micromanage from a distance, so she never saw me reading and rereading my contract and doing research on my rights and the consequences of breaking a contract.

I know that as of the moment I stepped off that stage, my contract was complete and fulfilled, leaving me legally free to do whatever the fuck I please. But if I let on that, I know that she would no doubt somehow ensure I could never escape. She would have people following me and keeping tabs on me more so than the regular security check-ins. She thinks she has me so far under her thumb that I would never even consider leaving. And that's exactly how I want her. Naïve and blind.

"Will do, Mom. See you in a few days."

I lead her with a guiding hand towards the door, subtly telling her to get the fuck out. She does with nothing more than a wave over her shoulder. She really has forgotten what it means to be a mother.

I exhale with a relieved breath when she's on the other side of the locked door.

"That was close."

"If she wouldn't have left on her own, I would have made her."

"I would have loved to see that but I'm glad she didn't argue more. If she goes willingly, she's less likely to return."

Luna side-eyes me like I'm speaking Klingon. I just roll my eyes at her. My mother is gone and there's only one night left between me and freedom.

Chapter 2

Lottie

Holy shit, is all I can think as I stare at myself in the mirror. My long blonde strands that have been my signature look for years are gone. My hair is short, not even brushing the tops of my shoulders with a soft wave, and I feel a million pounds lighter. The long strands of evidence of the hair massacre have been swept up and bagged, leaving no proof of a crime, and I'm dressed in the pale blue and white uniform shirt of the treatment team that showed up two hours ago.

I'll fit right in with the small group of women. They brought along girls who looked similar to me in height or hair color so that I could blend in with the group. No one will look twice when I leave with them. All I have to do is keep my eyes and face averted, and Luna will do the rest.

I can't bring much with me since that would be suspicious, an esthetician rolling out a massive suitcase that they didn't have when they arrived. So, I can only pack a small rolling suitcase that'll blend in with the other rolling cases of products they brought.

Because of that, I had to leave a lot behind. Maybe I can get it back in the future, like my vinyl record collection, custom-built guitars, and my father's guitar, which is my most priceless possession. I've only packed the necessities that would be too difficult to get in the small town like my favorite broken-in shoes, bras that fit just right, and professionally curated hair products, which will now last a lot longer with the lack of hair I'll have to deal with. Not to mention the amount of cash I have in my bag. Cash is untraceable, and I was told most of the businesses in Snowberry are cash-based.

"Are you ready?" Luna enters the bathroom and watches me through the reflection in the mirror.

"So ready I could barely sleep last night."

"Good. You have your plan, the map, and cash. Do you remember where to go and how to avoid being seen? What to say when someone recognizes you?"

"Yes. Keep my head down, don't talk to anyone if I don't have to, and if they recognize me, play it off like I'm a common girl who happens to look like a celebrity and get it all the time. I'm going to cross over to Caesars Palace, pick up a cab from the taxi line, and take it to the used car dealership. I'll pick something simple to blend in and then drive."

Luna nods approvingly. She wouldn't be as approving if she knew I also planned to make a little detour to the Caesar forum shops before catching that taxi. But I have to get more clothes than the few I packed, and I doubt there will be many places to get good-quality pieces in Snowberry.

I can't help it; I grew accustomed to wearing name-brand clothing over the years. I can't stand cheap materials and ill-fitting designs. I'll keep it basic, nothing flashy. Swear. Okay, maybe there'll be a few colorful dresses, but no red carpet-looks. I won't need those anymore. Definitely multiple pairs of jeans.

"Alright, let's get you out of here."

Luna leads me into the living room, where the five other women stand waiting patiently. I don't know how she convinced this many people to keep my secret. They must know who I am with all the security and secrecy, not to mention, ya know, my face and all. Since they were tasked with making me not look like me.

The other women position themselves in a group around me, sandwiching me between them so I blend in with the bland uniforms and cases. I grip my small, rolling suitcase at my side and take in a deep breath.

"Now remember, call me when you buy a new phone. Prepaid from a random stop-n-shop. No major chain stores and no long-term phone plans. Out of the box only," she clarifies. We've been over this already, but I don't argue and listen dutifully.

"I will. Thank you again, Luna. I'll update you and let you know if or when I'll return. All the emails are scheduled to be sent out tomorrow night, so no one should freak out until then. I'd advise you to be far away from my mother around that time."

I chuckle and try to smile, but I'm so nervous someone will stop me from leaving that it falls as fast as it arrives. They have no right to stop me. I'm an adult who can make choices for myself, but I know they would try. It's their job.

Stepping out from the protective camouflage circle, I wrap my arms around Luna as tightly as I can. I'm going to miss her and her stern looks. I don't expect her to return the hug, but she wraps an arm around my shoulders and squeezes.

"You'll be fine, Lottie, I promise. My friends will look out for you, and if you need anything, you let me know. I'll try to keep your mom in line while you're gone."

"Good luck. I haven't been able to do that in years; I don't know how you'll be able to accomplish it in days," I snort, releasing her from my death grip.

"Oh, I have my ways." She gives me a conspiratorial wink, and I believe she *does* have her ways.

"Just don't kill her, okay? I like you too much to see you imprisoned."

"You got it, kid."

I take my place again in the middle of the group and brush my hair over my cheeks, concealing my face as best I can without looking suspicious.

"Alright, ladies, you know what to do."

They huddle closer but not too close, and we all step as one towards the door. My heart races in my chest, beating erratically. This is it. I'm leaving. Finally. I can't believe it. My palms are sweaty, my knees are weak, and I feel like I'm about to bust out into an Eminem rap.

"Here."

One of the women with blonde hair a shade darker than mine but the same length hands me a disposable face mask.

"You look a little nervous. Wear this to conceal your face; no one questions it when someone wears one anymore. It'll help."

"Thanks."

I take the mask and eagerly tuck the elastic bands around my ears. I hate wearing these things and hated them even more when we were forced to during the pandemic, but I'm now happy about it. I'm happy that no one will look at me weird for walking around wearing one—at least until I get out of the hotel and across the street. Maybe I'll wait until I'm out of town, just in case.

Luna opens the double doors to the suite, and we all file out together. The guards posted on the outside of the doors side-eye our group and watch as we pass. Luna steps between our group and the head guard diverting his attention so he doesn't notice the one additional person in our party.

"Alexandria wants privacy for the next few days, so no one will be in or out except me. I'll be staying with her the entire time and will update you if anything is needed."

I send a silent thank you to Luna and keep moving forward with the group. The guards don't stop us. Why would they? They're there to keep people out, not in. Well, except for me.

We make our way to the elevator, waiting for only a few moments before one arrives. We then make our way down to the casino floor, where the others split off and head towards the parking garage, and I head towards the street exit that'll lead me to the bridge walkway to Caesars Palace.

I leave the mask on but unbutton the uniform shirt and shove it in a trash can once I get outside. Leaving me in a pair of black leggings and a plain white T-shirt.

The Forum Shops are on the opposite side of the casino, so I'll have to cross through the floor first. No one even looks twice at me. Just another body in the masses. They're all wrapped up in their own little worlds, gambling, drinking, partying. Jesus Christ, it's not even noon, and half the people in here are already drunk or still drunk from the night before.

It's been so long since I've been out in public without an entourage or screaming fans that it's a bit surreal. Just being another face in the crowd. It's like breathing fresh air after being trapped inside a smoke-filled room.

I make it to the shops without incident, and it feels like a bloody miracle. So, I quickly make my way through the shops, first into Louis Vuitton to pick up a suitcase—black, of course, to blend in—plus a new purse. What? A girl needs a purse. It's useful and practical.

After I have my luggage, I fill it with items from the shops, getting a few pairs of jeans for the first time since I was fifteen. I try not to spend too much time in each shop not wanting to linger in this city but wanting to get what I need. Once my two suitcases are full, along with a small weekend bag, I make my way to the taxi stand at the front of the hotel and head out of the city. By this time tomorrow, I'll be so far away and untraceable that no one but Luna can find me.

Perfect.

Chapter 3

Hunter

"Thank you, Dottie. I'll look into it." I hang up the phone with an aggravated sigh.

I do not need this today. It's burger day at Dottie's, which makes it much more disappointing that she called and informed me I would be missing out on my favorite meal. Now, there's an issue I have to attend to immediately.

"What was that about?" my younger sister Ginger asks innocently from where she sits across from me.

Her legs are crossed nonchalantly, and her ridiculously impractical heels sway with the light bobbing of her foot. Normally, she doesn't bother me during lunch, especially on Burger Day. But for some reason, she decided to just 'pop in to say hello.'

Ginger does a lot of work for the town through my office, but most of it is remote from her home office. She doesn't need to physically come into the office for any reason. I think she's doing it just to annoy me. It must be my lucky day because now

I have two things annoying me: my sister and the report of a suspicious male elf checking into the motel.

We don't get many elves in town, especially now that Vincent has failed to get me to sell my land to him; elves are unwelcome visitors. Truthfully, they're never really welcomed in Snowberry but more tolerated.

Elves are the scum of the non-human world, sticking mostly to large cities where they can swindle and steal to their heart's content. Most don't bother us here in our small, quiet town in the woods. There are a few in residence, but they don't partake in the crooked ways of their brethren. We still tend to closely watch them after they settle here, but those here have been for years.

This newcomer staying in the motel is undoubtedly one of Vincent's crew. Here to scout out new tactics to force me to sell or cause mayhem. I don't know why he has become so interested in our town and my property lately, but he'll never get an acre.

Whoever the mayor is always has their name on the deed to the land the majority of the town sits on. But I also happen to own the hundreds of acres bordering the town. The land has been in my family for generations, even before the town was built and established. We used it as a retreat for training our young to shift and hunt. As a place to escape the cities and return to our true form during the full moon and lunar eclipse. With so much of the world being modernized and developed, we thought it best to keep a piece untouched and hidden, just for us.

As time went on, though, it became clear we weren't the only species of non-humans who wished this, so the town was built here to become home to those who prefer a bit more freedom to be their true selves away from busy modern society.

I will defend this town and its residents with every breath in my body until the day I die. Neither I nor anyone in my family will ever sell our land to an elf. Especially one known for his illegal drug business.

I refocus on my sister while still waiting for a response. I weigh the pros and cons of telling her about the elf. It could cause gossip and concern around town, but if I don't tell her, the gossip will be astronomical, and I'll have to listen to one of Ginger's rants about keeping her informed. She's the resident hacker and know-it-all, so if anyone should know the elf is here, it should be her. Hell, she might already know about him.

"Dottie reported seeing a male elf check in to the motel. Someone she's never seen before and is concerned."

"Oh. Are you going to go over there and see what it's all about?"

Why does she sound so pleased with the idea? And why isn't she giving me the third degree right now? I raise an eyebrow at her, but she doesn't flinch; she just smiles at me in a way that I can't read. It could be genuine, but it could be a front. I can never tell.

"Yes. At least to get a name. Maybe introduce myself and welcome him to town. You know, just being the hospitable mayor."

I give my sister my best mayoral smile. She chuckles and fiddles with the rings on her fingers.

"Sure. Cause we all know how *hospitable* you can be," she says sarcastically.

Ginger knows exactly how I feel about unexpected newcomers in town. I hate them. I like to know when non-human *and* human visitors arrive. Most unexpected arrivals are passing through, lost, or looking for a place to hide.

Usually, Ginger knows before anyone when there'll be new

people in town, with her constant searching and sweeping of the internet. All non-human residents also know to inform her or the mayor's office when they have family and friends visiting. The only time we have an influx of unknown people is during the lunar eclipse when shifters somehow find their way to us and just show up for the week or weekend. Spending just enough time to shift and run and usually fuck.

"I don't know why there's an elf sniffing around town, but I'm going to find out. And then make him leave. We don't need any of their nonsense, only weeks away from the blood moon."

"I heard that. Last time wasn't so great."

I cringe a little at the reminder. She's referring to a few years ago, not long after I became mayor. We weren't exactly prepared for all the horny unruly shifters to flood the town, and things got a bit out of hand. We had to dust all the humans in town and alter their memories so none of them would call The Inquirer or FBI to report monstrous wolf creatures taking over the town.

I've been mayor of Snowberry for just over five years now, and although I've settled into a nice rhythm, it still feels a little unreal. I'm the alpha shifter, leader of all the shifters in town, and responsible for the safety and security of all non-humans—and by default, humans—under my care as mayor. As it has been the responsibility of all alpha shifters throughout history.

Being mayor just makes it easier for humans to accept the alpha's presence and involvement everywhere. However, dealing with all the other day-to-day responsibilities of being mayor isn't the most desirable.

At twenty-five, I was a bit young to be a mayor, but no age is too young to be an Alpha. It all depends on when a new alpha is needed, and the abilities and markers appear in that shifter. The last alpha had held the position for almost sixty years. Although he still had plenty of life left in him, his time in command was over.

Most people thought my older brother Ryder would become alpha since he is the oldest and far more mature, but he never developed the alpha power. Now, he's my beta and second in command, as well as the town sheriff. It suits him and his stern personality.

Our jobs and responsibilities have changed drastically over the centuries, but one thing will always remain. We are charged with keeping any and all non-humans in our pack safe. And now, in this new world where we are hidden from humans, it is also to protect our non-human identities.

"Well, I suppose you better get a move on then. Don't want to leave our new visitor unattended and wandering town alone. Who knows what kind of trouble he could get into."

Ginger stands, and I mirror the act, standing behind my large desk filled with files and papers and my overworked laptop, rounding it to follow my sister from my office. An office that, even after half a decade, doesn't feel like mine. Even though I've filled it with family photos and hung my college degree in business on the wall. I didn't choose the furniture or wallpaper, and it's all a bit old-fashioned for my taste. Maybe I'll update it this year and make it more modern.

As we leave, I trail closely behind Ginger, hoping to get a whiff of her emotions to find out what she's up to. I don't get much since she's become an expert at hiding them from me. I sniff the air behind her, but all I smell is a whiff of sickly-sweet anticipation. That could mean anything with Ginger. Especially with an unidentified elf making mischief in town.

We exit my office and cross into the lobby, where my two assistants sit at opposite desks on either side of my office door.

Donna sits to one side and Levi to the other. Donna has

been here since the town's inception in the early nineteen twenties, knows everything about everyone, and is best friends with Dottie—the other town gossip queen. So, it doesn't surprise me when she asks about the elf. I'm sure Dottie texted her before calling me.

"Are you leaving to see about that elf at the motel?"

"Yeah. Best to get it straightened out now rather than wait for him to cause problems."

Donna nods, pinching her lips together. Although Donna is pushing two hundred years old, she doesn't look a day over forty. Non-humans tend to age a lot slower than humans, creating a few problems in this technological world with all the cameras and records, but we manage.

Donna is a Mere, and much like us shifters, she has more than one form and can shift from one to the other as she likes. Replacing all of her mere attributes with human features. Light brown hair is pinned up in a neat and tidy bun on top of her head, and her matching soft brown eyes, which I know in her mere form, are pale lavender watch Ginger. Knowing there's always good gossip where she's concerned.

"Hopefully, it shouldn't take too long, so I should be back for my meeting with Mr. Peters this afternoon."

If I reschedule on him again, he's going to get suspicious, and I don't need a nosey human with too much time on their hands snooping around in non-human business. We already have to dust them with fairy magic more frequently than most since we live in such a small town. I don't want to dust him more than necessary and create more lies I'll have to keep track of.

Fairy dust is one of my most useful tools when trying to run a small, secluded town filled mostly with non-humans but also has a small population of humans who have no idea our world even exists. It comes from the wings of a fairy and is exactly what it sounds like: dust. More like a fine powdered glitter. Thankfully, it doesn't leave a glittery residue, or the entire town would shimmer like a disco ball in the sun.

Speaking of fairies, my other assistant, Levi, a fairy, flutters his wings and flitters over to stop in front of me. No one who isn't a non-human can see his true form, with his glittering translucent fairy wings, pointed ears, pearlescent cerulean skin, and pale white hair. To us, we see his true form, but to every human without the sight, they just see a regular human male, impeccably dressed with perfectly styled blonde hair and inhumanly bright blue eyes.

Non-humans can see the glamours others wear with just a shift of our eyes. It's like one of those pictures that changes to something else when you move just the right way, allowing us to see what humans see. Most of the time, we don't require it here in town, but it can be necessary at times.

"Here you go, boss. Messages from this morning."

"Thanks, Levi."

I shuffle through the stack of small papers, quickly scanning the neatly scrawled messages. Nothing that requires my immediate attention, and I can't wait till later. I return them to Levi as I don't want to lose them while out of the office.

"Put these on my desk, please? I'll handle them when I return."

"Sure thing."

He grins and takes the messages, re-straightening them into a perfectly neat stack while hovering just off the ground as he makes his way into my office.

Donna and Dottie have taken him under their wing lately and are teaching him the subtle art of professional gossiping. I despise gossip, but it is a helpful tool for keeping me informed about what's really going on in town. I don't care much about human gossip as long as it isn't anything violent. It's the non-human gossip I am most interested in.

Levi returns in a blur of blue shimmer skittering to a halt in front of his desk.

"I'm heading out now, too. Got my own errands to run, so I'll catch ya later. K?" Ginger says from where she stands with her back to the main entrance, one foot already out the door, ready to turn and run. I'm still not sure why she stopped by today. Usually, she either wants something or is delivering bad news, but today, she seemed to have no discernable purpose and is more than ready to run out the moment something interesting happens. Very unlike her, indeed.

"Sure, I'll walk out with you."

I say a quick goodbye to my two assistants and head out with Ginger. She turns towards her neon blue convertible Mini Cooper. It's an impractical car for the area, but she loves it. Plus, it's easy to spot from a long distance.

I grip her by the elbow to stop her before she can run away. Her scent spikes with a sour tinge of surprise before she quickly settles back into a calm neutral.

"Is there something going on Ginger? You never told me why you stopped by."

"No, nothing's going on. I just wanted to check in and see how you are doing. Nothing specific."

"Why do I not believe you?" I ask sardonically. It's never nothing with Ginger; there has to be an ulterior motive to today's visit.

"Believe me or not, Hunter," she shrugs noncommittally. "There doesn't always have to be a reason for things. I gotta go. See ya later, alright? Maybe we can go for a run this weekend?"

It has been a long time since we shifted and went for a run

together, and I could really use the time to quiet my mind and reset. I nod in agreement.

"Yeah, that sounds great. Maybe we can even convince Ryder to join us."

Ginger snorts, "Good luck with that. I don't think he's run with anyone in decades. Man likes his alone time."

Ryder is an extremely dedicated pack member and brother, but he tends to be more solitary at times, especially when he shifts and runs. We all participate, but Ryder always keeps his distance from the larger groups and to the furthest outskirts of our property. He has his reasons, I know, but I wish he would trust more in his pack, in me, to help him deal with his difficulties. Whatever they may be. I've tried to get him to speak about it in the past with no success. Unlikely that'll change any time soon. He's as set in his ways as I am.

Ginger gives me a quick hug and kiss on the cheek before heading to her car. Waving over her shoulder, she picks up her pace, hopping over the door frame and sliding into her seat without opening it. Like many shifters, she's tall, and her movements are graceful and swift. When she first bought the car, I questioned her comfort in such a compact vehicle, but she didn't seem to have any problems with it.

I turn to walk down the street towards the ten-room motel only a block away. Snowberry is small, and all the shops and businesses line the four main streets, which form a circle, or square, to be specific, around a small park. Keeping everything neatly accessible within a two-block walking radius. As a wolf shifter, I'm particular to walking and running, so the short distance isn't of any concern.

I pass by my father's photography and art store, *SnapShot*, the only grocery store in town, and the famous *Dottie's Drive-In Diner*. I sigh in mourning for the loss of my burger and fries but keep walking to the motel catty-corner from the drive-up restaurant. Maybe this will be a quick in and out, and I can stop and pick up a burger to-go on my way back to the office.

The Vacancy sign flickers as I enter the motel lobby, where I'm instantly greeted by the twenty-year-old front desk attendant, Amanda. She's a human with dark brown hair and tanned skin that I've known most of her life. She knows about the non-human world, her stepfather is a mere, and she has a half-breed younger brother. So she knows what I am and how things work around here.

"Hello, Mayor Evans. What can I do for you today?" she asks with a flirtatious bat of her lashes and a faint blush.

She's ten years younger than me, which isn't an issue considering how long we live in the non-human world, but she's still a kid, just barely out of high school. I try to make my features more mature and professional, so she doesn't think I'm interested. Leaning one elbow on the counter, I give her the most cordial smile I can muster.

"Hi, Amanda. I heard an elf checked in recently and was hoping to get some information on him."

"Of course," she chirps happily and pulls up his information on her computer screen. "He checked in about an hour ago under the name Roman, and he's in room three."

"Did he say what he was in town for or how long he was staying?"

She clicks on her computer again before answering. "He's booked for the next two weeks. Didn't say why he was here."

Two weeks is a long time for an elf to be in town. Putting him here through the blood moon. I hoped she would tell me it was just for the night, and he was passing through nothing more. Many times, non-humans seek out areas or towns with larger non-human populations to stay in when traveling. No such luck with this one. It's obvious he's here on Vincent's behalf.

Amanda turns to face me again. Perched on her tall stool, she sits straight and pulls her shoulders back, giving me a huge, wide smile.

I clear my throat and straighten my tie to give my hands something to do. Today, I chose a blue-patterned tie my mother gave me when I became mayor, which she says makes my ice-blue eyes pop. It's not required for the mayor to wear a suit and tie every day, especially considering how casual and laid-back our town is, but I like it. Makes me feel authoritative, as if I deserve the position and might be doing it right.

"Thank you, Amanda. Is he in his room now?"

She nods animatedly. "Yes. Hasn't left since he checked in."

"Great. Thanks a bunch."

I give her an appreciative nod, exiting the lobby without saying another word.

The motel is set up in one long line of single-story rooms down the side of the road, with parking spaces lined up in front of each door. There are a couple of cars in the lot. One is a black SUV that I know the elves favor, and it is parked right in front of room number three.

Now comes the hard part. Trying to be cordial without losing my temper and imposing my alpha power on the elf. Even not being a shifter, all non-human species feel our alpha power. It's something embedded in all our DNA. Shifters have always been the protectors, guardians, and militia. The alpha having the ability to push others mentally to bend to our will is sometimes necessary to ensure our pack's safety. Forcing the shocked, scared, and stubborn to do as we command to keep them out of the line of fire and out of harm's way.

I take a few deep breaths to calm my natural instinct to

command and bark out alpha orders before knocking on the door as gently as possible.

The male elf answers immediately, no doubt expecting my visit. He smirks, licks the pointed tip of one fang, and props a shoulder against the door frame, leaning to the side without a care. He's so relaxed that he doesn't even bother with a glamour. His pale gray skin and long, pointed ears lined with silver studs on full display. The black sclera of his eyes, drastically different from the white of humans.

He might be able to get away with his true form in the city thanks to cosplay and modern-day body modifications. But here? Here, the humans would freak out and stare. Another annoyance I don't need to deal with since donning a glamour is as easy as a thought.

"Well, hello, Alpha—sorry, *Mr. Mayor*. I was wondering when you would show up. I didn't think it would be this soon, but it saves me time."

The male crosses his arms over his chest, his fingers lined with silver rings that glint in the light. Again, he grins at me, all cocky malice. Fucking elves, thinking they can do whatever the hell they want.

"How about you save me the time and headache and just leave now?" I suggest with just as cocky a smile.

He scoffs a laugh and shakes his head, his long black hair swaying with the movement. Tisking, he focuses his yellow irises on me with a faux look of contrition.

"Sorry, Sparky, no can do. I have business in town that I just can't neglect."

"And what business would that be?"

He ignores my question, tapping his fingers against his bicep.

"You and I know you can't make me leave just to be here.

Why don't you scurry along, little pup, and go play house with the humans? If I need you, I'll make sure to whistle."

A deep growl reverberates in my chest, a warning to the impertinent elf. I can feel my body reacting to his blatant disrespect, nails hardening and sharpening into claws, canines elongating into fangs. Clenching my teeth, my lips curl back, flashing my fangs threateningly.

"Watch it, elf. If I feel my pack is threatened in any way, I can and will remove you from this town *with* force."

"Woah, down, Spot. I'm not threatening anyone. I'm just stating my right to be here." He raises his arms in a defensive position, acting all innocent.

I'm getting tired of the dog comments, but technically, he's right. We don't completely follow the laws of the human world, but we do have our own rules. One is that all non-humans are welcome until proven untrustworthy or dangerous. Until he does something against my pack and town he's allowed to be here.

No matter how much I want to kick him out right now, I don't have the right. And if I start ignoring the rules of our world and making my own, my pack will be unwelcome in other territories.

"Fine. But make sure you wear your glamour at *all* times. The humans here aren't used to such outlandish appearances. You won't blend in here in your true form." With even more false apology, he furrows his brow mockingly.

"Yes, of course. I wouldn't want to startle the poor, simple-minded humans." Finally, standing from his casual lean against the doorframe, he seamlessly transitions into his glamour, which isn't far off from his true form. His hair remains long and black, the silver earrings and rings remain, the gray pallor of his skin shifts tones to a pale tan, the fangs, claws, and ears all round out, and the bottomless black of his sclera fades away to generic human white while his irises shift from yellow to brown.

Even though I can always see his true form, I can also view his glamour when I choose. How else would I know he's wearing one or what he looks like for when humans describe him to me as a menace? Which they no doubt eventually will.

"Good. Keep it that way," I growl out between clenched teeth.

I want to impose my alpha power on him but hold back. He may be a cocky asshole, but he is abiding by our rules.

"I'm keeping my eye on you. So, watch yourself." Roman, if that even is his real name, lumbers a few steps back into the room and starts to pull the door shut. Before it can close completely, I stop it with my foot, halting its progress, leaving plenty of space to glare once more at the elf.

"Tell Vincent that no matter what he does, he's not getting my land."

Roman widens his eyes innocently. "I have no idea what you're talking about."

"Sure, you don't. Just deliver the message." He doesn't argue or deny my insinuation that he works for Vincent; he just shuts the door without another word. Once the door latches, I roll my neck, cracking the stiffness there. I may need a run before the weekend to relieve the growing stress from this new development.

Chapter 4
Lottie

The directions Luna drew out for me on the paper map didn't look like they led anywhere. The thick red line cut through what appeared to be undeveloped green space. The road to the town and the town itself don't exist on the map or Google Earth. I would never have found it if she hadn't given me turn-by-turn directions.

But I did.

The road was narrow but well-maintained. Once I turned off from the highway, it was hard *not* to find Snowberry. There is only one road in and out. Only one place you could end up if you dared turn down the empty road that looked like it led to a woodland cannibal's domain.

Luna had arranged for me to meet Ginger at the gas station at the town's entrance. I spotted her immediately in her bright blue Mini Cooper. She waved me down, and before I could step out to greet her, she ran up to the car, telling me not to bother getting out yet as we were going to go straight to the cabin, only a few minutes' drive away.

On the way to the cabin, I didn't see much of the center of town, but what I did see looked perfectly picturesque and adorable. I can't wait to stroll down main street, pop into the coffee shop, and sit at a curbside table, enjoying the quiet anonymity—assuming they have a coffee shop.

Shit. What if they don't have a coffee shop? Where will I feed my caffeine addiction? It's highly unlikely there's a *Starbucks* or *Dutch Bro's* here, but there has to be a locally owned café or something. At least, I hope to God there is. I have no idea how to make a latte.

Hell, I don't know how to make much of anything. I haven't had to cook for myself since I was a teenager. Looks like I'll be living off frozen dinners and whatever local restaurants they have. I hope the TV at the cabin gets the Food Network so I can learn how to cook while I'm here.

I follow Ginger down a residential street, her music drifting on the wind behind her. Thankfully, it's not mine. That would be awkward. The houses we pass are spread out and have vast green yards. A few people are out sitting on porches or walking down the street, but overall, it's pretty quiet. It is so different from the nonstop noise and hustle of Los Angeles.

Ginger's convertible turns down a neat gravel road, and I follow her closely. The road is lined with towering pine trees and splits at one point, and we take the lane to the left. We drive maybe half a mile more before the road dead ends at a small clearing where the most perfect cabin sits, sheltered by the imposing forest and colorful flowering bushes. It looks like a Bob Ross painting brought to life right in front of me.

I park and step out, stretching my cramped legs, never taking my eyes off the cabin. Celestial rays of sunlight shine down through the gaps in the treetop, lighting up the moss-covered roof.

Pure and exquisite silence greets me as I stand in awe at my new—temporary—home. There are no honking horns, sirens, airplanes overhead, snapping cameras with yelling paparazzi, and best of all no security team.

The heavy weight I've been carrying in my heart for years lifts, and my guilt for running away dissolves.

This was the right choice. This is what I need. It's what my soul needs.

"So? What do you think? It's pretty perfect, isn't it?" Ginger asks, stepping up to my side. I realize how tall she is.

I look up to her. I'm five feet eight inches and she's a few inches taller than me. She has to be close to or even six feet tall. I figure starting our relationship by gawking at her height isn't the best thing to do. So, I decide to wait to ask her exactly how tall she is until we get to know each other better. Instead, I answer her question.

"Yes, it is. Absolutely. Freaking. Perfect."

"Okay," she claps her hands and rubs them together like a cartoon villain. "Let's get your stuff inside, and I'll give you a tour."

We circle around to the back of my new-to-me silver Nissan. I bought the car at a used dealership on the outskirts of Las Vegas. Thanks to my many years of distrust and forced financial dependency, I had taken steps to establish a secret bank account. Taking money out of the account where my monthly allowance was deposited—that my mother had access to—and moved it to my secret account, as well as stockpiling cash in a hidden safe.

As of last week, when I left Las Vegas and separated myself from everything I've known for the past decade, I am physically and financially free to do as I please. There's no one watching over my purchases and transactions, telling me I should be shopping more, or asking why I withdrew so much cash and what I did with it. There's only me. And with how much I've squirreled away in a town like Snowberry, I'll be set for years. If I so choose.

Ginger effortlessly pulls my large suitcase from the trunk, followed by the smaller one, and looks at the minimal luggage and lack of...well, anything else. I didn't even stop to get groceries.

"Is this it?" She looks from my luggage to me questioningly. "I thought you were staying for three months?"

"Oh, I am. I just packed light. And I wasn't able to bring much, as you know."

Luna and I had to come up with a story to tell Ginger. Without giving too much detail and leaving it extremely vague, we simply said I am trying to escape an emotionally abusive relationship and require complete social separation and secrecy to start over.

None of it was a lie; my mother has emotionally abused me over the years in her obsessive need to control my life and profit from my hard work. I just didn't specify what type of abusive relationship I was escaping. Or who I really am.

"Of course, I understand. If you need anything, let me know. Anything you can't find in town can be shipped in. It may not look like it, but we do get mail here," she jokes, giving me a wink and elbow bump, lightening the mood. "Not Amazon Prime, but snail mail? We've got you covered."

My chest lightens and I laugh, "I will definitely let you know. But I'm really looking forward to a bit of simplicity and quiet. My old life was very...loud, and busy, and complicated. I had a lot of material possessions, and very few of them made me happy. Don't let anyone ever convince you that money buys happiness. I'm proof it doesn't."

I didn't mean to turn our first conversation into a sharing moment, but I feel I have to start off right this time. I don't want anyone to think I'm vain and materialistic. If I can, I'd even like to make a few friends to experience what it's like to make a connection with another person without the underlying fear that they're only my friends because of my fame and money. I've had enough of those people in my life; I don't need any more.

With Ginger easily carrying my two suitcases, I can pull out the Polaroid camera I bought to take a quick picture of my new home. I saw it in the old Radio Shack-type store I stopped in to buy a prepaid cell phone and just had to have it. I wanted to be able to take photos of my journey that were just for me. No one can hack in to access them; they won't be posted on social media sites or edited and photoshopped to perfection. Because they are already perfect in their one hundred percent authenticity.

Holding the camera up to my face, I peer through the viewfinder and snap the photo just as Ginger enters the frame, her back to me, long auburn hair swaying behind her. You can't see her face in the photo, and somehow, that makes it even more special.

I tenderly slip the photo into the notebook I've been using as a scrapbook and journal before shoving it and the camera in my bag. Slinging it and my purse over my shoulder.

Before I forget, I take out my new cell phone, which has only one number programmed into it, and pull up my messages. I type out a quick but unspecific message to Luna.

Lottie: *Made it. Everything looks great.*
Luna: *Good.*

I didn't expect a long response. Before I left, we discussed the less we said in texts, the better. That kind of thing can be discovered if someone really wants to. Phone calls can be more elaborate, but even those we keep to a minimum. Contact is only made when absolutely necessary.

By now, my mother has no doubt made the connection that Luna helped me. I'm sure she's watching her every move and action. It wouldn't surprise me if she hired someone to hack into her phone and try to track her calls and texts.

I slip the phone back into my purse. Ignoring it for the most part. It's nice not to check social media and news sites every hour of the day. They stress me out sometimes. All the constant pressure to keep up with trends and post the right thing at the right time. Not to mention the trolls. I hate those fuckers.

I catch up to Ginger, who's already opened the front door and is stepping inside.

I only have a moment to take in the large front porch before entering the cabin. There are two rocking chairs to one side that look well used, and the front door is painted a tranquil shade of soft blue. Everything else is bare wood. Looking as if the planks were pulled directly from the forest surrounding us.

Inside, the cabin is far nicer than I would have expected for a cabin in the woods. It's modern but rustic; still a cabin, but with updated appliances and amenities. A small but clean kitchen lines the right side of the space, with a petite dining table and four chairs. To the left is a cozy living room with a plush couch and stone fireplace. As I take in the space, the wooden floorboards creak quietly under my footsteps.

I don't immediately spot a television until I realize the framed photo above the mantle is a flatscreen in disguise.

"The TV has most of the streaming services loaded on it. No need to log in; it's all ready for use. There's also a collection of movies on the digital drive."

Ginger continues her tour, not waiting for me to catch up. Speaking over her shoulder as she moves through the living room and down the short hallway.

"There's only one bedroom and one bathroom, which I'm sure Luna told you," she calls from the opposite side of one of the few doors in the cabin.

When I step through the door, she's lifting my largest suitcase onto the bed. This bedroom is smaller than my closet back in Los Angeles, but there is still *plenty* of space. A small dresser and nightstand match the sturdy wood-framed bed, which is draped in a thick, colorful quilt. The large window opens up to the forest beyond, a perfect view first thing in the morning that I look forward to experiencing.

I'm going to sleep like the dead in this room, I just know it.

I set my bag down on the dresser and spin to find Ginger at the door, already on her way out. She's moving like a whirlwind from room to room.

"Here's the bathroom. There are towels in the hall closet, extra toilet paper under the sink along with a few standard toiletries. The water takes a minute to heat up, so don't jump into a shower right away, or you might freeze your tits off."

She laughs, and I peek through the bathroom door to see her opening and shutting the cabinet under the sink, flashing neatly stacked rolls of toilet paper. Other than the clawfoot tub, the bathroom is nothing extravagant. I can't wait to take a candle-lit bath in it with a nice large glass of wine.

Ginger scoots past me and back out into the living room, continuing her fast-paced tour. I wonder if she has somewhere to be, and that's why she's going so fast?

"There's plenty of chopped wood for the fireplace out back in the covered awning. I'll have one of my brothers chop more for you if you need more. Hunter is a volunteer fireman, so he knows his way around an ax."

"Oh, that's cool."

I barely enter the living room as she's already crossing to the kitchen, talking about the dishwasher and stove.

"Okay, so that's about it for the cabin. Pretty standard stuff. Are you ready to head into town to continue the tour? I thought I could give you the lay of the land and introduce you to some people in town. That way, you'll feel comfortable and right at home here in Snowberry. Plus, it'll help us get ahead of the town gossip."

I freeze, and my face falls. *Gossip?* A celebrity's worst nightmare. Rumors, lies, and stories could ruin a person's life in a matter of seconds.

"Gossip?" I ask on a thick swallow.

"Don't worry, it's just small-town nonsense. *Who's the new girl? Why is she here? Where is she staying? Where did she come from? Is she single?* You know, the normal nosey neighbor nonsense. Don't worry, Luna told me you want to stay offline and low-key."

She steps close and puts a reassuring hand on my shoulder, easing my tension. There's just something about her that makes you instantly like her. Hopefully, I can call her friend one day.

"It's all water cooler gossip. They're just bored people with nothing better to do. If we get you out there and answer all the questions before they even ask them, they won't have time to concoct crazy stories about you."

With a wide smile and a squeeze of my shoulder, she turns us towards the front door, which remained open throughout our two-minute walkthrough. Before Ginger is able to run me out of the cabin, I hurry back to the bedroom, grab my Polaroid camera, and sling it over my shoulder. I might find a few cute things to photograph on my first stroll through town.

Ginger hands me a keychain with one key on it and a small wood carving of a feather dangling from the metal ring. It's smooth under my fingers and looks hand-carved. None of the mass-produced machine-made crap from China.

"This is beautiful. Where did you get it?" I ask, still admiring the attention to detail in the lines and creases of the feather. I would swear I was holding a real feather if it weren't made of wood.

"My brother Hunter carved it. It's kind of a hobby of his."

"This Hunter guy sounds like a catch. Volunteer fireman, great at chopping wood and hand carving extremely detailed realistic feathers. What else can he do?"

Ginger snickers and gives me an *if-you-only-knew* look.

"Well, he also schedules his entire life, including when he does his laundry down to the minute. He never stays up past nine on weekdays and hates pie."

"Who hates pie?"

"Exactly. He's not nearly as appealing as he seems. When you meet him, don't let his baby blues fool you."

I've been surrounded by people who have been on covers of magazines and named in lists of The Most Attractive People; I doubt one wood-whittling mountain man with blue eyes will sway me. But I don't mention any of that to Ginger. Just nod along in agreement.

At her insistence, we ride into town in Ginger's car, leaving my Nissan at the cabin. The cool breeze flutters my short hair around my face as she whips around corners like a Nascar driver, parking in a small lot in what appears to be the center of town.

There's a small green space behind the lot with a gazebo at

its center, like every small-town hallmark movie ever made. I snap a quick picture before Ginger can pull her disappearing act and lead me away.

"Okay, well, first things first. We're going to go to the most important place in town. Dottie's," Ginger announces with her hands on her hips.

Gesturing with a jerk of her chin to the lot next to us, I look over to see a retro neon sign that reads *Dottie's Drive-In Diner*. A few cars are lined up in the parking spaces where servers on rollerskates perch window-mounted trays full of food on car doors. Food that I can smell from here.

My stomach growls in protest. I haven't had lunch yet, and the scent of fried heaven reminds me of that.

"Sounds like maybe we need to grab some food before I introduce you to Dottie," Ginger chuckles, leading me toward the heavenly scents.

Dottie's reminds me of Flo's from Disney's *Cars*, but in a great way. Everything is polished and shiny, with rounded corners in pastel pinks and mint greens. Pink neon lights line the angular sign and the entire border of the roof of the building. There's a small interior space with glittery pink vinyl booths, but most guests and activity are outside, either around umbrella tables or in parked cars. It's obvious the theme of Dottie's is retro drive-up, where you sit in your car and eat instead of going inside. I bet this place is hoppin' on a Saturday night.

I smile at the thought. I didn't even know places like this still existed outside movie screens.

Ginger and I enter the small interior and are immediately greeted by a petite, smiling redhead girl on roller skates wearing a retro-style uniform dress with "Dottie's" written on her left breast pocket in mint green and white. A small pocketed white apron tied around her waist.

"Hey there, Ginger. I wasn't expecting you today, only your brother, who I'm surprised I haven't seen yet."

"He had an unexpected issue to attend to. He was really bummed to miss out on his lunch. You know how he likes to stick to his schedule."

The server giggles and rolls her eyes good-naturedly, her high ponytail swishing behind her. The red strands curled at the end, bouncing lightly at the slight movement. "Oh, I know."

That's when she finally spots me, and her attention perks. Ginger said there would be a lot of interest in the new girl in town, and she wasn't wrong.

"And who's your friend? I don't believe I've ever seen you in town before."

"Becca, this is Lottie. She's renting our cabin for a few months."

"Really?" She turns surprised eyes on Ginger that seem to sparkle with mischief.

Wait, are they *actually sparkling?* Upon second inspection, it does look like twinkling glimmers in the bright green of her irises. That can't be right; it must just be the light hitting her right because there also appears to be a glimmer surrounding her.

"Lottie?"

"What?" I shake off the odd sensation of seeing something that isn't there and realize they are talking to me. "Sorry, what did you say?"

"I asked where you're from originally."

"Oh, um, Southern California," I answer vaguely.

The closer to the truth I can stay, the easier it will be to remember the lies. Lots of people are from southern California, telling them that much won't break my cover.

"Oh, how fun. This must be a big change for you."

"You have no idea," I chuckle at my own inside joke with myself, and the two women smile acquiescently.

"I've always wanted to see the city of angels. It sounds so exciting. All the celebrities and actors. I hear you can run into one just walking down the street. Is that true, Lottie?"

Becca beams with good-natured glee, unknowingly hitting a sensitive topic for me. I try to hide my wince and initial panic, shrugging it off.

"I wouldn't know. I don't live in the city."

I don't say anything else but take the opportunity to look around the space, hoping she will take the hint to change the subject. Thankfully, Ginger comes to my rescue.

"We were hoping to order some lunch and to speak with Dottie if she's around."

I internally thank Ginger for her well-timed diversion. She doesn't know it, but she just saved me from a very public panic attack. I'm not the best liar; I'm a singer, not an actress.

Becca's peppy attitude doesn't seem at all deterred by Ginger's redirect. Her smile is still stretched across her face, and that weird sparkle is in her eyes.

"Sure, go ahead and take a seat wherever you like, and I'll go get her."

Ginger thanks Becca, and she rolls away on her perfectly spotless white roller skates. We pick a pink booth against the window looking out to the street beyond, a handful of cars parked in the lot.

I slide in and put my purse and Polaroid on the seat beside me. The vinyl squeaks a little under my denim-clad legs as I settle in, feeling more and more like a normal girl the longer I'm away from LA.

Plastic laminated menus are on the table, and I pick one up

and review the options.

"So, what's good here?"

"Everything. Dottie's son Jared is the chef here, and he's amazing. Learned from a world-famous chef in New York. They only use locally sourced ingredients and fresh produce. We very much like the farm-to-fork movement here. There are a few farms just outside town; one raises pigs, cows, and chickens, which get sold at the butcher shop. If you're a meat eater, they have some amazing steaks and bacon there."

"I am. I can't cook them for shit, but I do love to eat them."

Laughing at my inability to grill meat, Ginger doesn't even look at the menu, probably having memorized everything already. I read over my options and decide on a classic BLT with a side of tater tots and cherry Italian cream soda. If the bacon is fresh butchered, it'll be delicious.

I'm also happily surprised to see an entire Italian section with spaghetti, pizza, lasagna, garlic knots, and various salads—not just garden or Caesar. Unfortunately, there is no sushi. I suppose beef and pork are easier to come by in Montana than fresh tuna.

We only wait for a few minutes before a woman comes bursting out of the double kitchen swinging doors, and she looks just like…

"Oh my God, you look just like Twiggy," I blurt out before the woman even reaches our table to greet us.

"Why thank you," she says in a sweetly appreciative voice, sashaying to stand at our table's side. "She is my idol," she preens while patting her short blonde pixie hair.

She's wearing large cotton candy pink and mint green acrylic daisy earrings that perfectly match her pink mod A-line dress and checkered mint green tights. Blending in perfectly with the décor of the diner.

I wasn't expecting someone so bright and colorful, but it makes sense now that I think about it. Dottie looks to be in her late thirties but has skin as smooth as a woman a decade younger. I'll have to make sure to ask Ginger later if she can tell me Dottie's skincare secret for keeping so young. There's barely a wrinkle on her face beyond the ones that appear at the corner of her eyes as a result of her wide smile.

"I'm Dottie, and you must be Lottie. Ha-ha, that rhymed. I'll definitely not be forgetting your name."

"Can I take your picture?" I ask, completely unable to stop myself. Holding up my Polaroid to show her what I mean.

Most people take selfies on their phones, but I don't want that. I want one of her to put in my book. Or maybe on the wall in the cabin. I could start a little collage of my time here.

"Why, of course, you can, honey. Here, get my good side."

She turns and poses in a very Twiggy-esque pose, with big, bold lashes, doe eyes, and a soft, relaxed mouth. I snap the photo, cementing the memory within four white borders.

Dottie slides into the booth next to Ginger across from me, propping her elbows on the table and resting her chin in her hands. She stares at me excitedly.

Desperately, I hope this fashionable woman doesn't recognize me.

"I hear you're stayin' at Hunter's cabin for a while. Does that mean I'll be seeing you around town then?"

"Yes. I plan on being here for a few months."

Concealing my nervousness, I fiddle with the strap of my Polaroid camera under the table, more concerned about meeting people in town now. I had hoped to remain unknown for a time. Blending into the forest and being ignored by most of the townspeople. Apparently, that's not going to happen, which puts me at risk of being recognized far sooner.

I really hope Dottie listens to disco music to go along with her nineteen-seventies attire. Maybe she won't know my music or name.

"Well, that sounds wonderful. It's a great time of year to be visiting."

"Why's that?" I ask, curious now if I've unintentionally found myself in a destination spot only known by word of mouth.

"Because of the season change. The temperatures are starting to drop, and the leaves will change color soon. Hopefully, you stay long enough to see the first snowfall. It's breathtaking."

I let out a breath of relief. A season change I can handle. Not some hidden, well-kept secret music festival. That would be the worst.

"I hope so, too. Living in SoCal, we don't get much snow, like, ever."

We all laugh because the thought of snow in southern California is ridiculous. I've seen it over the grapevine that runs through the mountains north of LA, but nothing farther south.

Becca rolls up to our table to take our orders. Ginger orders a triple grilled cheese sandwich that I make a mental note to try at some point. Over the next couple of months, I'll no doubt eat everything on this menu at least once.

It all sounds mouthwatering, especially since I've been on a strictly regimented diet for years. But I can't overload myself with fried food and grease, or I'll make myself sick. My favorite food is sushi, but it's about as likely I'll find sushi in Snowberry as a yeti walking through the front door.

Perhaps that's something I can teach myself to make. I mean, it's only fish and rice wrapped in seaweed, maybe with some cucumber or avocado. I won't be able to make the fancy rolls my personal chef would make with all the sauces and things I couldn't identify, but surely I could manage a basic California roll. Ironic since I ran away from California.

We sit and talk with Dottie as we eat our food, which is, as predicted, amazing. I don't get to meet the chef, her son, but Dottie promises she'll introduce me properly the next time I come in. I can't imagine her having a son old enough to be a professional chef.

I devour the perfectly crispy bacon and toasted BLT. I never knew tater tots could be on my list of favorite foods, but they are now. Especially covered in freshly shredded cheese and bacon bits with ranch. Ginger also informs me that I can buy them frozen from the grocery store and just pop them in the oven whenever I want them.

Add to mental shopping list.

Although, I'll probably accidentally burn down the cabin trying to use the oven. *Additional mental note; watch a YouTube video on how to use the oven.*

I learn that I *really like* Dottie. She's loud, colorful, and has all the tea on the entire town. She talks nonstop about this person or that rumor. Most are harmless, and I like this type of gossip about who was recently dumped and which recipe her baking rival will be using for their annual Christmas cookie bake-off. Christmas is still many months away, but I guess it's a big deal around here.

After an hour spent at Dottie's eating and chatting, Ginger walks me up and down the streets, pointing out the shops, what's sold inside, and which are her favorites. There are various types of stores and one or two empty storefronts. Thankfully, they have a coffee shop and a bakery. So, I don't have to worry about learning how to make the fancy coffees I've grown fond of.

Sing Sweet Nightingale

  I take a few Polaroids. One of Dottie's from the outside looking in through the window to the now empty booth we were just occupying. Then another of the bookstores, *Tall Tail*, with its jam-packed shelves, sat on the sidewalk outside the store. There's also a very inviting secondhand store called *Another Man's Junk*. It sounds a little pervy at first glance, but the meaning hits me after only a few moments of pondering. It's a secondhand store filled with antiques and the like.

  Sadly, we don't go inside any today. Ginger seems to be a little antsy as we walk, always looking around as if trying to find someone that she never spots.

  We make our way around the circle that makes up the central area of town before heading back to her blue Mini. I make a mental plan to return to the grocery store across the street from the parking lot to stock up my pantry and fridge in my car.

Chapter 5

Hunter

Something is up with Ginger, and I can't put my finger on it. Yesterday, she seemed to want to hang around for no reason, and today I haven't seen her at all. Who I have seen is that annoying elf, Roman.. He's already passed by city hall twice, making sure I saw him just so he could smirk and wave. Asshole. At least he's wearing his glamour.

Every day, I walk through town just to check on things. Today was my morning walk. I grabbed my morning espresso at *The Ugly Mug* first, then checked in at *Sticky Buns* for a bagel followed by quick pop into *Tall Tail Books* and *Another Man's Junk*, the secondhand store filled with odds and ends of all kinds.

Shanna, the owner, loves to collect things and bring them back here to sell. She's collected *many things* over the years. She keeps everything organized and neat, properly displayed on shelves and in cases. I wouldn't expect anything less from a Mere. They like to collect things and hoard them. Usually, they keep them hidden, their own little treasure trove. But some, like Shanna, have made it their career to collect and share their hoard.

It's only midafternoon, but my day is already getting to me. I don't know what it is, but it's like there are ants crawling under my skin. Every so often, the hair on the back of my neck stands on end, and I bristle. The urge to shift and run is a constant nagging in the back of my mind.

My brother Ryder shows up for his weekly check-in to review anything of note happening in town. Since the Sheriff's office is just across the hallway from mine in City Hall, he has a short commute.

Ryder sits in the chair opposite my desk, the same one Ginger sat in yesterday. His posture is far more rigid than her relaxed one. His spine is straight, and both feet are planted firmly on the ground.

Not for the first time, I think how he would have made a much better alpha than me. A much better mayor. He's the one who's logical and practical, strong and reliable. Not that I don't consider myself strong and reliable; he just always seemed the better choice. Traditionally, the position has always fallen to the eldest child, whether male or female, but not this time. This time, it was the middle child, the second son. Because of it, I've always felt a step behind where I should be. Second guessing my position and choices. Always trying to prove myself worthy. I only hope I've done so.

"Have you spoken to Ginger today? Or yesterday?" I ask as soon as he's comfortable. Well, as comfortable as he will get.

"No. Why?"

"Something is going on with her, and I can't figure out what it is."

Resting my elbows on the desk, I steeple my fingers

together in contemplation. I can't understand my sister on a good day, so trying to figure out her weird behavior now is nearly impossible.

"Did you ask her?" Ryder states plainly.

"Of course I did. She said it was nothing. Which, in female speak, usually means it's something. But I can't prove it."

"I could ask her if you like," he offers.

Ryder is a great brother, but he's not the type of person you sit down with and spill all your feelings to hoping for advice. His advice would be practical and blunt. He likes to confront an issue head-on and deal with it logically. You can't deal with emotions logically, no matter how often he tries. It makes him a great sheriff, though, making sure everyone stays in line and our secrets and families are protected. But he's not the best emotional companion.

That's the one thing I've always had that he hasn't, and it could be the reason I became alpha. I have more emotional capacity than he ever has. Taking into consideration people's feelings in my decisions, not just what's logical or practical.

"Thanks, but that's alright. I'm sure she'll eventually tell us, or whatever it is, will pass."

"I'm sure you're right. I can keep an eye on her for the time being. See if she does anything odd."

I nod in agreement. Maybe he'll see something I don't. Maybe she'll tell him something she wouldn't tell me.

"What else do you have to report? Anything new going on? Besides the elf."

Ryder furrows his brow. He's a stoic man, and his features are more square than my own. Our hair is the same midnight shade of black, though his is longer and more unkempt than mine. I don't think he even owns a comb, just uses his fingers to brush it back out of his face.

At fifty-five and thirty, we appear to be in our twenties thanks to our non-human slow aging. To a human, seeing us two together, they would guess us to only be a year or two apart. However, Ryder lacks the smile wrinkles a person of his age would normally have since he doesn't smile often. His mouth forming a perpetual flat line. I, on the other hand, smile constantly. I've always been an optimistic kind of guy, friendly and personable. It makes the whole shaking hands and kissing babies part of my job easy, I suppose.

My brother dislikes the presence of the elf as much as I do. Shortly after my initial welcome to the yellow-eyed cocky bastard, Ryder made one of his own. Received the same treatment and short, clipped answers as I did. Neither of us discovered his exact reasons for being in town. Although we both have our suspicions.

"Nothing notable. I did, however, notice something strange last night," Ryder says, pulling my attention to him.

I am immediately focused on only him and the next words out of his mouth. I don't like strange things happening in my town without my knowledge. There are many things we do that are normal to us and strange to humans, so if there's something strange to us, I need to know about it.

"And what would that be?"

"You weren't at the cabin last night, were you?" he asks.

"No," I answer immediately. "I haven't been to the cabin in weeks. Why?"

"I passed by there on a run last night and noticed a light on. Thought you might have been there for some reason."

An unsettling feeling rolls through my gut. Not another thing to deal with. This week is not going the way I planned. I frown at my brother, and my knuckles crack as I curl them into fists on my desk.

"No, it wasn't me. Did you ask Ginger?"

"No. I saw her in town for dinner last night, and she said she was going to her apartment to do some late-night work."

By work, he means hacking and searching for any information online about us that she needs to erase. It definitely wasn't her then. Once Ginger gets in her zone, there's no stopping her for hours. She'll sit at her computer glued to the screen until sunrise.

"I can go check it out," my brother offers.

"No," I interject. "I'll go. I need to run, so I'll check it out, sniff around, see what's going on."

Ryder nods. As my beta, he does as I decide without argument. Something as simple as checking on the cabin is no big deal. If there are people squatting in there, it's just as easy for me to remove them as it is for him.

"Anything else I should know about?"

His eyes go out of focus as he stares at my desk between us. "There's something different in town. Just a vibe. Dottie seems more excited than usual, which, of course, has me on edge. It's always something bothersome if Dottie is excited."

"What kind of vibe?" I ask.

Non-humans, especially shifters, pay attention to vibes, sensations, and feelings. It's an instinct thing; we follow them.

"I don't know. It doesn't feel good or bad, just...something."

"Okay. I'll keep an ear out. Thanks."

We finish with our weekly debrief going over the status of everyone and everything in town, ensuring all is well. After Ryder leaves, I last only another hour before I decide to leave for the day. The itch to shift is too great, and thinking of someone in the cabin sits on my mind like an anvil. I need to go.

I leave the office and drive home. When I pass by the turn-off to the cabin, I crane my neck to try and see down the path, knowing damn well I can't see anything from here. The road curves, blocking any line of sight. I'll just have to wait.

Pulling into my driveway, I park my truck and step out. Not wanting to waste any time, I strip naked on my large wrap-around porch. Folding my clothes neatly on the bench by the front door. No one lives around us for miles, so there's no one to catch me in the buff.

Besides, most non-humans are used to shifter nudity. Our clothes don't magically shift with us, unfortunately, so nudity is normal. If I were to stay dressed and shift, they would rip off like the Hulk, and ruining my clothing is unnecessary in this instance as I have ample opportunity to remove them.

The shift takes over as soon as I'm naked. Rolling up my spine and prickling at my neck where thick black fur sprouts and grows. When I was a pup, shifting took longer, getting used to reshaping bones and rearranging muscles. As I got older, it became easier. Now, the shift takes less than thirty seconds and with little pain. Sometimes, less than ten seconds if I'm motivated. My body, having long ago, acclimated to the process.

I stand on all four paws in my wolf form and shake my head, settling into the body that is just as much mine as my human form. Sounds intensify, and colors sharpen. Scents overwhelm my nose and something faint and sweet drifts on the wind. Something I've never smelled before.

Lifting my nose, I scent the air. The smell comes from the forest, and without much thought, I instinctively follow the smell.

Chapter 6
Lottie

Sitting in the rocking chair on the small cabin porch is my new favorite place. All I hear is the faint twittering of birds in the trees, bugs in the shrubs, and the creek of the chair as I rock back and forth. I've pretty much been sitting here all day.

I slept in and got up when I felt like it, letting the sun shining through the large window act as my alarm clock. The weight of the quilted blanking desperately tried to lull me back to dreamland.

It took a while, but I taught myself how to brew coffee in the machine on the counter with the grounds I bought at the grocery store last night. It wasn't great, but it wasn't horrible; only a few loose grounds made it into my mug. Then I cooked breakfast. Okay, I burned breakfast and ended up eating cereal, but I tried. That's what counts.

For the rest of the day, I did nothing. I sat, I read, I listened to music, and watched the light shift through the trees. And now the light is perfect: the witching hour, the few hours right before sundown when the lighting is ideal for photos.

This would be the perfect time to take a walk through the forest and take a picture or two.

Since I'm the one in control of my decisions now, I decide I want to go, so I'm going.

I pull on my brand-new lace-up ankle boots and an oversized cardigan, grab my Polaroid, and walk into the woods. Normally, I would think walking alone into the woods would be a bad idea, but Ginger assured me these woods are safe, and there are clearly marked trails I can follow.

I pick a trail and start walking.

The trees are tall and sturdy, and a few are larger around than I can reach with my arms. I hug a few just to check. I've never hugged a tree, and these ones look like they deserved it. A few needles and leaves cling to my hair and clothes, and I don't care.

The forest's smell is so clean and crisp compared to the smog-filled ozone of Los Angeles. I don't think people know what clean air is supposed to smell like anymore.

As I pass, I pluck a few pink flowers from the full bushes lining my path, covered with snow-white berries. I stop when I see a small white rabbit sitting on a log in a shaft of sunlight. As quietly as possible, I lift my camera and snap the photo. As soon as it hears the click and whir of the film developing, it hops off the log and disappears into the bushes.

The photo goes in my cardigan pocket, and I keep walking. It isn't long before I stumble upon a small patch of grass in an opening in the trees. In the center of the tiny field is a circle of mushrooms, a fairy circle.

Stepping gently over to it, I crouch down and line it up in my viewfinder. I take the photo, and as I kneel there waiting for the picture to develop, I hear a rustling in the bushes.

Sing Sweet Nightingale

Not five feet from me in the tree line, I spot two crystal blue eyes watching me, surrounded by black fur and a twitching nose.

The blood in my veins freezes along with every part of my body. You know how they say people either fight or flight when faced with conflict? Yeah, apparently, I'm the third option. Freeze in terror and mimic the most life-like statue ever.

The wolf doesn't move.

I don't move.

The forest doesn't move. Obviously, they're trees they can't move. But that's not the point. The point is everything remains still. One waiting for the other to make the first move. To breathe or flinch or piss themselves. I think I might be getting pretty close to the third option. Especially when the wolf takes a step out of the tree line. Bringing itself fully into view.

The beast is larger than any wolf I've ever seen, which is zero beyond the one I saw on Animal Planet. It has to be as tall as a Great Dane but wider and furrier.

It doesn't growl or lunge or bare its fangs at me. It just sits down at the edge of the clearing, watching me. I finally break free of my frozen state and jump back, standing braced to run.

Aren't you not supposed to run from wolves? Or is that only bears?

The wolf cocks its head at me, its ears remaining perked, listening. But its eyes look soft, curious. I take a closer look at them. They're so light blue that they're practically glowing against its black fur.

"Hey there, buddy," I coo, trying to somehow befriend a wild beast in the woods. "You're not going to eat me. Are ya."

I phrase it as a statement, more telling the wolf instead of asking. I'm sure I saw on some show that you're not supposed to show fear when dealing with a strange, unknown animal.

So that's what I do. I put on a brave face that I hope the wolf believes because I don't know if I do or not.

"You just out for a stroll, too? I know I'm enjoying the weather and the quiet. How about you? Any friends nearby I should know about?"

The wolf's thick fur ruffles as it shakes its head.

Did it just answer me?

"Can you understand me?"

It doesn't make another move, just stares at me with those piercing blue eyes.

"Of course, you can't. You're a dog. Dogs don't understand English."

It huffs what sounds like an annoyed disagreement.

"Sorry, wolf. Wolf, *not* dog."

The wolf lifts its head, and its pink tongue lulls out of its mouth. It may be a wolf, but it looks like a big dog, even with the pointy fangs.

"Cool. You're awfully pretty. Are you a boy or a girl?"

I bend my head to the side, trying to get a look between the animal's legs, but I can't see anything but black fur. When I look back up, I swear the wolf is giving me a; *did you really just try to get a look at my junk?* face.

"Sorry. That was rude. I guess I wouldn't want a stranger trying to look down my pants on the first meeting, either. How about I ask instead?"

It doesn't say or do anything.

"I'll take that as an agreement. Okay. Are you a girl?"

Again nothing. It remains motionless, its mouth closed and eyes unblinking.

"Alright. Are you a boy?"

Its mouth opens, and I swear it is smiling.

"Male. Awesome. Alright then. May I take your picture,

handsome fella?"

As slowly as physically possible, I lift the camera hanging at my side and watch the wolf, making sure he doesn't decide he's bored with me and has now decided to eat me. Thankfully, he doesn't.

I watch his intelligent eyes focus on my movements. When he doesn't do anything more than sit up taller and pose, I take that as a sign I can take his picture.

I snap the shot and watch as the photo develops. The light is perfect, and his blue eyes stand out among the darkening forest behind him.

"Wow, you're really photogenic."

The wolf stands, and before I can run, he's at my side, sniffing the photo and nudging my hand to show him. *This wolf is not a normal animal.* Lowering my hand, I show him the photo since that's apparently what he wants. He huffs at the image. Not sure what the hell that means. He likes it, maybe? Then, to my great horror, he rubs himself against my side. He reaches all the way to my ribs, and I lift my hands out of biting distance. Holding my arms over my head like I'm wading through water, trying to keep my cell phone dry.

He may be acting friendly, but I'm no fool. He's still a wild animal with meat-eating canines. Sooner than I expect, I find myself relaxing. His warm, soft fur feels nice against my side. The heat calms my racing heart, and I feel more and more at ease the longer he nuzzles into me.

I decide to take a risk and tentatively lower my hand to brush the fur at the back of his neck. It's lush and thick, and when I stroke gently, the wolf presses into my touch and makes a noise that sounds like a purr but isn't; it's more like a contented growl, low and quiet.

I guess he likes being pet, as most animals do. So, I do it

some more. Reaching up to his head but still remaining a good distance away from his mouth, I pet the short fur between his ears and lightly scratch.

This time, he lets out a soft whine, and his eyes close.

"You're a good boy, aren't you? Not scary at all. You just wanted some lovin'."

He nudges at my hand again, this time stretching his coarse tongue out to give me a little lick. I laugh because what else can I do? I'm in the middle of a forest, making nice with a wild wolf who seems to like me.

"Are these your woods? I'm sorry if I intruded on your personal space. I didn't know this area belonged to anyone."

I ramble on, talking to the wolf as if he were a person who could understand me. He's a better listener than most humans I've known. He sits and allows me to pet him for a few more minutes. By the time I'm done, I feel completely at ease with the beast. A creature I should be afraid of, but now I wonder how I ever feared him. He's calm and gentle and appears intelligent and curious. If he were a dog, I would take him home with me. But I doubt taking a wild wolf home would be a smart idea. Plus, I don't know if I'm allowed to have animals in the cabin.

"Okay, well, I have to get going now. It's getting dark, and I don't want to get lost on my way back."

He doesn't move but sits, watching me walk backward the way I came.

"Maybe I'll come back and see you again. Take some more photos."

The wolf lays down in a gesture that appears to be him saying, *I'll be right here when you return.*

"Bye then. Until next time."

I wave at the wolf lying in the grassy field, and only when I'm on the trail in the trees do I turn around and continue walking. I look over my shoulder as I go, checking to make sure the wolf remains where he was. He doesn't move the entire time.

That was the weirdest and most amazing experience of my life.

~Hunter~

After the blonde-haired woman leaves, I sit in the darkening meadow for a few long minutes. When I discovered the source of the alluring scent, I didn't realize it would belong to a person. Let alone a beautiful woman with golden hair and a soft, captivating voice. She smelled like gardenias and cloves with a hint of mint. I've never smelled anything like it before.

I should have stayed hidden in the shadows and bushes, but when she caught me watching her, I couldn't help myself. I wanted to get closer; to show her I wouldn't harm her. To rub my scent on her. I've never wanted to scent-mark anyone before. The instinct blared in my mind until I couldn't ignore it any longer, and I gave in, nuzzling and rubbing my neck against as much of her as she would let me.

My chest puffs with pride, knowing if any other non-human were to smell her, they would know she was mine.

Wait, what? Mine? She's not mine. I don't even know who she is. She did say she would be back, though. Maybe she's visiting someone in town?

I can tell by her scent that she's a human. I can only hope she knows about the non-humans. If not, then she'll never be mine, no matter how much my inner beast wants to claim her as such. My inner beast isn't as much of a separate being as it is my deep natural instinct. A part of me that doesn't weigh the pros and cons or make the decision that's best for the community. It's what I truly want deep down without limits or restrictions.

Standing, I shake off thoughts of the woman and her intoxicating scent. I need to check on the cabin. That's what I came out here to do, not get distracted by beautiful women I can't have. Turning toward the cabin, I run straight through the foliage, ignoring the path.

I make it to the cabin, and Ryder was right. There's a silver Nissan parked in the drive and lights on inside the cabin. I sniff around the grounds without getting too close to the cabin. I don't want to alert anyone inside to my presence.

There's not much to scent on the property this far away from the structure, just remnants of me and my siblings, and the lingering sweet scent in my nostrils of the blonde woman.

Turning, I sprint back in the direction of my house. I need to shift back and put on some clothes before I confront whoever is inside. Scratching at the door in my wolf form won't be helpful.

Although I could play the rabid dog angle and literally run them out, that could also turn around and blow up in our faces if they leave and start talking about a wolf attack. Instead, I'll go for the stern and demanding landlord.

The return to the cabin takes longer in human form since I have to stick to the paths and can't run as fast on two human legs as I can on four paws.

When I approach the cabin, the sun is almost gone from the sky. I catch a hint of gardenia, but it dissolves in the wind, blowing away as quickly as it came. My head swivels, searching for the blonde-haired woman, but of course, she's not here.

On the porch, there's a throw blanket draped across the arm of one of the rocking chairs I made a few years ago, and an empty coffee mug is sitting on the ground at its side. Someone is definitely here.

Sing Sweet Nightingale

My fist pounds on the door in a not-so-friendly manner, rattling it on its hinges. Whoever this person is, they're leaving *tonight*.

"Can I help you?" a timid female voice calls from inside.

"Yeah, you can tell me why you're in my cabin," I call out in a demanding voice.

"I don't know who you are, mister, but I rented this cabin fair and square."

The female voice grows a tad stronger but still cautious. As any female alone in a cabin in the woods should be when a man comes banging on her door at night.

"I highly doubt that."

My irritation is growing by the second. I don't care if it's a woman or a queen behind this door. I did not approve of her being here, so she needs to *not* be here.

Her voice grows a little louder and unyielding from behind the blue door when she replies.

"I don't care what you believe. It's true. So, would you kindly step off my porch before I call the cops?"

I have to smother a growl at her impertinence. "No, I will not step off *my* porch and the Sheriff is my brother. So why don't you get out here before *I* call the cops to have you forcibly removed for trespassing."

The door swings open and a woman I hadn't expected to see stands before me in a blur, engulfed in that scent I want to rub all over myself. The delicate floral aroma tinged with a tendril of my own unique scent marking.

"No, please don't do that. I rented the cabin from Ginger. I paid in full for three months, and she said everything was good. I'm sure if you call her, she'll tell you. I—"

I hold up my hand to stop her rambling and allow my mind a moment to process.

"Did you say Ginger?"

"Yes?" she says it like a question, like she's not sure she wants to confirm it was my sneaky sister who rented her my cabin.

I sigh, internally groaning. "Ginger is my sister. I'm Hunter. I own this cabin and the land surrounding it."

The tight pinch in her brow softens, and her shoulders sag, relieved. Apparently, my sister has been talking about me but not to me. I have a feeling this is the thing she was hiding from me. I knew she had a secret; I just wasn't expecting this.

"Oh, she told me about you."

"Did she now?" I ask, not at all surprised.

"Yes. She, however, did *not* mention you owned the property and had no idea I was here."

She gives me a sweet, innocent smile, and my heart does something funny in my chest. It pounds a little harder, a little faster. The ache grows and spreads like vines twinning around my insides.

Her teeth are pearly white and perfectly straight. Deep royal blue eyes stare up at me from beneath thick, fluttering lashes, and I'm thrown even more off-kilter seeing her now than when I first spotted her in the forest. Apparently, wolf me is more composed than human me.

"You say you've already paid?" I ask, breaking my silent gawking. My voice unexpectedly gravely.

She nods. I clear my throat and shift my weight from foot to foot, not sure what to do now. She's looking up at me with such hopeful anticipation. And for some reason, I don't want to crush her smile or make her leave. I want the opposite, actually. I want her to stay. I want to smell more of her intoxicating scent and feel her fingers run through my fur again.

"What's your name again?"

"Lottie. Lottie Pickle." She holds out her hand, relief lighting her face.

"Pickle?"

"Yeah, as in dill."

I laugh, and the sound surprises me, so I smother it. Taking her hand, I shake it. Her skin is soft and smooth under my fingers. I jolt at the sudden desire to touch more of her and the sharp static tingling that shoots through my body. Pulling my hand away quickly, I shove it in my pocket. Any woman who makes me feel that much with one touch is dangerous indeed. It's best if I don't touch her again.

"I suppose I don't have to call the Sheriff then. But I *should* call my sister."

That seems to comfort her, and she fidgets with the short ends of her hair before pushing a lock behind her ear. It falls loose instantly, and she pushes it back again. Obviously, the short length is unfamiliar to her. I like the blunt ends that look soft to the touch.

Damn it, Hunter, stop thinking about touching her.

"Okay, right. Well, sorry to interrupt your evening."

I shouldn't stay here any longer than necessary. Allowing myself such an indulgence will only make things more complicated. And I hate complicated.

"It's fine; it is your property. You're welcome to stop by any time."

Stepping off the porch, I back away, but Lottie follows me, stepping to the edge of the wooden planks and wrapping one arm around a column. I admit to myself—very quietly—that she looks rather good there.

"I shouldn't need to unless you run out of wood or something."

"Right, Volunteer fireman, good with an ax."

Lottie's scent catches on a breeze and washes over me. Causing unsolicited senses to perk up and pay attention. I rub the back of my neck, feeling a strange prickling, causing my hair to stand on end. Trying to smother the unwelcome sensation, I frown when it doesn't fully diminish.

"Right. I fear for what else my sister has told you."

"Don't worry, it's nothing embarrassing."

From the wicked grin on her face, I don't think she's telling the truth. But I don't ask. She can keep her secret if she knows something embarrassing about me but still smiles at me like that. I don't need to get to know her or start up a conversation. She's here. There's not much I can do about it at this point, but I should berate my little sister.

"Goodnight, Lottie," I say instead of the multitude of questions sitting on the tip of my tongue and cut the conversation short.

"Night, Hunter."

Lottie's smile wavers as she watches me walk away, then is replaced with a confused frown.

"Did you walk here?" she calls out to me, now a good twenty feet from the cabin.

"Yeah. My house is just about a mile that way." I point in the general direction of my house. "My brother and I live there. I own all the surrounding acres, nearly five hundred altogether."

"Wow. That's a lot of land."

"Yes, it is. Feel free to roam as you like. Most of the forest is safe, and if you need anything, well, I'm not far away. Or you could always call Ginger. I'm sure she'd be more than happy to help," I add, assuring her and myself that I don't have to be the one to help her.

"Thank you, Hunter."

"You're welcome, Lottie."

I like the way she says my name way too much. Which is why I'm going to be keeping my distance from Lottie Pickle. She's a human who obviously doesn't know anything about non-humans with sparkling ocean-blue eyes that want to suck me in and drown me.

There will be no sucking of any sort with Lottie. Sadly. But it's for the best. No matter how she smells or how my body reacts to her.

Chapter 7
Lottie

Today is my third day living in Snowberry, and I've decided I want to take a look around. When Ginger gave me her tour, I saw a few stores that looked appealing, especially the secondhand/antique store. I'm ninety-five percent sure I saw instruments in there, and I would pay anything for a guitar right now. Strumming fingers are good in a pinch, but nothing can replace the sound of an acoustic guitar.

After burning my coffee *and* toast and settling for a cold bowl of cereal, I decided my first task would be to hunt down real coffee in the local coffee shop, *The Ugly Mug*. The bakery across the street also has coffee but focuses on baked goods like pastries, cakes, and cookies. It serves only basic brewed coffee but a wider variety of teas, or so Ginger told me. whereas *The Ugly Mug* apparently makes all and more than a Starbucks.

Parking in the lot next to Dottie's, I take off on my adventure to discover more of the town and find the heavenly bliss that is espresso. I really need coffee; I don't feel like myself without it.

With my trusty Polaroid hanging on my shoulder, I straighten my spine and, with my head held high, walk confidently toward the smell of roasting coffee beans.

The Ugly Mug is the coolest coffee house I've ever been in. Nothing matches—*at all*—and I love it. The chairs don't match the tables, and the tiles lining the half wall surrounding the brewing area are different from each other, creating a chaotic but somehow cohesive design.

At least a hundred mismatched mugs hang on racks along the wall leading to the order counter. Above the first rack are painted instructions reading: *Pick a mug and a bean, then take a seat and let it steam.*

I suppose a good portion of them would be considered "ugly" by normal standards. Even though I think they're all rather amazing. There's one shaped like a donut with a hole in the center. One with tentacle legs that look like the mug would balance on them when sitting on a tabletop. One that has to be hand-painted by a toddler of what looks like people. Then I spot the one I'll be using today, a pink dinosaur with gold stars for spots on its spikey body. I think it's a T-Rex, but like a squatty chunky one. It's molded so the body of the dino is the majority of the cup. If I set it down on a table, it would look like it's sitting on its butt, the tail curling around to form the handle and a cute, rounded head protruding from the opposite side of the rim. It's perfect.

Picking my perfect "ugly" mug, I walk up to the order counter and slide my pink dino over to the guy behind the register. He picks it up and inspects it with a soft smile.

"This is a good one. If I remember correctly, it's from the Natural History Museum in London."

"What? Really?"

"Yeah, I'm pretty sure." The man looks at me, and his grin

grows into a wide beaming smile. "You're the new girl in town. Lottie, right?"

Wow. Ginger was right. Word spreads fast here.

"Yup, that would be me."

"Well, welcome to Snowberry and the *Ugly Mug*, where every mug is an adventure. Each mug we have is unique and was collected from all over the world by the owner. When his collection grew too large, he decided to put them to good use by creating a coffee shop. Because no mug should go unused."

The boyishly handsome barista, who looks to be around my age, gives a flourishing wave of his arm to the coffee shop around us with a megawatt smile that should be on a toothpaste ad. The white apron looped around his neck is painted across the front with his name in a very colorful and intricate pattern spelling out Tobias. It looks hand-painted, and when I glance at the other employees behind him, theirs are different and specific to them as well.

"That's pretty amazing. I've never seen such a place like this before. And if your coffee tastes as good as it smells, I'll probably be here every single day."

"Well, we look forward to seeing you every day. My name is Tobias, and I'm pretty much always here or at my husband's family greenhouse. If you're in need of the most beautiful flowers you've ever seen, you should check out *Daisy's*. Or if you just want to take a stroll through the gardens, you're welcome to do that as well."

Is this a normal small-town thing to be so friendly and open, or is it just a Snowberry thing? Either way, I am loving Luna more and more with every moment I spend here.

"A nursery with gardens? Wow. I didn't know this town had something like that."

"Absolutely. Daisy, my sister-in-law, runs the greenhouse

and nursery. She has a literal green thumb. If you ever have a free afternoon, swing by and check it out."

It's been so long since I've taken a stroll through a public park or garden that I can't even remember the last time I did so. There were perfectly manicured lawns and flowerbeds behind the mansion back in L.A., but even there, I had someone watching over me like a hawk. Security guards posted at either end, seemingly for my protection from outsiders getting in, but it always felt as if my mother had them there to make sure I couldn't get out.

Now, however, that isn't the case. I make my schedule, and it's wide open.

"All my afternoons are free. So, I most certainly will. Now, about this amazing coffee I keep smelling."

Making friends is definitely on my to-do list, but coffee is number one. After I'm well caffeinated, he is more than welcome to tell me his life story.

"Of course. Let's see what we have."

Tobias picks up my mug and inspects it between alternating glances my way. He seems to be figuring something out. I have no idea what he's doing but wait until he's ready to take my order. Which if he doesn't do soon, I might die.

"This is a good pick. You know you can tell a lot about a person based on the mug they pick."

"Really?" I ask. I didn't know mug divination was a thing.

"Absolutely. It's like a window into a person's personality and mood. For instance, this is my first time ever meeting you, but based on your cup choice, it is a great one; by the way, I can tell you're in a good mood today. That you're artistic and creative, have a silly sense of humor, and like pretty things just because they're pretty. You also like animals of the unusual or extinct variety."

I laugh because he's pretty dead on with his assumptions. Even though I haven't had a pet since I was a child, I've always loved animals of all kinds.

"You're really good at that. Is it a skill you were born with or learned?"

He shrugs and grins, his dark emerald eyes sparkling. *Again, with the sparkling?* I wonder if he's related to Becca over at Dottie's. Maybe it's a family trait.

"A bit of both. It's not as good as my ability to discern exactly what coffee you need."

"Need?" I question with one raised eyebrow.

I mean, I completely agree that I need coffee to function, but how would he know what I *need*?

"Yes. Although everyone has their signature coffee order, that's not always what they *need*."

There's something about Tobias, such as his relaxed posture and knowing gaze, that makes him appear wiser than any barista should be. It is as if he has aged wisdom gained through years of life experiences. Making him feel like a man far older than the mid-twenties he looks.

Curious to see if his coffee-discerning abilities are as on par as his mug divination, I give in and ask the question I know he's waiting for.

"Okay, I'll bite. What do I need today?"

Tobias squints his eyes and pinches his lips as he contemplates with a perceptive glint in his eye. "Today, you need something familiar but with a little extra sweetness to go with that pep in your step. A hot coffee to match the warmth already settling in your chest. You need something cozy but fresh. A latte with skim milk and a drizzle of caramel."

I'm stunned momentarily silent. No one has ever pinpointed what I needed so accurately. Everyone always focused on what others wanted and demanded, not what I needed. It may only be a coffee order, but Tobias has paid more attention to me in these five minutes than my mother has in the past ten years.

Trying to keep myself from crying like a lunatic because of a coffee order, I force a light laugh and smile, shaking away the weird sensation of finally being seen so that I can refocus on placing my drink order.

"Holy shit, you're psychic."

"Not psychic, but I do what I can."

The aged wisdom appearance transforms back into his boyish demeanor, and he once again becomes the perky barista he first was when I entered.

Setting my pink T-rex mug next to the espresso machine, he rings me up, and I pay.

Standing at the pick-up counter, I wait for this magical latte, watching the few patrons enjoying their own magical coffees. When Tobias hand delivers my pink T-rex mug, he stands waiting for me to take my first sip. When I do, I think my brain shuts off. It's that good. He gives me an *I told you so* wink and grin before returning to the register to help a waiting customer.

My pink T-rex mug and I take a seat at a table by the window with a view of the street beyond. I take a Polaroid of my T-rex coffee sitting on the colorful little table and add it to my growing collection in my notebook. Thumbing through the ones I've taken along this crazy journey into independence.

Considering all my recent experiences, I feel a little guilty about abandoning my fans, but I know if I were to tell any of them why I left, they would agree with me.

One of the photos stands out among the stack. One with a creature that should appear fearsome but only looks curious and a bit cuddly. I stare at it far too long as I sip my coffee.

Wondering where he came from and why he was so docile and friendly. Maybe he's been around the town for years and grown familiar with humans? Even knowing he could possibly be a violent beast that could easily tear my throat out, I still want to see the wolf again. His fur was soft and blacker than a starless night. The picture doesn't do him justice; I need to take another one. Closer up to get the distinct brightness of those sapphire eyes against his black fur.

Finishing my coffee, I return the mug and wave goodbye to Tobias as I exit the coffee shop. My insides are nice and toasty, warm from the latte and the new friend I made. Crossing the street, I pass by *Sticky Buns*, the bakery that smells sweet enough to give me a cavity just from smelling it, and then *Tall Tail Books*, which also has its own unique smell of leather and paper. A store for another day. Finally, I make my way to *Another Man's Junk* on the other side of one empty storefront.

The bell overhead jingles and announces my entry when I step through the front door. The store is filled with a plethora of unique furniture laid out to create a pathway around the store. Sturdy wooden shelves hold a plethora of objects. Items ranging from ceramic figurines and dolls to Tiffany lamps and all manner of nick knacks, and to my great pleasure instruments.

"Hello and welcome to *Another Man's Junk*; how can I help you find your treasure today?"

I'm greeted by a middle-aged woman with a large smile and a cardigan made up of crocheted squares with fish and shell patterns. Her chestnut hair is neatly braided and hanging long down her back.

"Hi. I was hoping to find a guitar if you have one."

"Well, of course, I have a few. Come on back this way, and I'd be glad to show you."

She waves for me to follow and starts twining her way through the store.

"I don't recall ever seeing you in town before. Are you new?"

Are strangers in town really that unusual? Do these people all have eidetic memories or something? Next, I expect to hear "I never forget a face" out of someone's mouth.

"Yes. just got here a few days ago."

"Well, that's wonderful. Do you plan on staying long?"

I have a feeling I'm going to repeat myself a few times before the day is over. It seems like every person I meet is going to ask me this. So, I decide to just get all the info out at once and avoid the back-and-forth.

"A few months. I'm renting a cabin from Ginger, or I suppose Hunter, actually. I'm Lottie."

"It's nice to meet you, Lottie. I'm Shanna. I am the owner and know every single item in this store. So, if you need anything, you just ask."

"Will do. Thank you, Shanna."

She continues chatting about the things she has in the store that I might be interested in, but my attention isn't on her words. Shiny objects catch my eye as I pass by displays, but none more interesting than the beauty of a holy grail sitting perched on a stand in the corner.

Surrounded by two other far less interesting guitars, the object of my every musical wet dream stares back at me, and I think I may be dreaming right now because there's no way one of the most sought-after guitars *in the world* is sitting untouched in a store in the literal middle of nowhere town. Although, that could very well be exactly why it is here.

"Is that . . . a pre-war Martin?"

The words barely escape my mouth, and I am in utter shock and disbelief. I must be hallucinating. Tobias must have slipped something more than just caramel into my latte. If this is what I think it is, this guitar is worth thousands of dollars—at an auction with the right bidders, possibly more.

"You have a good eye. That it is. Nineteen thirty-seven, to be exact. Only ever had one owner."

My feet carry me towards the Martin and as I get closer, I notice the intricately carved designs on the neck and head that I've only ever seen in photos. I wanted to purchase one in the past but just never got the opportunity.

"Can I touch it?" I ask like a child not wanting to get my fingerprints on a freshly cleaned glass window.

"Of course, you can. Take it for a spin. I make sure to keep all my instruments cleaned and tuned so customers can test them out before purchasing."

The wood is smooth, and the frets are cool to the touch when I pick up the guitar and hold it like a Fabergé egg. There's a strap attached, and I sling it over my head and let it settle against my hip.

"It's beautiful, almost in mint condition. Where did you find it?"

"It actually belonged to my father. He bought it brand new. Played it for years but has since moved on to other hobbies and no longer uses it. Is there something special about it?"

An incredulous chuckle rumbles in my chest.

"Oh yeah. Pre-war Martins are extremely rare and sought after for their perfection, for lack of a better word. There were only so many made, and collectors have been hunting for them for years. I've always wanted one, but—"

My sentence cuts off short when her words sink into my brain past the fog of wonder.

"Did you say your *dad* bought this guitar? Brand new?"

"Yes."

"In nineteen thirty-seven?"

With a cocked head, my brow furrows, and I stare at her questioningly. I suppose her father might have been alive then, which would put him in his nineties if he had been the one to purchase it as a grown man and not an infant. But she looks to be in her late thirties or early forties, so it's unlikely her father would be that old.

"Hmm?" she turns to look at me and startles. "Oh. Did I say father? I meant grandfather. It was my grandfather's. He was the reason I got into collecting and selling antique items."

"Oh. Okay."

What else am I supposed to say? You're lying? You said father, not grandfather? I don't know her; maybe she just misspoke.

"So, how do you like it? Is it what you were looking for?"

All mention of fathers and grandfathers is forgotten as I gush over the acoustic guitar in my arms. Strumming across the strings, I play a tune that's been rolling in my head for a while now but wasn't something the studio wanted to produce. They always wanted upbeat pop songs, not lovesick ballads that speak to how truly lonely I was . . . am.

"Yes. It is exactly what I am looking for. I'll take it."

"Wonderful."

Handing over the guitar to Shanna, she takes it to the counter to hold while I look around the rest of the store. Although there are many nice things, I don't need any of them. With the guitar, I'll have everything I could ever need.

Returning to the register counter, I pay for the guitar of my dreams and wish that my father could be here to see it and hear me play on the guitar, which I only know about because of him. The price for the guitar is far less than it should be, but when I offer to pay more, Shanna just brushes me off and won't take a penny more than the price on the tag.

I step out of the store with a guitar case in my hand and a smile so wide it hurts my cheeks.

Chapter 8

Hunter

I really need to stop thinking about Lottie living in my cabin, sleeping in my bed, on the sheets I've slept on many times, curled under my grandmother's quilt. Lottie is what we call a no-go zone. Getting involved with a female like her is just asking for trouble. Nope. I'm far better off keeping my distance and leaving her alone.

As I confirmed with Ginger in a very loud argument last night, she's already paid for the cabin for three months. There's not much I can do about that now. I could kick her out and refund her money; I have the right, but I don't want to. She seemed to want to be there so badly and didn't appear to be causing any problems. What's a few months?

The fact that she'd been there without my knowledge or any gossip reaching me proves that she wants peace and solitude in a location like Snowberry offers.

Lottie Pickle may spell trouble for me personally but for the town? She's harmless. That doesn't mean I'm not going to keep tabs on her. You know, for safety purposes. Not because I want to know more about her and possibly hear her captivating voice again. Not at all.

Halfway through my work morning, I realize I need something stronger than the bland brew from the break room coffee pot to get me through the day. As well as something to distract me from the desire to ask Ginger more about the allusive Ms. Pickle.

What a strange last name. How does a person end up with the surname Pickle? Were her ancestors pickle makers? It's not a common or even typical last name. *I bet I could easily find information on her with such an uncommon last name. I wouldn't even need Ginger to do a simple Google search.*

No. I shake the intrusive thoughts out of my head, shaking Lottie out of my daydreams even as I search the street and sidewalks for golden hair, striking blue eyes, and a whiff of her gardenia scent. Telling myself I'm just surveying the streets and nothing more.

This is going to be harder than I thought.

The Ugly Mug comes into view, and I quicken my pace, jogging the last few feet and rounding the corner to the door. You would think fewer people would be in a coffee shop this late in the morning, but you would be wrong. The coffee shop is just as busy now as it would be at eight in the morning. That is to say, about half a dozen people are sitting and drinking hot and cold beverages. It's a small town, so busy is relative.

I grab one of my usual mugs off the rack on the wall. A large, wide-rimmed cup, the exterior painted to resemble a pastel watercolor rainbow with a gold handle big enough to comfortably fit my larger hands. As a shifter and an alpha at that, I'm a little larger than the average male. So, I don't care that it's colorful and "girly." It gets the job done, and it's grown on me.

Tobias grins when I place the mug on the counter. He knows what it means when I choose this cup. I need coffee and a lot of it.

"That kind of day, huh?" he asks, ringing me up for whatever he thinks I need to drink today. I trust him to choose for me and don't question it. The only time I ever choose my own order is when I'm trying to remain on schedule and need to get in and out. Then, I stick to my go-to espresso—quick and efficient.

"Yeah. Too many new visitors in town so close to the eclipse."

Not for the first time, my thoughts venture to the elf wandering around town doing who knows what. So far, he hasn't stepped out of line, but it's barely been a couple days since his arrival. If I give it time, he'll slip up, and I'll be there to personally escort him out of town when he does.

"Ah, yes. I met our new resident this morning."

My heart drops to my stomach, thinking he's talking about the elf. But when I see his mischievous smile, I realize there's no way that who he's talking about. Which means he's referring to...

"Lottie was here?"

His grin grows wider. The bastard knew I already met her and wanted me to admit it. He is way too good at reading people and knowing things he shouldn't.

"Yup. She picked the pink T-rex mug. I like her. Her colors were vibrant and happy. She's going to fit in perfectly here."

Fairies see emotions as colors around an individual, like an aura. Tobias being a rather old fairy who's been around the world a time or two is very good at reading people. To hear hers is so bright doesn't surprise me. But I shouldn't care what color her emotions are; she's just another visitor in town and nothing more. How she's feeling should play no part in my day.

And yet here I am, with warm tingles spreading through my gut. I'm pleased to hear she's in a good mood, and I wonder if our interaction last night had anything to do with it.

Damn it, Hunter, get your shit together. She's just a girl, nothing special. Get over it. You shouldn't care whether or not you have anything to do with her happiness.

I put on an air of indifference and pay for my coffee, feigning disinterest. "Oh, is that so?"

"Absolutely. There's something about her that conveys... rightness."

He says that last word as if he has thought it over thoroughly and settled with rightness. I can see his eyes shifting around me no doubt seeing flashing colors around me displaying my erratic emotions. Since I don't even know what I'm truly feeling right now, I'm sure my colors are a kaleidoscope, ever-changing from one to another.

My brows pinch together in confusion. "What does that mean?"

"Many things."

He says nothing more but keeps a tight smile on his lips, which I know means there is more, but he can't say what. Some fairies, especially the older ones, tend to have special abilities like a sixth sense. Tobias can just tell these things about others but doesn't always know the why. I've asked him to explain in the past, but he says it's more of a feeling, a knowing that someone is good or bad, lying or telling the truth, or in this case, "right." He doesn't know facts or specifics, so I don't ask for further clarification.

Nodding, I slacken my features to hopefully hide my irritation with his vague words. And maybe calm my emotions so as not to blind him with my flashing colors.

Sing Sweet Nightingale

When my cup is set on the pick-up counter, I eagerly scoop it up and gulp down a large swallow. The coffee is hot and strong but laced with a subtle sweetness. I have no clue what it is, but I drink it, and it settles my rattled nerves, at least for a few minutes.

As I stand looking out the window drinking my coffee, I spot the cause of my inner maelstrom casually strolling down the sidewalk, smirking at every person he passes. He doesn't seem to be doing anything unscrupulous at the moment. But I frown when his sights lock on to someone down the street, and his stride picks up pace. Craning my head, I try to see around the parked cars to the person who's grabbed his attention so thoroughly.

My blood boils when I realize who the golden-haired woman practically skipping down the street carrying some sort of case is. Lottie Pickle.

Fucking hell.

I don't immediately bolt out of the coffee shop and stalk over to them. There's nothing that says he can't look at a woman walking down the street. She's not even a citizen of Snowberry, just a visiting human. She is of no importance to him or me, but I have to hold back my growl when I spot him intercept her path.

Why do I want to protect her as if she is one of my pack? She's an outsider, a stranger, a *human*. I shouldn't care either way if he speaks to her. And yet, the last half of my coffee is gone in two gulps, and I walk out the door in their direction before I even know I'm moving. Tobias' quiet laughter trailing behind me.

Lottie's face comes into focus the closer I get, and I realize her smile is forced and doesn't reach her cobalt eyes. Her posture isn't any better. She's closed off and leaning away from him. She doesn't want to speak with him, and he's pushing himself on her.

She's dressed in skintight, high-waisted jeans with delicate tears in the thighs, exposing slivers of tanned skin. Skin is also visible across her ribs where her jeans end and her cropped little black sweater begins. Tanned skin taunts me with its golden glow, beseeching me to touch and taste.

As soon as I'm close enough, her gardenia scent washes over me, and unbidden, my cock twitches in my slacks. I ignore the irrational appendage and focus on her other scents. Her emotions. The sweet floral of her scent tainted by bitter irritation.

You would think he was touching her and forcing her physically with the fire that ignites in my gut. I want to sink my fangs into his throat and rip. I clench my jaw to keep from doing just that. He still hasn't done anything wrong. My hands ball into fists, and I feel the prick of my nails becoming claws in my palms.

Taking a deep breath, I steady myself before I speak. Loud and clear directly behind the elf.

"Is there something I can help you with?" I growl out in an aggressively polite tone.

The elf spins to face me, not having noticed my abrupt approach. A disingenuous smile crossing his thin lips.

"Mr. Mayor, so good to see you again. What are you doing wandering the streets in the middle of the day? Don't you have other more important mayoral things to be doing?"

He rolls his hand in a flippant gesture of indifference. I really want to ring this male's neck and rip his head from his body. But I can't, not yet anyway. If he touches Lottie, however, I may not be able to stop myself with how my inner beast is responding to her.

Shifting in the middle of town would be irresponsible and

reckless. That doesn't seem to matter right now, and I really need to get my shit together. This is fucking ridiculous. I'm acting like an uncontrollable pup eager to wag my tail and roll over for this woman and strike down any male who dares get close to her.

Mustering all the self-control I've deliberately acquired over the years, I check my anger and urges. Settling for restrained displeasure in my tone when I speak.

"Checking on the well-being of my residents is *very* important to me."

He licks his lips and smirks, shoving his hands in his pockets and casually leaning back on his heels. The action only fueling my hatred for this elf and diminishing my dwindling patience with his arrogance.

"Oh, I bet her well-being is important to you."

Chapter 9
Lottie

Out of all the things going on right now that require my attention, like the skeevy man who was just hitting on me, the thing that grabs my interest is the mayor title he used towards Hunter. In our previous conversations, he and his sister failed to mention that little tidbit of information. It would have been nice to know I'm renting the mayor's cabin and hanging out with his sister.

Hunter turns his attention to me and ignores the rude man between us.

"Is this man bothering you?"

I could tell Hunter was an attractive man last night on my front porch—or rather *his* front porch—but now, in the full clear light of day without the evening shadows hiding his features, I can see he is a heartthrob. Tall, well-built, with a strong jawline and thick black hair that looks soft even in its smooth styling. I see now why Ginger warned me about his baby blues. They are mesmerizing. Like two ice-blue diamonds adrift in a dark sea beckoning me.

It's not only his eyes that mesmerize me, but his deep and low voice, which reverberates through my bones and echoes in my chest. Something about it makes my toes curl when I hear him speak, as if his voice is comprised of the most perfectly in-tune note ever to be played. It's seductive, and the strange pull I felt towards him when we first met tugs once again at my chest, urging me towards him.

However, the deep scowl on his face and his obvious rising anger convey less-than-pleasant emotions on his part. I can't tell if he's mad at the man for being pervy or at me for taking time out of his busy day Mayoring.

I didn't ask you to come to my rescue, Mr. Mayor. I was doing just fine and was just about to tell him off when you showed up and interrupted my well-scripted refusal.

The words die in my throat under his scrutiny, and every ounce of bravado and eloquence flies right out the door with that well-crafted refusal.

"Oh, um, well. . ."

The flirtatious man reaches out an arm and wraps it around my shoulders. I instantly cringe and try to pull away but don't get far. His arm is like a vice and oddly cold. A strange man hasn't dared to touch me in years, and for a moment, I wish Luna were here to pry his hand off me and break his fingers.

"Of course not, we're just having a friendly chat. Getting to know each other. Might even get some dinner together later tonight."

The scowl on my face must be deep because Hunter's expression grows harder and angrier seeing it. He reaches out and, with a strong hand, grabs the guy's shirt collar and pulls just hard enough to force him to remove his arm from my shoulders or risk knocking me over. I take the opportunity to step a healthy distance away out of reach.

Hunter drops his grip on the man once he's repositioned himself, placing his bulky body between us. The man now too far away to try to touch me again. Interesting. That's the type of maneuver I would expect Luna to pull. She said she knew people in this town. Perhaps that meant more than just Ginger? Was Hunter, at one point, a bodyguard as well?

That sounds like an interesting story—a bodyguard turned Mayor— it would make a good movie. They could get Henry Cavill to play Hunter.

"Hey, easy on the threads, man. No need to ruin the Gucci."

I poke my head around Hunter's massive body, taking in the man's shirt that he's smoothing down with one hand, and I don't know how I hadn't noticed before. Usually, I'm really good at spotting brand labels. Only weeks away from my former lifestyle, and I'm already forgetting it.

Hunter ignores the man's protests and scowls at him. Not giving two shits about his precious Gucci. "Don't touch people who obviously don't want to be touched," he practically bellows, standing his ground and still blocking me like any bodyguard I'd ever known would.

"You're the one who was touching without permission. And how do you know she didn't want to be touched?" the man with the death wish counters. *This guy is really dim, isn't he?*

"Anyone with eyes could see it."

"You wanted me to touch you, didn't you darlin?" the stranger asks sweetly as if it were unbelievable that a woman wouldn't want to be touched by him.

He might be physically attractive on the outside, but something about him that rubs me the wrong way.

"No. I most certainly did *not* want you touching me. Now or ever."

He pulls back in mock surprise, gasping and clutching his Gucci shirt as if he'd been insulted in the worst way.

"Sweetheart, you wound me."

"I'm not your sweetheart, and I'd appreciate it if you kept your clammy hands to yourself," I bite back.

I've always wanted to tell people like him what I really think of them, but I couldn't say anything with so many reporters always surrounding me. One wrong word in the press and my sweet, good-girl image would be ruined. If they knew the mouth, I had on me.

"Ouch. Feisty. I think I like you even more now. Are you sure we can't renegotiate the no-touching policy? Maybe add in a biting addendum."

Hunter actually growls in front of me, and his muscles bunch and tighten. Yeah, he was definitely a bodyguard in a previous career. But none of my past protectors ever made my insides quiver because of a growl. A sexy as hell growl. I don't even think a man has ever growled around me before. I kind of like it.

"Don't even think about it, Roman. She said no touching that means *no touching*. Am I understood?"

The timber of Hunter's voice changes and rumbles in a low and threatening way. It's not even directed at me and a chill rolls down my spine. Heated desire mixing with the cold stillness of submission. My insides warring between doing as he says and having my way with him.

The man, Roman's countenance completely changes. His playful smile flattens, and his casual posture straightens and hardens. It even looks like his eyes become darker.

"Yeah, I get you."

Roman's eyes shift to me, and his previously sweet flirtation turns into lewd leering paired with a suggestive biting of his bottom lip. My skin pebbles with goosebumps along the path his eyes take down my body, physically disgusted with his perusal.

"Sorry, sweetheart. Maybe we can play another time."

He really is that stupid, isn't he?

"Not likely," I state as firmly and rudely as possible.

He sighs but shrugs, finally taking backward steps away from us. "Too bad. You taste delectable. It would have been fun."

Hunter bristles and takes a half step towards Roman. The move is an obvious threat. He takes his position as mayor seriously. *Or is it specific to me?* The thought melts the previous chill, bringing me right back to boiling hot aroused.

Something deep inside me churns with delight at the prospect—something I've never felt before—not a gut feeling or heart thumping. This is something new and unexpected—feral. I don't have time to process the sensation before my attention is drawn back to the man in front of me.

"Move along. I'm sure you have *work* to do. You know, the reason you're in town," Hunter bites out at the still retreating man.

"Of course. Until next time."

Roman takes one last look at me and Hunter before spinning on his heel and sauntering in the opposite direction, whistling as he goes. Not in the least concerned with the irate Hunter still glaring at his back.

That was an extremely odd interaction. It seemed like they knew each other and weren't on the friendliest of terms.

"Are you okay? He didn't do anything inappropriate, did he?"

Looking up, I notice Hunter has turned to face me, and staring into those blue diamond eyes, I have to suck in a breath to steady my erratic heartbeat before answering.

"Yeah, I'm fine. He didn't do anything. We had only been talking for a minute before you arrived. He just sort of walked up to me and started flirting. It was kind of off-putting."

Hunter nods, grimacing, but quickly smooths over his expression into a soft neutral, all previous emotions now gone. The anger and throat-slashing wrath that I sensed in him before now replaced with a polite, calm demeanor. Doesn't make me any less attracted to him, I notice.

"I would steer clear of him in the future," he says.

"Why is that?"

He doesn't answer immediately seemingly determining his response. After years of dealing with people who tell half-truths and keep pertinent information from me, I can tell he's not going to answer candidly.

"He's not a trustworthy person. A bit of a cad. It's best to just not get involved with him."

Although I believe him and his opinion of Roman, I also know there's more to it than he's telling. I watch him for a moment, trying to understand more about this man I just met who so adamantly defended me without question with such heated veracity, then instantly went cold again.

At least I'm not the only one having hot flashes.

"Okay. I believe you. He wasn't exactly my type anyway. Too pervy. He probably has like five STDs and ten illegitimate children."

Hunter's stoic demeanor cracks, and a bark of laughter bursts from him, surprising me with its warmth. It sinks into my skin and slivers into my bones. I want to hear more of it, but he buttons his lips tight when he realizes what he just did. But the lightness in his eyes remains. Surprised by his reaction, he flounders for a moment and redirects the conversation, gesturing to the guitar case in my hand.

"What do you have here?"

"Oh," I smile brightly as the excitement I had in the store renews. "This is my new guitar. I just bought it."

"You play the guitar?"

"Yeah. My dad taught me as a kid, and I've been dying to play lately. I usually play all the time, but since I didn't bring a guitar with me, I really missed it."

"Do you sing, too?"

My heart stutters, and my brain short circuits. The question isn't one I thought I would have to answer. I suppose I brought it upon myself with the whole guitar purchase. Anyone would ask it. Hunter just doesn't realize what a loaded question that is for me. If I were to admit I sing, would he ask to listen? Would he then recognize my voice? What then?

I realize I've been standing here silent, Hunter looking at me expectantly and probably thinking I'm crazy for longer than normal. It's probably best to just admit it and deal with the consequences.

"Yes. Sometimes. You know, just for fun, in the living room. *Alone.*"

There, that wasn't too weird. Right? Totally normal response.

"Oh. Well, that's a shame. The local bar, Blue Moon, has a rather popular karaoke night. I'm sure everyone would love some new blood in the mix. There's only so many times you can listen to Dottie sing ABBA off-key before your ears start to bleed."

His easy-going reply has my nerves settling and shoulders relaxing.

"I don't know, I like ABBA."

"You won't after hearing her belt out Dancing Queen off-key for the hundredth time. It really is an assault on the senses.

Just know," he adds in a lighter seriousness. "That if anyone else finds out you can sing, you're going to get a lot of guilt tripping and peer pressure to participate. So, if you don't want to sing in public, I'd hide that guitar before someone sees."

At his declaration, I start looking around the street to see if anyone is watching us. A few people are mulling up and down the street and in the storefronts. Thankfully, we're in front of the empty shop with a for lease sign hanging in the window. No one within our immediate vicinity. It's still possible someone may have already seen me with the guitar case, though. Hopefully, not Dottie. It sounds as if she is the karaoke queen and the instigator of all strong-handed entries.

"Will do. So, you're the mayor, huh?" I ask, diverting attention away from me and moving it to him. Hoping to bypass any more talk of singing, especially in public.

His cheeks pinken, and he makes a noncommittal noise in his throat, which makes me giggle. This strong, attractive man is bashful about being the mayor.

"Yes, I am. I guess I'm just not used to telling people they usually already know," he admits with a smothered grin.

It's like he's trying not to smile too much. He keeps catching himself and pulling back into a neutral expression. Reverting into a disinterested posture, yet he continues to appear interested. The signals he's giving are very confusing indeed. I can't tell if he's interested, not interested, impartial, or just being friendly. Perhaps it's part of his mayoral duties? It's all too confusing to understand.

"And mister handsy?" I tilt my chin in the direction Roman went. "Where does he work? If there's somewhere I should avoid, I'd like to know."

Hunter scoffs and even sneers. "He's not a resident of Snowberry. Just passing through. Hopefully, he'll be gone soon."

"But you know him. Have you met before?"

"In a manner of speaking. I know his boss," he says vaguely.

More half-truths. I have a feeling Hunter keeps a lot to himself. I doubt he'll answer, but I decide to keep asking anyway, just in case he deigns to divulge any important information.

"And who is his boss?"

"No one you need to bother yourself with. Just steer clear of him and anyone with him, and you'll be fine."

Hunter refortifies his stiff posture and takes a step back, making space between us that says everything his words keep mixing up.

Not interested.

My heart sinks a little, and the part of me that reacted to his voice and attention churns with melancholy. I realize I want him to be interested because I'm interested.

"Anyway, have a nice day, and if you have any issues around town or with the cabin, you can contact Ginger or my office at Town Hall."

He keeps backing away, taking measured steps back in the direction he came from. Probably a good thing. Getting involved with someone right now isn't a good idea. Not only because of the train wreck of a relationship I just got out of but because I'm literally living on the lamb right now. I have no idea what my future will be, where I'll be, what I'll be. A pop star, a musician, a recluse, a nobody.

Everything may seem calm on the surface, but underneath the pristine exterior is a maelstrom of chaos and uncertainty. Of fear for the future and the day when someone recognizes me and the paparazzi reappear. Or the day when my mother finds me and manipulates me back into submission. That is my greatest fear. Not being able to retake control of my life without my mother stealing the reigns right out of my hands.

I love music, I love singing. But being a celebrity is not what I want my future to be. It's a life filled with lies, greed, and loneliness. That's not what my dad wanted for my life. He wanted me to be happy, to love, and to enjoy life. I haven't been happy in years. I smile and wave and sing songs about love and happiness, but inside, I've been slowly cracking and losing pieces of myself. I just want to find them all and assemble them back into something resembling a person.

Ever since I arrived in Snowberry, I've felt like I've been slowly regaining who I used to be before all the fame and money. Who I am and what I want out of life. I don't know if I'll want to go back to my old life in three months. Living life like everyone else has been . . . easy. Nothing has been easy since I became Alexandria—pop superstar. Going to the grocery store, picking out my own clothing, *dating*. All of it required a dozen people and a security plan. But life here is easy. Simple.

Well, sort of simple. The mayor is making it less simple with his damn baby blues and seductive voice, and confusing behavior.

"Thank you. I guess I'll see you around town sometime," I say in farewell to Hunter's retreating form.

"Maybe," he says noncommittally; that makes me think he doesn't want to be seeing me around town any time soon. Or at all.

He gives me a little wave, and I pinch my lips into a thin line at the man who is more confusing than a pig in roller skates.

Since I am heading in the same direction as Hunter, I wait until he's made it far enough down the street that I won't appear to be following him when I resume walking. I take the opportunity to admire his firm backside, which flexes with each stride of his long legs. Not because I'm interested, but because it was in my line of sight. It's his own fault, really.

When I cross the street and turn the corner, I notice his tall form far down the street, bounding up the stairs to a white-wash brick building that is obviously town hall. He walks really fast. Must be those strong legs of his.

After stowing my guitar in the trunk of my car, I head to the next stop on my to-do list. I've been going through a lot of Polaroid film lately, and when I noticed the camera shop, I knew I would be going there sooner rather than later. I just hope they have the film I need.

SnapShot is on the opposite side of the parking lot from Dottie's and only a twenty-foot walk from my car. Inside, I find more than just cameras and film. There's a whole section of art and craft supplies. Colored pencils, paints, canvases, sketchbooks, and pens.

Bypassing the paint, I head straight for the film by the back counter. I'm surprised by how many film options they have. Nowadays, everyone uses digital cameras or their smartphones. It's nice to see such an extensive inventory of film and film cameras. As a matter of fact, I don't think I see any digital cameras at all. Old school. I like it.

"Hello there. Welcome," a male voice calls out, startling me.

I jump and spin in place, facing the voice. No one was in here when I entered, so he must have come from the back room because I didn't hear the bell at the front door ring after I entered.

"Hello."

"Can I help you find anything today?" the man behind the counter asks.

He's classically handsome, with jet-black hair that's

graying at the temples. I can't tell exactly how old he is, as his characteristics could make him younger or older. I'm going to go with older, maybe around the age my dad would be if he were still alive.

The thought warms me to him immediately. Associating him with a father figure. With his welcoming smile and friendly attitude, he doesn't seem to be just for customers.

You know how sometimes, when you meet a person, you get a vibe? Well, his vibe is nothing but positive feelings. He puts off an air that makes me instantly like him. Kind of like Ginger.

"Yes. I'm looking for Polaroid film."

I hold up my white and blue Polaroid Now I-Type instant camera.

"Well, isn't she a beauty? Polaroids are one of my favorites. I absolutely have some film for you."

Stepping out from behind the counter, he walks down the next aisle and stoops. By the time I circle the chest high shelf and join him he stands holding a small box with the polaroid rainbow across the middle.

"Found it," he proclaims, handing the box over to me. "Do you need more than one?"

Each cartridge only holds eight photos, and at the rate I'm using them, I'll definitely need more than one.

"Yes. A couple if you have them. Maybe three or four?"

"Not a problem."

Bending down, he produces three more boxes of color I-type film and hands them to me.

"You take a lot of photos?"

"Recently, yes. It's kind of become a new hobby of mine."

The man walks back behind the counter, his broad smile still in place. I follow, unable to resist smiling in return. Placing the film, my camera, and purse on the counter, I pull out my notebook, which holds the majority of my photos.

"I've been taking them everywhere I go. Some around town as well."

He takes the film boxes and starts ringing them up, typing the prices into a register without internet or a barcode scanner. I spot a credit card machine behind the counter that doesn't look like it gets much use.

"Really? Any good ones?" His tone conveys true interest, not just polite conversation.

Flipping through my notebook, I pull out a couple of my favorites and lay them out one by one for him to see.

"I took this one of my coffee this morning. This one at Dottie's when I first arrived. Then there's the cabin I'm staying in."

He nods and inspects each one as I lay them out. Smirking at one of the cabins, laughter evident in his eyes. Then I place the final photo down, the one of the wolf. He picks it up and holds it in front of his nose for a closer inspection.

"I took that one in the forest where I'm staying. The wolf was surprisingly tame. He let me take his picture, then even rubbed against me and let me pet him."

"Really now?"

With the photo still held in his hand, he looks up at me in disbelief, eyebrows raising and the smile on his face amused. His dark eyes saying something I can't decipher.

"Is that weird? I sure as hell thought it was weird, but when he didn't bite or maul me, I figured maybe he was used to being around humans."

"Oh, he's definitely used to being around humans."

Shocked at the familiarity in his words, I look at him, my forehead pinching in confusion.

"You know the wolf? Has he been around a lot?"

"He's definitely familiar to the town. There are a lot of them in the woods, actually. We know them; they know us," he explains nonchalantly like it's a normal everyday thing to be friendly with wild wolves.

"So, I shouldn't be afraid of him then?" I ask.

It would make me a lot more comfortable knowing that one interaction wasn't a fluke and that if I cross paths with the wolf again, I don't have to fear it. For some unknown reason, I've been feeling drawn back to the woods ever since meeting the wolf.

"Not at all." The man looks me over, studying me. He grins as he sets the photo down on the counter with the rest of them.

"I'm sorry I never introduced myself." He extends a hand across the counter to shake. "My name is Michael. I'm Hunter and Ginger's father."

"Seriously?" I blurt out before I can stop myself with my hand halfway to his, frozen in shock.

There's no freaking way he's Hunter's dad. He can't be that old. If I remember correctly, Ginger said they have another brother who's older than them both. He must have been really young when they were born.

Michael chuckles and doesn't seem offended by my outburst. He closes the distance between our oddly outstretched hands, clasping mine in his. His hand is far larger than mine, and his grip is solid but gentle.

"Sorry. It's just—you don't look old enough to have a grown son as old as Hunter."

"Well, thank you. We live a healthy life and stay active. I think that's what keeps us young at heart."

He releases my hand, and it drops uselessly, resting on top of my purse on the counter. What some people in LA wouldn't pay to bottle whatever it is he's using to stay young. It has to be something in the water because Dottie didn't look as old as Ginger made her out to be, either.

"I actually just ran into your son before coming here," I admit.

Michael doesn't immediately speak. Just continues smiling and watching me.

"And, was he friendly?"

Odd choice of words, but whatever.

"Um, well, when we first met last night at the cabin, he tried to get me arrested for trespassing. But today, he was polite and helpful. I'm not sure he would consider us friends exactly."

Michael chuckles, and it ends on an exacerbated sigh. "He can be a little uptight sometimes. He takes his position as mayor very seriously and doesn't like when unexpected obstacles appear. New people in town always make him a little edgy. He'll get over it."

It's nice to know it's not just me. The inner part of me that was saddened at Hunter's initial distancing lightens. So, he's just a stickler for the status quo. Doesn't like change or waves in the water. That's fine with me. I don't want to cause a disturbance.

"I know," Michael proclaims suddenly, surprising me with his optimistic tone. "Why don't you come over for dinner with me and my wife? We can invite Ginger, Hunter, and Ryder, my oldest. You can get to know them, and they you. I'm sure once Hunter is more familiar with you, he'll be more friendly."

"Oh, I don't know—" I start to decline his polite offer, but he cuts me off before I can finish.

"Nonsense. I insist. Why don't we plan for this weekend? Say, Friday night? Saturday is karaoke night, and I know Ginger doesn't like to miss it."

I fumble my words, trying to find a way to reject the invitation, but nothing comes out. I've never received such a heartwarming invitation before. Most people only want me to attend their event to draw the media's eye to them. Bringing them the attention that always follows me everywhere I go. But Hunter's dad only wants me there to get to know each other better. How can I say no to that? And I secretly want to see Hunter again. Maybe his dad is right; if he gets to know me, he'll be more inclined to be my friend.

"Okay, then. Friday it is."

"Perfect. I'll let everyone know and don't worry about anything. I'll have one of the kids pick you up, say five?"

"Sounds great."

As long as that kid is Ginger.

I pay for my film in cash and chat for a minute longer with Hunter's dad before venturing back to my car. I think I've had enough excitement for today. Plus, I really want to get home and test out my new guitar.

I drive back to the cabin with swirling thoughts of Hunter, guitars, dinner with his parents, and the unexpected fluttering in my gut of anticipation.

Chapter 10
Hunter

Today was going so well. With no surprise, little sister visits or detours to coffee shops or public exchanges with Lottie or the elf. My routine falling back into place where it should be, everything running on schedule as usual. Things going smoothly around town for once. Until now. Even before his features come into view, I can tell who the man standing on my porch is as I pull into my drive.

Why the fuck is Vincent here? I was pretty sure I made it abundantly clear last time he was in town that if he ever showed his face here again, I would tear it off with my teeth. Apparently, he has a death wish because there he stands without a glimmer of fear in his cold black and silver eyes. Not even deigning to wear a glamour. All of his sickly-gray skin visible.

Most elves don't have a healthy pallor to begin with, but for some reason, Vincent's is even duller and sicklier than others, making him appear one foot in the grave even though I know he's nowhere near a natural death. He wouldn't allow it. Extending his life by extricating magic from pixies, sprites, and fairies for his own benefit—and not in a humane way, either. From what I hear, most don't survive his 'treatments.'

Just makes me want to kill him that much more. And now that he's willingly stepped foot on my land after my last warning, no one would fault me for killing the arrogant male.

The only thing that keeps me from immediately disemboweling the elf on my front porch is the exuberant amount of security he's brought with him. Not only elves but fairies, shifters, and nymphs as well.

I know I can take them, but the odds aren't weighed in my favor, one against a dozen. Even as an alpha, I may be able to disperse his men, but he would be long gone by that time. The coward. Never fighting his own fucking battles. Brute strength only goes so far against fairy dust and nymph magic. I'd rather wait until I at least have Ryder around to even the playing field. He's one of the more feral fighters of our pack; even with his passive daily demeanor, his inner beast is one of the most vicious I've ever met. Even though he hasn't shifted around me in years. At least not fully, only partial shifts.

My truck is barely in park and turned off when I jump from the driver's seat and stomp in his direction.

"What the hell are you doing here? I thought I made myself clear to you and your minion crawling around town; I'm not selling, and there's no amount of money you can offer that will make me change my mind."

Vincent's answering grin is all self-satisfying superiority.

Fucking prick.

"Come now, Hunter, I'm sure we can find something enticing enough to persuade you."

"No. Now get off my property."

Sing Sweet Nightingale

I point an aggravated, sharp-clawed finger down my driveway and away from my home. My body already trying to shift into my true form to fight the male trespassing on my land. He's pushing his luck stepping foot on an alpha shifter's land. After our pack, our land is the most sacred to us and is highly protected.

"Is that any way to greet a guest? I thought shifters were all hospitality and cordiality? No? Your mother would be ashamed."

We're only hospitable to invited guests, and he damn well knows that he is not welcome here. *Ever.*

"Say one more word about my family, and I will not hold myself back. You will be faced with my alpha wrath whether I want it or not."

He shakes his head disapprovingly, like a scolding teacher. "You should really get that temper of yours in check. Might get you into trouble one day."

Alpha rage is not something that can be controlled. It's instinctual, and holding it back takes every ounce of control I possess. A control I was forced to learn after an unpleasant incident when I allowed my inner beast to take control. A mistake I'm not going to make again. No matter how much I want to let it loose on this asshole.

"It already has in the past. I must admit I'm rather fond of unbridled rage and bloodlust when directed at my enemies. I like having beings with such power in them at my command." Vincent's eyes are dark and assessing as he looks over my strained posture and fisted hands.

I say nothing because I fear speaking will distract me from restraining myself and unleash the bloodlust he seems so fond of. Vincent, it seems, has plenty to say for us both.

"I just wanted to come by and see if there weren't some

way we could work out this little disagreement between us like mature males. You have all this land just sitting here in disuse."

He waves a grand sweeping arm at the forest surrounding us as if it were a barren wasteland with no purpose. It has a purpose and a deep connection to a lot of non-humans. Many would be lost without this land to roam freely. Numerous sprites and pixies have made it their permanent home. They can't live in modern society. They aren't shifters or humanoid enough to pass for humans, even with a glamour. Most can't even speak words like we do. They're more magic and creature than the rest of us. Harmless in most cases but can be deadly if attacked or frightened. Their magic is the purest of all the non-humans.

I know this is part of the appeal to Vincent and why he wants the land. Which is just one more reason for me to keep it far out of his reach. He wants to defile it with his abominations—atrocities grown from the mixing of non-human magic and natural psychotropic plants to create his special breed of potent drug. The richer in magic the land is, the stronger it'll be.

Not in my fucking lifetime.

"My land gets plenty of use that doesn't involve stripping it to grow drugs. I am completely content with what I have and don't need anything more. Especially anything you have to offer."

"It's a real shame. I could use a shifter as powerful as you in my organization. You could make real money working for me. Have any female or male you want; live wherever you please. Not have to answer to whimpering simpletons complaining about roadside garbage and flickering streetlights. Don't you want to put your alpha power to good use? Commanding strong shifters and enforcing your will? That's what an alpha was meant to do after all. Lead. Command."

I sneer at the insinuation that I would associate myself with scum such as him. Or that I would ever stoop so low as to work for him.

"No thanks."

Vincent ignores my refusal *again*, strolling over to the carved wooden bench swing hanging from the rafters of my covered porch. Sitting he crosses one ankle over his knee getting comfortable. His black loafers polished to an annoying shine.

"Why must you insist on remaining in this backwater town wasting away?"

"I like backwater towns. They're cleaner than gutter cities."

Vincent winces mockingly. Pursing his thin lips and glaring at me through slitted eyes, the silver of his irises nearly swallowed whole by the surrounding black.

"I tell you what. You think on my offer, say for the next two weeks. And I'll be around when you're ready to accept. After that, I can't promise my offer will remain as juicy as this. Or as civil."

"Juicy as what? Unless I'm mistaken, you haven't made any offer, just vague statements."

He chuckles and grins. "See, that's why I like you, Hunter. You come to work for me as a general in my ranks, commanding your own pack of elite shifters for whatever amount of money you want, and in return . . . I get your land. That's all I want."

Before I can reject yet another asinine offer, he stands and crosses the porch to where I've been standing on the steps, glaring.

"Don't answer now. Just think about it."

"My answer won't change. It'll be the same in two weeks as it is today."

"We'll see."

Shoving his hands in the pockets of his pristinely pressed suit pants, Vincent ambles by me, not a fucking care in the world. Completely comfortable in his assumption of my inevitable acceptance as his football team of minions coalesce on the two black SUVs parked in my driveway. He stops at the rear passenger door of one and slips on a pair of mirrored sunglasses, flashing his fangs at me with a grin.

"See you around, Alpha."

"Better not. If I see you in my town, it won't matter how many people you have with you, I will kill you."

His smile doesn't falter, and his hands don't shake. Anyone else receiving a promise of death from an alpha shifter would be shitting their pants, but not Vincent. Death threats are a daily occurrence in his world.

"You say the nicest things," he mocks in a saccharine tone.

I don't move until the two black vehicles are out of sight. Letting out all my pent-up anger in a roar and one swift right hook to a column supporting the awning. It splinters and breaks clean through leaving small dangling pieces at the top and bottom. Sharp pieces of wood strewn across the deck.

Damn it. Now I'll have to make a new one.

The shift that began the moment I first saw Vincent continues to crackle through my body. I can't hold it back any longer. I need to let it take over and run it out. As quickly as possible, I pull off my shirt and pants, tossing them on the ground, not bothering to fold them neatly as I usually would. There's no time. My inner beast needs to be set free. So, I let it.

I release the hold on my control and allow my instinct to take over. The shift rolling through my body faster than it ever has. Flying right by basic unassuming wolf straight into my full true form. Ginger likes to refer to it as "beast mode" or "beast form."

Sing Sweet Nightingale

My height stretches to over nine feet tall, knees reversing direction, popping into place as I settle on my hind legs. My arms and hands elongate, tipped with razor-sharp claws, while thick black fur sprouts from every pore covering my entire body. Jawbone cracking and growing to form my snout. The sharp point of my fangs curl around my lower jaw, and a snarl works its way from my chest out my throat.

I take off into the forest, crouching to propel myself forward with my hands and claws. The trees fly by in a blur as I run. The anger already beginning to dissipate the farther into the forest I go.

I don't consciously pick a direction and don't even realize where I'm heading until I slow on instinct. Standing on my hind legs, I slowly walk towards the small clearing where I first met Lottie days ago. Then when I arrived the meadow was empty, this time it isn't.

Before I see her, I hear her. The gentle strumming of a guitar and her sweet, melodic voice carry through the still forest. Her voice is perfection. It floats through the air and slivers into my bloodstream. The sound is melancholic and uninhibited. Her words laced with a feeling of freedom. A sweet singing nightingale. It eases my simmering rage, cooling it to nothing more than a tepid puddle.

Her scent is stronger in this form, my enhanced nose inhaling deep and pulling every bit of her into my body as possible. It sends tingles through my nerves, and impulses I've never felt course through me with my desire for more of her. More of her scent, her voice, and her soft touch threading through my fur. The need to claim a blaring alarm in my mind that I have to silence. The growing lust a fire I need to put out.

I shouldn't be here.

I shouldn't spend any more time with Lottie than I already

have. Especially alone, especially in this form. Realizing I'm still a nine-foot beast, I take in a deep inhale laced with gardenias, clove, and mint and shift down to my basic wolf form. I can't shift to human; I'd be naked and would freak her out just as much as my true form.

That's probably what I should do. Walk out into the meadow butt-naked and say something lewd. She would definitely keep her distance if she thought I was some sort of exhibitionist perv stalking her in the forest. But that could cause so many other problems... Unassuming wolf form it is.

Within a few silent steps, I'm at the edge of the meadow, listening to her sweet voice. I don't want to interrupt; I want to hear more of her singing—more of her pure essence. Her words sound familiar; I think she's singing a song I've heard before.

"And I don't want the world to see me.
Cause I don't think that they'd understand.
If everything's made to be broken.
I just want you to know who I am."

Iris by The Goo Goo Dolls, but in a way I've never heard it before. Softer, quieter, more vulnerable. Sadness and joy mixing in a swirl of scents. Sugar and salt. Like flakes of sea salt on caramel chocolate.

Stepping into the clearing, her singing stops, and her head whips around to search out the source of the disturbance. When she spots me, her startled expression transforms into a smile so sweet, so heart-stoppingly brilliant, it almost knocks me on my ass.

"Hello there, handsome. I was worried I wasn't going to ever see you again."

Lottie is angelic in the golden rays of sunlight creeping in through the tops of the tree canopy. Her blonde hair glows like a beacon, drawing me to her light. The dark blue of her irises glittering like the surface of Blue Agate Lake only a few miles away, bringing the feeling of being adrift in the sea of her smile churning in my gut. A rapid pattering in my chest is the only indication that I still live.

No matter the logical reasoning I have as a man to stay away from her none of it matters when I'm in this form or my true form for that matter. I can't deny my inner beast's desire for her. The draw to her. Her sunshine hair and ocean eyes and nightingale voice. And finally, I give in with all of me. Relenting to my demanding inner self. If this is where my soul wants to be, then, at least for now, this is where I shall be. Sitting at her side and rubbing my neck against her shoulders. Scent marking her like I never have another. At least for today. Her presence the only thing reigning in the temper and anger Vincent brought on. The only thing keeping me from relapsing into uncaring oblivion.

Tomorrow, when I get back in the office and am once again a man and mayor and thinking with a straight head, I'll resume faking disinterest.

Chapter 11
Lottie

The wolf is back. And this time he's less wary of me. I suppose I am of him as well. I don't fear him now, not after Michael's reassurance that he won't hurt me.

The large black wolf walks right up to me, rubbing against my shoulders and then my neck. I reach up and scratch his scruff and pet him in greeting. Tilting my head into his neck when he decides he wants to get as close to me as possible.

Is it weird to befriend a wild animal like this? I should be cautious and frightened, but I'm not. The animal's presence soothes me in a strange way that nothing else ever has. I don't think about it too much; it'll only baffle me more than I already am. And I kind of like the idea that I made friends with a big bad wolf all by myself.

On this trip to the woods, I brought a blanket since I planned on staying awhile to play and absorb the world around me. The wolf arrives as I'm lounging and playing a favorite song of mine, but I immediately change to a less depressing tune.

The wolf lies down at my side, wrapping his large furry body around mine protectively. Circling around my back, his head is lowered to eye level on my right. The mass of the deadly beast at my back makes me feel safe.

"Would you like to hear a song I've been working on?"

He perks up, and I swear there's understanding dancing in his blue eyes. Glacier blue eyes that regard me with such humanistic intelligence. They remind me of the nickname they gave Frank Sinatra because of his distinct eye color; Ol' Blue Eyes. His snout is so close to my face he could easily lick me from chin to temple. He doesn't, though. Just sits patiently waiting.

"Blue eyes as bright as a glacier in the middle of the ocean. Would you mind if I gave you a name?" I ask the animal whom I know can't speak or likely understand me.

"Your eyes remind me of Frank Sinatra's; they called him Ol' Blue Eyes. So, how about I call you Frank?"

The wolf chuffs and scowls. I didn't even know a wolf could scowl, but he does it.

"Okay then, not Frank," I giggle. "How about Sinatra, then? I need to call you something other than wolf."

He bumps my elbow with his nose and rests his chin on his crossed paws.

"I'll take that as a yes. Alright then, Sinatra. Shall I sing you a song?"

A deep rumbling sound emanates from Sinatra's chest as he remains motionless, patiently waiting for me to play.

"Okay, but don't judge. I've only got a vague idea of the lyrics so far. But the chorus has been dancing around in my head since I arrived."

I settle my pre-war Martin guitar on my crossed legs, tucking my bare feet under me, and strum out the beat that

I can't seem to get out of my head. Humming along with the rhythm where I think the lyrics should go. Adding in a couple words and short lines that come to me in the moment. I jot them in my notebook, sitting open at my side for later.

"So? What do you think?" I ask Sinatra.

This time, he does stick out his tongue and licks my exposed knee through the rip in my jeans. It tickles, and I chuckle at the strange sensation of the wet and rough texture.

"I take it you liked it then? I haven't written anything like this in a long time. Haven't been able to."

Sinatra tilts his head at me in question. Fuck, this animal is more attentive than my entire legal team. I chuckle at the thought and the way his brows appear to furrow.

"I had a very controlling boss, who also happened to be my mother. She wasn't very . . . understanding. She didn't want to listen to my opinion even though it was my life she was fucking with. All that mattered was her and what she wanted. It made it hard to write music from the heart if you know what I mean."

Sinatra snorts and shakes his head. Okay, I guess he doesn't know what I mean.

"Living a life that isn't yours is something I wouldn't wish on my worst enemy. Living a lie slowly kills a person from the inside out in a way that is unrecognizable until it's too late. I just hope I caught it in time to salvage some semblance of the life that I want."

I admit my deepest pains and fears to the wolf sitting and listening motionless at my side. It feels nice to tell someone. To verbalize the feelings I dared not admit out loud before is cathartic. If I hadn't feared my mother getting ahold of session notes, I would have sought out a therapist long ago to speak to. Nothing in Tinsel Town is private. Some way or another, it would all get out in the worst way.

I suppose dawning a disguise and running away isn't much better, but at least the team back in LA can make up whatever the hell they want to explain my absence.

"That's why I'm here," I tell him, trying to explain further. "I wanted to escape my old life. See if I want to start over somewhere new or maybe return, but make, like, a million changes. I still haven't decided yet. But that's what the next few months are for."

Reaching up, I smooth a hand over Sinatra's head, the soft suede fur there shorter than the rest.

"I think I kind of like it here, though. What do you think, Sinatra?"

He perks his ears up and stares at me.

"Should I stay, or should I go?"

With a growl-like purr, he places his head on my thigh, pushing the guitar to the side.

"Okay. I guess that means I'm staying. At least for now."

Laying back, I ease onto Sinatra's large body and relax against him, setting my guitar to the side and nuzzling closer. His fur is softer and silkier than any I've ever felt before. He doesn't smell like dog like I thought he would. Instead, he puts off a deeply relaxing scent of wood shavings, leather, and spicy musk.

I had imagined my time here in many different ways; snuggling with a giant wolf inhaling his weirdly pleasant scent in the middle of the forest was not one of them. But I think it's the best one.

Picking up my Polaroid, I turn it around and point it at myself, shifting so Sinatra's head is next to mine.

"Smile."

I click the button and wait for my selfie with the wolf to develop.

Sing Sweet Nightingale

~

Tonight is my dinner with Ginger's family. All of them, *including* Hunter and his sheriff brother, I haven't met yet. Dad always said it's prudent to make a good first impression. And although I didn't make the best first impression with Hunter, I can still salvage one with his mother and brother. And perhaps have a redo with Hunter if I'm lucky.

Deciding not to arrive empty-handed and having nothing else to do today, I take Tobias' advice and find my way to Daisy's, the local flower nursery. Since none of these businesses are online, I asked the counter girl at *Sticky Bun* for directions.

I really wanted to taste what was creating the delectable scent I smelled the other day. The cinnamon bun I ordered was devoured in less than a minute, it was that good.

If I'm not careful, I might get addicted. Not a bad thing, in my opinion. Mother always cut sweets out of my diet. Pretty sure I haven't eaten real sugar in over five years.

The nursery is easy enough to find since I only have to make two turns to get there, and Calliope, the friendly girl from the bakery, was very helpful with directions. The road has no sidewalks or lane markings but is paved. It twists a few times before Daisy's comes into view.

When Tobias mentioned a nursery and gardens, I had pictured generic rose bushes, neatly graveled paths, and rows of plants in plastic pots like at *Home Depot*. Maybe a small wooden greenhouse for the more exotic plants. Something simple.

Daisy's is not that. The greenhouse is massive. Beautifully curved panes of glass form a birdcage-style dome at least two stories tall. The structural beams are painted white, the shape standing out amongst all the varying colors surrounding and filling it.

Even from the parking lot, I can tell the greenhouse is filled with exotic blooms in a rainbow of colors. Vines crawl up the walls and twine around lattices.

Surrounding the opulent greenhouse are gardens of potted and planted flowers. Wild in nature but somehow tamed to stay within their borders. A few people meander down rows, picking and snipping flowers and placing them in woven baskets.

Off to the side, away from the center of activity, is an adorable two-story house painted white to match the greenhouse right down to the climbing vines on its walls.

There's a hand-painted sign at the entrance that reads *Daisy's Gardens.*

Bypassing the outer gardens, I head straight for the greenhouse. The closer I get, the clearer the inside becomes, and I notice butterflies flitting about everywhere—not just the basic tiny gray and brown ones, but giant orange monarchs, vibrant blue and yellow ones, and purple and pink ones. They float through the air like bubbles.

I'm so busy gawking at the butterflies I almost run into the woman standing at the entrance holding an empty basket in her hands.

"Oh my gosh, I am so sorry. I was so focused on the butterflies I didn't see you."

"It's okay. That happens to me sometimes, too," she says in a soft and wispy voice. "I'm Daisy."

So, this is the elusive Daisy.

Daisy extends out her hand in greeting, and I accept it, marveling at the green ink filagree vine tattoos spiraling up and down her soft brown arms. I notice they reach all the way up her neck and down her thigh. Her torso, which I'm sure holds more tattoos, is hidden under a light wash denim overall, the shorts cut almost daisy-duke style. How appropriate for someone named Daisy. She even has flowers tied in her hair. Daisy is the epitome of a flower child.

This town is filled with extremely unique and interesting people. I didn't even see a tattoo parlor in town, so she must have gotten those done somewhere else.

"I'm Lottie. I'm new to town, and Tobias said I should come check you out."

"That was awfully sweet of him. He's my brother-in-law, so he feels the need to tell everyone to come here."

Daisy smiles shyly and giggles so faintly it sounds like chimes tinkling in the wind. Her abnormally green doe eyes widen with delight as she grins at me.

"Have you come in for something special today? Or did you want to take a look around? I'd be glad to give you a tour. Normally, I hide within the greenhouse tending to the plants, but my brother forced me to stand here and greet customers today. Says I need to be more 'social'." She uses air quotes and rolls her eyes playfully. "I would love an excuse to not stand here anymore."

She looks at me expectantly; honestly, I could use her help.

"A tour and help picking a bouquet would be wonderful."

"Wonderful. What is the occasion? What are the flowers for?" She hands me the empty basket in her hands and loops her arm through mine, dragging me into the greenhouse. Acting like a friend I've known for years rather than a woman I just met thirty seconds ago.

"Oh well, I was invited to dinner, and I thought it would be nice to show up with flowers as a thank you."

"That's a wonderful idea. Who are you having dinner with? Maybe I can help pick flowers they'll like."

"Do you know everyone in town?"

Considering I'm going to the mayor's family's house for dinner, I'm sure she knows who they are. The town is small, but could she really know everyone?

"Basically. I may not hang out at Dottie's or attend karaoke night, but I've lived here my entire life. It's a small town," she adds in a conspiratorial whisper as if it weren't obvious.

With a whisper of a smile on her lips, she shrugs and steps us to the side out of the main entryway to make way for a couple with baskets bursting with flowers. I look down to make sure I don't trip over the vines stretching across the ground, noticing Daisy isn't wearing any shoes. She must have really tough feet walking around on all this gravel and dirt all day.

"Oh well, it's um, Ginger's family. I met her dad, Michael, at his shop the other day, and when I told him I was renting his son's cabin, he invited me over for a get-to-know-them dinner."

"Oh. You're staying at Hunter's cabin? He doesn't rent it out that often, especially to—strangers."

She says strangers as if that wasn't the word she wanted to use. I take another look at Daisy, trying to read her body language, hoping it'll tell me something her words aren't. The pink peonies in her shiny brown hair sway with her movement, and I notice tiny vines wrapped around the strands.

I wonder if she does that on purpose or if it's a result of spending so much time around the plants. The end of her ear pokes through her hair with her movement, and it looks pointed, like an elf from Lord of the Rings. That is until she brushes her hair back over it, obstructing my view, so I can't confirm it is actually pointed. It could have just been my imagination. It's been rather active lately.

"Okay, well, Hunter's mom is a fan of snapdragons and Tsumugi roses. So why don't we start with those? We have a lovely selection to choose from."

Daisy guides me with the arm still linked with mine down another aisle, circling through the large building to a section filled with all kinds of blooms. I have no idea what a tsumugi rose is. I picture the standard rose in my mind but am pleasantly surprised when Daisy stops in front of a section bustling with large, full blooms. These Tsumugi roses have more petals than a normal rose and they're thinner and more rounded. One with soft, buttery yellow petals catches my eye. Reaching out, I brush a finger along the delicate petals.

"This one is lovely. Very nice choice. Yellow symbolizes friendship, so this would be a great color for starting a new friendship. They would go really well with these white ones."

Daisy and I begin to pick out the best blooms for the bouquet—more her than me. The stems and blooms seem to lean towards Daisy as she brushes her hand over them and leans in to smell them, searching for the perfect bloom.

She says everyone I pick is 'not ready yet,' whatever that means. So, I let her sift through the flowers, choosing the ones she deems ready. Although I do pick out a few of my favorites and add them to my basket, which is now bursting with flowers.

Daisy is face-first into a bush full of roses, trying to find the last perfect bloom, when someone bumps into my side. Turning, I have to look up to meet the eyes of the man standing next to me—bright baby blues.

"Hunter. What are you doing here?"

"Found it!" Daisy calls out and places the white flower in my basket. "You know what? This is going to need a vase and maybe some greenery for fullness. Eucalyptus would be perfect." She rambles, focused on the flowers, only finally noticing Hunter staring wide-eyed at us when I don't reply to her.

"Oh, good, Hunter, you're here. You can show Lottie where the snapdragons are while I fetch the vase and eucalyptus. She's getting them for dinner with your parents tonight. You know where they are, so I'll just find you. Okay?"

Daisy is speaking far faster and more animatedly than she had when I first met her at the front door, and the sudden turn of events has my head spinning to watch her skipping away on her bare feet, leaving me alone with Hunter. The only man in the world whose baby blues have made my stomach flutter as much as the butterflies overhead.

"You're coming to dinner at my parent's tonight?" Hunter asks, shocking me back to awareness.

"Yes. I thought you knew since your dad said you would all be there."

He groans but smothers it quickly. "I knew about dinner but not about you attending. My dad left out that bit."

"Oh, well, now you know."

"So, it seems."

"Don't sound so excited about it."

One side of Hunter's lips quirk at our back and forth before he forces it back to neutral.

"Well, I suppose I should show you the snapdragons. And I guess I won't be needing these."

He holds up the few Tsumugi roses he had collected. They're a soft pink that would match well with my yellow ones. I hold out my basket to him.

"Would you like to add them to mine?"

Surprised at my offer, he nods and adds them to my basket. Sitting next to the yellow and white, they do fit in perfectly.

"I don't think I'm going to need many snapdragons at this rate," I chuckle. "Especially if Daisy is getting greenery to fill in the gaps. Your mom is going to end up with a huge centerpiece instead of a bouquet."

Hunter shrugs and gestures in a direction that leads out a side door into the gardens beyond. "That's okay. She loves flowers. She won't mind."

"Good because I would feel bad telling Daisy I didn't need all her precisely picked choices."

A semblance of a grin crosses his face, and Hunter's tight posture doesn't seem as stiff. "Yeah, she tends to get a little overzealous when it comes to flowers and plants. I can barely get her to have a five-word conversation with me if it isn't about something growing out of the ground."

Laughing, my initial nervousness fades as we walk and talk casually. The other times I ran into Hunter, he was polite and courteous but short, not stopping to have a full conversation with me as if he couldn't spare the extra minutes. I'm sure mayors are busy, but still. Maybe this could be our redo first impression.

"Were you only here to get flowers for your mom?" I ask, subtly trying to discover his relationship status. Not that I need to know that for any specific reason; I'm just curious.

"Yeah. I haven't attended a family dinner in a few weeks, and I know my mother will give me the third degree about it. I thought softening her up with flowers might help. But, now I think I have an entirely different reason to fear dinner tonight."

We walk slowly down an aisle bursting with sunflowers, and I stop to squint up at him in the sunlight.

"Why is that?"

"Oh, um, well, you know how parents can be when they invite a girl to dinner and don't tell their single son about it. This wouldn't be their first time doing something like this."

So, he is single.

"You think your parents are trying to set us up?" I blurt out, shocked that was his first assumption.

"Well, I mean, maybe. It's just..." he fumbles with his words, and I notice a slight pinkening of his cheeks. It's sweet. "They've done it once or twice before. It wouldn't be my first dinner ambush with a pretty girl who thought she was on a date with me."

He thinks I'm pretty? Or am I reading too much into that?

Keeping my eyes trained on him, I shake my head faintly, smiling up at him. "I promise I was not expecting this to be a date of any sort. I too have had my fill of parents setting me up."

"Really? A beautiful girl like you needs help finding a date? I highly doubt that."

I'm surprised by his open compliment, but he doesn't cringe back at his words for once. Gazing down at me with clear curiosity and interest.

So, he is interested.

"You'd be surprised. There's a lot of fakes and phonies out there. Plus, I didn't know my mom had set me up until we broke up." Turning away from his now piercing gaze, I trace the outline of the tiny sunflower pedals, not wanting to talk about Asshat with Hunter any longer.

"So, you're single then?"

My head whips around to find him blushing, his gaze flicking everywhere but in my direction. He's flustered again.

"I mean, sorry for prying; that's none of my business—"

"Yes," I practically yell at him, wanting him to know I am *very* single.

His floundering stills to an astute alertness, his complete focus directed at me.

"I am single," I clarify, just in case.

Hunter nods, and his embarrassment shifts to something

heated and focused, intent. My internal temperature rises under his heated stare, causing my throat to go dry. I swallow, trying to lubricate it. Hunter's eyes shift to my mouth, watching my tongue lick at my lips.

Clearing my throat, I try to bring the conversation back around to something less... personal.

"I was under the impression your father was just being nice and wanting to welcome me to town. Help me get to know a few people, so I don't feel like such a stranger."

I use the word Daisy did to describe me, trying to discern if he thinks me a stranger at this point.

Hunter begins walking again, guiding us without even having to look where he's going. Knowing exactly where the path dips and turns.

"Oh, yeah, of course. You're probably right. That's likely more accurate than my theory."

He lets out a forced laugh, and on a long, heavy breath, his shoulders pull tight and then go slack, not quite sure what they want to be. I like flustered Hunter; it makes my awkwardness less awkward. With a lighter but suggestive tone, I decide to mess with him just a little, hoping to break the thickening tension between us.

"However, you know your dad far better than I do. I could be completely wrong, and he could be secretly planning our wedding."

"What?!" Hunter barks out, eyes widening and feet faltering, coming to a stuttering stop in the middle of the path.

"I'm just kidding, Hunter, relax." I muffle my laughter and try to cover my smile with my hand. The look on his face has my heart lightening, and his brows drop dramatically when he realizes I'm fucking with him.

"Oh, ha ha, very funny. You're just full of jokes, aren't you?"

"Sometimes. If the situation calls for it and you seemed a little tense. I just wanted to loosen you up."

I tap his elbow with mine and see him doing just that.

"See? That wasn't so hard. Oh, look. Snapdragons."

I point to the row next to us and realize we're in the middle of the snapdragon area. Somehow, I had walked past half of them without even noticing.

We find a section of snapdragons that we think would go well with the colors we already have going in the basket and choose a few stems. When I notice Hunter's large hands and body absent from my periphery, I stand up straight and turn in a circle, looking for him. Spotting him about ten feet away, staring into the thick forest of trees that surround the gardens.

"Hunter?" I call, but he doesn't respond or even flinch. Just stands stock still staring, hands fisted around a stem of snapdragons, crushing them between his fingers.

"Hunter," I call louder, trying to get his attention.

He finally turns his eyes in my direction but doesn't budge his stone posture.

"Are you okay?" I ask, coming to his side and looking out in the direction he was staring.

His eyes turn back to the trees and glare daggers. I try to see what he sees, but to my eyes, there's nothing there.

"Is there something out there? I know there are wolves around here, but I was assured they were harmless."

Hunter grunts and shifts his body in front of mine to block my view of the forest.

"Everything's fine. Thought I saw something, but I was mistaken. Come on, why don't we go find Daisy. She probably got distracted by a wilting vine and forgot about your vase."

His body remains taut, but his expression softens, and he even gifts me with a small smile without trying to smother it, and I completely forget about whatever he might have seen in the trees and allow him to guide me away. His hand settles on the small of my back and heats my skin where it makes contact.

The sensation trickles through my body and makes my nipples harden under my shirt as a needy throb starts between my thighs.

Holy fuck. I have never been turned on so fast before and by only a hand on my back. He's not even touching my skin, and it feels like he's caressing my naked body with his tongue.

Next to me, Hunter takes in a deep inhale and growls low in his throat. The vibration reverberating through his hand, still connected to my back, only intensifies the heat growing in my body. The tumbling of my stomach and quickening of my heart add to the turmoil inside.

Large fingers curl gently but possessively into my shirt, pulling it tighter against my chest. Displaying the points of my nipples through the soft material.

Before I can even attempt to comprehend what the hell is happening, Hunter's searing touch is gone from my back, and he's taking a large step away from me, clearing his throat and trying not to look me in the eye.

"I'll see if I can find Daisy. You wait here."

Without waiting for a response, he walks away and disappears inside the greenhouse to find Daisy. Leaving me hot and panting and wet in the panties, standing here like a fool with egg on my face.

What the actual fuck was that?

Chapter 12

Hunter

No fucking touching. What's so hard about that to remember? I knew it the moment I made contact with her that I was fucked. But I was so distracted by what I saw in the tree line that my sanity fled briefly. A moment too long, and I slipped. My tentative control fucking slipped.

Touch is very personal for shifters, especially between sexual partners and lovers. We like to rub our scent on each other, so all others know who we belong to and to not even think of touching what isn't theirs. With the soul of a beast at our core, we tend to be very possessive.

The moment she heated under my touch, I could smell her arousal. There was no way I could suppress my growl of approval. Even surrounded by flowers, I could still smell her distinct scent mixed with my own from when I rubbed against her yesterday.

It had made my inner beast extremely happy to smell the mixture of our scents, and it had drawn me right to her. I hadn't planned on talking to her, but she was in the damn Tsumugi rose section, and the stupid hose tripped me, knocking me into her. I was only trying to get a scent of her emotions. Those scents were weaker underneath her heavenly smell, and I had to get closer to discern them properly.

She was happy again, only sugary sweetness this time. No salt.

I could kiss and kill Daisy for her brash pushiness. Nymphs aren't always as observant of people. They are generally more concerned with plants and animals, as that's what their magic is connected to.

Daisy is only a half earth nymph, unable to use a glamour for very long. Thankfully, her non-human characteristics can be explained as tattoos or style choices. I doubt Lottie realized the flowers were actually growing from her hair or that the green tattoos shifted slightly on her skin when she got excited about her plants and flowers.

Still, I can't be angry with Daisy for pawning Lottie off on me. I was able to speak with her as a man rather than a wolf, and I was unable to answer her questions with more than just a growl or headshake. It's nice. It shouldn't be, but it fucking is.

I had to get away as fast as possible, but the beast inside nearly forced me to take her in my arms then and there and claim her as mine. I don't know what the fuck is going on with me lately, but it's causing me to lose focus.

I find Daisy hiding in the back, indeed distracted by the dry soil in an enormous potted plant with dozens of vines growing out of it and up the wall. I send her in Lottie's direction with instructions to help her finish her bouquet for my mom.

I can't go back to her, not now. My dick is so hard I have to readjust before making my way to my truck. My knot already swelling. Something it rarely does so fervently, no matter how horny I've been in the past. The scent of her arousal turned me hard in an instant, preparing to respond in kind and make use of her growing desire, and apparently wanting to do more than just satisfy her physically.

Normally I only feel the need to fuck and mate this strongly during a blood moon which only happens once every four years or so. Even though the lunar eclipse happening in less than two weeks is a blood moon, this is something else entirely.

If I hadn't left, I have no fucking idea what would have happened.

You probably would have bent her over and rutted her right there in the middle of the snapdragon garden. That's what would have happened, you fucking moron.

Her influence on me is greater than I thought it would be. She's just a human; how can she affect me like this? Only a possible mate should make me act like this. Pulling at that thing inside us that makes us more than human. Calling to my soul in a way that relays . . . rightness. There's that word again, the one Tobias used to describe Lottie. But she couldn't be a possible mate. As far as I know, mates have always been other non-humans, whether they be shifters or something else. I've never heard of a mate pull from a human. Is that even possible?

Fuck this is so messed up. I should call Fynn and ask him. He knows everything about this kind of shit. With his nose always buried in those books of his and his extensive personal collection of historical non-human records, maybe he'll know what this means—what this is. Until then, I'll just keep my distance. Better to not cross a line I can't come back from until I know I want to.

And no fucking touching.

Touching potential mates activates mate bonds and begins the process. If a mate bond were possible with a human, I can't touch Lottie until I know how it will affect us. I can't start something so precious and important with a woman who has no idea what it means. *Can I?* No, that would be wrong. Even though I want to touch every inch of her body so badly, my skin itches with irritation from not doing so immediately.

Is this how the mating pull works? Driving a male insane until he gives in and falls to his knees in subluxation just to get a taste? Would she even feel the other end of the pull as a human?

Fuck this is so confusing. I need answers now. Pulling out my phone, I text Fynn, asking if he's available to talk. He doesn't like when his reading and research are interrupted by ringing phones. I text and wait for his response.

My feet stop abruptly halfway to my truck in the parking lot, and I curse. I still have to go to dinner tonight with her there. For a brief moment, I contemplate calling my dad and having him cancel the whole thing or bailing at the last minute and ignoring their phone calls. But that's a dick move. Lottie doesn't deserve that.

She's right that my dad is just trying to help her acclimate. If I bail, it will just make things weirder and my family more suspicious. Ryder and my dad won't say anything, but I'll never hear the end of it from Ginger and Mom.

Looks like I'm going to dinner, whether it's a good idea or not. But first, I need to call Fynn.

~

Although I had resigned myself to attending dinner tonight, I was taken off guard once more when my father called and asked if I would give Lottie a ride. You know, since I'm *so close* *and she doesn't know where she's going. It's only polite.*

Sing Sweet Nightingale

I make sure to wear thick jeans to help restrain the inevitable hard-on I'm no doubt going to have at some point tonight, pairing it with a black button-down shirt, cuffing the sleeves, and popping open the top button to be more comfortable.

Sadly, my call to Fynn resulted in few answers regarding my predicament. He didn't have any immediate information on hand. Recalling hearing something about a non-human feeling the mate pull to a human, but he has to check his records to be sure. Never one to jump to a conclusion without all the data first. Once he knows more, he'll call to tell me. Until then, I just have to hold my shit together. I can't make any assumptions or take any actions with Lottie until I know more.

Telling her what I am and the world I come from is a big step, and I need to ensure she is what I believe she is before sharing such private and guarded information. It's not just me that could be affected by such a revelation.

It's not unusual for non-humans to marry and have children with humans but a mate bond isn't something I've heard of others having with a human. It's very sacred and strong. Not what you would consider rare among non-humans, but it also doesn't happen for everyone. To find a mate is an incredible thing and can't be ignored. At least not for long. If a mate pull is ignored for too long, it disintegrates, and you may never find one again. Although possible, it is very improbable.

At half past four, I leave my house to get Lottie. Ryder leaves at the same time, heading to our parents' house early. He hates being late. We live together in the large house I own. It might not be normal for siblings to live together among humans at our age, but in shifter families and communities, it's very common, especially since Ryder is my beta.

It's typical for the beta to live with the alpha even if they aren't related. Makes it easier to communicate and handle situations that may arise. We don't just deal with our own pack and town. If needed, we could be called upon by other alphas for assistance, and being close to my beta just cuts down on the hassle.

He doesn't give me words of encouragement or assurance, just a simple "see you there," and he's gone in his truck down the driveway without a backward glance.

I make the short drive to Lottie's—*my* cabin. *When did I start thinking of it as hers?* This is already not a good start to the night.

I park my truck and get out, walking sluggishly to the front door, dreading this night and her mood. I did ditch her at Daisy's earlier. Hopefully, she's not upset about that.

Raising my fist, I stop just inches from knocking on the door. Lottie's voice drifts through the open window, and I hear my sweet nightingale singing again. This time, it's something more upbeat and newer. I've heard this song before but can't place it. I'm sure they've played it at *Blue Moon*, or maybe it's one of the songs Ginger blares on her radio as she drives through town.

I stand frozen, listening to her move about the cabin and sing the poppy song a cappella. I can feel her joy, and it echoes through my heart, lifting the weight of dread that sat on it. I feel lighter and more optimistic about the evening now.

When my fist finally falls and I knock on the door, Lottie's singing immediately stops. Not ten seconds later, the door swings open, and there she stands. The calm her singing just created is washed away by burning lust, and I'm glad I situated myself in my jeans before arriving.

Long, lean, tan, bare legs pull my eyes from her face, unable to look at anything else. She's wearing some sort of skirt or dress that hits her mid-thigh. The hem is flowy and has some sort of floral pattern on it. I don't really know. My attention is still on her thighs, which are now pressing together. And there's that scent of arousal again.

Fuck, it smells amazing. Sweet, heady, and floral. I want to taste it. Taste her.

I just barely suppress another growl and forcibly remove my eyes from her legs, roaming up her body over the dark maroon deep V-neck sweater she's wearing, and stop and stare when I reach her eyes. It's better than staring at her bare legs, but not by much. Her denim blue eyes are large and round, and her bottom lip is pulled between her teeth. She's nervous as well as excited.

"Hi," she says, breaking the silence between us with her soft voice.

What is it about her voice? What is it about her?

"Hello, nightingale," I say dreamily in response. Clearing my throat to regain my composure. "You look beautiful tonight."

"Thank you. Why do you call me nightingale?"

"Because of your singing. It was beautiful, like a nightingale. You're going to have a hard time avoiding karaoke if you sing like that."

She blushes but also averts her eyes. Her scent shifts as a dash of fear enters the mix, souring her sweetness. Why is she so afraid to sing in front of others? She's obviously good at it. I would sit and listen to her sing anything for as long as she would let me.

"Well, as long as you don't tell anyone, I think I can manage."

I will gladly keep it our little secret if she doesn't want me to tell anyone. I like being the only one to hear her sing. I like that that part of her is just for me.

I mimic zipping my lips and locking them. That appeases her, and the fear evaporates from her scent. Good.

"Are you ready to go?" I ask, the ease of our interactions growing with every conversation we have that I don't run away from.

"Yes. Let me just grab the flowers. Oh! I also bought some wine."

She spins, her short hair fanning out in an arc as she jogs into the small kitchen, returning with a bottle of red wine in her hands.

"It was the best they had at the grocery store, so I hope it's okay."

I'm no wine connoisseur, but I recall having a conversation with Ginger regarding a bottle of wine at the store that was priced at five hundred dollars and that I swore would never sell. No one in town is that fancy or willing to spend their money on such a splurge. But Lottie doesn't seem to be affected by it all.

"The one that cost five hundred dollars?" I ask, just to confirm.

"I know," she starts with a frown. "I would have gotten something better, but it was the best I could do on short notice. I hope they like it."

She thinks a five hundred bottle of wine isn't acceptable? My parents and Ginger will be more than pleased to partake in the wine. Her lack of concern for its price, however, *is concerning* to me.

For the first time, I take a moment to truly look at Lottie, ignoring her enticing smell and hypnotic eyes and noticing the purse with the LV logo on its side. I don't know what brand it is but even I can tell those letters translate into multiple zeros on the price tag. Not to mention the quality of her clothing, which looks brand new, lacking the normal wear and tear of well-used clothes. Yet the Nissan sitting in the drive has seen better days, not fitting in with her put-together attire and high-dollar wine purchase.

She's told me as Hunter the wolf, or Sinatra as she named me, about her past, family, and reason for being here, but it never sounded like she was rich. Her easygoing attitude and lack of snobby superiority add to her personable nature. One thing that I've noticed through my dealing with the wealthy is that they don't tend to possess it. What she told me was vague, though. Never mentioning what her job was or what happened to spur her on this journey into self-discovery.

A hundred questions are poised on my tongue, but I can't manage to say anything other than, "I'm sure they'll love it."

Hopefully reassuring her that her willingness to spend so much on a gift for my family will be well received and appreciated.

Lottie smiles and tucks the bottle of wine under her arm, turning to the small dining table where a large bouquet in a yellow vase sits. It's large but tasteful. Lottie must have had to twist Daisy's arm to get her to hold back like this.

Before she can lose her hold on both the vase and bottle, I step into the cabin to help her. Instantly, my senses are overwhelmed with Lottie. Her smell, heat, and very being have taken over every inch of the space. I don't completely hate it.

Grabbing the vase, I make sure not to touch her hands. I can only imagine my reaction to touching her skin after what happened in the gardens.

"Thanks."

"You're welcome. I hope you're not mad at me for leaving you with Daisy earlier. I got a call and had to leave to take care of some business," I lie, hoping she believes me.

Lottie just smiles and shrugs it off. "It's okay. Daisy helped me finish. I understand. You must be busy as mayor."

"It can get . . . consuming at times."

Lottie leads us out of the cabin, pulling out the carved feather keychain from her purse to lock the door. I follow behind her, exiting and waiting for her on the porch as she locks the cabin securely.

I stare at the keychain in her hand, and she notices.

"I heard you made this," she says, dangling the wood feather from her fingertips, which took me hours to carve.

I nod, shifting my weight on my feet. I want to get in the car and get this night over with, but at the same time, I hope it'll never end.

"Yeah. It's a hobby. Something to do when I have free time. I also made those rocking chairs." I motion with my head indicating the chairs, not wanting to risk dropping her thoughtful gift by releasing my two-handed hold on it.

"Really?" Her surprise lifts her eyebrows almost to her hairline.

"Is that so hard to believe?"

"No. It's actually quite impressive. I just didn't know you made larger things."

Her cheeks turn a ruddy pink that goes well with her maroon sweater, making me want to press my nose into her neck and inhale her skin and that pink tint. Gripping the glass vase a little too tightly, I refrain from doing anything so rash.

She's only human; she wouldn't understand my need to smell her and rub my scent all over her, I remind myself. *Just be cool until you hear from Fynn.*

"It just depends on my mood. Sometimes, focusing all my concentration on something small and detailed helps me shut out everything else. Quiets my mind in a way."

"I know what you mean. It's like when I'm playing my

guitar. It takes me out of my own head for a while."

Her pink lips turn up, and her tender smile is so small but sparking so much inside me. I stand there like a complete idiot, staring at her and her mouth until she rolls her lips between her teeth, smothering a mischievous grin at me.

Without a word, she turns and finally steps off the porch, heading for my truck. I follow like a trained pup, without question, opening the passenger door and holding it, waiting for her to slide in. I desperately want to reach out and offer her my hand, but I am unable to risk skin-to-skin contact.

The height doesn't seem to bother her, and she climbs into my truck with ease, tucking her skirt under her thigh and running her fingers along her pebbling skin. My eyes trail the same path as her fingers, mindlessly handing her the flower vase. It takes a hesitant moment for me to be able to detach my hungry gaze from her flesh before closing the door, trapping her and her scent in my vehicle. Which I know will linger long after tonight.

Chapter 13
Lottie

Hunter's family home is stunning in a charming, picturesque way, that I'm learning is standard for Snowberry. It sits on a plot of land that keeps a football field of space between it and the nearest neighbor. The two-story home is reminiscent of the cabin I'm currently staying in. Made of large slats of dark wood with a peeked roof line and dormers. The trim is painted a deep green, allowing the house to blend in with the trees around it.

It only took about five minutes to get here from the cabin, mainly because Hunter drove exactly the speed limit. I suppose that, as mayor, he needs to set a good example. I didn't mind the unhurried drive, enjoying the confined space with Hunter. The smell of fresh-cut pine mixed with a leathery, spicy scent fills the cab of his pick-up truck, which I like.

That burning attraction I've had around him only grows with every interaction. Each minute adding to the strange pull in my chest that developed at some point in our short time together. Luring me to close the distance between us.

It scares me how I react to Hunter. So many years spent around people I can't trust who only want to use me for their advantage has me squashing any growing desire I have for him. Trust doesn't come easy to me anymore, and I shouldn't allow myself to get too close to these people. Even though I want to be their friend, I can be nothing more. My life is too complicated, too messy to drop that nuclear bombshell on their lives.

When we arrive at his parents', Hunter opens the door for me again like a gentleman but doesn't offer his hand to help other than to take the vase from me. Once again, he carefully avoids touching my hand as he grasps it with his much larger one.

Instead of knocking on the front door, he immediately announces our arrival with a loud call into the house.

"Mom, Dad. We're here." His voice booms through the house in a way that feels familiar.

"We're in the kitchen," calls a familiar female voice.

Guiding me through the house, I follow behind Hunter's bulk until we enter a large, spacious kitchen filled with people I know and don't know.

An older woman, who I assume is Hunter's mom, strides towards him, arms open wide to match her happy smile. Embracing Hunter with a veracity I personally haven't felt since my father's last hug. Hunter holds the vase out of the way to avoid dropping it on the floor. Her golden auburn hair clipped up out of her face in a haphazard bun that almost falls in her face when she pulls away from her son. She rearranges it before noticing the flowers in his hand.

"Are those for me?" she asks, kissing her son's cheek, fawning over the flower arrangement, and sniffing the bouquet.

"Yes. But they're not from me. Lottie picked them out for

you."

Attentive eyes turn to me beside him, and her smile widens, if that's possible. Hunter's mom is tall like Ginger but not nearly as tall as her son, with a face that looks too young to be a mother of kids as old as hers. Faint wrinkles appear around her eyes as she continues to smile at me and her son.

"Thank you so much, Lottie. I'm Sophie Evans, but you can just call me Sophie. It's so nice to meet you." Sophie grasps my free hand without waiting for me to even lift it, squeezing warmly. "My husband and daughter told me all about you but didn't mention you were so beautiful."

"Oh," I blush, tucking my chin into my chest. There have been thousands of people in my life telling me how beautiful, sexy, and gorgeous I am, but none I ever believed as sincerely as Hunter and his mother complimenting me.

"Thank you." I try to laugh it off and not be totally awkward. "I also brought you this."

Shoving the bottle of wine in her hands, she finally releases mine to take it and inspect the label.

"Oh, my goodness. How thoughtful, thank you."

The wine diverts their attention enough to allow us entry farther into the room, where I'm introduced to Ryder, the oldest brother, the last of the Evans family. A man who has the same striking features and build as Hunter but with eyes so dark grey they're almost black. His hair is just as black but longer and more unkept than his brother's neat cut style, and if possible, his posture stiffer. He doesn't seem unkind just a bit stoic. Not very chatty either, leaving all the talking to his relatives.

Ginger greets me like an old friend with a tight hug and pulls me to a bar lining one wall of the living room. Popping open the bottle of wine with a flourished practice before pouring glasses for everyone except Ryder, claiming he doesn't like the taste and will stick with his beer.

"Wow. Isn't this that fancy expensive bottle they had at the market?" Ginger asks, holding the bottle up to her face to read all the small print.

"It was the best one they had, so, yes? I'm not sure." I sip on my glass of wine, the taste smooth but sharp at the same time. I've never heard of the brand, but it's good.

"This bottle cost like five hundred dollars, Lottie!" she exclaims, tentatively placing the bottle on the wooden bar top.

I hold my breath, waiting for a sneer or the backhanded comments that I'm used to. What I get is quite the opposite.

"You shouldn't have spent so much. We would have been fine with a ten-dollar bottle. You don't need to waste your money trying to impress us. We're easily impressed out here in the sticks."

A giant breath of relief deflates my lungs. They aren't insulted I didn't spend more on a gift for them. They actually seem concerned that I spent so much. Is my perception that skewed due to my glitzy life in a gilded cage?

"It really wasn't a big deal. Sometimes, it's nice to splurge on something to share with others."

My excuse is enough to pacify them, but they seem to sip their wine slower now, appreciating every drop that much more. I take a hearty chug to help ease my nerves. Sitting at the bar, Ginger sits next to me, but Hunter takes up a position standing at the far end, keeping a healthy distance between us, but his eyes are always trained on me, even if it's through his periphery. Every time I bring the glass to my lips, I see his attention flick to me to watch, then instantly look away.

"So, tell me, Lottie," Sophie starts, pulling my attention away from Hunter and his odd behavior. "What brought you to our little town of Snowberry? We're not exactly a tourist destination."

"No, I suppose you're not," I agree, fiddling with the stem of my wine glass, steeling my reserve to answer a plethora of personal questions I may have to lie about.

I don't want to lie to them. They seem like nice people, inviting me into their home and being so welcoming. But there are things I can't tell them, not if I want to retain my secret identity. I wonder if Batman ever felt this guilty lying to his friends.

"A friend of mine suggested it. She knew I wanted to get out of the city and away from everything for a while. Said I would love it here. So, she got in contact with Ginger and arranged for me to rent the cabin."

"That was nice of her. What's her name? Do we know her, Ginger?"

Sophie looks to her daughter for confirmation. I look at her, concerned that this is going to lead somewhere I don't want it to. If anyone knows Luna and what she does, they may guess who I am, or at least that I'm more well-known than I let on.

Ginger side-eyes me, pausing before answering. "Uh, no. No one you know, Mom. Just an online friend of mine."

I can feel my heart beating in my throat and exhale slowly, easing my growing anxiety.

"Oh, I see. Well, we're certainly happy to have you here. How long are you staying?"

"A few months." I sip my wine, hoping she doesn't ask anything about my past.

"And how are you liking town?"

Now, this question I can answer. Anything about town is easy to talk about. It has nothing to do with my past or my future—just my present.

"Town is amazing. I'm pretty sure I'm in love with Tobias

at the Ugly Mug. I'll drink any coffee he puts in front of me."

"You and everybody else in town. He is a godsend. We're lucky to have him," Sophie gushes.

It's no surprise to me that he's well-liked in town. If he worked in the city, they would always have a line out the door and around the corner. Having a coffee superpower puts him above Superman status. A flying man in a cape is nothing compared to the perfect cup of coffee every single day.

A ding echoes from the kitchen, and Sophie excuses herself to see to dinner. Ginger and I remain at the bar, discussing getting coffee and breakfast together sometime soon. Hunter and his father talk quietly at the opposite end of the bar; Ryder stands nearby but doesn't participate in any conversation.

He's an interesting man, Ryder. His sheriff badge is clipped on his belt next to an empty gun holster, no doubt being careful and professional not having it near while drinking. He may not be talkative, but at least he's responsible.

Ginger shifts topics from coffee to alcohol, specifically drinks served at the bar in town, Blue Moon. I have a sinking feeling I know where this is leading.

"Saturday night is karaoke night. You should come," she holds up her hands in supplication before I can argue. "I promise you won't have to sing. Just come, hang out, play some pool, and have some drinks. It's a great way to get to know the rest of the town. Pretty much everybody goes."

I gnaw on my lip, unsure how to decline politely. Looking up, I see Hunter watching me from down the bar, still conversing with his father but with one ear perked in my direction. He wants to know if I'm going to agree to go.

"Everybody goes?"

"Yup. *Everybody*. Even grumpy Ryder over there comes in for a few beers and a game of darts. There's more to do than just sing out of tune."

Ginger watches me from over the rim of her glass and then follows my gaze, which keeps lingering in Hunter's direction. She inhales deeply and smiles before taking a sip of wine.

"You know, Hunter usually shows up, too."

"What?" I ask a little too loudly, drawing Hunter and his father's attention.

Ginger waves them back to their own conversation and turns her back to them, ignoring their twin looks of interest.

"I don't know why you think I would care if Hunter attended. He already mentioned it to me before. It didn't sound like he cared much for it. Said he couldn't stand to hear Dottie sing anymore."

My attempt to brush off her keen eye fails, and her expression grows more intrigued. Damn it. Should have feigned ignorance and kept my mouth shut.

"Is that so? Well, I think he might change his mind if you were there."

The wine I was just drinking to cover my blabbering nearly comes out of my nose. I cough to clear my throat of the blockage before trying to speak again.

"Why would you say that?" I finally manage around a horse throat.

"Oh, just a feeling. Plus, he stares at you a lot."

"He does?" I can't hide the astonishment and interest in my voice, but I try to anyway. "I mean, he's just curious about me. Being the new girl in town."

"Sure, he is."

I can tell Ginger doesn't believe me, but she doesn't push it. Thankfully, our conversation is cut short when her mother announces that dinner is ready. We all file into the open dining space connecting to the kitchen, where a spread fit for a

Thanksgiving feast covers the large family table.

A roasted chicken is surrounded by mashed potatoes, steamed vegetables, macaroni and cheese, grilled Brussels sprouts, and biscuits, each place set and waiting.

The family arranges themselves in their seats while Ginger directs me to sit. I expect her to sit down next to me, but instead, she rounds the table and takes the seat across from me next to Ryder, leaving the one at my side available for Hunter. Ginger gives me a conspiratorial wink, and I glower at her mouthing *traitor*. She laughs and ignores the telepathic berating I'm giving her.

Hunter sits down next to me, fidgeting and shifting his chair to put a few inches of space between us. Not even allowing for an accidental grazing of our thighs. Bummer. I want to feel that surge of electricity I felt in the flower gardens at Daisy's. It was shocking but extremely pleasurable. Even just thinking about it has my core clenching.

Next to me, Hunter takes a deliberate inhale, and his fists clench where they rest on the table next to his plate. He's facing forward, and I can't get a good look at his expression, but it looks pained.

"Dinner smells delicious, Mom." The words rumble out of his chest, and he clears his throat when Ryder gives him a puzzled expression.

Well, I think it's a puzzled expression. That's my best guess, anyway. It's subtle, the slight raising of one eyebrow and direct glare in his direction. I could be wrong. He could be agreeing with his brother because dinner does smell delicious.

Sophie sits to my right, and she smiles at her son warmly. "Thank you, Hunter. Everybody dig in. Food's only gonna get cold."

Everyone eagerly reaches for dishes and serving spoons to

fill their plates. I pick out a biscuit and wait to fill my plate until the others have first.

Hunter turns to me, holding a mac-n-cheese-filled bowl in one hand and a serving spoon in the other, looking down at my single lowly biscuit on my empty plate. "Would you like some mac-n-cheese?"

"Yes, thank you. I was just waiting my turn."

"Nonsense," Sophie chimes in from my side. "Take what you like before these heathens eat it all."

There seems to be plenty of food to have leftovers, in my opinion. Do they really expect to eat *everything*? Watching Ryder pile his plate nearly three inches high and Ginger's plate not far behind him, maybe they will.

Shifting my biscuit to the side, Hunter scoops a spoonful of cheese and noodles onto my plate. Not nearly as much as on his, but still a hearty helping that I'm sure I won't be able to finish. Before I can reach for the chicken, Hunter beats me to it, placing a leg and slice of breast on my plate at my instruction.

Once everyone has a full plate, mine completely served by Hunter, there isn't much talking for a few minutes. Everyone enjoying the home-cooked meal with its mouthwateringly amazing flavor, if I do say so myself.

"So, Lottie," Sophie starts, setting down her fork and taking her wine glass in hand. "Tell us about yourself. What do you do for a living?"

Fuck, fuck, fuck, fuck, fuck.

"Oh, um . . ." I stall, trying to come up with a good lie that never comes, so I settle with the only thing I can think of. "I'm in between jobs right now."

"Really? Are you looking for a new career or just taking a break?"

"Uh, maybe both. I'm not sure if I want to stay in the

same position, but I love the industry. So, I might try to find something else within the same area."

Keeping my answer vague, I infuse a little truth into my story. I do love music; I love singing, composing, and writing. The part I don't like anymore is the fame. When I was fifteen, my mom told me I was going to be a famous singer, and I was excited about it. It was fun for the first couple of years until it became too much. Too many photo ops, interviews, security details, tour performances, stalkers, and lonely nights alone in my mansion hiding from my mother and her demands. If I could make music without all of that, paving my own path and possibly releasing more records under the guidance of a new manager, I would gladly remain in the music industry.

Most musicians are always looking for the spotlight and record deal with the world tour, but until you've had to do it, you don't realize how demanding it is and how strong you have to be to succeed without losing yourself.

"What industry would that be?"

Ah fuck. Walked right into that one.

As I'm mentally fumbling my emotional football, Ginger picks it up and runs with it in the opposite direction.

"Maybe Lottie will become a photographer. She carries her Polaroid with her everywhere. I'm surprised she doesn't have it with her tonight."

Thank you, oh wise and loving Ginger. If she would let me, I would create a religion around her and build her a neon blue church on a hill to bring her designer shoe offerings every Sunday.

"That's how I met her. She came into the shop looking for more film," Michael tells his wife from his place at the head of the table on the opposite side of Hunter.

His lips stretch into a coy grin as he looks my way. As if we have some sort of secret inside joke I'm unaware of. Maybe because I told him about Hunter?

I'm so curious about that look that I keep silent, wanting to know where this is going.

"She showed me a few of her photos she's taken around town." He pauses to shift his eyes toward Hunter, who has gone extremely still watching his father. "She even took a few around the cabin that I found very beautiful. Great composition. You wouldn't happen to have any of them with you now, would you, Lottie?"

Michael turns his attention back to me, smiling broadly. Since he's smiling and not in a malicious manner, I'm assuming he's not mad about the photos, so I concede.

"Yes. I have a few of them in my purse. I've kinda been collecting them in a notebook and carrying them around."

I dig into my purse hanging on the back of my chair, where I hooked it when we sat down to eat, pulling out a small stack of Polaroids I took around the cabin and town, even though he specifically asked for the others. One by one, I hand them to Sophie, listing off where I was even though I'm sure she knows all of them. The last one is the photo of the wolf in the forest the first time I met him.

"I was honestly shocked I was able to take this one." I hand the photo over to Sophie, and her eyebrows shoot into her hairline. A reaction I myself had when meeting the wild wolf. "I stumbled upon this wolf while taking a walk in the woods by the cabin. He was surprisingly docile and friendly."

Sophie grins and covers her smile with her hand, pinching her lips together. If I didn't know better, I would say she's trying not to laugh. But there's nothing funny about the photo. Is there?

"Oh, yes. He's very docile... very friendly. I've never known him to let anyone take his photo, though." Sophie says, then hands the photo over to Ginger, who barks out a loud, sharp laugh before slapping her hand to her mouth.

I frown at her. That's an unusual reaction to a photo of a wolf.

"Oh my. What a handsome wolf." Ginger's eyes stray from the photo in her hand to Hunter sitting next to me, wide and glittering with humor. "Wouldn't you say so, Ryder?"

Holding the photo to the side so he can see it, her gaze remains on Hunter. Her lips are pulled between her teeth, and her shoulders shake with unreleased laughter.

Ryder grunts and returns to his food, shoveling in another bite. "It's just a wolf, Ginger. Nothing exciting about that."

Ginger smacks him on the shoulder, and some of her bubbling humor fades, but not all of it. She still retains her glittering, teasing eyes. When I look around the table, it seems I am being left out of the loop because both her parents also seem to have a knowing look on their faces while trying to cover it up with cups or forks full of food.

Hunter, however, is still as a stone statue next to me and appears to be glaring murderous daggers at his sister, his cheeks turning a flattering shade of pink.

What the actual hell is going on here?

"Am I missing something? Is there something about this wolf that I should know? Because he's come back again since then, and if he's going to start foaming at the mouth and eat me, I'd like to know."

Ginger laughs again and hands the photo back to her mother, who takes another look before passing it on to me. No one but Sophie seems to be able to answer my questioning concerns for my life.

"No, no. He won't eat, bite, or do anything of the sort to you.

He's a kind, sweet wolf who will probably be more protective of you than threatening to you."

"He might hump your leg if you let him get too friendly though," Ginger snickers from behind her wine glass. "Ow," she flinches and scowls as if someone just kicked her under the table.

"How come you all seem to know this wolf personally?"

Everyone but Ryder looks at each other waiting to see who will answer. Michael is apparently the chosen one to speak for the family.

"He's lived in this area for many years, and we see him on occasion. Feed him sometimes." He smiles. "Like I told you before, you're completely safe with him. Ignore my daughter's comments she's just pulling your leg."

I turn slightly in my chair to get a better look at Hunter the only one to not make a comment on the wolf and its presence in town. "What about you Hunter? Have you seen the wolf before? He was on your land."

Hunter lets out a slow breath and finally faces me, easing his tight posture just a bit. The pulse in my neck picks up pace when those damn baby blues lock onto me. But before he can open his annoyingly kissable lips to answer, Ginger chimes in from across the table.

"Oh, he sees him the most. They're great friends. Aren't ya big bro?"

Hunter's eased expression pulls tight again, and his mouth puckers in annoyance. I don't have siblings, but from his expression, I can only imagine this isn't the first time he's looked like he wants to ring his sister's neck.

To his credit, he doesn't respond to or acknowledge her jab that I don't understand.

"Yes. I've seen him before. You're perfectly safe with him.

Like my mother said, he's a bit protective of humans on his land."

Ginger muffles another giggle. I and Hunter ignore her. I'll have to ask her later why she thought this was so funny.

"Thanks. I'll keep that in mind when I see him again."

Hunter nods, turns his eyes down, goes back to his plate, and attempts to finish the last couple of bites.

I take one lingering look at the Polaroid of the wolf before slipping it back into my purse.

For the rest of the evening, there's no more talk of the wolf but plenty of talk about the town and, unfortunately, more of myself. At least as much as I'm willing to divulge. Simple things like relationship status and favorite meal I've eaten at Dottie's so far.

They're all entertained by my stories of burnt toast and microwave dinners. I'm invited over for dinner again whenever I'm pining for a home-cooked meal or even cooking lessons. Which I gratefully accept. Planning for a day next week to come back over for Sophie to instruct me on proper oven use and a few simple low-ingredient meals. She also says if I bring my toaster over, she'll explain the settings and see if we can resolve the burnt toast issue.

At the end of a long and wonderful evening, Hunter drives me back to my cabin, walks me to my door, and bids me a quick good night before high-tailing it to his truck.

He may have attempted to seem uninterested and avoided physical contact, but I can still tell he wants to know me better. He just doesn't want to admit it. Even though I know it's a bad idea, and I should also be attempting to keep my distance from the hot mayor, I just can't stop the growing desire that makes my pulse flutter and core clench whenever I get close to him.

Chapter 14

Hunter

What the hell is Ginger doing at my house on a Saturday morning? After dinner last night I'm not particularly thrilled to see my little sister pulling up my driveway, top down, music blaring as usual—something poppy and catchy, from what I can tell through the window.

Opening my front door, I greet Ginger, who is wearing sweatpants and a t-shirt, since I wasn't expecting visitors today. She hops out of her car and strolls over to me, spinning her keys on her finger and whistling the tune of the music that was just playing from her speakers.

"Hey there, bro."

"What are you doing here, Ginger?"

She frowns at me and pouts, stopping on the bottom step of my porch. Her gaze catches on the broken column, and she raises an eyebrow in question.

"Don't change the subject. Why are you here?" I reiterate, crossing my arms over my chest and not allowing her to distract me with discussion of Vincent and his presence in town, which I'm sure she is well aware of.

"You promised to change the oil in Minnie."

Right. She asked if I would do the oil change on her Mini Cooper, which she so cleverly named Minnie, and I agreed. I sigh and rub a hand over my face. I really don't want to deal with her today, but I did make a promise.

"Why can't you get this done at the auto shop in town?"

"You know exactly why. I will *not* deal with *that man*."

That "man" she's referring to is Luca, the shifter who works at the auto body shop and gas station in town. He didn't do anything wrong to her precious car; however, he may have asked her out on a few occasions, and for some reason, Ginger is extremely adamant about staying far away from him.

"I don't know why you can't just tell him you're not interested like you do all the other guys who hit on you," I grumble, stepping off my porch and rounding to my detached garage.

Pressing the code into the keypad, the rolling door begins to slowly lift, exposing my organized workshop within. I'm a little OCD when it comes to my tools and workspace. I'm not a mechanic by any means but I like to be prepared for any issue that may arise around the house. I also store many of my woodworking tools and wood scraps here.

"I want nothing to do with him. I don't even want to be within sniffing distance of him."

Not a completely unusual thing for a shifter since we have a very strong and sensitive sense of smell. However, in a small town, she can't completely avoid him. She can avoid the auto body shop but can't control where he'll be elsewhere in town while she's present.

Personally, I don't really give two shits about her personal issues with Luca; she can evade him as much as she wants. But is it really necessary to have me do all her oil changes?

"Do I really need to do this? Can't you just go to the auto shop when he's not there?"

Ginger smirks at me, narrowing her eyes, and cocks out one hip, propping her hand on it.

"Do you really not want to change my oil? Or do you just not want me to bring up the whole picture in the woods thing with Lottie?"

I growl a warning, signaling I very much do *not* want to talk about it. She, of course, ignores my warning as little sisters do, just wanting to annoy me more.

"It really was a flattering picture of you. Did she take any more?"

Keeping my back turned to her, I sift through my shelves, searching for the items I'll need to do her oil change. I don't answer her question because if I lie, she'll just know by my smell, so why bother even trying? But I sure as hell am not going to tell her Lottie took other photos, *selfies* even.

"Oh my god," comes Ginger's breathless and gleeful surprise. "You totally did take more photos. Tell me, what were they? Did you pose again? Did you roll over and let her scratch your belly?"

"Ginger." My warning comes out low and laced with a growl.

"Oh, fine, you boring old stick in the mud. You're no fun. Lighten up." She leans her back against the shelving unit I'm mindlessly staring at.

I don't even think what I need is on this shelf, but I don't really see what's in front of me. All I can see is Lottie and me in the forest, fearing that Lottie may at some point show Ginger the other photos since they seem to be getting close.

Turning on my heels, I switch to another shelf and find the oil, drip pan, and funnel.

"Pull your car up to the garage. I don't want a mess in my gravel."

"Yes, sir." Ginger mock solutes and scrunches her face up in a comically stern and serious expression.

While I get to work changing her oil, Ginger sits on the rolling stool by my workbench and begins scrolling on her phone. I can only guess the multitude of things she could be doing on it. She may often act like an immature baby orangutan, but the girl is a computer genius. A few of our connections with non-humans in government positions have reached out in the past asking if she wanted to come to work for them, helping control the flow of information at a higher level. Each time, she turns them down. For some strange reason, she wants to stay right here in small-town Snowberry. Which surprises me with her love of high-end fashion and all things glamourous.

I always thought she would skip out of town as soon as possible so she could go to the big city and live the flashy life I always thought she wanted. Even with her teasing and loudmouth, I love my sister and am happy to have her in town with us. Even if she makes me change her oil because she has some sort of beef with the mechanic in town.

"Are you coming to karaoke tonight?" Ginger asks without looking up from her phone and spinning on the stool. Rolling from one side to another.

"Not likely. This week's been long, and I think I might just stay at home and relax."

"Go for a run, maybe?" she offers coyly.

I grunt in response.

"That's too bad," she sing-songs.

I know she's bating me, but I also know if I don't ask, she'll find a way to tell me anyway or dance around the subject until I give in and ask just to make her stop.

With an exasperated sigh, I ask what I know she wants to hear. "And why is that, Ginger?"

"Because I convinced Lottie to come with me."

My hand stills while tightening the lid back onto the oil drain.

Thankfully, I'm under Ginger's Mini Cooper right now, and she can't see—and hopefully can't smell—my interest. Trying to play it cool, I finish tightening the cap and slide out on the wheeled creeper from under the jacked-up car.

"And why would that matter to me?" I ask as casually as possible while wiping the oil and grease from my hands.

"Because you like her." She pauses for dramatic effect before continuing. "And she likes you."

My hands almost freeze again mid-motion, but I catch it quickly and keep moving.

"Oh?"

"Mmhmm."

I catch sight of her from the corner of my eye. She still has her phone pulled up in front of her face, but her eyes are watching me over the top of the screen.

"You should really come by. I think it'll be fun. Since Lottie doesn't want to sing, we'll probably have a few drinks, hang with the girls, and maybe play a game of pool." She makes her tone overly nonchalant, but I know every word is very deliberate.

Shifter males have a weakness when females play billiards. All the bending over and reaching around and stick fondling. It's a sweet kind of torture we all love to enjoy.

My cock twitches in my pants, liking the idea of watching Lottie bend over and slide a cue stick through her fingers. It stiffens slightly, and I shake the image from my mind, not needing Ginger to bear witness to the desire I'm sure she's already scented.

"Great! I guess we'll see you there then. We should be there between eight and nine. We're going to grab a late dinner at Dottie's first. Can't drink on an empty stomach." She rubs her stomach dramatically before returning her attention back to her phone.

I don't respond. She knows I'll be there, so I return to her car, lowering it off the jack and filling it with quarts of oil. When the oil is filled, I toss the empty containers in the recycle bin, grabbing a rag from the workbench next to Ginger.

Unintentionally, I look over her shoulder at her phone as she's slowly spinning on the stool and do a double-take at the images I see on the screen. It looks like Lottie but with long hair, a very short and sparkly outfit, a microphone in hand, and a plastic smile on her face.

"Why is there a photo of Lottie on your phone?" I demand a bit too loudly.

"What?" Ginger jumps in surprise and spins to face me, holding the screen to her chest, trying to hide it. "I don't know what you're talking about that wasn't Lottie."

"*Yes*, it was."

"*No*, it wasn't."

"I know what I saw, Ginger."

"You must be getting old then because it wasn't Lottie," she argues adamantly, standing and slipping the phone into her back pocket.

"Ginger," I snarl.

"Hunter," she mimics snidely.

"Show me the phone, Ginger." I don't hesitate to infuse my tone with alpha command because I know she will argue and fight with me tooth and nail and never give in.

Ginger scowls at me and releases an aggravated tight breath through her nostrils. Slowly reaching into her back pocket she pulls out her phone and hands it to me. I swipe it open; it's locked.

"Unlock it."

She grumbles and does as I command. When she hands it back to me, the screen is unlocked and is open on an article titled "Pop star Alexandria enters private retreat after World Tour." *What the fuck?* Who is Alexandria, and why does she look just like Lottie?

I read further into the article, quickly skimming its contents. It talks about how the pop star hasn't been seen out in public since her last concert in Las Vegas a couple of weeks ago and how it's rumored she entered some sort of celebrity retreat where there are no cell phones or internet access.

I scroll down further and stop at the photo of this *Alexandria* person. This one is a close-up instead of a full-body shot, her hair pulled back behind her shoulders. Even with all the makeup and hair styling, I recognize those eyes, those lips, the curve of her cheek. It's Lottie.

Then realization strikes me, and I turn on Ginger, who's standing and leaning against my workbench, her arms crossed over her chest defensively.

"Who was the friend of yours that referred Lottie to stay here?"

Ginger shrugs and diverts her gaze off to the side, avoiding eye contact. Her scent shifts, and I smell not only her anger but also her anxiety. Before she opens her mouth, I know she's about to lie.

"Just an online friend, no one important."

"Ginger," I groan and sigh, already reaching the end of my

patience.

"Luna, okay. It was Luna."

"Are you freaking serious, Ginger? You let Luna convince you to allow a world-famous pop star to stay in my cabin?"

I hand her back her phone and run a hand through my hair, gripping the ends, trying not to rip it out in frustration. This is not what I need right now. Vincent and his men lurking around town, the blood moon lunar eclipse in less than two weeks, and now a world-famous pop star using my cabin as her personal vacay spot? None of this is going to end well.

I begin slowly pacing, trying to expel the anxious energy building under my skin, threading my hands together at the back of my head.

"Don't worry, Hunter. She wants to be found even less than we do. Luna told me all about her before she ever got here. She's hiding out from the world just like us. Her mother is a tyrant and forces her to work non-stop. Her contract just ended with the record label, and she wanted out. This was the only way she could get out without interference.

"Luna said she'll probably stay a few months, get her ducks in a row, and either return to LA or go her separate way. She just needs somewhere out of the limelight, away from all the gossip rags and fans, to figure things out."

Ginger takes a deep breath, and her tone becomes softer, pleading for understanding.

"Lottie doesn't want the celebrity status; she just wants to be normal. You've spent time with her. Do you think she would tell anyone about Snowberry? Or us, for that matter?"

I stop pacing and face my sister, considering her argument. She has a point. I would have never thought Lottie was a famous singer. Rich, yes. That was obvious with her clothes and expensive wine purchase. But a fame-seeking celebrity?

It's just not who she is.

Ginger stares at me expectantly, hopefully. Her shoulders turned inward, preparing for my denial and rejection. She's befriended Lottie and wants to continue being her friend. Not because she's a famous singer but because she's a nice person.

"No. I don't think she would tell a soul if we asked her not to. Wouldn't even need fairy dust. She'd keep it secret," I admit, my arms falling loosely at my side as I give up my stressing.

Ginger's shoulders relax and separate from her ears.

"Exactly. So please don't make her leave. Don't say anything about it. Just act like you don't know. Come to Blue Moon tonight and treat her like any other person."

Her posture relaxes even further, her spine straightening. Her scent returns to her normal mix of spicy sass and sweet sisterly teasing.

"Or maybe not any other person. Maybe a special person. Perhaps a girlfriend or even a m—"

"Don't even say it, Ginger." I pause, taking in a steadying breath. "She's human, I don't even know if that's possible."

Her eyes widen, not expecting me to admit such a thing.

Grinning around pinched lips, Ginger holds up her hands in surrender, saunters to the driver's side of the Mini, and climbs in. Hopeful anticipation gleaming in her eyes.

"We'll see you later, big bro. Don't forget to shower beforehand. You smell like motor oil and dirt."

With a wink, she starts her car and backs out, making a U-turn to head down my gravel driveway.

I stand there staring at the fading taillights of the mini and don't move an inch until the dust has settled and all sounds of Ginger have dissipated. Pushing off from the workbench, I stride towards my front door, thoughts of Lottie—A.K.A. Alexandria—spiraling through my mind.

I realize that even knowing who she really is, I don't want her to leave. I want to spend more time with her, no matter her past. Now, my singing nightingale makes more sense. Of course, she sounds amazing. She's a professional—a world-famous pop star.

Our conversation at dinner last night runs through my head again. She said she was in between jobs and was trying to figure out what she wanted to do for the future. Thanks to our conversations in the forest while in wolf form, I already knew about her controlling mother.

Until there's a reason for me to be concerned about Lottie's presence causing problems in town, I'll do as Ginger asks. If anyone can keep a secret, especially about a secret identity, it's a shifter.

Chapter 15
Lottie

I can't believe I agreed to come to karaoke night. I'll admit, dinner was a lot of fun. Dottie joined us and introduced her son, Jared, who looks the same age as her. I still don't know what kind of magic she possesses to look so youthful.

It's eight thirty when we walk through the front door of the local watering hole, *Blue Moon*. The bar is already half-filled with people. Some I've seen around town, and some I haven't. Thankfully, karaoke doesn't start till nine, and I don't see Dottie yet, so I have enough time to have a few drinks and hide out in a corner where no one will notice me.

Ginger leads me to the bar along the back wall, passing by two billiards tables, a few dart boards, and cocktail tables. There are booths against the right wall and a small stage in the back corner where I assume karaoke takes place. No doubt, it's also where live music plays from time to time.

We perch on tall barstools where my feet dangle, and I rest them on the bar rail. The smooth wooden bar under my hands is clean and lacks the sticky, unpleasant texture most bar tops always seem to possess. Behind the counter, one of the most gorgeous women I've ever seen mixes drinks without even looking, adding flourishes and bottle spins effortlessly. Her cobalt blue hair floats around her brown mocha skin in fluffy waves as she spins a bottle full of alcohol in her hand and pours a generous helping into the glass.

Ginger calls to the woman who waves with her free hand and finishes the drink she's making before walking over to greet us.

"Evelyn, this is Lottie. Lottie, this is the best mixologist you'll ever meet. Her drinks are to die for."

"Well, I don't know about all that, but I do like to play around with ingredients. It's nice to meet you, Lottie. I've heard gossip around town about this mystery woman staying in Hunter's cabin. It's nice to finally put a face to the name." Extending her hand, I shake it quickly in greeting. Noticing her nails are painted the same cobalt blue as her hair.

"Nothing negative, I hope."

"Not in the least."

Evelyn's smile is wide and genuine. Up close, her skin appears to shimmer in the low light as if she's covered in body glitter, but like two days later, after you've tried to wash it off but a layer still remains. Her eyes are so bright, light blue, that I wonder if they're contacts. Either way, the combination of hair color, skin tone, and eye color is striking.

For a petite woman, she carries herself like an Amazonian queen. Strong and confident, shoulders back and chin high. And not in the false way I used to do while walking onto a stage to perform when I just wanted to turn and run away.

Over the last few years, performing has become more of a mechanical action for me. Robotic, if you will. I'd plaster on the smile, do the dance moves, and sing the songs, rarely feeling the emotions I displayed while on stage or that were being portrayed in the music. I'd become so disconnected from it all. It was painful, loathing the thing I had loved so much. All I want is to enjoy music again. Being here in Snowberry has made falling back in love with music easier. To feel more than numb.

Right now, though, I'm not feeling the music, and if someone tries to force me to sing karaoke, I may have to fake a stomach bug and sneak out the back. Possibly explosive diarrhea if they don't believe me.

"What can I get for you two lovely ladies tonight?"

"We would like two blue moons, please," Ginger orders for us.

I have no idea what's in a blue moon, and I don't care as long as it contains alcohol.

"Coming right up."

Evelyn grabs two shot glasses and a few bottles from the bar, free-pouring alcohol and other mixers without measuring, adding something blue to tint the clear liquid.

"Oh hey, looks who's here," Ginger nudges my elbow and points with her chin behind me.

I turn in my seat to see Hunter and Ryder sliding into a booth on the opposite side of the bar. They just arrived, and Ryder keeps his eyes trained on his brother, his back towards us. But Hunter's gaze catches on mine as if he knew exactly where I was.

A breath catches in my throat as heat washes over me. My nipples pucker under my dress at the sudden, unexpected arousal. Since when could a glance turn me on?

The temperatures have been dropping day by day, but it isn't the cooling air that causes goosebumps to pebble across my exposed skin. Ginger came over to pick me up before dinner and insisted I wear the one semi-casual cocktail dress I brought. The hem hits mid- to low thigh, making it a little more demure than the miniskirts I wore back in Cali. The material is silk chiffon in a soft robin's egg blue. The natural waistline balances the lower neckline, creating a sexy but modest look.

We're in a local small-town bar, not a high-end rooftop nightclub in Vegas. I don't need flashy or glitzy here. Even in what I would consider a casual look, I can tell I'm still a bit overdressed compared to the rest of the crowd. There are some women in dresses, but they're relaxed and informal.

Under Hunter's attentive gaze, the dress doesn't make a difference; I feel naked. Like he can see through any fabric I could place over my body.

Hunter's chest rises and falls in a deep breath I can see even from across the bar and the heat in his eyes intensifies. I swivel on my seat and look away before I do something stupid, like swoon so hard I fall off my seat and flat on my ass on the floor.

Yeah, let's not do that. I'm supposed to be flying under the radar, not drawing attention to myself.

My drink, a blue moon, sits on the bar in front of me. It's definitely blue, but it's also smoking and . . . glowing? That can't be right; I have to be seeing things. It's just the colored lights over the bar making it appear to be bioluminescent. Right?

Lifting the glass, I stare at it in awe, trying to discern how the hell they managed to make it smoke and glow without adding anything else—not even a clump of dry ice.

"This is amazing. How did you make it do that?"

Evelyn grins, spreading her arms wide on the bar and watching me in amusement.

"A mixologist never reveals her secrets," she says.

"I thought that was magicians?"

"Them too."

I take an experimental sip of the smoking blue moon. It's sweet, then sour, and then it burns on the way down in the best way.

"Holy crap, that's good."

"Careful," Ginger warns. "They're stronger than they seem. It'll sneak up on you if you're not careful."

Against her own advice, Ginger takes a large swallow of her blue moon before grinning at me. I take another drink, too, this one larger than my first, but I sit my glass down on the bar afterward to keep from drinking too much. I can already feel the warmth growing in my chest and trickling down to my stomach.

"What do you say we go say hello to my brothers?"

"Oh, I don't know . . ." I start to rebuff but don't get the chance to finish when Ginger stands and strides right over to her brother's table. "Okay, I guess we're going over."

Steeling my spine and trying to push down my growing attraction to Hunter, I slide off my stool, bringing my blue moon with me. My sneakered feet land on the floor, and I smooth my skirt down my backside, making sure not to flash anyone unintentionally.

My white Prada sneakers are soundless as I make my way over to the booth. Ginger's already seated next to Ryder, leaving the seat next to Hunter wide open just for me.

I slide into the booth, and even with Hunter scooting all the way in my thigh still brushes his denim-clad one under the table. I feel it tense, and I shiver.

Hunter smells amazing. That same woodsy, leathery musk from when he drove me to his parents last night. I don't know what it is about him specifically, but the smell of him only makes my arousal intensify.

"Hello, Lottie. Are you having a good night?" Hunter asks in his gravely baritone.

"So far."

"Good."

We sit awkwardly side by side, looking but not looking at each other. My fingers mindlessly fidget with my glass, trying not to pick it up and chug the blue drink to give myself a bit of liquid courage. Hunter doesn't have a drink yet, so his hands rest on the table folded tightly in front of him.

Our uncomfortable silence is broken when a server approaches to take the guys' drink order. They both order beers and once again, when the server leaves, we return to our wordless staring. Ryder doesn't seem the least bit uncomfortable with the silence. I think he rather prefers it. Ginger also doesn't seem bothered by it because she's busy shifting her bright eyes between Hunter and me, suppressing a grin. She's either trying not to speak to see how long we let this go or is trying to decide what to say to make this even more awkward. I don't have to wait long to find out which.

"Doesn't Lottie look pretty tonight, Hunter? When I saw that dress in her closet, I told her she just had to wear it." Ginger props her chin on her palm, elbow on the table, a teasing, playful grin spreading across her lips.

She's staring at Hunter, waiting for him to reply while I turn beat red from ear to toe. Poor Hunter flusters next to me but only takes a moment to recover and pull himself together.

"Yes, she does. It's a very lovely dress." Hunter turns to look down at me, running his gaze quickly down and back up. "It was a perfect choice."

The blush that started with Ginger's question now intensifies, but this time, I smile. My heart flutters in delight instead of embarrassment.

"Thank you, Hunter."

"You're welcome."

The server returns with the guy's beers, and after we all partake in our drinks, the conversation begins far less awkwardly this time. We talk about dinner at Dottie's and upcoming plans for the week, of which I have none—other than meeting with Sophie to learn how to cook.

"I can't believe you burnt toast. You literally just turn the nob down to a lower setting, and that's it. Burning toast has to be intentional."

"Well, I'm sorry I'm not a toast connoisseur, okay. I never really had to cook before. Someone else always did it. Cooking is just not my forte. I'm hoping maybe a few lessons with your mom can give me enough knowledge to make basic meals, so I don't always have to order takeout."

Ginger laughs openly, relaxing more with each sip of her drink. I'm following right along behind her, drinking slowly but feeling the warming effects of the alcohol.

"Mom will definitely teach you a thing or two. She is an excellent cook."

"Well, I look forward to not burning my toast anymore. Cereal gets real boring real fast."

Hunter, who had remained quiet but attentive, finally eases into the conversation, and I feel the previous weirdness drifting away. The easy friendship and camaraderie freely given by these siblings makes me feel like a real friend and part of their community.

"If you're looking for a good breakfast, you should try Morning Star Café. Their breakfast platters are exceptional."

Ginger and even Ryder nod in agreement. I haven't investigated the café yet and am going to have to now. Even if Hunter's mom teaches me how to cook properly, I don't think it'll ever be a skill I perfect.

Halfway through our drinks, a blur of pink twirls up to our table. It isn't until she stops that I realize it's Becca, the waitress from Dottie's, rolling up on her skates. Different from the pure white ones she was wearing before, these ones are pale pink, with each wheel being a different pastel color.

"Hey, Ginger, Lottie, boys. What are y'all doin' over here sitting around? I thought we were gonna play some pool?"

We had told Becca our plans for the evening when we were eating dinner. She mentioned meeting us here to play a few games of pool with us, but Seeing Hunter made me completely forget about it.

"Of course we are," Ginger agrees happily. "But that makes an odd number; we need four to play teams." She gives her brother a knowing smirk from across the table.

"How about it, Hunt? You willing to join us for a game?"

Hunter doesn't answer immediately, Ginger doesn't flinch, and Becca pouts, hoping to sway him with a sappy face and large stuck-out bottom lip. He ignores them both and looks at me. I give him a soft, reassuring smile.

"You can be Lottie's partner," Ginger adds in a sing-song voice.

"Sure, sounds great," he finally agrees, and my heart does a little pitter patter.

"Woohoo! Let's go before someone else nabs the open table."

Becca rolls away, and I watch the redhead in her skintight jeans and roller skates wheeling towards the empty billiards table. Moving so smoothly, it's almost as if she's gliding on an invisible wind, barely having to propel herself along.

"Does she wear those skates all the time?" I ask Ginger. "I thought they were just part of her uniform for Dottie's?"

"Oh, they were. She just decided she liked wearing them a little too much, and now she wears them practically everywhere. We've all kind of gotten used to it."

Ginger shrugs and slides out of the booth, and Hunter and I follow suit. Ryder remains silently sitting in the booth as we carry our glasses to a table near the pool table, claiming it as ours, and begin setting up for the game. Hunter stands next to me as we choose cue sticks.

"Have you played before?" he asks as I test the weight of one of the sticks.

"A few times."

I've played far more than a few times, but I've learned it's best not to brag to a man about how much better you are at something than them. Hurts their masculine pride.

"Are you two ready to play, or are we going to stand around all night?" Becca calls from behind us.

We choose our sticks and turn to meet her and Ginger at the table, where they've already begun racking the balls.

"What are we playing?" Hunter asks.

"Straight pool. Nothing fancy, basic rules. Rotating each turn between team members."

"And what do we get if we win?"

Ginger laughs, leaning on the table for support. The idea of us winning the most hysterical thing she's heard, apparently.

"You want to make a wager?" she asks incredulously through her chuckles, staring at Hunter with disbelief. "You're a shit player. It wouldn't be fair to bet against us. I only partnered you with Lottie because I thought it might get you two close. Not because you could win."

Hunter scowls and grumbles low in his chest, frowning at his sister. Her lips quirk in a teasing grin.

"Is that so?" I insert myself between the two siblings,

leaning on my stick like a magical staff, one hand propped on my hip in challenge.

Ginger raises an eyebrow at me, intrigued. "Yeah. That's so."

"Well, I think we could beat you."

Leaning close enough to my ear, I can feel his breath fan across my skin. Hunter whispers, "Are you sure about this, Lottie? I really am a shit player. I was just trying to have a little fun."

When I turn to look him in the eyes, our noses brush and he leans back a fraction so we're not touching but close enough that one small movement would cause us to kiss. I try to ignore the heat pooling in my gut and the ache between my thighs. It doesn't completely work but it's enough that I can speak.

"Yeah. I got this."

Hunter inclines his head and straightens at my side, prepared to stand by me at my word. I like that he trusts in me so freely and doesn't try to argue. He just waits patiently, supportively.

I look back to Ginger, who looks as happy as a clam. She thinks she's going to win. Hunter must be a really horrible player. I wonder why he agreed to play then if he was just going to embarrass himself?

"Great. And what shall we wager?" she asks, twisting the cue stick between her fingers rolling the smooth wood back and forth.

Normally I would wager money, but that doesn't seem appropriate. So, I look to Hunter for assistance. He's beaming at his sister with malicious glee.

"If we win, I don't change the oil in your car anymore. Or the coolant or anything else for that matter. You have to take it to the auto shop like a normal person or do it yourself."

Sing Sweet Nightingale

Ginger's smile falls, and she glowers at her brother, her eyes squinting dangerously in his direction. That doesn't seem like a big deal to me, but from the look on her face there's something else to it that I'm not getting.

"And if I win," she begins, keeping her fiery gaze locked on Hunter. "You have to sing karaoke. Song of my choice."

My body goes rigid, and my heart sinks to the pit of my stomach.

I told her I didn't want to sing.

"Both of us?" I ask shakily.

"No. Just him. He never has, and I want to hear his lovely singing voice."

My racing heart eases back into a normal rhythm, and I breathe a sigh of relief. Even if we lose—which we won't—it will only be Hunter on stage. I can live with that.

"Agreed." Hunter reaches out a hand and shakes Ginger's; Becca and I watch on as the siblings have a silent stare-off, not sure if they even remember we're still here. This seems to have become something between them, and that's fine with me. I'm just here to have a little fun with new friends, that's all.

We all take up our positions, and Ginger waves to the racked balls on the table.

"Age before beauty."

Hunter snickers and shakes his head, turning those baby blues on me. They're lighter, softer than when he was standing off with his sister.

"Would you like to do the honors? As I said, I'm not the best."

One side of my lips curls up, and I internally apologize in advance to Ginger because she is not prepared for what's about to happen. I may be horrible at cooking, but years spent hiding out in my house with no one to keep me company and too much time on my hands gave me ample opportunity to perfect my billiards skills.

"I would love to."

Hunter steps out of the way and leans back against the wall nearby behind me. I ignore his watchful gaze and instead focus on Ginger and Becca on the opposite side of the table, waiting patiently to see what happens.

Lining up my shot, I get the cue ball right where I want it, sliding the stick through my fingers until I know I have the right amount of speed and strength. I snap the point of the stick against the white polished cue ball, and it spurs into action. Rolling across the green felt it smacks into the other balls with a loud crack.

The balls scatter wide, and two sink into pockets right away. Stripes.

"Holy shit." I hear Hunter's stunned surprise behind me, but I watch as realization washes over Ginger's face. Her snarky arrogance and smug smile vanish in mere seconds.

I line up my next shot and sink one more ball before I scratch, and it's their turn. A deep, throaty chuckle tickles my spine as I go to stand by Hunter.

"You're a freaking shark," Becca blurts, laughing lightly, not nearly as upset about it as Ginger.

"Why didn't you tell me you were so good at pool?" Ginger mopes.

"You didn't ask."

Chapter 16

Hunter

I have never beaten my sister at billiards. She's always been better at it than me. But tonight, I think she might actually lose. Granted, not directly because of me, but I'll take the win however I can get it. Especially if it means I don't have to deal with changing her oil or windshield wipers anymore.

We only have one more ball to sink to win, the eight ball. I stand back, allowing Lottie to line up her shot, and the sight is a welcome one. Lottie leans over the table, thrusting her backside out in my direction. I don't pay attention to what's happening on the table because all my focus is on her beautiful ass. The swaying blue material of her dress brushes against the backs of her thighs in a way that has my pants growing tighter.

I wasn't kidding when I said it was a pleasurable torture to watch females play pool. Seeing Lottie bent over all but presenting herself to me has me practically panting. I've been hard the entire game and have had to discreetly adjust myself so as not to draw attention to it.

My hand tightens on my stick, and it creeks under the pressure. Lottie's skirt rides up just far enough to glimpse her creamy thighs that rub together with every slight adjustment she makes to her angle.

I can easily imagine her in this very position, down on all fours in the middle of that grassy meadow in the forest. Her voice hoarse from screaming my name, and her pussy bared for me, wet and ready. The urge to growl and purr is too great to suppress, and I feel a rumbling vibration in my chest. Thankfully, the music and chatter of the bar are too loud for anyone to hear. The place has gone from partially full to almost overflowing with people.

My perfect view is suddenly hindered by the body of another male, leaning in to speak with Lottie. She must have already taken her shot, and I didn't see it since I was focused on her ass and how I'd like to see it bare except my claw marks.

My insides bristle at the thought of another male near my female. But I stay still; he's only speaking to her, and if I were to make a claim on her publicly like this, there would be talk around town. So, I clamp down on my desire to wring the nymph's neck and clench my jaw tight to stop from barking out an alpha command at him.

The nymph, now leaning in dangerously close to Lottie, is one I'm very familiar with. Kai isn't a full-time resident of Snowberry but visits regularly for the equinox, which happens not long after the blood moon. I hadn't known he was back in town already. He's a cocky bastard and a relentless flirt. He'll hit on anyone that strikes his fancy, and Lottie, being new in town, would be considered fresh meat to him.

I don't expect Lottie to reciprocate his flirtations, but when he leans in to sniff her and runs a finger down her exposed arm, I can't stop my body from pressing forward, a warning growl building in my chest.

"I don't care who you smell like, sweetheart; you are too delicious to ignore," Kai utters softly enough that Lottie furrows her brow in confusion at him.

She's a human, and Kai knows it, but he still says stupid shit like that anyway.

"Kai," I bark out his name in a low warning tone. Nothing aggressive ... yet.

"Hunter. Didn't see you lurking there. Is this one yours? So sorry," he says in mock defense with a shit-eating grin but wisely removes his hand from Lottie.

He knows damn well I was standing here and even just admitted knowing who she smelled like—me—and yet still tries to play it off innocently. As if he was completely unaware.

"Didn't know you were back in town," I say instead of the litany of clarifications he seems desperately in need of.

Putting him in his place in front of Lottie and the other humans present in the bar tonight would be too much of a hassle, and I don't have enough fairy dust with me. Although I could easily ask for more from Becca. Even though she was on my sister's team playing against me just now, Becca is always willing to help. She was a great help to me four years ago during the last blood moon disaster when we had to go around town dusting the humans. She and Levi worked in tandem to help get everything back to normal. Making sure we got to the humans quickly and efficiently replacing their nightmare fuel memories of horny wolf beasts with ones of less scary wild dogs running through town.

Kai shrugs and smiles in Lottie's direction, still not giving up on his flirting. "Came early, felt like getting away from the city and ... things for a while."

He's most likely referring to the demands of his uptight

family. Kai comes from a long line of *purebloods*, as they like to call themselves. Nymphs who only mate and procreate with other nymphs. No cross-species mating and definitely no humans. To them, humans are for fun, not for mates or children. They think humans weaken their blood and species and they're not completely wrong.

When a non-human breeds with a human, the offspring are a mix of the two, half and half. Like Daisy, she's half earth nymph and half human. Her ability to use a glamour isn't as strong, her senses are not as sharp, and her appearance is a blend of her two parents, giving her more human characteristics. For example, her shorter pointed ears rather than the long, elegant points of most.

Whereas a pairing of two non-humans results in a child of one or the other. If a fairy were to mate with a shifter, their child would be either a fairy or a shifter, not a mix of both, except in the occurrence of two different types of the same, like nymphs. There are many types with different magic, and their magic can mix when they mate. Kai himself is a mix of animal and fire nymph.

Kai follows his family's rules and restrictions but is less prejudiced than some of the older generations. They come to Snowberry to celebrate in the old way for the equinoxes and solstices, leaving their manors and mansions to "slum it" with the common folk. Everyone looks forward to the seasonal celebrations as it isn't only the nymphs who partake.

"Well, as nice as it is to see you again, Kai, we're in the middle of a game, so how about you take your shameless flirting elsewhere for the time being? Okay?"

The cocky nymph chuckles and wisely takes a step back. Running his fingers through his long red hair that he doesn't try to hide through his glamour, he deftly avoids his glamoured invisible horns. An amused fire dancing in his eyes, his fire-nymph side showing. I think that's part of why he enjoys stirring up trouble so much. Fire nymphs like to spark flames and watch things burn sometimes.

"No problem, Boss. I think I see a few willing ladies right over there calling my name."

He winks at Lottie before sauntering over to the bar, his striped tail swishing behind him. He's already setting his sights on another female, another human. I think he purposely seeks them out to piss off his family since they dislike them so much.

"Who was that?" Lottie asks, pressing close to my side.

Her arm brushes mine, and a bolt of pure desire shoots through my body, reawaking my cock. I shiver and step to the side so it doesn't happen again, no matter how desperately I want to touch her skin.

"That was Kai. His family has a vacation house in town. They visit a couple times a year."

"Oh," her voice sounds curious but disinterested in him personally, which makes my chest swell. "He was very . . . friendly."

Lottie's giggle is just as musical as her singing, and I can feel her amusement as if it were my own. Light and airy, a soft tickling in my stomach.

"Yeah, he's friendly, alright. With *everyone*. He's relatively harmless, though. You tell him no, he won't push it. He might flirt and sweet-talk you, but he won't be forceful. You don't have to worry about him," I tell her, knowing she must be concerned after the whole Roman incident.

"That's good to know."

I stare down at her, and when our eyes lock, we stand there silent and motionless for a few moments before Ginger's snickering snaps me out of my stupor.

"So, did we win?" I ask, redirecting my attention back to the game at hand.

"Oh, yeah. We did."

Turning, I take in the table; all stripes and the black eight ball are gone, and four solids remain.

"You are my hero, Lottie Pickle."

She smiles, and a fierce protectiveness for this woman floods my veins. *I'll do anything to keep that smile on her face.*

"I try."

"How about two out of three?" Ginger offers, trying to salvage her loss.

"What? You want to lose twice?"

Lottie's burn finds its mark, and Ginger's jaw drops while Becca hisses in laughter.

"Okay, miss smarty-pants. You just think you're such hot shit because you managed to beat me once, but that doesn't mean you can beat me twice."

I can see Ginger's competitiveness growing, and I know she's going to demand a rematch, but I won't let that happen. One game is enough torture for the night.

Stepping between the two, I hold out my hands in surrender. "All right, how about we get a few drinks and sit down for a bit? There'll be plenty of opportunity to play again later."

There won't be a later.

All the girls agree, Ginger more reluctantly than the others, but I manage to persuade her with offers to pay for the drinks. We find a table far away from the karaoke happening on the corner stage, and the girls sit as I go to the bar to order the drinks. Ryder joins me, a silent companion as he assists in carrying all the glasses to the table.

The girls all wanted blue moons, Evelyn's specialty. Lottie is still amazed at the glowing drink that she can't figure out.

None of us tell her how she does it, of course, because it's part of Evelyn's magic.

She's a nymph with earth and animal magic, a mixture that gave her bioluminescent abilities. With just a touch, she can temporarily give things the ability to glow like bioluminescent fish or fungi.

Settling in with our drinks, we fall into light conversation, commenting on whoever is on stage attempting to perform. Lottie is gifted with one of Dottie's performances, which she claps to wildly, asking for an encore, much to everyone's dismay but to Dottie's delight. And, of course, Dottie is more than willing to oblige.

"Don't encourage her. She has enough confidence as it is and very little talent to back it up," I chide playfully.

The drinks have relaxed everyone, even Ryder, whose stoic features crack the tiniest bit at our banter.

"Oh, nonsense. She enjoys it; let her enjoy it. There are so few great joys in life."

So very true.

Although the girls keep their attention focused on the stage or each other, mine and Ryder's swivel around the room occasionally. Checking to ensure everything is copasetic.

Everything seems to be going great until a duo of younger girls take the stage and start singing some poppy song I don't know. Since Lottie sits right next to me, I notice immediately when her demeanor shifts from easy and relaxed to quiet and stiff. I eye her, worried she's sick or perhaps she saw something non-human I hadn't caught, which freaked her out.

Looking around, no one's glamour seems to be slipping. I look back at Lottie, and I can smell her panic. It's sticky and clammy, smelling like damp mold. It curls my nose, and now I'm starting to panic. I look to Ginger only to see her in a similar but less frantic state. She's eying Lottie warily but trying not to show it.

I finally catch Ginger's gaze and try to convey my concern without words. Thankfully, my sister understands my unspoken expression.

She puckers her mouth, pinching her lips together widening her eyes while microscopically tilting her head in Lottie's direction, then towards the stage where two females are destroying whatever song they're singing.

I don't understand her meaning. *She doesn't like the song?*

I frown at Ginger, lost to her wordless communication. She tries again with the same move but more aggressive. It doesn't make it any clearer.

Next to me, Lottie abruptly stands and stutters before blurting out, "I need some fresh air. I'll be right back."

No one has time to respond before she's practically running out the door.

Ginger seat hops until she's sitting next to me where Lottie just was. Leaning in, she whispers low in my ear so no one else can hear.

"That's one of *her songs*. You know, *Alexandria*."

Lottie's secret identity.

Fuck.

"Go after her," Ginger hisses.

I don't hesitate, I go after her. But when I burst out the front door, my panic increases when I don't immediately see Lottie. She's not here.

Chapter 17

Hunter

Lottie isn't here. Her sweet scent of gardenia and panic linger, but I don't see her. I follow her scent as it crosses the street to the parking lot and continues. I finally spot Lottie halfway across the small park, heading toward the street that will lead her back to the cabin.

Picking up my pace, I jog until I catch up with her. She's moving fast but not fast enough to escape me.

"Where are you going?"

Lottie jumps at the sound of my voice and halts, not noticing I had approached her.

"Oh. Hunter. Hi. Sorry, I just . . . don't feel well. Thought I would walk it off and head back to the cabin."

I know she's lying. Firstly, because of her scent—it spikes when she lies. Secondly, I know it has to do with hearing her song at karaoke. But I can't tell her that; she doesn't know that I know. Probably doesn't know Ginger knows either. And it seems she would like to remain as anonymous as possible while here. So, I don't try to argue with her excuse.

She starts walking again and I easily keep pace.

"I'll walk you. It's dark out, and you shouldn't be out here alone."

"I thought Snowberry was a safe place?"

I smother a smile at her ferocity. She is a feisty one.

"It is. But it would make me feel better to walk you. It would ease my mind knowing you made it home safe."

She doesn't stop but slows to a normal pace. Her eyes stray to me, and I can see her processing my request. We cross the street, and I don't allow her to get ahead of me.

"I guess that's okay," she finally relents when she realizes I'm not going anywhere but with her.

"Good. I would hate to have not walked you home and found out you got lost in the woods trying to find your way back."

A small smile cracks her worried expression, and she seems to loosen a bit. Her scent shifts back to the gardenia clove I love so much. I take a deep inhale, and the scent calms the beast inside, who is raging to protect Lottie and destroy whatever made her so afraid.

When Lottie doesn't offer any other conversation, I take the hint and walk beside her in comfortable silence. Just being near her and knowing I'm protecting her soothes my soul.

The night has fully set in now, and the sky is a dark, inky color. Stars sparkle overhead, and the waning moon casts a silver light over the dark street.

There are streetlamps in town and some in front of homes, but the rural side streets don't have any manmade lights to illuminate the night. My shifter-enhanced vision is more than enough for me to see every crack and dip in the road. Lottie seems to be having more trouble traversing the uneven pavement and lack of sidewalk. A few times, I reach out to steady her elbow, and the one time I make contact is the most pleasurable moment of the evening.

When we reach the intersection of the road that branches off and leads to my property and the cabin, we have to cross the street. Lottie follows behind me, but the moment the asphalt ends and the dirt and gravel road begins, Lottie trips.

She shrieks and falls onto her hands and knees, cursing under her breath.

"Are you okay?" Reaching down, I try to help her up, avoiding touching as much skin as possible. It's difficult, considering how little her dress really covers.

"Yeah, I think I'm okay. Just tripped in a hole I didn't see."

She stands and tries to put weight on her legs, but one practically buckles under her.

"Ouch, shit."

"What?" I ask, panicked that something is broken.

"I think I twisted my ankle."

My eyesight is enhanced, but I'm no doctor, and I can't tell if there's something wrong with her ankle just by looking.

Lottie tries to walk on it, and again, she crumples, hopping on her opposite foot and reaching out to steady herself against my side.

It's torture to feel such pleasure touching her and guilt for her pain.

"Great. This was such a good day, too. What a crap way to end it. Maybe I could . . ." she trails off, trying to position herself against me so she can hop on one foot.

That is not acceptable.

Crouching down, I scoop Lottie into my arms, cradling her against my chest. The feeling of holding her so close and touching so much of her skin sets my entire body on fire. I make sure to hold her high enough that she won't press against my groin and feel the massive hard-on now testing the limits of my jeans' durability. The material presses hard against my knot, which is already swollen and ready for a good rut.

I smother a curse at the torturous sensations flooding my body.

"You don't have to carry me; I'm sure I could manage to make it back to the cabin. If you just give me an arm to lean on, I'll be fine."

I grunt disapprovingly.

"Not a chance, Lottie. I'm carrying you, and that's final."

My fingers tighten on Lottie's side and thigh where I hold her, allowing for no argument. She doesn't fight. Wrapping her arms around my neck, she draws her chest closer to mine and presses her beautiful breasts into me. I can feel her warmth where we connect; a growling purr emanates from my chest.

"Did you just growl?" Lottie chuckles close to my ear.

"No," I lie because I can't very well admit to my beast liking her close proximity and that the growl was a purr of contentment.

Lottie giggles again, getting comfortable in my hold and settling in my arms like she belongs there.

She does, my inner beast agrees.

Lottie's fingers roam the breadth of my shoulders, tentatively at first but more boldly when I don't stop her. The soft touches both heaven and hell in my current predicament.

"I bet carrying me doesn't even phase you, does it?"

"Not really."

"I haven't seen a gym in town. How do you stay in shape?" she asks, her fingers circling the collar of my shirt, momentarily grazing across the bare skin beneath. My cock pulses in time to her touches, and the light of the waning moon isn't helping the situation.

"I have a home gym, and I like running in the woods around my house."

"I like running. It was the only part of my workout regimen I didn't mind doing. Always felt so freeing." Lottie looks up at me, and I catch her gaze out of the corner of my eye. Her lips are parted, and her tongue pokes out to lick them. "Perhaps we could go running together sometime."

My feet falter under me, and I almost trip and fall on nothing. Running and chasing a female is a primal desire all male shifters possess. Female shifters love to tease and cause chase. To hear Lottie offer to run with me has my inner beast perking up in interest, flashing images of Lottie running through the moonlit trees, stripping her clothing, and laughing with unbridled joy. Of me catching her and pinning her to the moss-covered ground, licking her from nipple to pussy, and making her scream in pleasure before flipping her over and plunging my knot deep inside her.

Fucking hell, this night is going to kill me.

"You okay?" Lottie's concern washes the sharpest of the desires from my mind, but most remain to taunt me as I continue walking. Trying to right myself.

"Yeah, fine, just caught my foot on a root."

I decide I should probably pick up my pace. Every moment she spends in my arms is one more moment for me to fantasize about all that I want to do to her.

We make it back to the cabin, and while still in my arms, Lottie unlocks the door, and I walk us into the cabin. She left a light on in the living room so I can see easily while sitting her down gently on the couch.

"Let's take a look at that ankle." Reaching up, I switch on another light next to the couch and kneel down in front of her.

Her ankle does look swollen but isn't red or purple, so it's nothing major. Still, my instinct demands that I make this better. That I relieve her pain. Removing her shoe and sock as gently as possible, I rest her bare foot on the floor.

"Don't move. There's a first aid kit in the bathroom. I'm sure I have some salve or something we can put on it and then wrap it."

I don't wait for her to agree before I stand and make my way to the cabinet under the bathroom sink and find the first aid kit. I intend to wrap her ankle but plan on using the small bag of fairy dust in my pocket and not some human salve. I can't risk her not healing properly. I'll just have to put my sleight of hand to the test when applying it.

Readying my dust hidden in the palm of my hand and the prop salve, I return to the couch and find Lottie sitting right where I left her.

Kneeling down in front of her once again, I gently lift her injured leg with my free hand. She winces at the movement.

"Sorry," I mutter, hating that she's in pain. That won't be the case for long.

I infuse the fairy dust with my intentions—healing her twisted ankle and removing any swelling—and cup my hand gently around the tender flesh. I take a small dab of the ointment and press it and the dust into her skin, holding it there, waiting for the magic to take hold. When I'm satisfied it has, I quickly wrap the ankle in the athletic bandage I also took from the first aid kit.

The wrap is more to conceal her rapid healing than assist in healing, as she might suspect.

"There. You'll be good as new in the morning. It wasn't even that bad."

Lottie looks down at her ankle regarding the wrap. She

shifts it slightly from side to side testing it.

"You're right. It's already feeling better. Thank you."

Her ocean eyes catch on mine, and the desire that I had momentarily forgotten due to tending to her injury returns in full force. I hold perfectly still, fearing moving might cause me to do something I shouldn't. Like, kiss her.

In my current position, kissing her would be easy; she would only need to lean forward a short distance.

"You're welcome." The words come out rugged and hoarse, intense craving thickening my throat.

Lottie scoots to the edge of the couch, and I don't dare move as her face comes way too close to mine. Her unique scent spikes with a surge of heady lust. The hairs on my arms stand on end with her near proximity and that scent. My fingers itch to reach out and claim her.

I dredge up every ounce of self-control I still possess and remain still waiting to see what she does next.

Her eyes fall to my mouth, and I suck in a breath. When my lips part, hers do as well. Her chest rises and falls with her labored breathing.

In a move I wasn't expecting Lottie leans in and places a soft kiss on my cheek. My eyes shut as I experience the purest ecstasy I've ever felt, my body melting and hardening all at once.

I reach up and grip the couch cushions on either side of Lottie, trapping her in the bracket of my arms. My claws are no doubt poking holes in the material.

I couldn't care less about the state of my couch cushions because Lottie didn't pull away after she kissed my cheek. She remains with her cheek almost against mine; all I'd need to do is turn my head for our lips to touch.

Once the thought enters my mind, I can't stop it. My head

begins to turn, seeking out her lips, and my brain nearly short-circuits when I feel her lips, soft and willing, make contact with my own. Just a soft brush that quickly becomes more.

Lottie leans into the kiss, pressing firmer against me. My mind blanks, and nothing else exists except for her and this kiss. Her hands grip my shoulders, pulling me closer, and I don't fight it. My inner beast purrs in approval at the turn of events.

I press closer to Lottie, deepening the kiss. Discovering what she likes and giving it to her. When I tilt my head, seeking more, she allows it. When I trace my tongue over her bottom lip, she parts them for me. Allowing me to slip my tongue inside and get my first real taste of her.

I groan at the contact as our tongues press for dominance. I can't stop my body from pressing closer to hers, spreading her knees and closing the distance between us. My hands find their way from the cushion to her hips, gripping tight and pulling her to me. The heat of her core radiates against my lower abdomen, and I groan again.

Lottie lets out a breathy whimper that nearly breaks my fragile control. It does, however, bring me back to my senses. Breaking off our kiss, I breathe heavily, pressing my forehead to hers, inhaling her air, and trying to calm the need to claim and rut her right here and now.

I can't do that. She doesn't know what I am, and what I would do to her would frighten her. Not to mention, human males don't have knots.

She needs to know what I am before I can take this any further. But of course, I can't tell her that either. Not until I know if this pull I feel towards her is real. If it's even possible for a human to be a mate to a shifter. At this point, I don't even fucking care anymore. I consider telling her exactly what I am—risks be damned—before I return to my senses.

Not like this. I can't tell her like this. I have to figure a few things out before I can even consider telling her anything.

"I can't," I manage to get out between breaths.

Lottie flinches, and I hold her tighter before she can pull away. She manages to lean back enough to look me in the eye.

"Not that I don't want to," I clarify before she can jump to any conclusions. "I just can't right now. Not tonight. There are things . . . it's complicated."

Lottie nods, her eyes softening, and the slight frown on her kiss-swollen lips eases.

"I understand complicated."

For a long minute, we remain like this: holding on to one another, not willing to let go just yet. But I have to; if I don't, I never will.

Disconnecting from her, I reluctantly pull farther back and slowly stand. I don't want to leave her; my inner beast certainly doesn't want to leave her.

I take another step away, and my beast threatens to take control and claim his female, the one he believes to be his mate. Fuck I really want to let him. Because he's me, and I'm him. I want to claim her; I want to call her mine and see my mark on her flesh and feel her presence in my soul.

Not yet. Just a little longer, and I'll get answers from Fynn, and then I can make a decision. *Just wait a little longer, Nightingale. I'll make you mine; I know I will.*

"I should go. I'll check on you tomorrow to make sure that ankle is healing."

I don't wait for a response. If I do, I may never leave, but I do hear her soft, lilting voice as I leave.

"Goodnight, Hunter."

My resolve almost cracks, but I manage to make it outside

and into the tree line before I allow the shift to take over.

Chapter 18

Hunter

For the next few days, I keep my distance from Lottie. After that kiss and touching so much of her skin, I don't think I can control myself around her. I have to wait until I can speak with Fynn, which needs to happen immediately because the throbbing in my balls is only growing with every passing hour I don't go to Lottie.

My affection for her has escalated far faster than I expected. Not just from the possible mate pull and physical attraction but for her sassy humor and open friendliness. For the way she infuses so much emotion into her singing and her brazen courage befriending what she believes to be a wild wolf.

Discovering her hidden identity should put me off Lottie completely. Celebrity and fame are the opposite of the type of life I have or want, as a non-human and by personal preference. It seems so tiring and stressful to be a celebrity. The whole adoring fans and constant cameras on you bristles my fur.

As the alpha, I hold a position of leadership and command,

sometimes adoration, but not celebrity. I still have my personal space and privacy. No one is trying to snap photos of me cleaning my truck from a hundred yards away with a telescopic lens—at least, I don't think they are.

It's easy for me to understand her desire to escape all that. And part of me wants to ensure she has it. Has everything that she desires, both emotionally and physically.

My inner beast is becoming restless, and I don't blame him. Luckily, Fynn texted me last night to inform me he has some information on the whole human/non-human possible mate situation. I made plans to meet him for lunch at Dottie's today but first I have my weekly meeting with Ryder.

My brother seems particularly moody today. His frown more severe than normal. Instead of sitting motionless and calm across my desk from me, he's fidgeting, something he never does. Tapping his heel on the floor, making his knee bounce in quiet agitation, he rolls his shoulder, and winces when he rotates it too far.

"Everything okay, Ryder?" I ask tentatively. He's not likely to give an answer, but I try anyway.

"Yeah, I'm fine. Why do you ask?" With that snippy, sharp tone in his voice, I don't think he's anywhere near fine.

"You seem on edge more than usual. Something wrong with your shoulder?"

He wrinkles his nose and frowns, shifting his shoulder again, trying to compensate for his perceived weakness.

"Hurt it on a run over the weekend. It's nothing. Already healing. Don't worry about it."

"Seems like more than that is bothering you. Anything I should know about? Maybe that girl you mentioned before? The one snooping about."

On our way to *Blue Moon*, Ryder mentioned another new

girl in town. This one is sneaky and snooping around like she's looking for something or someone. He assured me she wouldn't be an issue, but I'm not sure about that.

Ryder growls in irritation, his fists tightening on the chair's armrest. I haven't seen this much emotion from Ryder in a long time. Whoever this girl is, she is rubbing Ryder in all the wrong ways. Could be good for him.

"I'm handling her. She's more of a nuisance than I thought she would be, but nothing I can't manage."

"Who is she anyway? Why is she here? No one else seems to be talking about her, which is concerning with how gossip works in this town."

Normally, when there's a newcomer in town, *someone* says something, but this woman has been particularly low-key and keeping to the shadows. Either that or Lottie is redirecting everyone's interest since she's been around me and my family so much.

"She's an online blogger." He hesitates, visibly battling with himself over how much to divulge. "A conspiracy theorist of sorts. The kind that believes in the paranormal and alien."

I bristle, my spine going rigid. Those are a lot of words I don't like hearing in one sentence.

"And she's here because?" I prompt.

"Heard rumors and theories about the eclipse. Nothing concrete. I think Ginger's taken down her site a time or two."

He's trying to play it off as insignificant, but it isn't. Nothing is too small or unimportant to give our full attention to when it comes to the safety of the town and our people. Our pack.

"Well, fairy dust her and get her out of town. We don't need a nosy human with theories about the paranormal snooping around right now. With the eclipse and the elves, we have more than enough to deal with."

For the first time since I became alpha my brother doesn't immediately agree to my orders. He hesitates, clearing his throat and averting his eyes.

I squint at him, trying to read the unfamiliar expression on his face. He wants to fulfill my order but also . . . doesn't.

"There are circumstances that may prevent the use of fairy dust in this situation." Is all he says.

"Are you going to elaborate?"

"Not yet."

I frown in confusion at my beta. I'm not sure what the hell is going on with him lately. He was on edge at Blue Moon on Saturday night, and now he's acting cagey, not wanting to disclose pertinent information regarding a possible threat to our secrecy.

I let out an exasperated sigh. I really don't have time for this. He needs to get his shit together and handle it.

"Can I trust that you'll handle this?"

Ryder's posture goes taught, and his eyes flash to mine, determination sharpening them to an acute focus.

"Yes, of course you can. You focus on the elves and Lottie. I'll deal with Tess."

"Tess?"

"The woman, that's her name. Though I prefer to think of her as the pain in my ass."

My laugh almost slips past my lips; I don't think I've heard Ryder make a joke.

"Well, just make sure this pain in the ass remains yours and not mine."

"Understood."

If Ryder says he can handle this, then I'm going to let him; I already have enough on my plate as it is.

"Just keep me updated. And if you need Ginger's assistance

with any online removals, just let her know."

Ryder jerks his head in a quick nod, agreeing. Now that that is settled, I can focus my attention on Fynn and this whole mate bond with a human thing. I haven't told Ryder about it yet, but I probably should.

"I'm meeting with Fynn for lunch," I begin. "He has some information he looked into regarding a possible mate bond."

Ryder doesn't speak, but his brow furrows ever so slightly in curiosity. Clearing my throat, I press on, knowing what I say next could possibly change many things for us. Personally and as a race.

"I may or may not be feeling the mate pull towards Lottie. I've never heard of such a thing occurring with a human, so I asked Fynn to look into it. He said he found something, so hopefully, by lunch, I'll know for sure if it's possible."

Ryder looks shocked and more than a little intrigued. He's leaning forward, his hands gripping the armrests.

"I didn't know that was possible," he says more to himself than me.

"Neither did I. Which is why I enlisted Fynn's help. I'll let you know what he says. If it's possible to have a mate bond with a human, we need to know and need to let everyone else know."

Nodding in agreement, Ryder silently leans back into his chair, the tensing of his muscles slackening as he eases back.

We are far less interested in anything else happening in town for the rest of our meeting. Nothing is as important as my possible mate bond with Lottie and a snooping blogger in town. Oh yeah, and Vincent and his goons can't forget them. Not that he'd let me.

Fucking hell, I need to figure out how to get him to leave and stop trying to buy my land. I could try fairy dust, but it's more of an immediate fix for memories that were just formed, usually within the past hours or days, sometimes weeks. It's been known to work on a few memories as far back as months. But beyond that, the memories are too difficult to alter; they blend and weave with other memories, events, and people, making it too hard to completely remove a specific detail.

Perhaps I can create a new memory of him accepting my refusal and agreeing to never attempt it again. Or I could just kill him, that would make me and my inner beast feel better, but it'll just piss off his entire organization and bring more trouble to my doorstep. No, convincing him to leave and never return would be best. I just don't know how I'm going to accomplish that yet.

I finish my meeting with Ryder, who stomps out, a man on a mission to deal with this Tess woman, while I fill my time until lunch finally rolls around.

The bell chimes happily overhead as I enter Dottie's. Becca greets me with a wave and smile, gesturing me in when I tell her who I'm here to meet. She rolls out the door on her skates, food-filled tray in hand, heading towards a parked car.

When I walk up, Fynn is already sitting in a booth waiting for me. Fynn is a tall but lean man, his hair kept long and straight, similar to his true mere form, but a more natural light brown hue instead of the silvery gray.

As usual, he has his nose in a book, completely unaware that I've arrived until I sit down across from him, and the movement draws his attention.

"Hello, Hunter."

"Fynn."

"Would you like to order some food? I thought I would wait until your arrival just in case you were hungry."

"Yeah. Sounds great."

Flagging down Becca on her way back to the kitchen, we place our orders, knowing the menu backward and forward. Fynn takes his time situating his tea, and I can't take his slow pace any longer.

"Well? What did you find out?" I ask impatiently, my inner beast ready to claw his way out of my chest if I don't find out soon.

Fynn takes a sip of his tea and positions it to the side, pulling out his leather-bound notebook filled with curling script and bits of paper tapped to its pages. Opening the notebook, he finds the right page and begins.

"According to my research, a human and a non-human can have the mate bond if there is non-human blood in the human's near to immediate ancestry."

My heart flips in my chest, my pulse beating out a staccato rhythm a marching band could keep beat to. Lottie can be my mate; it isn't impossible. I'm momentarily rendered speechless but quickly find my voice. I need to know more—everything.

"What exactly does that mean, *non-human blood in her ancestry?*"

"It means that somewhere in her family tree, a few generations before her was a non-human who procreated with a human. Resulting in a half-breed who then most likely went on to marry and procreate with a human. Lottie may not have any characteristics or magic associated with her ancestors because of all the human blood diluting it, but it's still there, however minutely."

My mind is reeling as I try to absorb and process all the information Fynn is so casually revealing. Lottie has non-human ancestors, and because of that, she has just enough non-human blood in her heritage to allow for a mate bond to appear.

"But how? Why? I thought mate bonds could only appear with full-blooded non-humans?"

Fynn nods calmly, stirring his tea as if we're discussing the weather and not a complete shift in the future of our race.

"That used to be the case, but apparently, over the last couple of decades, cases such as you and Lottie have been popping up across the globe. I think it's part of our evolution. Our numbers have been dwindling with so many humans filling up the world and the non-humans forced to hide from them. Our species at the beginning of its extinction.

"I believe this change has occurred to help us produce the next generations. To ensure the continuation of our kind. If we're able to bond with humans and not just create half-breeds through copulation, we may be able to restrengthen our people."

What he's saying doesn't make sense to me, especially since non-humans have been "copulating" with humans for centuries. We've always mixed with them, and there have always been half-breed children as a result. Where do you think people with webbed toes came from? Mere's mixing with humans. But I don't interrupt. I listen intently, just as Fynn expects, and he continues.

"Every time a non-human has crossed with a human, the resulting offspring are half-breeds, a weakened version of the full-blooded non-human. However, if a mate bond is formed between a non-human and a human descendant of a non-human, I believe the resulting child will *not* be a half-breed or weakened by the human blood. Something to do with the mixing of essence, soul, and blood."

"Wait," I interrupt, knowing he hates it when people interrupt his speeches, but I need clarification. "So, you're saying if Lottie and I were to complete a mate bond, our children would be full-blooded shifters? Not a half-human half-shifter like before?"

Fynn looks at me like I'm a complete moron because he just explained it, but I need it spelled out in layman's terms.

"Yes. That's what I just said." A small frown creases his brow as he looks at me.

Fynn is one of the smartest meres I know, but sometimes he's too smart for his own good. Missing obvious social cues and forgetting not everyone's brain thinks like his.

"Now, I can't confirm this hypothesis without testing if, of course, but from the accounts I've managed to find, that seems to be the result."

The thought is shocking. Once, we lived out in the open among the humans, and our numbers were great, our kind just as prominent. Now, we're a fraction of a percentage of what we used to be. To be able to replenish our race would be astronomical. So much so that it could mean that, at some point in the future, we could live out in the open once more. Maybe not in my lifetime, but perhaps in my children's, considering how long we live. We're patient and don't mind playing the long game.

Before I can ask another question, the bell over the door jingles, and out of habit, I look up to see who entered. First is the woman I can't get off my mind, who pulls me to her and smells like desire incarnate, igniting my blood with fiery lust. The one and only Lottie. The second is the male I wish to never see again who douses my internal fire with icy hatred. Vincent.

Chapter 19
Lottie

Walking into Dottie's, I almost trip on the threshold. Staring right at me is Hunter and his gaze is as sharp as a predator seeking out its prey. The heat simmering there blisters me from the inside out, and I almost melt into a puddle. My nipples tighten, and a needy throb pulses between my legs. This man does things to me that I didn't think were possible outside sappy love ballads and country songs.

The moment I enter the door with Ginger and the man who was polite enough to open it for us, that heat fizzles and cools to barely an ember.

Did I do something wrong? Is there something on my face?

I start to reach up to check my face but notice Hunter's line of sight isn't focused on me. Following his narrowed gaze, it lands on the man behind me. He's smirking and smoothly steps around me and Ginger heading for Hunter and the other man sitting at his table.

Ginger grips my elbow and steers me toward an empty

table far from Hunter's, I make sure to sit at just the right angle that I can still see his profile.

It's been three days since I kissed him on the couch at the cabin. I have no idea what possessed me to act on my desires, but I did. I couldn't help it. I wanted to kiss him so I leaned down and pressed a soft kiss to his cheek thinking that would be acceptable. Innocent enough as a thank you for carrying me home and taking care of me. I didn't mean for it to escalate, but I am so happy it did. I thought he was happy about it, too, even though he broke it off and left abruptly.

I can only hope I didn't scare him off with my brash actions. Ever since the first moment I met him I've been drawn to him and even though getting involved with a local probably isn't the best idea, it also sounds like a wonderful idea. Every time I imagine it my panties get damp, my heart races, and my breasts ache. You'd think I hadn't had sex in ten years with the way my body reacts to Hunter and just the thought of being with him.

The man who entered behind us sits across from Hunter, and he doesn't look too happy about it. Neither does the man he sat next to. They obviously know each other, but like the pervy man who hit on me in the street last week, they don't seem to like each other very much.

Ginger's trying to draw my attention away from Hunter and the other men, but I don't hear her, I'm too focused on watching Hunter to see if he will look at me again. Give me a sign of how he feels. He's too fixated on the new man at his table that I don't see much directed at me.

"Lottie!" Ginger scolds, pulling my attention back to her.

"What?" I laugh out at her big sister tone.

Ginger is fast becoming a good friend, and I know when the time comes for me to leave, it will be hard to tell her goodbye—even harder to say it to Hunter.

Maybe I won't have to.

This is my life now. There's no one controlling where I go or when. If I wanted to, I could stay. Right? Would I be accepted here as a permanent resident? My only family is my mother, and I wouldn't mind her never knowing where I live. Maybe, just maybe...

"Stop staring at my brother. It's weird."

"I'm not staring." I was totally staring. But quickly return my attention back to Ginger sitting in the booth across from me.

"Oh, sure, okay." She rolls her eyes comically as she speaks. "So, what would you call that doe-eyed sparkle look you're giving him?"

She crosses her arms on the table and cocks her head at me. The long waves of her auburn hair shifting over one shoulder at the sarcastic movement.

Scoffing I blush a little but try to give her a comeback as sassy as her question.

"I call it astute observation. It never hurts to know your surroundings."

Her laugh rings out around us, and it's contagious, my own joining and mixing with hers. The lightheartedness I feel in this town has me feeling like a completely different person than I was only a few weeks ago. I haven't worn a single rhinestone or sequin since, and although I still love shiny, pretty things, it's nice not to have to put on a show every minute of every day.

Our lunch progresses easily, we order our food and I covertly watch Hunter from the corner of my eye. His conversation doesn't seem to be going well. The man who was originally sitting with him gets up and leaves, but the man with the long black hair who entered behind me remains. His posture relaxed, confident. While Hunters seems tense, but he too leans back in his seat hands resting loosely on his strong thighs. A concealed fury resting just below the surface.

Ginger excuses herself to go to the restroom and I don't think I'm going to get any better opportunity today to speak with Hunter. I thought about going into his office in town hall but was too nervous to interrupt him at work. Popping by to say hello while at lunch is far more casual and easy. Even if he's currently frowning.

I stand, and as steadily as possible, make my way over to his table. He doesn't notice me until I'm practically on top of him, his conversation with the other man cutting off abruptly as his eyes flash to mine.

"Hi, Hunter."

"Lottie. Hi," he responds a little nervously.

"I hope I'm not interrupting." I look at the man across from Hunter, hopefully relaying my apologies.

"No interruption at all, beautiful. We're just having a friendly lunch. Discussing a few … personal matters," the man answers coolly, the picture of laidback nonchalance, a wide smile spreading across his thin lips. "I'm Vincent, by the way. And you're … Lottie?"

Vincent extends his hand out, tilting his head in question as he says my name.

"Yes, that's right." Extending my own hand in answer it's quickly intercepted by Hunter's. His long fingers curl possessively around mine as he pulls my hand out of Vincent's reach.

"Did you need something, Lottie?" Hunter draws my attention away from Vincent's polite but flirtatious smile. His own smile pulls at the corner of his mouth, his eyes soft and inquiring.

"Oh, I was wondering if you would like to join me for a run

this evening?"

Hunter's eyes widen, and his lips part in surprise. The hand still holding mine tightens ever so slightly but loosens just as quickly. His thumb rubbing small circles against my skin mindlessly.

"I remember you said you like to run, and I haven't run in a while and thought it might be nice to have someone who knows the woods to run with so I don't get lost," I ramble trying to explain away my sudden invitation without sounding like a weirdo or too eager to spend more time with him.

Hunter's eyes shift between mine and momentarily flash to Vincent, narrowing before returning to me. Those lips, that I now know from personal experience are soft and perfectly kissable, pull into a flat line.

"I don't know if I'll be able to. I have . . . a lot of work to attend to."

"Nonsense," Vincent cuts in. "The lady wants to go for a run safely through the woods. She needs a guide. We wouldn't want anything to happen to her. She's so sweet and lovely. Perfect prey for a hungry predator."

That low guttural growl that surprised and enticed me on Saturday night when Hunter carried me to the cabin emanates quietly from his chest. Sometimes I think Hunter is more beast than man when he makes sounds like that. And my traitorous heart and pussy only like him the more for it.

His eyes immediately return to me, the growl cutting off abruptly. His words softer than expected when he speaks.

"Maybe some other time. But please don't go running in the woods alone. He's not wrong about predators."

The edge of my lips quirk, and I try to hide my grin. "I'm not afraid. I'm the beast whisperer, remember?" I joke.

Hunter pulls me closer still holding the hand he intercepted speaking softly. "That may be, Nightingale, but still. Humor me."

Since it appears to mean so much to him that I don't go running in the woods alone I acquiesce to his request with a slight nod.

"Good."

Reluctantly, he releases my hand which tingles with heated pinpricks in his wake. A hand threading through my limp arm at my side makes me jump with surprise as Ginger appears next to me, an absurdly broad smile on her face.

"So sorry for the interruption, boys. We'll let you get back to your conversation and lunch." Ginger pulls on my elbow trying to gently guide me back to our table. "Come on Lottie. Our foods getting cold."

Awkwardly, I wave at Hunter, barely able to squeak out a goodbye as Ginger drags me back to our table. Looking over my shoulder, I see Hunter and Vincent watching our retreat. Both interested for different reasons. Although I have no idea who Vincent is, his gray eyes linger on me. A knowing and unpleasant glint gleaming there. A shiver runs across my skin and down my spine so forcefully I turn away with jerky movements. Returning to our table and cooling food.

~Hunter~

"What a juicy little peach that one is. All honey and sugar." Vincent licks his lips while stile ogling Lottie as she sits at her booth with Ginger, tasting her lingering emotions as elves do. To them, instead of scenting emotions like shifters, they taste them on their tongues. If he had managed to touch her, he could have altered her emotions with his slimy magic and he would no longer be breathing and smirking across the table at me.

The alpha rage burning in my gut spreads to every nerve ending, readying for a fight. This male is looking at what is mine, and I don't like it.

"Eyes off her. *Now*." I force my voice to remain low, but I can't contain the growl in my tone, nor the alpha power that forces Vincent to comply. His scowl is venomous. Hating that I forced him to comply. It doesn't matter how much money or property or cronies he has, all must obey the alpha command.

"She seems very important to you for a simple human. Is there something you want to share, *Alpha*?" He spits out the last word like a curse.

"Not with you, *Elf*."

Vincent bristles at my reciprocated tone and sits taller in his pink vinyl seat.

"You have till Thursday next week to accept my offer before things get messy. Though, I would recommend an earlier response if you don't want to see anything untoward happen to that tasty little human over there." Vincent licks his lips again, no doubt trying to absorb the remnants of Lottie's sweetness and lust I scented on her.

"Careful. Threatening a member of my pack is cause for retaliation," I threaten right back at him.

He scoffs and chuckles low and menacingly.

"Oh, Hunter. She's not a member of your pack. She's not even a resident of the town. She's an unattached human passing through. You have no claim over her."

My blood freezes in my veins. I've already claimed her as mine internally. The moment Fynn told me it was possible, that was it. To me she's already a member of my pack, my future mate, my future wife. But to other's she's just a human. Fair game. At least until I claim her fully, cementing the mate bond between us. A factor that I highly doubt I'll be able to complete in time to avert Vincent's attempt to use her against me without fear of retort.

"She's still in my town, and as mayor I can protect the residents of Snowberry," I claim, even though it's weaker than my initial warning.

"What are you going to do? Arrest me? Do you even have a jail cell here? I have every right to interact with sweet Lottie as much as I wish. And until her status changes, I will do just that."

Threatening words won't do me anymore good here than they already have. I have nothing left I can control him with for the time being. Something I need to rectify. Until then, I'll have to keep a close eye on Lottie.

Vincent stands to leave a triumphant smirk on his sharp featured face. And I can't help but offer one more threatening warning.

"Watch yourself, Vincent. You're in my town, and I protect what's mine."

His smug expression doesn't falter as he drags one sharp claw across the table's surface, leaving a jagged line behind and giving Lottie one more cursory glance on his way out. His guards fall into step behind him as soon as he exits.

Thankfully Lottie isn't looking at the elf, but laughing with Ginger, and the frenzied rage that was building subsides at the sight of her joy.

I will protect her no matter what. I don't care if she isn't officially a member of my pack or resident of Snowberry. She is mine. Mine to protect, mine to keep, mine to please. And if he attempts to put one finger on her, I will not hold myself back. I will do what's necessary, consequences be damned.

Taking one last longing look at Lottie, I force myself to

stand and leave the restaurant without stopping to speak with her like I desperately want to do.

I'll see her again tonight. I know I said I was busy, but that was a lie. I've cleared all my evenings of former commitments to be free to visit with Lottie in wolf form. Tonight will be no different. Except I'll be posting outside the cabin all night standing guard, just to be sure.

Chapter 20
Lottie

Now, I know I said I wouldn't go for a run in the forest alone tonight, but that doesn't mean I can't go on a walk to visit with my favorite wolf. I've taken this path on several occasions and know well enough by now not to get lost. With Sinatra at my side, I doubt any other predators will attempt to approach me.

Slipping on my cashmere sweater and scooping up my Polaroid and guitar, I make my way into the woods. The sun is still out for at least another hour or two, so there is plenty of time to go for a walk and return before dark.

The walk to the meadow takes ten minutes at a brisk pace. When I arrive, Sinatra is already there waiting for me. He sits in the center of the circle of late afternoon sunlight, ears perked and eyes focused. As soon as I step over the threshold into the clearing, his tongue lulls out of his mouth, and he stands to greet me.

Rubbing his head and neck against my hand, arm, side,

back, and finally, chest. Seemingly assuring himself of my presence. Scratching his neck and head, I praise the beautiful animal and giggle at his antics. He's like a giant cuddly dog greeting his owner when they return home from work.

My heart lightens, and that comforting feeling of peace the wolf always brings washes through me, and I forget that Hunter rejected my offer earlier today.

"You are such a good boy, aren't you, Sinatra. My sweet boy. You always want to spend time with me, don't you?"

Sinatra bounces on his front paws in agreement. His black fur glistening in the sunlight, ice blue eyes glinting. Whoever says animals don't have personalities never had a pet. Because this wolf has such an obvious personality. Protective, friendly, cuddly, sweet and thoughtful.

"That's what I thought. Although I don't blame him for his work. He is the mayor, after all. That has to be a demanding job. Or at least I would think so. I don't really know what a mayor does, but I'm sure it's important."

Sinatra follows me to the soft, mossy grass area I usually sit in and circles me until I settle. Plopping his massive furry body down so close to me, he almost knocks me over.

Laughing, I push at Sinatra's black fur body, trying to give myself a little space.

"Scoot back, Sinatra. I need a little room. Especially if you want me to play for you again."

He doesn't move back but lets me scoot forward to get comfortable.

"What should I play today?" I ask my wolf. "The Eagles? Fleetwood Mac? Elvis? Sinatra?"

Sinatra doesn't respond to any of the artists, so I choose one for us: *Witchy Woman* by the *Eagles*. I strum through the chords at a leisurely pace, letting my eased mind control the speed and style of the song.

Sinatra sits watching me, and halfway through the song, he lowers his head to his paws at my side, ensuring the side of his snout presses against my thigh, keeping me warm and cozy.

When the song is over, I mindlessly play random songs and chords that drift in and out of my mind.

"Have you ever met Hunter, Sinatra? He lives in a house not too far from here."

I look down at the wolf, who is watching me closely, listening intently. So, I continue.

"He's the mayor of the town. I'm sure you've seen him. His family seems to know you pretty well, so I'm sure you have." I pause, thinking about Hunter and his restrained smile and baby blues, his dark hair that's almost as black as Sinatra's fur.

"I think I may have a crush on him," I admit. "There's something about him that's . . . alluring. I feel drawn to him. Especially when he speaks, and growls."

Sinatra nuzzles his nose against my hand because I stopped playing, and I laugh, picking back up on my incoherent strumming.

"The deep gravel of his voice sends tingles through me in a way that makes me all . . ." I huff out a shaky breath, "well, horny."

Sinatra's head perks up, and I swear he's staring at me in shock like he knows what I said. My face flushes, and I giggle, embarrassed to admit such a thing to a wolf.

"Don't look at me like that. I'm sure there are lady wolves that get you all hot and bothered. It's natural. But with Hunter, it feels more than just natural. It feels deeper. I don't know how to explain it. I just know when I look into his eyes and hear his voice... And don't get me started on the way he smells."

The wolf cocks his head at me in question.

"He doesn't smell bad. Actually, he smells divine."

Just remembering the sound of his deep voice and the smell of his intoxicating scent goes straight to my clit, and my nipples peak under my sweater. I have to rub my thighs together to ease the sensations growing there.

Sinatra leans closer to me as I cuddle down into his fur. Forgetting the guitar in my hands and halting my playing.

"I don't know what to do about it, Sinatra. He seems interested but denies himself. I know he's a good man. A bit protective. I've had plenty of guards in my life who were protective, but something about him is more possessive. More personal.

"He's also very confusing, but sweet. His family is amazing. Spending time with them last week had me realizing what I've missed out on with my own family ever since my dad died."

My mood drops from horny to sad, thinking of my dad always does that. We missed out on so much together. Who knows what my life would have looked like if he were alive. I probably wouldn't have become Alexandria.

Sensing my shift in mood, Sinatra lifts up on his front paws and begins nosing at my cheek and neck, licking and tickling me. My guitar is pushed to the side as I wrestle with Sinatra, laughing hysterically and trying to get him to stop. His wet nose and fine fur only add to my torment.

The wolf stands over me as I lay flat on my back laughing, when he stops abruptly. Planting his four paws on the ground around me, he stands over me like a shield, caging me in. His head goes straight up, matching his ears. His pink tongue pulls back inside his mouth as his nose twitches, sniffing the wind. A small growl begins to rumble in his chest just above me, and I can see his lips pull back, exposing wicked, sharp fangs.

Sinatra is focused on something in the darkened bushes that I can't see from my position on the ground. But when I try to stand, Sinatra positions his body to stop me.

That growl that began quietly now rumbles loudly, but that's not all that's loud in the meadow. I hear snapping and cracking, and then I see the impossible.

The wolf standing over me appears to be *growing*.

I don't believe it at first, but in the next moments or minutes, I don't know how long, there no longer stands a wolf but a beast. A giant creature that resembles a wolf but towers over even the tallest human I've ever met. His hind legs are tall and powerful, and his front paws become fingered hands with razor-sharp claws. A mixture of man and beast that is extremely angry. Thankfully, it doesn't seem to be aimed at me, but that doesn't stop the ear-piercing shriek that wrenches itself free from my lungs.

I scramble, trying to put as much distance between myself and the beast.

"Holy fucking shit! What the actual fuck?"

Curses slip free unhindered as I freak the fuck out. What the hell am I looking at? Is this creature Sinatra? The beast retains my cuddly wolf's black fur and ice-blue eyes but none of the sweet demeanor and playful personality.

Scuttling back on my ass and all fours like a crab, I manage to get a few feet away before the beast leaps forward at the bushes he's been eyeing. He doesn't break through the greenery to take chase of whatever was there. Only stopping once he reaches the very edge, growling and snarling and howling at whatever is pissing him off.

My heart beats fast and hard in my chest, causing me to freeze in fear. Again, I'm faced with the option of fight or flight, and again, my body reacts with motionlessness.

Come on, Lottie, get the fuck up before it turns around and sets its sights on you.

I don't move fast enough, and the beast turns to face me as I reach for my guitar to use as a weapon if I must. It breaks my heart to ruin such a beautiful instrument, but my life is more valuable. I'm not completely stupid.

I scramble into a shaky standing position, brandishing my guitar like a bat.

"Stay back. I swear I will bash your head in if I have to."

The beast doesn't listen and slowly lurches forward on his massive back paws. But speed doesn't matter with his size. He's no longer snarling or aggressively exposing his teeth. Blue eyes lose their bloodthirsty glint, replaced with concern.

Concern? This beast is concerned? I must be losing my mind. Spending too much time with Sinatra, thinking this creature is concerned with my emotional state.

But his clawed hands lower into a position I would expect a human to make to a cornered animal, trying to soothe it. The menacing growl settles into a quiet growling purr—a sound far too comforting and reassuring to be coming from such a creature—and it almost lulls me to lower my makeshift weapon as the beast steps closer.

"No!" I scream swinging my guitar at the beast's head. "Don't come any closer."

It growls. I growl. I swing the guitar wildly unseeing, and the growl turns into a voice.

"Stop, Lottie! It's me. It's Hunter."

Immediately I stop my frantic swinging to see Hunter standing before me. Or almost Hunter. His body is disproportioned—too tall and hairy, his nails like claws, and I see his knees snap forward, forming human legs from the double-jointed legs the beast had.

"What the fuck?"

Was the beast Hunter? Was Sinatra the beast? Would that make Sinatra Hunter? I am so fucking confused right now.

"What the hell are you? Were you that thing just now?" I scream at the—yup, completely naked Hunter.

Holy fucking shit. Hunter is naked, and goddamn, is he gorgeous. Ripping muscles flex and tighten across his chest and defined abdomen, and lower his . . . wow. That is his cock. Yup. Large and stiffening cock. *Fuck*.

I look away from his groin, trying to refocus on the important issue at hand. A beast just shifted into Hunter, right in front of my eyes.

Hunter ignores his nudity and my staring, keeping his hands lifted and palms up as he approaches me.

"Please put down the guitar, Nightingale. I know how much you love it, and I don't want you to ruin it," he says in soothing deep tones.

It's then I realize I'm still holding my guitar over my head ready to bash it into him. I lower it to my side, and Hunter reaches out to pry it from my clenching fingers.

"That's it, just relax," he coos.

"Relax? How can I relax after what I just saw?" My voice is high-pitched and scratchy from screaming.

"If you calm down, I can explain."

"Explain?" I shriek. "This better be one good fucking explanation because that was completely fucked up."

Hunter nods slowly. His expression shifts from pensively worried to a calm resolute.

"Yes, I can see how you would think that. I didn't mean to shift in front of you, but . . . there was a threat I couldn't ignore."

I have no idea what he's talking about, but I latch on and roll with it.

"Shift? As in, you changed from Sinatra to the Beast?"

"Yes," he admits, drawing out the word. "Then into my human form."

He gestures to himself with his free hand, not holding my guitar, and I reflexively look down and get another eyeful of his massive package that doesn't seem to be shy in the least. I quickly avert my gaze again because looking at his cock has me thinking all kinds of inappropriate things.

"I don't understand," I say, a bit calmer now but still just as bewildered.

"I know. I'll tell you everything, but not here." Hunter looks around behind me as if checking for threats.

Is he checking for threats? He said something about a threat he couldn't ignore.

"Why don't we go back to the cabin and sit down? You can ask me all the questions you want, and I'll answer them. Okay?"

He gives me a sheepish smile, and those damn baby blues lure me in and have me nodding my head, agreeing.

"Here," he extends my guitar out to me. "Take this. I need to shift to walk to the cabin."

Accepting my guitar, I raise an eyebrow at him. Why does he need to shift back? And does he mean back into the giant beast? He seems to read my thoughts and chuckles.

"Unless you want me to walk back like this?" He waves a hand at his nude body again. This time I don't take the bait and check out his dick again. "It'll be easier if I'm in wolf form. I'll shift back once we get to the cabin, and I can put some pants on."

"I don't have any pants that'll fit you," I blurt out because, of course, that's the most important thing to be thinking about right now; what pants he'll be wearing.

Hunter chuckles again and shakes his head. "I keep some in

the linen closet just in case."

"Oh, okay then."

I wave at him to get on with it so we can get to the cabin and I can get some answers. He shakes his head again, smiling. A smile I realize isn't restrained or tight. It's open and easy. I like it.

Oh yeah, great time to be swooning over his smile, Lottie. Pay attention.

Hunter shifts once again before my eyes, this time into Sinatra, the black wolf, instead of the massive scary beast. It's only once he's fully furry again that I don't know how I didn't see the resemblances before. Black fur, light blue eyes. Then again, I also didn't know werewolves existed five minutes ago, so yeah, there's that.

Tentatively Sinatra, or rather wolf Hunter, paces forward and nudges my limp hand with his wet nose, giving me those damn puppy dog eyes.

"Oh, don't start with that. I know who you are now. And— Shit! I just told you all that stuff about *you*!" I smack myself in the face and groan loudly. "I am never befriending a wild wolf in the woods ever again."

Hunter chuffs in what I assume is a laugh and turns to leave the meadow. Turning back only to yip at me when I don't immediately follow.

"Yeah, yeah, I'm coming. Such a demanding mutt."

Hunter jerks his wolf head back to me with a scowl and growls, ending in a whine.

"You deserve that for what you did. You're the one who lied here, not me. If anything, I was overly honest with wolf Hunter."

Wolf Hunter whines again but continues on his path back towards the cabin. I pick up my discarded Polaroid camera, slipping it and my guitar strap across my chest, following in step behind a fucking werewolf.

Chapter 21
Hunter

This was not how I planned tonight to go. Spend a little time with Lottie in the forest, secretly follow her back to the cabin, and watch over her all night from outside in wolf form. That was the plan. Not shift into my true beast form to scare off the two elves lurking in the shadows, trying to catch me unaware and do who knows what with Lottie.

Vincent had made his threat not six hours ago, and his men were already seeking her out and hunting her down. I don't even want to think of what they would have done if I weren't there. With their ability to alter people's emotions through touch, they probably could have made her go willingly if they had gotten their cold, gray hands on her.

My fur stands on end thinking about it, and I slow my pace, keeping at Lottie's side, not wanting the elves to try for a second time tonight.

Before, when I would walk at her side, she would reach out and pet me. Rest her hand on my back or neck, mindlessly stroking my fur, the feel of it warming my insides and calming my inner beast. She does so now but stops after a few moments as if realizing she had done it unconsciously. She doesn't do it again, shoving her hands in her pockets to prevent it.

The walk back to the cabin is far quieter than my previous walks with Lottie. Now that she knows who I am and that I understand everything she's saying, I guess she doesn't want to share any more of her secrets and private thoughts, as she did when I was just an ordinary wolf.

I don't immediately shift to human form when we arrive at the cabin, walking in on all fours and heading for the linen cabinet in the hall. I sit and stare at the door, waiting for Lottie.

"Are your clothes in there?" she asks. I nod.

She opens the small closet and digs around until she finds the stack of clothing on the top shelf. Pulling it down, she hands it to me. Taking the bundle of clothes in my mouth, I quickly trot to the bathroom to shift and change.

When I exit in human form, wearing a pair of gray sweatpants and a white t-shirt, I find Lottie attempting to brew a pot of coffee. And I say attempting because she's got the grounds in the machine without the filter.

"You need a filter for that."

She jumps at the sound of my voice behind her, gripping her chest over her heart. She's still wearing the soft as sin sweater I rubbed my scent all over when I first saw her tonight.

After the afternoon I had, I needed to do it to assuage my growing mate pull. I needed to feel her and to have her smell of me. Just in case Vincent needed any further confirmation that she is mine.

"Must you be so quiet and sneaky?" she scolds.

"Sorry," I chuckle. "I didn't mean to be. Here, let me do that."

Without waiting for her snappy reply, I gently reposition her by her hips to the side and take over making the coffee. Grabbing the reusable gold filter from the cabinet, I clean out the machine and restart the process properly.

"Oh. I was wondering why my coffee was grainy," Lottie admits quietly, while also watching my movements intently, memorizing the process for later.

Once the coffee is properly brewing, I turn and face Lottie. Leaning against the counter, I grip the edge at my sides to keep from reaching out to hold her. She stands a few feet away, her arms wrapped protectively around her middle as she eyes me up and down. I don't mind her perusal of my body. Just as I hadn't when she did it before when I was naked. My cock responds in the same way now as it did then. Thickening against my thigh and making itself known through the thin material of my sweats, having nothing to restrict its upward progression as I didn't think to store underwear with my backup clothes.

"Are you a werewolf?" she asks blatantly, not a hint of fear in her expression, only sheer determination.

"No. I'm a shifter."

"Aren't they the same thing?"

"Not even close."

"Hmm. Could have fooled me."

I did. I think internally, but don't dare verbalize. I hate knowing I was lying to her, but I'm glad she knows now. I don't have to hide from her anymore, and maybe if I can explain everything...

The coffee pot gurgles behind me, filling the carafe, the only sound in the quiet cabin I once used as a retreat, and now is coated in Lottie and her scent.

"What is a shifter? How did you become one? Are there more of you? How many forms do you have? Are you immortal?"

"Woah, woah, slow down."

I raise my hands in surrender, unable to control my smile around her any longer. I tried to hide it before, not wanting to allow myself too close. There's no way to suppress it any longer. Just being near her and smelling her sweet gardenia scent has my smile instantly forming.

"You said you would answer all my questions, so…" She sits at the small table and primly folds her hands on the tabletop, sitting alert and clear-eyed. "Start answering."

Running my hand around the back of my neck and around my chin, feeling the scruff starting to sprout there, I take a deep breath and start answering.

I tell her what I am, that I was born this way, that there are many others like me and others different from me, and I clarify that I am not immortal, although I will live far longer than any human.

When she asks about the others I mentioned, the coffee finishes brewing, and I pour us each a cup, setting the sugar and creamer I find in the fridge on the table in front of Lottie. And then, I settle in the chair across from her for a long conversation. Trying my best to explain as plainly as possible about shifters, meres, fairies, nymphs, pixies, and elves. Not getting into the nitty gritty tiny details but the basics of each and how we disguise ourselves with glamours or shifting to human forms.

"Wow, I was not expecting all of that." Lottie finally says when I'm finished with my explanation. "So, what about Big Foot? Is Big Foot real?"

"No," I scoff. "That's a myth. But yetis are very real. They remain in the far north, where they can easily hide in the extensive wilderness and snow. They can't shift like us or glamour themselves either, so they like to remain more hidden."

Lottie's jaw drops, not expecting that answer.

"And Chupacabras?"

"Nope."

"Vampires?"

"Hell no."

"Leprechauns?"

"Yes. Sneaky little buggers."

Again, Lottie is shocked when I confirm the existence of something she thought was completely fictional.

"Unicorns?" she asks hopefully.

"Sadly, not anymore. They were hunted to extinction many years ago."

She makes the cutest frowny face and pouts her lips out in a way that has me focusing on them, my cock stirring in my pants at the sight. I remember what those lips felt like against mine, what they taste like, and I want another go at them. This time, I won't pull away or stop.

"So, what was the threat in the forest you couldn't ignore?"

Her question has my thoughts going from hot and horny to cold and angry. If I ever see those elves again, I will rip every one of their piercings out one by one.

"There were elves in the forest watching you."

"Why?"

I shift in my seat and bring my mug to my lips, only to realize it's empty. Setting it down, I brace myself for another conversation that might not be as easy for her to accept.

"Do you remember the man you met this afternoon at Dottie's? Vincent?"

She nods but remains quiet, dutifully listening like an A-plus student. *I bet she got great grades in school.*

"Well, he's an elf and not a very nice one. Not that many of them are nice to begin with. He wants to buy my land for his drug business, and I won't sell to him."

"Good. We don't need any more drugs on the streets. I bet he would ruin this town and the forest if he were to get his hands on it."

My heart instantly warms at her declaration. She doesn't know Vincent from a stranger, but she's already against him, and that comforts me. She can't be easily persuaded into helping him—at least not without his magical interference. Which reminds me I should warn her about that, but Lottie continues with her questions before I can.

"So what were they doing in the forest tonight? Searching your property?"

"Not exactly." Lottie watches me, completely rapt, and I see now why she's my mate. Smart, patient, curious, understanding, as well as beautiful, and graceful, with the most enchanting voice I've ever heard.

"They were looking for you."

"Me?" Her eyes practically bulge out of their sockets as her entire face shifts in surprise. "Why would they want me? I didn't even know they existed."

"That would be because of me."

She cocks her head to the side like any curious pup would. "How so?"

"Because he could tell at lunch that you're important to me. He wants to use you to get me to sign over my land to him."

The ferocious scowl that contorts her face is almost comical but also welcome. She's feisty and isn't going to wilt under the pressures being thrust upon her. Perhaps years of superstardom have strengthened her to deal with such pressures.

"What an asshole. I can't stand manipulative, underhanded people like him. Don't you dare let him control you or your decisions. You have a right to tell him no, and he should respect that." Her voice increases to nearly a shout.

Her fury is clear, not only in her words but in the death grip she has on her mug. I fear she may throw it across the room at any moment in disgust and frustration.

Yes, she will be a worthy mate indeed. I can't wait to see her handling arguments between citizens in town over everything from property lines to celebration decorations. She'll demand respect and fairness that they'll willingly obey, even without an alpha command.

"I don't plan on letting him strong-arm me. But I also won't let him use you or hurt you. I should also warn you about him, not just because he's a scumbag but because of the magic all elves possess."

Lottie furrows her brow, and her eyebrows drop low over her eyes. For someone who just learned about the non-human world, she is very calm and more concerned about things like Vincent ruining the forest with his drugs than a man who can shift into a giant wolf beast.

"They have the ability to alter a person's emotions through touch. They can make you feel happy, sad, scared, aroused. They can't control your actions but they can shift your emotions to be more amiable to their suggestions."

Her eyes widen in realization, and she sucks in a sharp breath. "That's why you pulled my hand away when he tried to shake it."

"Yes. I didn't want him to try anything with you, but . . ." I trail off, trying to figure out how to tell her the rest of it. "But I also didn't want him touching you *specifically*."

"Me? Why? Because I'm a human?"

"No, not just that. Among non-humans, we have mates. And I don't just mean friends or spouses, but *bonded mates*. A person who is perfectly matched to our inner selves. Our other half that is perfectly made to be our partner, lover, and friend for the rest of our lives."

Lottie sits still across from me, her hands wrapped around her coffee mug, completely engrossed in my words. I like her attention on me, and I like being able to tell her all of this. Even though I hadn't planned on telling her so soon—at least not tonight in such a manner—a part of me is glad I slipped and shifted in front of her.

Nothing in our laws says we can't tell a human what we are; only that if that human is a threat they must be dealt with. Usually with fairy dust and memory-altering. In extreme cases, death, but nothing like that has been necessary in decades. At least not in Snowberry. I can't speak for how non-humans elsewhere deal with their issues.

"When we meet that person, we feel what we refer to as the mate pull. It's like something inside of us attaches to that person and ties an invisible string between us. That string tightens and shortens, forcing us closer and closer together.

"You don't have to act on the pull, but not doing so can be very emotionally and physically painful to sever. Although it can be done, most don't ignore a mate pull. Being somewhat rare, although not singular. A possible mate could appear again if the first mate pull isn't solidified. Most don't risk finding an even rarer second mate to ignore the first."

Clearing my throat, I take a fortifying inhale and slowly release it, preparing myself for the final part of my explanation.

"When I first met you, I felt this pull. I didn't think it was a mate pull because you're human. I can tell by your scent. To my knowledge, at the time, we couldn't have mate bonds with humans. But it kept growing and pulling me to you. So, I asked a friend of mine to do some research, and today at lunch he told me what he discovered.

"He says we can have a mate bond because somewhere in your lineage not too far ago, you have an ancestor who was non-human."

"Wait, hold on," she says, holding up a hand, stopping me, and briefly closing her eyes before opening them to narrow on me. "You're saying my like great-grandpappy was a non-human?"

"Or something like that. Could have been a great-grandmother." She laughs, the sound airy and high-pitched.

"So, I'm part non-human?"

"Apparently so, yes."

Her eyes go distant, and I'm surprised she's more concerned with the non-human ancestor than the whole she's my mate thing.

"What kind?"

"What kind what?" I asked, confused by her question.

"What kind of non-human am I?" she clarifies.

"I have no idea. We would have to do a deep dive into your relatives to figure that out."

"Hmm."

That's it? That's all she has to say is hmm?

"You're taking this all very well. Are you sure you're not in denial or having a breakdown or something?"

Lottie shrugs, standing to refill her coffee mug. She stands by the counter, and I swivel in my chair to keep her in my line of sight.

"Maybe I am. But how am I supposed to react? Should I be crying or screaming? I mean, it's strange but kinda cool to know that the creatures I've always assumed were fictional actually exist." Her eyes widen with a twinkle, and the edges of her lips curl up. "I can't wait to see a real fairy and mermaid."

"They don't like being called mermaids. Especially the men. Just call them meres or mere folk is fine," I correct.

The mermaid title is something a human came up with eons ago because they saw a siren in the ocean, who usually happen to be female and devastatingly beautiful with a voice that can make anyone walk into a stream of lava if they so desire. Sirens are among the deadliest and most powerful non-humans because of their voice and ability to control any race to do anything they want.

I don't get into the whole history of sirens versus meres and the human term of mermaid. That'll be for another day, as will a lesson on types of fairies and nymphs. First, before all that, though, I'll have to go over me being an alpha. For now, I just want to get her to understand what being a possible mate to a shifter implies.

"Do you understand everything I've told you about mates and the mate pull?" I ask tentatively redirecting the conversation back to where I need it to be.

Deep ocean blue eyes find mine, and they turn from cool breezes to boiling pools. Her scent shifts from neutral to sexually excited. I inhale deeply, loving her lust-tainted scent. Her pheromones instantly harden my eager and overly excited cock.

A growl rumbles in my chest and throat as my eyes drop to watch her pretty pink tongue poke out and lick a drop of coffee from her lips.

"Careful, Nightingale, I have a very acute sense of smell, and your arousal only makes me hard."

A bright pink blush flushes her cheeks, and she turns her head, trying to hide behind her mug. Pink looks good on my Nightingale. I'd like to see all of her flushed that color.

Lottie clears her throat, and I can tell she's trying to subdue her arousal, but I can smell her growing wetter, and it makes my cock throb in my sweats. The soft material brushes against my engorged head and knot. Another thing I'll have to explain when the time comes. Because it will. Now that she knows what I am and I know the mate pull is real, Lottie will be mine.

"I kind of understand. I . . . I feel the pull too. I just didn't know that's what it was. I just thought I was attracted to you . . . and horny."

I chuckle. Oh, the pull will definitely make us both extremely horny. It helps when creating the bond and for procreation, of course.

Standing from my chair, I cross to her and pluck the coffee mug from her hands, setting it on the counter behind her. Leaning in, I trap her between my arms and press my body flush to hers. Loving when her scent spikes with spicy arousal.

"It makes me horny too," I admit, punctuating my confession with the softest press of my hips to her stomach so she can feel just exactly how horny.

Lottie's chest rises with a sharp inhale when she realizes I'm pressing my cock against her. Her eyes go glassy, and the urge to slide my cock inside her and bite the soft tan skin of her neck is so demanding I have to clench my jaw and my hands to stop myself from doing so.

"Wow. It feels even bigger than it looked."

"I was only half hard before," I breathe the words against her skin as I bend down to run my nose along her jaw.

The pull appreciates the skin-to-skin contact. Which, of course, only intensifies my desire and hers. I want to act on my throbbing lust, but I need to make sure she has no more questions before I do because I may not be able to stop myself once I start. Instead, I press a tender kiss along her jaw before pulling away to stare down at her.

Lottie isn't short for a human female, which means she comes up to my shoulders, which I like. With those long, lean legs of hers, she'll be able to make the chase far more enjoyable when the time comes.

"Do you have any other questions for me?"

Her eyes shift back and forth, searching mine, and I can see when she comes to a decision.

"Can I see you again? In the beast form?"

Chapter 22
Lottie

He wasn't expecting me to ask that. Hunter's eyebrows shoot up, and the surprise is clear in his expression. But I do want to see him again. I want to know all his forms. It scared me before when I didn't know who he was. Now that I know it's Hunter, and he won't eat me—and we're possible mates, I still need to wrap my head around that one—I want to see it again. See him again.

Learning about the non-humans is shocking but exciting. I don't know why he expected me to be freaked out about it. I look forward to learning all about his people and finding out which type each person I've met in town is.

Wait. If he's a shifter, that means Ginger is a shifter, as are his brother and his parents. Now it totally makes sense why they were laughing at the photo of Sinatra I showed them. Because they knew it was Hunter. They were messing with him. I think I like them even more now.

Hunter stares down at me for another long moment,

reading the determination on my face. Now that he's told me he has three freaking forms he can shift into at will, I want to see them all. And since I've seen plenty of human and wolf Hunter, I want to see beast Hunter. What he calls his true form.

"You really want to see it?" He obviously doesn't believe I would really want to, based on the slight down-turning of his lips.

"Of course I do. It is you, and you are it, and I want to see it now that I know it's you. I'm curious. I didn't really take my time to inspect you before."

I give him a warm smile, hoping he doesn't say no. He turns in place, looking around the cabin, but still hasn't removed his lower half from pressing against me. His hard erection still firm against my lower stomach, just above my pubic bone. Since I'm a bit taller than most girls, our hips are almost lined up. But he's still taller, just over six feet, if I'd have to guess.

He seems to come to a conclusion with a sharp incline of his chin.

"I guess I could show you in here. I'm rather big."

"I noticed."

I gently rock my hips, pressing into his cock, and he groans.

"I wouldn't do that unless you want to see my beast with a massive hard-on as well."

I'm taken aback by his statement, not even considering he would also be aroused in his beast form. I bet his cock is huge as a beast. The thought has me considering rocking my hips against him again just so I can see it. Hunter must realize my intention because he puts both hands on my hips, stopping me from doing just that.

"Nah ah, you naughty little bird. Not today. Maybe later I'll show you, but as a human it's unlikely you'll ever experience it."

Now I'm really curious.

"You sure about that? Have you seen how big baby heads and bodies are? Human females can handle a lot."

Those baby blues sharpen and narrow on me, going dark as he absorbs my meaning.

"You are going to be the death of me, sweet Nightingale."

I smile and bite my lip, enjoying this far more playful and open Hunter. However, in wolf form, this was his personality, just without words.

"I think you'll live, as will I."

Reaching out, I place my hands flat on his chest and press him back. He doesn't resist, and I stop once we've reached the open area between the kitchen and the living room—a space large enough for his true form to fit without breaking something.

I hope.

"Show me your beast, Hunter," I whisper close to his chest and feel the vibration from the growling purr there.

Extricating myself, I step back, giving him plenty of room to shift.

The tempting man—shifter—before me smirks and reaches down to peel his t-shirt off over his head. Taking his sweet ass time and drawing out the motion. Flexing every muscle needed and unnecessary to complete the action. Tossing the shirt away on the floor before reaching for the waistband of his pants.

"You giving me a strip show?" I raise an eyebrow at him and his fingers that linger just under the waistband of his sweats.

"No. I would just rather not tear through my pants when I shift as I'll need them after."

I should have known. He was naked when he shifted before, so he obviously would need to be naked again.

Steeling my backbone, I lift my eyes, keeping them firmly

glued to his face as he drops his pants to the floor and kicks them away.

It takes a lot of self-control not to look down to check out the appendage that felt thick and large against my stomach. It isn't until the fur starts to sprout across his body and I hear cracking and popping as his body changes and shifts that I allow my gaze to roam his changing form. Taking less than a minute, Hunter once again becomes the hulking beast I first saw in the forest.

This time, my heart beats heavily in my chest with a different emotion. Awe at the majesty and beauty of the beast before me. He's beautiful in a deadly way. His posture is hunched over to accommodate his massive size. I imagine he's nine or ten feet tall if he were to stand up straight on his hind legs.

Crouching forward, he carefully places his clawed hands on the wood floor, his new position bringing us face to face. His eyes are still that unfathomable azure filled with wary caution, waiting for my reaction.

My hand extends out and I connect with his furred neck that's so thick around my hands would barely touch were I to wrap my arms around it. The fine hairs are just as silky soft as Sinatra's had been and just as inky black. Flexing my hand, I let the strands filter between my fingers, and Hunter's eyes close briefly at the contact.

His head and snout are as big as my torso, but he keeps his mouth shut, probably trying not to scare me with his pointed teeth I got a flash of before.

Hunter relaxes into my touch and bends even lower, pressing the top of his head against my chest. I lean down and rub my cheek against the finer fur between his tall, pointed ears. Wrapping my arms around as much of him as I can.

A soft, contented whine echoes through the room. Hunter's

beast form practically going lax in my arms.

I rub my face against him again since he seems to like it, and he makes the sweet sound again.

"You're beautiful," I whisper into this fur, but being so close to his massive keen ears, he must hear me.

We remain in that position for a few moments before I pull away and take a longer look at the rest of him, circling his huge body. I do manage a quick peek between his legs, looking for this mystifyingly massive cock he spoke of, but I see nothing but a bulge under his fur.

I continue my perusal, inspecting his hindquarters and double-jointed legs, which I imagine can run very fast. Then I notice his surprisingly bushy tail, which wags when I brush my hand down it.

Just a giant cuddly dog.

Running my hand over his hip and up his back, ending at his shoulder and neck. I can see the fur rise along his spine as if my touch elicited a form of goosebumps. This seems likely the case when he does a whole-body shiver and shake. He brings his giant snout back to press against my side in the same motion he did as a regular wolf. It must be a shifter thing.

"Okay. You can change back now."

Just as quickly as before, his body transforms from beast to human in a graceful fluidity that speaks of years of practice. And once again, before me stands a naked Hunter.

I keep my eyes trained on his face, not allowing myself to look down until he turns and bends over to pick up his sweats. I hadn't gotten a good look at his backside yet, and I am not disappointed when I ogle his firm round ass. It flexes as he slips each leg into the pants and then conceals it under the gray material. Shame, someone as physically stunning as Hunter should walk around naked constantly.

He comes to stand directly in front of me, not touching, just watching.

At a loss for what to do, I shift on my feet. Now that he's shown me his true self and exposed his deepest secrets, I suppose it would only be right to do the same.

"Since you've been so honest with me about who you are, I should probably tell you who I am."

"I know who you are, Lottie," he says, stepping another inch closer to me.

"You might think you know me because of everything I told you when you were a wolf, but . . . there was something else I didn't mention about who I really am."

Closing the distance between us, Hunter reaches up and cups my cheek. His palm is large and warm. I can't help but lean into him, the touch eliciting a wave of pleasurable tingles across my skin.

"I told you. I know who you really are. Alexandria."

The warming pleasure vanishes under frigid shock. His smile only softens at my stunned expression.

"How did you know?"

"Ginger," he admits the one word as if it's all the explanation needed. It's not.

"But how did she know?"

Even as I speak the question, the answer comes to me; the only way she could have known was if someone told her, someone like...

"Luna," both Hunter and I say at the same time. I frown up at him, his thumb brushing gently over my jaw.

"How do you know Luna?"

"I've helped her out on assignments in the past. When I was younger, before I became Mayor. Shifters sometimes call on other shifters, especially alphas, to assist on jobs."

"Wait," I interrupt, pulling his hand away from my face so I can think straight, holding it in mine between us. "Luna is a shifter?"

Hunter repositions our hands, threading our fingers together and pressing them to his chest.

"Yes. Why do you think she makes such an effective bodyguard? Shifters are instinctually protective. We are the guardians of non-humans. It's in our blood."

"That sneaky little..." Biting my lip, I glower down at our entwined fingers.

Luna is going to hear it from me the next time I talk to her. I've shared everything with her, intimate personal things that no one else knows, and she never told me. A thought occurs to me as I'm mentally chastising Luna for not sharing this world with me: Hunter said he did jobs with Luna in the past.

Upturning my gaze back to Hunter, I look at him from beneath my lashes.

"Did you ever work with Luna guarding me? As Alexandria?"

I'd like to think I would have remembered Hunter, but honestly, I don't know most of my security team beyond Luna. She rotates them in and out and brings in extra when needed for shows and events. He very well could have been on a security detail for some awards show I attended, and I never knew.

Hunter shakes his head. "No. I haven't done jobs for her since I became mayor, and I think she started working for you around the same time. So, I wouldn't have been on any details for you."

"Oh."

That makes sense, I suppose. Makes me feel better for not remembering him if he had.

"Have you known who I was this whole time? Have I been walking around like an idiot thinking no one knew when really everyone knows? *Does* everyone know?" My voice squeaks and cracks as panic sets in. "Fuck, this is not good. The media is gonna get wind of this, and then my mother is going to show up."

"Shhh. It's okay," Hunter soothes, calming my spiraling babble, releasing my hand to rub up and down my arms in reassuring strokes. "No one but Ginger and I know. And I didn't know till I saw your photo on her phone the day after dinner with my parents. I forced her to tell me. Don't worry. There'll be no media showing up here if I have anything to say about it. As you can imagine, a town filled with wolf shifters and fairies doesn't exactly like a lot of media attention."

My racing heart calms at his gentle tone. At least I won't have to worry about being outed to the gossip rags and websites.

My mind races and spirals, imploding with all the new information. There's a lot to digest about non-humans, Hunter being a shifter and knowing I'm Alexandria, this whole mate thing, elves wanting to use me as leverage against Hunter to gain his land, and so much more. The sheer overload of information has me dizzy.

"I think I need to sit down."

Gently, Hunter wraps an arm around my shoulders, guiding me to the couch and helping me sit.

"I know this is a lot of information, and you're taking it exceptionally well. Why don't we just take it easy for the rest of the night? I'll make us some dinner, and we can talk or not—it's up to you. In the morning, I'll have Ginger come over, and she can explain the things I can't."

Inhaling lung fulls of air, the lightheadedness passes, and I nod.

"Okay, good. I'm also going to stay here tonight. To keep

an eye on you. I was going to watch the cabin from outside as a wolf, but now that I'm here, I'd much rather sleep on the couch than in the dirt outside."

Hunter gives me a roguish smile, and the last bit of my uneasiness vanishes. I give him a flirty smile in return.

"The couch, huh? You're not going to try and convince me to share the bed with you?"

"No, little bird. When we share a bed, I won't need to convince you. You'll be pulling me by my tail to join you."

"That's awfully confident. You sure about that?"

Hunter leans in and brushes his lips against my neck in the faintest of touches. Breathing heat against my skin that prickles in response.

"I am very sure about that Nightingale."

His words are a brand on my skin, and I believe every single syllable.

"Now, let's see what you have that we can make into an acceptable dinner."

Hunter removes his lips from my flesh and stands from the couch, taking with him the lust that nearly consumed me at his words.

Shaking my head clear of the lust-filled fog his voice created, I watch him cross the small space to the kitchen.

"You can cook?"

"Of course. You didn't think my mother was the only one, did you?"

With that Hunter proceeds to make me the first cooked meal in my kitchen since I arrived.

Chapter 23
Lottie

Just as he promised, Hunter slept on the couch and didn't once try to sneak into my room and share the bed with me. Unfortunately, I wouldn't have minded snuggling up close to him in human or wolf form. They're both very cuddly.

I spent a reasonable amount of time staring out my window last night, unable to fall asleep with everything running through my mind. Eventually, my eyes grew heavy, and I fell into a deep, peaceful sleep.

The smell of coffee—non-burnt coffee—brewing lulls me from that sleep. Soft golden rays of sunlight slip in through the picturesque window.

Stretching, I slip out of bed and make my way to the kitchen. There's already a fire crackling in the fireplace, warming the small cabin and keeping away the cold chill of the autumn morning. September in southern California isn't nearly this cool. I'm thankful Luna warned me of the weather before coming so I could pack warm pajamas.

Hunter stands in the kitchen, his back turned to me, his head tilted to focus on something on the stove. He's still wearing the sweats and shirt from last night, and I take a moment to admire his firm ass through the flimsy material. Just as nice as it was last night.

"Good morning," I call out, pulling his attention from the stove.

He turns, and his face brightens with a wide smile. "Good morning, sleepy head. I was wondering when you were going to wake up."

The clock hanging on the wall reads eight-fifteen. That's not that late. My brow furrows, and I look back to Hunter, who's still smiling at me but keeping a watchful eye on the pan before him.

"It's not even nine. How early do you get up to think eight fifteen is late?"

He shrugs and returns to stirring the contents of the pan, giving me his back once again. I take another lingering look at his butt before crossing to see what he's cooking.

"I'm usually up and out of the house by seven. Early bird gets the worm and all that," he chuckles.

"Well, I don't like worms," I state, peeking around his shoulder to the stove. "Whatcha cookin'?"

"Breakfast," he says, like I couldn't tell that.

"Obviously, but what specifically?"

Hunter steps to the side to show me the pans. One pan has scrambled eggs with chunks of green veggies, and another has bacon and sausage. I'm pretty sure I didn't have any of those things besides the eggs in my fridge.

"Where did you get all this?"

"My house. I woke early and made a quick trip since you had nothing beyond cereal."

Inhaling the delicious aroma, my stomach grumbles greedily. Hunter laughs and leans over to kiss the top of my head as if it were the most natural thing in the world. Out of shock I don't respond because I have no idea how to. Our relationship seems to be shifting drastically, and although I'm not opposed to it, I have no idea what we are to one another.

"Why don't you get some coffee and take a seat, food will be done shortly."

Nodding awkwardly, I go to fill my cup and sigh with delight at the taste of the warm, bitter bean juice—so much better than the burnt dirt water I was making.

I sit and watch Hunter move around the kitchen, completely at home in the space. Though I suppose he would be, this is his cabin after all. I'm sure he's spent many days and nights here to know exactly where every teaspoon is kept.

He makes two plates and a cup of coffee, then sits across from me at the small dining table.

The food looks mouthwatering.

"Dig in," he commands with a wave of his fork, already piled high with eggs.

He shoves the full fork in his mouth, and I follow suit, moaning when I bite into a perfectly crispy piece of bacon. We don't talk much as we eat, and it isn't until Hunter's cleared the plates and refilled our coffee that he does.

"I've asked Ginger to come over and keep you company today, maybe answer any remaining questions you have. I hope that's okay."

"Yeah. That would be great. I'd love a girl's day."

And I can ask her all the other questions I didn't have the nerve to ask Hunter specifically about the possibility of being a mate and whatever the hell that entails.

We don't have to wait long before Hunter stands, as if he

heard something outside, listening carefully before grinning down at me.

"Ginger's here, or almost. She's just down the driveway."

Wow, can he hear her that far away and distinguish her car from others? Remind me never to whisper secrets anywhere near a shifter.

Slipping his hand into mine, he helps me stand and pulls me into the circle of his arms. A move so simple and yet so monumental, again with the ease and comfort of someone who's done it a thousand times. Apparently, he's done distancing himself from me.

His embrace is strong but comforting, a presence that eases me deeper into his embrace. Wrapping my arms around his waist, I allow him to hold me and myself to hold him. As strange as this all is, it's also easy. Right. And I haven't had either of those things in many years.

Leaning into his touch, I rest my cheek against his chest, which swells against my face with a deep breath. His heart a steady beating drum in my ear, further drawing me in.

Pulling away just enough to look down at me, Hunter bends to nuzzle his nose against my temple.

"Be good today, Nightingale. Stay with Ginger, and don't go anywhere alone. I still don't know if Vincent's men will try anything again. And I couldn't forgive myself if something happened to you."

The part of me that prickles at trying to be controlled eases only at the sound of the concern in his voice. For him, for now, I'll do as he asks. But I will not let this Vincent asshole ruin everything I've gained. I will not allow anyone to ever control my life again.

"Fine. But only because you asked so nicely. Don't expect me to follow commands like a trained dog just because you gave them."

His chest rumbles with a chuckle between us, and I can feel the smile on his lips as he presses them closer to my skin.

"I wouldn't dream of it, little bird."

Those inquisitory lips of his make their way down the side of my face and don't stop until they find mine. Pressing soft but firm with a greedy tenderness that makes my knees go weak. Thankfully, Hunter is holding me, or I'd make a fool of myself by falling to the ground at his feet. The kiss deepens, his tongue brushing against my lips and then stroking inside. He tastes like bacon and coffee.

My body tingles and burns with desire, my nipples hardening to stiff peaks, which rub shamelessly against Hunter's hard muscles, causing him to groan into our kiss. His cock thickens against my stomach, only making my desire grow, my panties getting damper by the second.

The kiss goes on until there's a knock at the door. I don't know how long we stood there, but the spell is broken the moment Ginger's loud and demanding voice booms from the other side of the front door.

"Open up, you horn dog. I can smell you both, and I'd rather not walk in on anything involving my brother's naked ass."

We both laugh, and Hunter only releases his hold on me after another small peck on my lips. His erection tenting his sweats in a very obvious display of his response to our little make-out session. Gripping his cock through his pants, he adjusts himself, tucking his hard length up so it at least isn't an arrow pointing directly at me and what we were leading up to had she not interrupted.

Turning to the front door, he calls out to his sister. "No one is naked, you perv."

He opens the door and waves for Ginger to enter. She does

so with the flourish of a spring chicken. Dressed in another of her fashionable outfits with thigh-high russet suede boots that almost perfectly match her hair and an ivory sweater dress that flares from her narrowed waist. Her high fashion ensemble is out of place among my flannel pajamas and Hunter's sweatpants.

"Hello, darlings. Everything tucked away?" she asks haughtily as she saunters into the cabin, travel coffee mug in hand.

Hunter grins and shakes his head at his sister, stepping through the open door behind her.

"Be good, Ginger, and stay put. I'll text you when I know something."

With a longing look filled with blatant carnal promises, Hunter backs out of the cabin. Leaving me flushed and horny while his sister looks on with amused mirth.

"So, Hunter finally told you he was your big bad wolf, huh?"

I roll my eyes at her but chuckle. Hunter is never going to live that down.

~

"Okay, so let me get this right," Ginger and I have been sitting for over an hour now discussing things, primarily mate things but also about Hunter being an alpha, and I think I have it all figured out. Maybe. "So, mate bonds are formed differently for each type of non-human that can have mates, but for shifters, it starts with a smell?"

"Yes. Smell and scent are very important to shifters; it's our first indication of a mate pull."

"Okay, so you smell this person, and they smell like extra super awesome. Then if you touch that person, the mate pull increases, making you, like, extra horny and sensitive to their touch?"

That would explain why Hunter was so adamant about not touching me. He was trying not to get turned on or further progress the mate bond. I wonder why I can feel its effects as well? Because of my non-human ancestry? From what it sounds like, I shouldn't and don't have any non-human attributes other than a lingering blood connection to a long-dead great-great-grandfather or grandmother. I shouldn't be affected in the same way he is. For now, I keep that to myself. At least until I learn a little bit more about their world.

"Basically, yes. Or so I've been told. I haven't experienced it myself," Ginger confirms.

She is way too excited about all this, and I'm not sure if it's because I am—or used to be—a celebrity, because she's my friend, or because she just really likes watching her brother squirm.

"Okay. After the touching thing to solidify the mate bond, we, or the couple, would have to . . ." My cheeks redden as I recall what comes next. "Mate under a full moon, and during climax, the male will bite the female to complete the bond."

"Not the male specifically but the more dominant partner, sometimes that's the female. But either way, yes. The chase builds the desire and anticipation. Chasing is a bit of a kink for shifters." Ginger winks at me conspiratorially, and I think back to when I asked Hunter to go on a run with me. Does he think I was propositioning him? Was I?

Ginger continues, completely ignoring my wide-eyed stare.

"Once they chase and fuck the mixing of DNA and essences, it connects the two on a biological and magical level we don't quite understand. We know that once the bond is made, the one with the shorter life span gains the life span of the other."

Right, because shifters live hundreds of years, as I've just learned. And others, like the fairies, can live for thousands. Non-humans also age slower than humans, which is why Dottie looks the same age as her son even though she's eighty-freakin-five years old. I'm thankful to learn Hunter isn't older than he appears; he actually is thirty, but Ryder, on the other hand, turns out to be fifty-five. Damn, I wish I aged like them.

I suppose if I mate with Hunter, I will.

That's a thought that'll stop you in your tracks. Mated to a wolf shifter and able to live for hundreds of years. The idea isn't unappealing. Although scary, it is still intriguing.

Ginger continues with her mate bond explanation. "Not only do they gain the same life span to ensure they spend the most time together, but they also gain a type of sixth sense. Able to *feel* the presence of their mate. Like a locator beacon. As well as being able to feel when they're in physical pain. It's an old connection meant to allow one to be able to find their mate if they were in trouble to protect them."

She rolls her head to give me a sardonic look from her spot on the couch next to me. "If you haven't noticed by now, shifters are *very* protective."

"Oh, I've noticed."

"Anyway, that's about the gist of things when it comes to shifter mates as far as I know," she concludes, tilting her head to rest on the couch.

"So, nothing weird happens to the mates, at least physically? I wouldn't sprout fur and a tail if I were to complete a mate bond with Hunter?"

Just saying it out loud has a lump forming in my throat. I'd barely been considering getting involved with Hunter for a short tryst, and here I am, talking about forming a permanent mate bond with him, even though I've only kissed him twice.

Ginger barks out a laugh, lifting her head to stare at me.

"No, you won't sprout a tail and start howling at the moon. The change is only internal, nothing external. You would still be you but for much longer than anticipated."

"That doesn't sound so bad."

Again, my cheeks redden as I mentally prepare to ask another intimate question. "And the *mating* part. Do they do that in their true form?" I tentatively ask, hoping she doesn't realize what I'm really asking.

"Usually, yes. The bonding ritual has traditionally been done in their true form."

So, if I were to go through with a mate bond ceremony with Hunter, he would be in his true form? With the monster cock he mentioned before? I may have jokingly teased him that I could handle that, but in truth, it sounds frightening to even attempt such a feat.

I sink into the couch cushions, curling my knees up against my chest and wrapping my arms around them. I changed out of my pajamas and into leggings and a sweater, which are not nearly as stylish as Ginger's, but these days, I go for comfort over style. Mostly.

Nibbling on my cuticle, I stare off into space, trying to figure out how something like that could possibly work without damaging my insides.

How deep can a cock go before it starts to cause damage? I've seen those giant foot-long *dildos, but can people really fit that whole thing inside?* With my mother overlord, I never got to participate in the orgies and sex parties celebrities like to partake in behind locked doors away from the media. So, my experiences with sex and kinks land more on the average Joe spectrum rather than the experienced, knowledgeable kinky.

Ginger must notice my inner turmoil because she chuckles,

drawing my attention to her amused expression.

"Not with you though, Lottie. Since you're human and far smaller than Hunter in his true form, he would shift down for you. To whatever degree you both wish. He can retain certain characteristics if you like that kind of thing. Claws, tail… girth." She wiggles her eyebrows at me, and I blush even further.

I do kind of like his tail.

"He can be fully human or not. As I said, most take their true form but not always when there are differences. Evelyn is a nymph, and her mate is a shifter. She was able to take him in his true form because of her magic, but he still shifted down some to accommodate her size."

"Are all non-human couples mated? Hunter said something about it being somewhat rare."

She shakes her head and adjusts the hem of her dress across her crossed knees.

"There are many who are and many who aren't. Most just get married as humans would. Pledging their love and lives to one another. Some participate in the act of a mate bond ceremony but don't actually form the mate bond. It's a great gift to find a mate."

Ginger sighs wistfully, and her expression becomes one of yearning I understand. We all want that one person who fills in the gaps, who completes you and compliments you perfectly, who loves you unconditionally, and who protects and supports you no matter what.

Supposedly, Hunter is that to me, and I am to him. Made for one another, a perfect partner. I can't say it isn't tempting, that he isn't tempting. Because he is. I want him; I can't deny that. To have him and to be loved and accepted for hundreds of years together? That's something I can't ignore.

"Well, that's enough of that; let's talk about something

else. Like, can you get me access to couture lines direct from the designer?"

With that, we fall into an easy conversation about fashion and designers and what it was like to attend fashion week in Paris. Ginger forces me to promise to take her one year, which I do. Even if I decide to step down from the limelight, I am still Alexandria and can get into any fashion show I want.

Chapter 24

Hunter

Ryder seemed notably captivated by our conversation this morning. When I left Lottie's, I ran straight home to change and find Ryder. There's never anything I keep from my brother and beta. He needed to know about mate bonds between us and humans. If this is not a one-off thing, others may feel it too, and we want them to know it's real.

He seemed distracted a good portion of the time and took off without a word. He must still be dealing with that blogger he told me about. With the blood moon only a week away, there are also more shifters showing up in town, and he has to deal with them as well. I leave that all to him. For now, I need to focus on Lottie and Vincent and what the fuck I'm going to do about both.

I know what I want to do with Lottie. I want to chase her through the forest and pin her beneath my hulking form and rut her like the beast I am. I know I can't take her in my true form; she's too small and fragile, and I'd never do anything to hurt her. But I can chase her and pin her to the ground and fuck her as a man. It'll be just as satisfying.

But I also want more. I want to know if she talks in her sleep, what her favorite movie is, her greatest fear and deepest desires, how fast she can run, whether she wants children and whether she plans on going back to her life as a famous pop star.

That last one is a rather pressing issue. It would be difficult, but I'd make it work if she wanted to return to LA and continue her career as Alexandria. I could pose as her bodyguard. My inner beast wouldn't be pacified with anything less. As her mate, I would be her best protection. But it would also be difficult.

There are non-humans who are successful celebrities, so it can be done. None of them are alphas, though. I may complain about the day-to-day responsibilities as mayor, but I would never change it. I'm an alpha. I'm born to lead and command. If an alpha doesn't have a pack, they can go insane. Literally, if that were to happen, I would be useless as a mate to Lottie. And that won't suffice. I'd have to create a new pack. I'd have to leave Ryder and Ginger, my parents, Donna and Levi, Dottie and Fynn. I've established my pack here; leaving it now would be painful.

Not having my mate could be more painful. I would eventually get past the physical pain of the separation as long as we never solidify the bond. But the emotional pain of knowing I had the opportunity to have Lottie for a mate and let her slip through my fingers would destroy me.

I can go back and forth in my head all day, but nothing will be solved until I work things out with Lottie. Until she definitively tells me yes or no. Until then, I'm no longer going to restrain myself. I won't deny myself her touch and affection.

Her smile and laughter. Her lighthearted kindness and easy-going banter. Her sweet, enchanting voice. That is if she ever sings for me again.

I will learn everything there is to know about my mate and give her every pleasure our bodies demand. I will show her what it will be like to be mated to an alpha, to *me*.

Fuck, I never thought I would find my perfect mate. And unless she denies me, I will make her mine. I'll just have to be very convincing.

It's been hours since I left Lottie with Ginger, and I can just imagine what my sister has filled her head with. Not that I think she would speak badly of me; she loves me. She loves Lottie, and I'm sure would love for us to be mates. I'm more concerned she told embarrassing stories of our childhood and frightened her with stories of the mating ceremony.

Knowing you're going to be hunted and chased through a forest in the middle of the night under a full moon to be mounted and fucked by a nine-foot-tall wolf beast and then bitten while orgasming can be overwhelming for some. For others, it's arousing. Just thinking about chasing Lottie through the dark woods, hearing her heavy breaths and echoing laughter, has my cock hardening in my pants again.

That's going to be happening a lot more now. The more I touch and smell her, the more my body will respond, hoping to fuck and mate. I don't blame it; Lottie is sexy as hell.

Stuffing down my growing desire, I reprimand myself and adjust my cock to a more comfortable and less visible position. It won't go away completely, but at least I can minimize my reactions around my siblings. In private, alone with Lottie, I'll wear my boner like a badge of pride. Showing her exactly how aroused she makes me isn't something I am embarrassed by.

This time, I don't walk to Lottie's cabin but drive over in

my truck, tossing an overnight bag in the back seat with a few changes of clothes. I don't plan on leaving Lottie's side until this Vincent situation is handled. Making her leave the comfort of her space in the cabin won't help her to trust me, so I figure sleeping on the couch for a few days won't hurt. Maybe once she's more comfortable with the idea of us, I can bring her to my house and show her where she might live if she were my mate.

My house is nice—two stories, large spacious rooms, with a multi-car garage—but I'm sure it doesn't hold a candle to whatever mansion she lived in back in Los Angeles. I can only hope my humble abode doesn't offend her.

She seems happy enough in the small cabin so I think she might like my house. But will she be okay sharing it with Ryder? At least until he marries or finds his mate.

Arriving at the cabin in mere minutes, I'm glad to see both Ginger and Lottie's cars still parked outside. Which means they didn't leave, or they did and came back safely. Either way, my mate is here, safe.

Looking around the clearing, I sniff for signs of elves or any other presence lurking in the shadows. I neither smell nor hear any, which pacifies my protective instinct for the time being.

I don't even knock as I enter through the front door. She better just get used to me being around because I don't plan on leaving—ever.

Both Lottie and my sister are curled up on the couch, talking and laughing. My Nightingale's sweet laughter rings out like the purest joy. It absorbs into my skin and settles itself deep in my heart.

"Hey, Hunter, did everything go okay?" Ginger calls over the back of the couch, causing Lottie to turn her luminous smile in my direction.

The sight of her nearly makes me speechless, but I manage to force out the words. "Yeah. All good."

"And Vincent?" Lottie adds, a small bit of her smile dampening at the mention of the elf.

"Nothing yet. Wherever he's hiding out, he's keeping quiet and letting his henchmen do his dirty work."

Ginger growls, and a matching scowl sours her expression. I feel the same way about the bastard, but I can't do much until he makes a move. Attacking an elf of his stature without "provocation" (at least what they believe to be) would be dangerous and invite even more mayhem upon our town.

It's best to wait him out. Eventually, he'll cross a line, and I'll make sure he feels the full force of my beast when he does.

"All right, love birds. I have some things to take care of. Gossip blogs to suppress and Reddit pages to irradicate."

Ginger stands from the couch, scoops up her purse and travel tumbler from the end table, rounding to meet me. She presses a kiss to my cheek and then winks at me. *What the fuck is she winking for?*

"See y'all later. Remember," she turns to look over her shoulder at Lottie. "Mom's house tomorrow, ten a.m. cooking lesson."

Lottie nods her head adamantly her smile broadening and flashing her white teeth. I want to argue against her going out tomorrow, but she'll be with Ginger and me at my parents' house. Because I'll be going with her. I'll be going with her everywhere for the next week at least. But I plan to keep her here in the cabin, safe and secure, until Vincent gives up and leaves town empty-handed once again. Or until I make him.

Ginger zips out of the cabin like a whirlwind, shutting the door behind her, leaving me and Lottie alone once again. Just the way I like it.

"Hello there, sweet Nightingale. What did you and my exasperating sister do while I was gone?"

My feet move swiftly, carrying me to the couch to sit by Lottie's side. As if I've done it a million times, I place a soft kiss on her temple in greeting. She accepts it, not pulling away or pushing me away. I take it as a win, tilt her chin up with my knuckle, and press another kiss to her lips this time. Infusing it with all the pent-up lust she stirs in me.

When we pull apart, Lottie's lips are swollen pink, her eyes are unfocused, and her breath comes in short pants. The best part is the pink flush spreading across her cheeks and down her neck.

"Um, what was the question," she asks in a daze, her eyes focusing on my lips as if she wants to kiss me again.

Later, sweet Nightingale. I'll kiss you all you want.

"What did you and my sister get up to while I was gone?" I repeat.

"Oh. Not much. Just talking."

"About?"

"You. The mate bond. Fashion shows in Paris."

I chuckle and settle on the couch, pulling her into my side and getting comfortable. I could stay like this forever, especially when she snuggles into my side and makes herself comfortable.

"Fashion shows in Paris, huh? She blackmailing you into taking her? Don't let her push you around and force you to do things you don't want to. She can be a bit demanding at times. Especially when it comes to fashion."

She snickers and rests her head on my chest just under my shoulder. My arm finds its proper place around her, holding her close. I like snuggly, affectionate Lottie.

"She's not blackmailing me. I offered to take her whenever

she wants to go. It doesn't matter to me. The fashion is interesting, but it was never really my scene. I only ever went because it's what my manager and publicity team thought I should do to better my image and popularity. To be seen in the most prestigious fashion shows hob-knobbing with a-list celebrities."

She inhales deeply and her body goes lax on the exhale.

"I hated going to those events and parties and acting like I was so excited to be there. It was exhausting."

I rub my thumb along the soft fabric of her sweater covering her arm in a soothing motion that seems to quell her growing displeasure. She will no longer do things that displease her. Only pleasurable things when I'm around.

"You don't have to take her. She won't be mad if you tell her no."

"I know. But maybe with her at my side, I'd actually enjoy it."

The thought that Lottie is making plans with my sister that far in the future is encouraging. That means she wants to be around that long.

"I will gladly play bodyguard for you if you want to go. Hell, maybe I'll even rope Luna in to do some private work for me this time."

Her giggles cause goosebumps to rise across my flesh, and again, I'm struck with just how much she affects me. It must be the mate pull. It has to be because no one has ever elicited such volatile reactions from me.

We fall into a comfortable silence, neither one of us moving from our position on the couch, and I take the opportunity to relax, to just be and feel what it could be like with her as my mate. My inner peace only broken when Lottie speaks.

"So, what shall we do for the rest of the day? I've been dying to go into the bookstore and pick out a few books. And we could swing by The Sticky Bun for an afternoon snack. Maybe go for a walk after when we get back."

I hate to burst her happy bubble, but we won't be doing any of that today or anytime soon. If she wants something from the restaurants in town, I'll have Ginger or Ryder or one of my assistants drop it off for us.

"We're not going anywhere. We're going to get comfy and stay right here. We can have my assistant Levi bring us something later if there's something specific you're craving."

"If he could rustle up some sushi, I would love him forever. But why can't we just go get it ourselves?" Lottie's tone becomes sharper but confused.

"Because Vincent and his men are still running around town, and I'd like to keep you safe from whatever he may have planned until he leaves. So, until then, you're going to have to stay here under my protection."

Lottie jerks from my arms so abruptly that she practically falls off the couch in her retreat.

"What? Are you trying to tell me I have to stay here and can't go anywhere? At all till you say it's okay?"

From the sharp tone of her voice, I gather she's not happy about my decree, and I tread carefully in my response but maintain my decision.

"Yes. It's dangerous with Vincent trying to make a play for you, and it's easier to keep you safe here, in the cabin."

"No!" Lottie practically yells and stands from the couch, putting distance between us. Distance I don't like.

She was just so open and accepting, and in an instant, I pushed her away. I don't care if she's mad at me as long as she's safe and protected within these four walls.

"Yes. It's the most defensible position."

Sing Sweet Nightingale

"No! I will not have another person making decisions for me, telling me what to do and when. Controlling my every move and life, all under the pretense of protection and what's best for me. No! Not anymore, never again.

"My mother did it for so much of my life, and I will not let anyone take control again. Every minute I lived under her rule, I felt like I was suffocating, dying slowly under the weight of her thumb. You may think you know me and my life, Hunter, but you don't. I'm not some pampered princess on a mountain vacation. I ran away from my life. Left without a word and didn't tell anyone where I was going or for how long, or even if I would ever return. Because that's the only way I could escape her control. To break free from her tyrannical rule.

"I'm finally in control of my life, my body, and my future. And I will not give it up because some prick with a Napoleon complex wants to throw his weight around to try and strong-arm you into giving up your family land."

During her speech Lottie began to grow more and more agitated. Fisting her hands and gesturing wildly to emphasize her point. Now she deflates, expelling all her pent-up frustration and anger, staring down at me with wide hopeful eyes. Eyes I can't look away from, eyes that latch onto my soul and grip tight.

"I will not do that again. I *will* be going to *Sticky Bun* and the bookstore. I'll concede to no forest walk, but I will be going into town, and you can come with me or not. But I will be leaving in ten minutes. So, if you want to keep me safe, you'll be ready to leave when I am, or I'm going alone."

My mate has claws, and she is not afraid to use them. I hate the idea of her being out in the open for Vincent to get to, but her ferocity and defiance turns me on.

Whatever it is that chose Lottie for me chose well. She has

spirit and spine and a determination to be in control of her own life that I admire. An alpha needs a strong mate to put him in his place every once in a while. I suppose that time just came sooner than expected.

A low growl grows in my chest in appreciation for this woman standing firm in front of me. Standing, I encroach on her space, filling it with my body and scent, hoping it does as much to her as hers does to me. When I see her pupils dilate and her throat bob in a swallow, I know it has at least some effect.

"Very well, Nightingale, I will go with you to town. But you must stay in my sight at all times. Am I clear? This, I will not budge on."

Her shoulders drop, and she puckers her lips. I can tell she wants to argue, but she won't. She'll give me this much.

"Very well," she grumbles. "But you can't rush me, and I decide when we leave and where we go."

She points her index finger in my face, and I bend down to nip on the tip, giving her a small growl for good measure.

"Fine."

"Fine."

Lottie steps out of the reach of my pheromones and makes her way to the bedroom to get ready to leave. I watch her ass in those skintight leggings the entire way.

Chapter 25
Lottie

Blowing up at Hunter and unpacking all that baggage onto him at once was not intentional, but it was necessary. If this is going to work out between us in any way, he better learn right now. I will not let him boss me around. Alpha or not. No one will ever control me again.

Hunter begrudgingly drives us into town, parking on the street directly in front of Sticky Buns. He doesn't have to say it, but I know it's to minimize the opportunity for an attack. Keeping the car close and easily accessible for a quick getaway. I've been guarded by professionals enough in my life to spot such things. It doesn't bother me because he's doing as I demanded.

Sticking close to my side, he leads us into the bakery, opening the door for me and washing me in its heavenly, sugary aromas.

We walk up to the counter and get in line behind a few people already waiting. A few other patrons are sitting at the colorful tables, enjoying their pastries and sweets. I mostly ignore them, reading over the menu and today's specials, but I can see Hunter's head swiveling to identify every single person present. His brow furrows when he spots a woman with vibrant red hair sitting alone at a table positioned almost exactly at the center of the shop.

I give her a cursory glance. Curious as to why Hunter would be interested in her. I don't feel jealousy at his perusal because he doesn't look very happy to see her, whoever she is.

She has long red hair tied up in a high ponytail. She's dressed completely in black, wearing a leather jacket that makes her look like a badass. Her dark-lined eyes are sharp and perceptive.

The line in front of us moves, and my attention is drawn away from the mystery woman as I follow the progression.

Should I get another cinnamon roll or an apple fritter? Ooh, maybe a lemon tart. They all sound so good. I wonder if Hunter will think I'm weird if I order all three.

Amidst my internal debate on baked goods, the line has moved up again, and Hunter leans down from behind me to whisper in my ear.

"Order whatever you like and find a table. I need to go talk to my brother outside for a minute."

I look up to spot his brother Ryder pacing outside the bakery, more emotion on his face than I've seen from him. He's irritated and . . . angry? His hands propped on his hips, and his body changes direction in his pacing, but his gaze remains firmly fixed on the bakery interior. Weird man.

"Okay," I agree, not wanting to get in the middle of whatever is going on between them.

Hunter steps away, and the person ahead of me finishes placing their order. I step up to the counter, ready to order an outrageous amount of sweets.

"Hi Lottie, what can I get for you today?" asks Calliope from behind the counter.

She greets me with a genuine smile, and I return the gesture. She was extremely helpful and friendly when I needed directions to Daisy's and recommended the best cinnamon roll I've ever eaten. So, I think I can trust her.

"Hi, Calliope, I would like to get a cinnamon roll, apple fritter, lemon tart, and blueberry muffin, please. Oh, and a large milk."

"Okay, would you like anything else? Or are you two sharing?"

I giggle, not at all ashamed to admit they're all for me. "They're all for me, but if he asks really nice, I might let him have a bite."

Calliope rings me up, and as I'm digging for my wallet, a new voice appears at my side.

"Hi there."

I turn to find the badass redhead standing next to me, one hand leaning on the counter and the other on her hip as if she's been there the whole time. She's shorter than me, but I would bet she could win a fist fight with a bear for how tough she looks.

"Hello," I manage, not quite sure what to make of the woman.

"You're not a local, are you?" she asks. But I have a feeling she already knows the answer. Hopefully, she doesn't know who I really am.

"No. Well, not yet. I'm considering relocating, though," I admit. Something I haven't even told Ginger or Hunter yet. Somehow, telling a stranger seems easier.

She nods and purses her lips, looking me over before eyeing

Calliope behind the counter.

"I'm Tess. Also, not a local. Just visiting. I heard this is a great place to view next week's blood moon."

She extends her hand, and I shake it awkwardly. Her grip is like steel, and I was right; she is tough.

I don't have time to form a response like, *'What the hell is a blood moon?'* before she's speaking again. She's very forward and confident, which is something I admire in a woman.

"So, have either of you seen anything strange around town lately?" Tess asks.

"Um, like what?" asks Calliope, just as lost as I am. Her face scrunching under her thick-rimmed glasses.

"Oh, you know, weird things. People doing weird stuff, acting odd. Maybe people with weird markings or strange creatures in the woods at night?"

What in the actual hell is she talking about? Creatures and weird markings? She couldn't be talking about non-humans, could she?

"I don't think so," I squeak out in response. I don't like the way this conversation is going.

"So, no werewolves then?" she asks blatantly.

"What?" The word comes out shaky and high-pitched.

I did not expect to have to deal with this sort of thing so soon after learning about shifters and non-humans because I'm sure that's what she means. What else could it be? I thought Hunter was a werewolf at first, too.

"You know, hairy beasts that change under the full moon and hunt people for sport."

This is oddly not the weirdest conversation I've had today, but definitely the most awkward.

Calliope and I look at each other. She wears an expression similar to my own. Shock, confusion, and a bit of knowing reluctance as if she and I know the same secret. Perhaps we do. She could be a non-human, and I wouldn't know it since I can't see through their glamour.

We stare at each other for long moments, both with our mouths opening and closing, trying to decide what to say. Thankfully, Calliope speaks first.

"No, no werewolves or anything of the sort. Nothing like that around here," she says with a soft nervous laughter in her voice.

"Nope haven't heard of such a thing since I've been here," I agree, solidifying my tone and shaking my head. Hoping I sound more assured than I think.

"Oh, okay. Well, if you hear anything, let me know. I'll be around for a while."

Tess straightens from her casual leaning position and anxiously taps her fingers on the counter. Looking at us with unmasked suspicion.

Shit, was that not convincing enough? How do I deal with this situation?

Thankfully, I don't have to figure it out because Tess excuses herself with a quiet muttered thanks and briskly walks away.

"What was that all about?"

Calliope shrugs, eyes wide and just as baffled as me.

Not a moment later, Hunter steps up behind me, pressing his body close to mine. His heat pressing into my back, a comforting presence I'm starting to grow used to.

"Did you place your order?" he asks, placing a tender possessive hand on my hip.

"Yeah, but I haven't paid yet."

"Good."

Pulling his wallet out of his back pocket, he starts to count out bills. I start to protest, but his commanding voice cuts me off.

"Add a cinnamon roll and coffee, please."

Calliope taps on her screen, adding the items to the order. When she announces the price, Hunter holds out the cash to pay.

"I have money; I can pay for my own," I protest.

"I know, but I'd like to pay for you if that's alright."

His tone garners no argument, no matter how much I want to point out that I have millions of dollars sitting in my secret bank account doing nothing and serving no purpose. The least I can do is buy my own food. After all, I have been contributing to the local economy nearly every day by eating out and buying coffee from the Ugly Mug. At this rate, I could probably sustain the entire town with my meal purchases alone.

I bite my tongue, not wanting to start an argument over who has more money. It would only be embarrassing and announce to everyone my financial status, which is not necessary. So, I let him pay for my pastries and follow him to sit at a table toward the back of the shop. From here, we can see the entirety of the bakery and everyone in it, including Tess, the rather strange and forward redhead.

Scooting closer to Hunter, I lean into whisper because I don't know who in here knows about non-humans and who doesn't.

"That girl was asking about werewolves."

Hunter grunts and purses his lips as if this isn't news to him.

"You know who she is?" I ask, furrowing my brow up at him.

"Yeah. Ryder's been dealing with her ever since she came into town the day after you did. She's a paranormal blogger on the hunt for werewolves. Which are wolf shifters. He's handling it. That's why he's outside pacing like a caged wolf right now."

I look through the large front window and spot Ryder across the street, frowning towards the bakery as he paces back and forth like a prowling beast. He doesn't look happy. Taking only three large steps before pivoting one hundred and eighty degrees and repeating the movement in rapid succession.

Eyeing Tess, I see her actually sticking her tongue out at Ryder and waving at him with her fingers. Ryder stops still, and I can see his muscles flex and grow from all the way across the street. There is definitely something going on there.

"You sure he can handle her? Kinda looks like she's getting under his skin."

"Yeah, he's fine. Ginger is keeping an eye on her blog and posts to ensure she doesn't mention anything about Snowberry or the blood moon next week."

Again, the mention of the blood moon. What the hell is it? Obviously, I assume it's a moon phase, but why blood?

"What is a blood moon?" I ask, hoping we're not around too many people for him to tell me.

"It's a lunar eclipse that happens twice a year, but every three to four years, there's a special eclipse called a blood moon where the full moon turns blood red. It has something to do with the earth's atmosphere and the sun's rays, but I don't really understand it. You'd have to ask Fynn about all that."

The Blood Moon doesn't have anything to do with being a wolf shifter. But it affects them? Or do they celebrate it? Maybe it's part of their religion? Do wolf shifters have a religion? Do they pray to some moon goddess or something?

"And you celebrate it?" I ask, not voicing the cacophony of additional questions growing in my head.

"In a way, yes."

He gives me a scathing look that suggests their celebration is more than drinking and dancing in the moonlight.

"And who's Fynn?" It seems like a safe question to ask in public.

"He's a good friend of mine. Likes to read and knows things. He's a mere, and I'm sure he would be delighted to meet you. I kind of had to tell him about you when I asked him to do research on the human mate bond subject. So, he knows who you are. But don't worry," he adds quickly before I can berate him for telling others my identity. "He won't tell anyone. He doesn't care about your past career or anything like that. He's more interested in books and how all this is possible."

I'm not happy he told another person who I am, but he says Fynn is reliable, and I believe him. For some strange reason, I trust him.

"Then I would love to meet him."

Calliope appears and places our pastries on the table, set on delicate white plates with tiny cartoon drawings of cupcakes, croissants, and other cute little sweets around the edge of the plate border.

We fall into easy conversation about nothing specific. Hunter devours his cinnamon roll in three large bites and sips on his coffee as he tells me about being mayor and growing up in a small town. How everyone is always in each other's business but also how it's nice to be able to call on your neighbor when you need help removing a dead tree stump from your yard or how everyone shows up with a plate of food when they smell someone cooking bar-b-que.

I tell him how my neighbors filed a lawsuit against me for planting trees that shed leaves in their yard over the fence line. I stay away from topics like my singing career and mother, one because I don't like talking about them and two because I don't want anyone to overhear and connect the dots.

After finishing at the bakery, he takes me next door to *Tall Tail Books*, and I pick out half a dozen books to take home, which Hunter dutifully carries with a smile on his face. While we're there, he introduces me to Fynn. I hadn't imagined meeting him this soon after Hunter telling me about him, but I guess that's how small towns work. He's polite and curious but quiet, getting lost in his search for a book not five minutes after meeting me.

Chapter 26
Lottie

Cooking with Sophie and Ginger is the most fun I've had in years. Even though Hunter insisted on driving me here, he did leave for a good portion of the time I was learning to cook. I'm thankful for this because I made a fool of myself more than once. But now I can successfully cook scrambles eggs without turning them to rubber, make toast and coffee without burning it, and even a chicken casserole. It's a lot easier than I thought it would be, but it still took me two tries to get it right.

Sophie also made chocolate chip cookies that smell heavenly. She promises to teach me to bake on another day. Apparently, that deserves its own lesson.

Hunter strolls into the kitchen just as we're cleaning up. I slide my near-perfect chicken casserole in front of him on the kitchen island and smile proudly.

"Look what I made."

He sniffs it and hums appreciatively.

"Go ahead, take a taste."

Handing him a fork, he doesn't hesitate to plunge it into the creamy cheesy noodles and chicken. The bite is more like an entire serving size on his fork, but he fits it into his mouth easily, his eyes widening in surprise at the taste.

"Tastes just like Moms."

Which is the biggest compliment he could give me. Last night, when he stayed at the cabin with me, he made dinner for us again since I'm apparently useless in the kitchen. *Well, maybe not anymore.* His cooking skills still far succeed my own, though, and probably always will.

Spending another night under the same roof as Hunter and him still not doing more than being thoughtful and sweet and giving me nothing more than toe-curling kisses was infuriating. How dare he get a girl all excited and leave her hanging.

I know he wants more with me and I him. Every moment I spend with him increases it threefold. His scent, the deep timber of his voice, the feel on his body so close to mine but not touching skin to skin. He's fast becoming a drug, even more addicting than the cinnamon rolls at *Sticky Bun's*.

Hunter chews and swallows and immediately takes another mouthful.

"That good, huh?"

"Mmhmm," he mumbles through a mouthful of food.

Watching him eat something I made, and it being good, makes my heart all fuzzy inside. Before he can protest, I snap a Polaroid for my growing collection of memories. All I've ever known is music; it's all I've ever been good at, and it's all I was allowed to do. Being able to make something else with just as much of myself in it as my music is a new sensation. One that I'd like to repeat.

Sophie pulls the cookies out of the oven and barely sets them on the cooling rack before all three of us reach to grab one. Hunter shoves the entire thing in his mouth in one go while Ginger and I take more reasonable bites of ours. They're warm and gooey and fill my stomach with warmth beyond just their temperature.

I feel a wholeness growing inside when we leave Hunter's parent's house. One that makes me smile for no reason and sticks with me the entire way back to the cabin, containers full of leftover casserole and cookies at my feat.

"I have a surprise for you," Hunter says as he helps me out of his truck when we arrive home.

"Really? What is it?"

I love surprises. He could say it's something as simple as a walk in the woods and I'd be excited for it. I wouldn't mind if he shifted back into wolf form and we went for a walk.

"The library puts on a movie under the stars night in the old abandoned drive-in theater. The screen is on the ground, and no cars can drive in there anymore. It's become overgrown with grass that is decently comfortable on a blanket or in a folding lounge chair. They're having it tonight, and I thought we could go."

My heart races with excitement, but I don't want to be too obvious that I'm excited to go out to see a movie. He may not know it, but the only movies I've seen in a theater were movie premiers I was forced to go to, and most of them sucked. Going to a drive-in wasn't even on my list of things to do while living incognito, and now I'm wondering why it wasn't.

I try to mask my elation with calm interest.

"And that's not too exposed for you?" I tease. He chortles.

"No, I think I can handle one night at the movies. Besides, we'll be surrounded by lots of other non-humans and humans. We'll be completely safe. Vincent won't start anything in a group like that. He may be an asshole, but he doesn't like to deal with so much collateral."

The thought has me cringing. Just thinking about Vincent hurting all those innocent people has me hating him even more. Shaking the horrible mental image of screaming townspeople from my brain, I focus on the fun movie-under-the-stars aspect of my evening.

"What movie are they showing? Please tell me it's something good and not something lame like *Mission Impossible*."

"*Mission Impossible* is not lame. But no, they aren't playing any Tom Cruise movies. They like to play old classics that are appropriate for all ages. This week is *The Wizard of Oz*."

"That sounds great, I love that movie. I don't think I've watched it since I was a kid."

Hunter grins as we enter the cabin, casserole dish in hand.

"Good. Cause that's not the only surprise I have for you."

"There's more?" I squeal in uncontrolled delight.

"Yes, but you have to wait till later to get the rest."

Pouting out my bottom lip, I give him my best puppy dog eyes. I love surprises, but I hate waiting to get them. He just shakes his head at me as he puts the casserole in the fridge.

"That's not going to work, Nightingale. You're just going to have to wait. But I promise you'll love it."

"I better."

Hunter's expression turns playful as he stalks over to me, trapping me against the back of the couch with an arm on either side.

His nose skims down my neck, and tingles prickle across my skin. Pressing a soft, lingering kiss against the crook of my neck, I shiver.

"Promise," he whispers against my skin, his lips never breaking contact as he lingers there, practically absorbing into me.

Sing Sweet Nightingale

How I could so easily fall for this man. With his sultry words and easy affection. Not to mention the body on him that radiates heat against mine and is corded with muscles that flex and shift and taunt me to touch them.

Maybe soon I will.

~Hunter~

Lottie is the most impatient surprisee ever. For the whole afternoon she tries to get me to tell her the other surprise, which I don't. What good is a surprise if you know what it is? Plus, I enlisted my sister to help organize the surprise, and I don't want to get Lottie's hopes up if Ginger isn't able to deliver my request.

For a movie in the woods, Lottie sure did dress up for the event. I told her she didn't have to, but she insisted she was comfortable, and that's all that matters. The plunging neckline of her jumpsuit far too low to be worn without a shirt underneath, but she does it anyway. The black lace of her bra that thankfully covers enough to not flash anyone, beckons me to tear through it with my teeth and release her perfect breasts hidden beneath. The practically sheer white sweater she wears over the ensemble isn't nearly enough to quash my growing desire or divert my gaze from her.

We couldn't arrive at the drive-ins soon enough. I need something to distract me from staring at Lottie.

The makeshift movie theater doesn't have any parking, and you can't drive up to it like you used to be able to when it was a functioning drive-in theater. Meaning we have to park in the lot across the street from the firehouse and high school on the corner. The old road leading to the theater is no more than a narrow dirt path that curves behind the high school sports field to the repurposed space.

I help Lottie out of my truck as she loops her Polaroid camera over her shoulder. She's almost as bad as my dad, carrying her camera with her everywhere. I appreciate that it's instant and not digital. I don't have to worry that any of these photos will appear on Instagram, the bane of my existence.

She looks me up and down with a quizzical expression on her beautiful face, the ends of her short blonde hair brushing her jaw.

"You said this is like a blanket on the ground situation, right?"

"Yup."

"So, where's your blanket?"

One corner of my mouth quirks up, and her expression shifts from questioning to amused.

"I've got it covered. Don't worry."

Her lips purse in a stifled smile, but she doesn't press me to tell her. Perhaps since we're here now she has enough patience to wait until we walk down the path.

Placing her hand on my bicep, I pull her close to me and guide us down the path. Thankfully, Lottie has more sensible taste in shoes than my sister, and we make it to the grassy field relatively easily.

There are already a few dozen people here, their blankets spread across the ground and couples paired up close together while they wait for the movie to start. As usual, Dottie has set up a snack table offering free popcorn, water, and an array of toppings to make "gourmet" popcorn.

Lottie gasps at my side, and I turn to find her wide-eyed and smiling so big I'm sure I can see every one of her teeth.

"Wow, this looks amazing. Can we get some popcorn? I love dipping mine in nacho cheese."

"Of course, but first, let's find our spot."

She nods and lets me lead her to the far back corner, slightly separated from the majority of the people clumping closer to the screen. I like having a little space from everyone, and being out of direct ear shot of others will benefit us both. I don't plan on sitting silently watching the movie. I'm going to use every opportunity I have to get to know Lottie better.

Nestled against a fallen tree trunk, I find the next surprise I have planned for Lottie. A large thick blanket is spread across the ground a few pillows propped against the trunk with a small cooler sitting nearby. Which hopefully holds surprise number three.

"Here we are," I announce when we approach the impeccably set up picnic. Ginger did good, I'll have to thank her. She's never going to let me forget it.

"Is this for us?" She kneels and scoots onto the blanket, making herself comfortable and setting her Polaroid camera to the side, not even waiting for me to confirm it's ours.

"Yup. All ours. I like to have my space. Plus, I like having a backrest, but I also want to cuddle with you and keep you warm. Because once the sun goes down, that thin thing you call a top isn't going to keep you warm."

Her laughter is bright and warm, and I bask in its ease. Sitting down next to her, I lean against the plethora of pillows, making sure to press myself up close to her side. She doesn't protest and reciprocates the gesture, settling in and getting comfortable. The act has my inner beast growling in pleasure. Lottie may be coming around to the idea of us—the idea of being my mate.

"How did you do all this?" she asks.

"Ginger helped."

"Well, remind me to thank her because this is great." She

takes in the nest of blankets and pillows my sister assembled. I'll admit it is very comfortable.

"So, what's in the cooler? Is it another surprise?" she asks eagerly.

"As long as my sister was able to acquire what I asked, then yes. Go on, open it up."

Sliding the cooler in front of her, she sits up and lifts the lid, her eyes going wide at its contents. The special meal I asked Ginger to pick up from Jared for tonight.

"I know our little town isn't anything close to Los Angeles, but you mentioned wanting sushi the other day, and I thought maybe I could give you something you're missing."

She reaches in and pulls out a clear container filled with rice-wrapped sushi rolls. I'm not a sushi expert by any means, but they look good to me. I had no doubt Jared would be able to make them even though they don't offer them on the menu at Dottie's. He is an extremely talented chef, and I had full trust he could if he had the ingredients. I'm just happy he was able to on such short notice.

"Oh my goodness, Hunter. This is the best surprise ever. I love it. Thank you. Sushi is my favorite, and I have been craving it. Where did you get it? I haven't found it anywhere in town."

My chest swells, and my spine straightens ever so slightly under her praise. I was able to give her something no other could.

"I have my connections. I am the mayor, after all."

"Well, you may have to introduce me to your connection because if this tastes as good as it looks, I'm going to need more."

"I'll give you anything you ask of me, Nightingale."

A blush pinkens her cheeks, and she ducks her head self-consciously. So, unlike her outgoing personality. For someone who's been in the spotlight a good portion of her life, it's interesting to see her shying away when it's just the two of us.

"Well, are you going to eat it and tell me how it tastes?" I ask when she sits staring at the container of food without opening it. "How will I know it's any good if you don't tell me?"

Her posture eases, and she opens the lid, picking out a roll and popping the entire thing in her mouth. Her eyes close, and she moans around the food in satisfaction.

"Good?"

With her mouthful, she can only nod vigorously and doesn't pause to speak once she finishes chewing before shoving another roll in her mouth.

Note to self; buy Lottie as much sushi as she wants.

Chapter 27

Hunter

When Lottie finished most of her sushi, sharing some with me because she's that thoughtful, we went over to pick out our popcorn before the movie started. She couldn't just decide on one, so we have three bowls laid out on the blanket at our side: one with M&M's, marshmallows, and chocolate syrup, one with nacho cheese, and another just plain buttered popcorn.

Right now, on the screen, which sits slightly askew on the ground, Dorothy has just found Munchkin Land, and Lottie sings along under her breath with the songs. Even muffled her singing draws me in, and I find myself watching her more than the screen.

She's tucked under my arm, and I was right about her getting cold when the sun fully set and had to pull the extra blanket my sister was smart enough to leave for us over our laps. The position is the most comfortable I've ever been in. I rarely attend the movie under the stars night, but with Lottie at my side, I'll attend every single one.

Becca walks by and waves but doesn't stop until Lottie calls out to her.

"Hey Becca, could you take a picture of us please?"

Becca, ever willing to help, especially when it comes to anyone's dating life, eagerly agrees.

"Of course." She skips over and takes the camera from Lottie's outstretched hand.

Scooting back against my side and pressing close, Lottie positions herself just right for her photo. I watch her until Becca draws my attention, counting to three before taking the photo. I manage to look at the camera and smile when she clicks the button and the light flashes.

"That is going to be such a cute photo. You two look so good together." Turning her attention towards me, Becca eyes me warmly. "It's nice to see you out and about more Hunter, outside of your mayorly duties. You should do it more often."

Her eyes shift briefly to Lottie, who is too busy watching the photo develop to notice.

"I think I will," I agree.

Silently adding a promise to myself that'll only happen as long as Lottie is around.

"Have a good night. I'll see y'all at Dottie's."

"Night, Becca. Thank you."

Lottie waves to Becca as she returns to her blanket with her mate, a male nymph she's been mated to for at least a century but still acts like newly mated young. Making out in public and being all gushy. It's cute, envious even. That envy slowly evaporates when Lottie melts into my side. *That could be mine, too.*

I look down at the Polaroid in Lottie's hand, which is still developing, but I can see the image slowly appearing. The clearest part is our smiling faces, with the dark background keeping all the focus on us. Becca is right; we do look good together.

The last thing I want to do is ruin a good mood, but there are a few things I want to know about Lottie and why she's here. She mentioned rather animatedly that her mother was extremely controlling of her life, but why abscond to a hidden town in the woods and evade all contact with anyone?

"Lottie, can I ask you a question?"

Her dark blue eyes turn upward to catch mine, and she remains relaxed and at ease.

"Sure."

"Why did you leave LA? I know you said your mom controlled a lot of your life, and you wanted to get away from her, but why leave completely? Why hide out here and cut all communication with anyone? Don't you miss singing and your life there?"

Her gaze slides away from mine, focusing on the almost fully developed photo in her hands. She seems to draw strength from it somehow. On a deep exhale, she begins her story.

"It's not just her control over my schedule and wardrobe. She's highjacked my life, made it something I didn't want. Doing everything that she decides would make the most money and create the most fame.

"When I was fifteen, and she told me she got me a record deal, I was ecstatic. I wanted to sing and play and spread my music. Like most singers and musicians, I thought that was what I wanted. To land a record deal and hear my music on the radio. And for the first few years, it was. It was great. I wrote my music and sang what I wanted. Mom helped with wardrobe choices and handling all my bookings.

"It started so subtly that it took me five years to realize I had completely handed over all the control to her. When I was twenty, I wanted to create a new album with a new look, something I was very excited about. I took it to my mom and team, and they immediately shut me down and told me what I was to create. What would sell the best, and what the fans would expect. They convinced me I was wrong, and they were right, and I should trust them.

"Trusting them was my first mistake. But at that point, I was so far under their thumb if I tried to do anything, they would easily negate it before anything could come of it. That's when I began to pay closer attention to everything. To watch and listen. Realizing I was just a tool and puppet for her to get what she wanted. My wants and desires had nothing to do with my own career."

Lottie sighs and brushes her thumb over the polaroid she continues to stare at while she speaks.

"After that, everything became a task. I wrote and sang the songs they wanted, wore the clothing they chose, went to the events they rsvp'd to, and even dated men *they chose*. My life was no longer my own.

"I still love to sing, but my desire to do so dwindled. I could never lose my love of music. It's too deeply rooted in my soul, but performing was no longer what I want to do. A famous pop star is not what I want to be. It's not what everyone thinks it is. At least not for me. It was lonely and depressing, with no possibility for a future of any kind other than the one she designed for me. No husband, no children, no happy home or family holidays. She wants me to work nonstop forever. Her perfect little workhorse.

"When I discovered my contract would be ending, I knew that would be my only opportunity. And talking with her wouldn't work. It never has. I needed to escape, to be completely free from her and all the people she surrounded me with who did her bidding and didn't care about my wellbeing, only their paycheck and compliance with her demands.

"Well, all except Luna, that is. She's the only one who ever listened to me and spoke to me as a person instead of a machine made for performing like a wind-up doll."

Finally, Lottie looks up to meet my eyes, and I remain quiet, waiting for her to finish. Somehow knowing she needs to get this off her chest.

Her expression is so raw and exposed, and I want to tell her she's worthy of the life she always wanted, whatever that may be. Singing, performing, hiding out in my cabin, being my mate, having a family, or returning to Los Angeles. It's her choice, her right to decide.

"I know it sounds so stupid complaining about being rich and famous, but that doesn't matter when I'm not living my own life. I'm just a robot they programmed, and I just got sick of it."

"Everyone's life is different, Lottie. Yours shouldn't be considered any less than another's because your circumstances differ. Everyone deserves to be in charge of their own life choices, no matter who they are."

Tucking Lottie even tighter under my arm, she lets her head fall to my shoulder. Her body fits perfectly against mine. The characters on the screen continue their journey down the yellow brick road, and we're both silent for a brief moment.

"Thank you, Hunter," Lottie whispers.

"For what?"

"For not calling me a whiny, entitled diva."

"Why the hell would I call you that?" I blurt out a little louder than I intended. The fact that she thinks I would ever call her that is offensive.

"Because that's what my mother called me when I complained about it to her."

A growl of annoyance rumbles in my chest, and my jaw ticks. "Well, your mother isn't worthy of being related to you."

She giggles softly, and the sound subsides my growing anger. Her mother sounds like a total waste of space, and I'm glad she was able to get away from her. No one should be made to feel worthless in their own life.

~Lottie~

Even with my long-winded confession, it can't ruin my night with Hunter. The movie, the stars, the popcorn, and sushi! I can't believe he got me sushi. It could very well have been the best sushi I've ever had. But I think the best part is cuddling under the blanket with Hunter. His body radiates warmth, staving off the chill of the cooling evening temperatures. They won't be able to do this much longer with the cold weather continuing like this.

After our little chat, we settled in to watch the movie. We're about three-quarters through it now when Hunter breaks the silence.

"Would you be up for another surprise?"

I pop up like a jack in the box and stare at him like he couldn't have asked a more redundant question.

"Of course, I would love another surprise. Surprises are my favorite."

He chuckles. "Good. Um, this one is a little different from the others. But how would you like to be able to see all the non-humans in their true forms? Beyond their glamours?"

My jaw drops and just about unhinges.

"Is that possible?"

"Yes. The fairies have dust that their wings produce that can be used to do many things. Giving people the sight is one of them."

"Oh my god," I said, turning to face him. I can't believe what he just said to me. "You have fairy dust? Like Tinker Bell?"

He chuckles again. I know I probably sound like a child, but how could I not? He just told me he's going to use dust from a fairy's wing to magically give me the ability to see non-humans as they truly are. Of course, I'm going to think of Tinker Bell. The dust might not make me fly by thinking happy thoughts, but that's okay. I'm still living out every little girl's fantasy right now.

"Yeah, a little like Tinker Bell. I think the author of *Peter Pan* knew about non-humans and incorporated a few details into his story. I'm sure if you asked Fynn, he could confirm it."

"Yes, absolutely, yes. Please fairy dust me."

I'm eager and know it, but it only seems to widen Hunter's smile.

"Okay, okay, hold your horses."

He shifts, sitting up, and digs below the blanket into his pocket, producing a small drawstring pouch. I spin in place to kneel, facing him.

"Eager little bird, aren't you?"

"Yes. Yes, I am, and I'm not ashamed to admit it. Fairy dust me." I try to speak as quietly as possible, but my enthusiasm may have gotten the better of me.

Shifting to put his back towards the majority of the people around us, Hunter pours a small amount of fairy dust into this open palm. It shimmers like the finest glitter in the moonlight with a slight blue tint to it.

"Don't worry, it won't stick to you like real glitter. It absorbs into your skin, completely invisible. Are you ready?"

"How does it work? Is it a specific type of dust? Does it only give people the sight? What else can it do?"

I have so many questions, but Hunter just shakes his head, trying to hide his grin.

"In time, you'll learn everything you want to know. For now, just know that the dust doesn't do anything until I infuse it with intention. I want to give you the sight, so when I use the dust on you, that's what will happen."

Nodding, I hold my tongue to ask all my questions later. Hunter holds his hand and the dust up to his face and gently blows the shimmering powder in my face. I don't feel a physical sensation of it coating my skin, but a cold tickling sensation like snowflakes settling against my cheeks and melting into my pores.

Nothing seems to happen at first. Everything looks the same until an iridescent film coats my vision. The world wavers and when it resettles, there aren't just people sitting in the field watching the movie anymore.

Gossamer wings of various colors protrude from backs, antlers and horns curl from heads, and tails twitch under skirts and blankets. There are skin tones in every shade, not just the ones I'm used to but purple, blue, green, and . . . pink.

"Becca is completely pink!" I quietly exclaim.

The woman I know as a spunky redhead with glittering green eyes is pink from head to toe—not just hair but skin and wings, all in varying shades of bubble gum and cotton candy pink. The male sitting next to her doesn't have wings, but he does have pointed ears, blue markings on his skin, and dark hair that shimmers blue under the moonlight.

I was just expecting the fairies to look like themselves but with wings, and they most certainly do not. I have no idea what the people with tails and horns are, but some have stripes and interesting markings all different from the next. Of course, I can't tell who else is a shifter since they have a human form, not just a glamour to conceal themselves. So, of the people who still look like people, I don't know who is human or not.

"Yeah, she likes to call herself the love fairy. She's tried to set me up on dozens of blind dates, all of which I declined after the first." Hunter repositions himself back at my side, leaning against the tree trunk, looking around the field, and then back at me, watching for more reactions.

"What was wrong with the first?" I ask.

There are so many beautiful creatures to look at now in the field that I can't pull my rapidly shifting eyes away from them, but I try to hold as normal a conversation with Hunter as I can.

"She was my cousin."

"What?" Laughing, I turn to face him, wondering how she couldn't have known they were cousins. "I mean, I guess some people are fine with that, but how did she not know?"

"Becca doesn't make matches so much as she thrusts two single people together and hope it sticks. Her intentions are good, but none of her mismatched pairings have stuck yet. Though that doesn't stop her from trying."

Turning to look at the fairy, I find her with her mouth glued to the male's she's with. Apparently, they've seen the movie before and don't mind missing it.

"Apparently, whoever made her match was much better at it," I comment off-handedly.

Hunter's answer comes at the end of a muffled chuckle. "He's her mate. No person matched them; I guess you can say they matched themselves."

Mates are a strange concept I'm still wrapping my head around. Me supposedly being Hunter's mate is an even stranger concept, but one that is growing on me every day.

A partner who gives without taking, a man who loves me unconditionally. A bond that will allow me to live for hundreds of years. Who wouldn't want that?

I catch sight of Hunter from the corner of my eye, watching me with an expression none have ever given me. It makes my heart race and my skin heat.

Quickly, I divert my attention away from him and back to the others before his heated stare can cause more than a fluttering in my chest.

I feel more than see Hunter lean closer to me as the soft touch of his finger runs up my arm and shoulder, tracing an unknown pattern on my collarbone. That thing I was trying to avoid by looking away now stirs deep in my gut. Causing a yearning to grow between my legs.

Hunter inhales deeply, pressing his nose close to my throat, before letting out a guttural groan.

"You smell . . . torturous."

"Not exactly the word I thought you were going to use," I mutter, a little distracted by his lips on my neck.

"There are many words I could use to describe your scent, delicious, arousing, wonderful, alluring, distracting. But at the moment, it's torturous."

His breath is hot against my skin, and a shiver runs down my spine. I'm staring at the movie screen but can't see it. I can't see anything; only feel it. Feel the desire stream through my body, the lips pressing against my throat, my fingers digging into my thighs, and the wetness beginning to pool there.

With another deep breath, his arm reaches behind me and grips my hip, pulling me closer. His words are a growl in my ear.

"Like I said, torturous."

Nothing comes out of me except a pitiful whimper that does

something to Hunter. He stands abruptly and lifts me up with him. His arm remains tight around me, holding me upright.

"Come, Nightingale. I think it's time we left."

"But the movie isn't over," I protest weakly.

"It is for us."

Leaving behind the comfortable blankets and treats, I nearly forget my camera, but grab it before Hunter guides me back through the field and down the narrow dirt path back to his truck, holding me tightly the entire time.

Chapter 28
Lottie

I squirm in my seat the entire ride home, the need and desire building the closer we get to the cabin. The short drive feeling like an eternity.

It's easy to discern what Hunter craves because it is the same thing I crave. And if the brief glimpse of him rearranging himself in his pants is any indication of what's to come, I greatly look forward to arriving.

My leg bounces with anticipation the closer we get, but the moment the truck is shifted into park, the anticipation which hummed in my veins now causes me to freeze—a reaction I'm becoming accustomed to. *I should really work on that; it won't always work out in my favor.*

Thankfully, Hunter doesn't seem to care I haven't moved because he rounds the hood of the truck and opens my door, reaching in a hand to grip mine and help me out.

Once in motion my body no longer resists me or Hunter. I latch onto his shoulders, and without hesitation, he leans down to press a possessive and needy kiss to my lips. Searching and seeking that friction we both crave. Our bodies pressed flush against each other. His hard cock sandwiched between us only making me wetter.

His touch is intoxicating; the more I have of it, the more I want. The pull, that string tied from him to me, is growing shorter and tighter, causing the tension to grow and multiply. My body is pulsing and throbbing with need.

His lips are relentless as he commands my body. His tongue slips between my lips, demanding entrance, and I allow it. Opening to accept him. The sensations throughout my body intensify with each artful stroke of his tongue against mine. My pussy clenches, and I shamelessly grind against his erection, hoping if I stand on my toes it'll press against my clit.

He holds my waist tight, not allowing me to dry hump him like I want.

"Soon, Nightingale, I'll give you everything you want," he whispers against my lips.

In a haze of kissing and groping, we somehow end up inside the cabin. I don't recall unlocking the door or walking in, but we end up inside all the same.

I pull at Hunter's shirt, trying to pry it off over his head. He chuckles at my attempt as it gets stuck on his shoulders. He removes it completely and reaches for my thin sweater, which I slipped on over my jumpsuit. Once removed, it reveals my lace bralette underneath.

Hunter growls at the sight as I greedily run my hands over his exposed torso. The hard line of his abs creates a pattern I trace running up to his pec and around his nipple. A stuttered sound rumbles in the back of his throat at the touch. That sound goes straight to my pussy, making it throb eagerly.

I fumble with the button on Hunter's jeans, but before

I can undo them completely, he stills my hands, his fingers wrapping gently around my wrists. I look up at him, pouting with the need to get him naked. I thought we were both on the same page. We both want this, crave it. He said so himself. So why is he stopping me now?

He must read all of this in my expression because he lifts my hands and presses them flat on his chest, pressing a kiss to my cheek.

"Don't worry, Lottie, I very much want to strip you bare and have you in every position. But there's something you should know first that I don't think my sister told you about."

Waiting patiently, I look up at him. I know we can't solidify the mate bond this way, I made sure to confirm that with Ginger. We have to be under a full moon, and he has to bite me. Just having sex won't do anything other than give us both great pleasure.

"Male shifters have a slight deviation in our anatomy from humans, even in our human form."

I frown, my gaze wandering over his body, trying to figure out what could possibly be different. I saw him completely naked in the forest when I first shifted in front of me, and I don't recall seeing anything different. Everything was where it was supposed to be. Albeit, he was larger than any man I've ever been with.

The thought has my mouth watering wanting to see it again, feel it. In my hands, in my pussy.

"Stop looking at me like you want to eat me, little bird, or I won't be able to explain properly."

Dutifully, I focus my eyes back on his and roll my lips between my teeth to try and still my movements. Once he repositions his hands on my backside, locking me in the embrace of his arms, he continues.

"Male shifters, on our cock, we have what's called a knot. It's a thickening swell at the base that locks inside our partner during sex. Helps to . . . keep everything inside, to promote fertilization and pregnancy. Not to mention it feels fucking fantastic. We think it stems from our beastly wolf nature since we're the only non-humans to possess it."

My mind is whirling with this new information. I've heard of such things from books, mainly fictional. Perhaps those books aren't so fictional after all. The image of him pressing inside me and filling me so fully, locking us together, has me rubbing my thighs together.

He may think these things will scare me off or make me second guess being with him. They won't. If anything, he's bolstering his chances.

I bite my lip, letting my hands roam back down toward his pants.

"I'm okay with that. Sounds fun."

Hunter's growling groan echoes through the dark cabin, his eyes never straying from mine. His chest rises and falls with heavy breaths, and I swear I can see his canines elongate under his parted lips.

"It will be, but not tonight."

"What?" I stop my southward venturing, again confused by his words.

"Are we or are we not having sex tonight?" I ask, completely surprising myself with the stubborn pout in my tone.

Hunter only laughs and grips my ass tighter, pressing me harder against his still impressive erection.

"Oh, we're having sex, little bird. I'm just not going to knot you tonight."

My brow furrows, pulling severely between my eyes.

"But you just said—"

"I know what I said," he interrupts. "But it's not going to happen tonight. I just wanted to warn you before you saw it."

Leaning down, he brings his lips close to my ear and slips his fingers down my backside and between my thighs, rubbing at my pussy through my jumpsuit.

"When I knot you, it will be when we solidify our mate bond. After I chase you naked through the forest and pin you to the ground, bent over under a full moon. Your perfect ass on display, and your pussy dripping with need for me. Then and only then will I give you my knot and my teeth, sinking both inside you. Because if I were to knot you now, I would never let you go. Until then, having the rest of me will have to suffice."

A shiver rushes through my body at his words. Being a musician, I greatly appreciate words. Thoughts and feelings being made vocal for a partner to hear, to understand, and to feel. Spoken in his deep, gravely timber only makes them that much more effective. The visual of his description plays out in my mind like a flip book.

I know that if he were to chase me and catch me, I would let him do anything to me because I know I would like it. I would want it. I already want it.

"From the feel of it, you are more than sufficient."

I emphasize my point by gripping him hard through his jeans. He straightens and glares down at me with hungry eyes, a blue so piercing I can almost feel them penetrate my chest, straight into my heart.

Without words, he says everything he needs to. Pulling down the straps of my jumpsuit and I slide it off till it sits in a pile on the floor at my feet. Leaving me in nothing but my underwear. I do the same, finally able to unzip his pants and let them fall down his hips to join my clothes on the floor.

Hunter lifts me by the backs of my thighs, and I wrap them

around his waist as he carries me to the bedroom. Our lips locking in our need for each other.

He falls onto the bed, me beneath him, his hands bracing him over me. Not waiting for him, I pull my bralette off over my head and throw it to the floor. His head immediately drops, and the tip of his tongue runs over the peak of one nipple. I groan at the sensation. My nipple hardens further when he sucks it into his mouth and nips at it with his teeth. The pain and pleasure of it shoots straight to my clit, and I tighten my legs around his waist, rubbing my pussy against his cock.

The hard length pulses, held back only by the thin cotton of his boxer briefs. Reaching down, I grip him between us, feeling far more of him now that his pants aren't in the way.

His shaft is thick and hot, and it twitches in my hand when I give him a tight squeeze. Hunter groans and releases my nipple, moving to the other, repeating his torturous process.

My hand wanders farther down, feeling for this knot of his; it's hard to miss when the base of his cock thickens to the point I can't touch my fingers together when I grip it. His mouth pops from my breast, and he growls, pressing his forehead in between my breasts, and his hips rock against my hand.

"Fuck Nightingale. I'm not even inside you yet, and I already want to go back on my word. If your hand feels that good around my knot, your pussy will feel even better."

Again, his hips rock, thrusting his cock in my hand. The shaft sliding up and down, each time I make sure to cup and grip his knot. He seems to like that.

With a growl, Hunter leans back, removing his cock from my hand, and stands practically ripping his underwear off, revealing himself fully to me. This time, I take my fill looking at him. There are no lights on in the bedroom, but moonlight streams through the window, illuminating him enough for me to see clearly.

He looks like any other man, well, not just any other. His wide chest leads to a tapered waist, and that desirable Adonis v. His cock stands proud at attention, hard, thick, and long. At its base is the knot I felt. A bulge thicker than the rest of him that only makes me want to sit on it more.

A needy whimper escapes my throat, the wetness in my panties embarrassingly growing. Hunter's nostrils flare, and I swear his eyes glow in the moonlight.

In one swift motion, he removes my damp underwear and relishes in my nudity, admiring every bare inch of me. I don't flinch or cover myself. I want him to see me. As he's appreciating me, I appreciate him.

"You're beautiful, Lottie. My perfect Nightingale. I want to stand here and look at you for hours, but I fear I don't have the willpower to resist you for that long." Hunter's voice strains at his admission.

His hands slide up my inner thigh, and he brushes a finger over my wet center. I moan at the startlingly sharp shock wave it sends through my body. He does it again and circles my clit, making me shake. My fingers dig into the quilt under me, and my back arches.

"So responsive. How about if I do this?"

I'm staring at the ceiling and can't see what he's referring to, but I feel it a moment later when his tongue licks up my pussy from bottom to top and when he suckles on my clit. I scream a surprised moan as I writhe under him.

"You smell the sweetest when you're aroused for me. I wonder how sweet you'll smell when you come for me."

Hunter returns to licking my pussy, and my mind blanks under the ecstasy.

Chapter 29

Hunter

Lottie's smell and taste are driving me insane. I know I said I wouldn't knot her, but that's all I can think about doing at this moment. Once I get inside her, it'll be damn near impossible not to, but I want the first time to be for our mate bond. It may sound ridiculous to some, but I've never knotted a female. Fucked, yes, but I never felt the overwhelming desire to thrust my knot inside her and lock us together.

It's not something reserved specifically for mate bonds; plenty of shifters knot when having sex. It's pleasurable, so why wouldn't they? I just never wanted to until now, until Lottie.

I take my time feasting on her, enjoying her squirms of pleasure and moans of ecstasy. When I sense her growing close to her peak, I slip a finger inside her and tease her clit with my tongue. Her breathing intensifies, and her thighs tighten around my ears.

"Oh, fuck Hunter. Yes, don't stop. Oh my god, more," she demands, and I give my Nightingale what she wants.

Curling my fingers inside her, I suck on her clit, and she comes apart around my tongue. Screaming out her orgasm as she convulses and quivers. I don't stop my thrusting fingers until the last tiny shockwaves of her orgasm subside to quit mews of bliss.

Her taste is heavenly, and the smell of her heady release has my knot thickening and aching for release inside her. My body senses my mate and wants to release my cum inside her. The feeling is so overwhelming and strong that there's no room for anything else in my mind and heart at the moment. I'm completely consumed with Lottie.

"Fuck. I was not expecting that," she mutters breathlessly.

Crawling up her body, I wedge my hips between her thighs and rub the length of my cock through her wetness.

"I'm not done with you yet."

Kissing her, I slip my tongue into her mouth, and she moans against me. Her talented hands sliding around my shoulders, her nails digging into my back. My hips thrust of their own accord. I growl at the feel of her heat against me. It's so fucking good it almost has me coming right then and there.

Lottie cants her hips matching my movement, shifting to line up her entrance with the head of my cock. She groans when it slips inside her. Her slick desire easing my entrance.

"More," she whispers in a needy but demanding tone.

"Fuck. Lottie, easy baby. Slow down. You're too tempting. All I want to do is rut into you, but I don't want to hurt you."

"You won't hurt me. I want it all, Hunter. I don't want slow."

Pushing infinitesimally more inside, I don't allow myself to thrust fully inside her yet.

Sing Sweet Nightingale

"Are you sure? Once I get a full feel of you, I won't be able to hold back."

"Yes. I want you, Hunter. Do it, fuck me."

I don't hesitate; my battle with my desire to be gentle losing to my need to have her. Giving her what she wants, I thrust deeper. Impaling myself inside her tight pussy. Her back arches, and her walls tighten around my cock, squeezing me, pulling me deeper. Wanting more. With each fluid thrust, she takes more of my control with it.

Our breaths mingle as I hover over her, trying to retain my control and not thrust fully, seeding my knot inside her. I said I wouldn't, not yet. And at this moment, that's all I want to do. The beast inside me demanding it. It wouldn't solidify our bond, not without my bite and the full moon, but I want the first time she takes me, the first time I feel a female around my knot, to be our bonding.

She wriggles and rocks her hips, wanting more. Leaning back on my heels, I lift her hips to meet mine, watching where her body takes my cock. The sight is erotic and ignites the primal part of me that knows she's my mate.

Mine.

My thrusts become harder, faster, and erratic, pumping my cock into her until I reach my knot. Bumping it against her clit with every thrust in a way that makes her squirm and scream.

"That's it, little bird, scream for me. You like it when my knot rubs against your pretty pink clit don't you?"

"Uh huh," She nods and groans again when I press deep, stopping when all but my knot is inside her.

I press down and swivel my hips. The movement causes us both to moan in pleasure. My balls tighten at the sensations. The smells and sounds fill every one of my senses until all I know is her and us. The feel of her soft skin against mine, the smell of her desire mingling with my own, the sounds of her pleasure ringing out unhindered, and the taste of her still lingering on my tongue.

"Come for me my sweet Nightingale. Come on my cock and squeeze me inside you. I want to smell your cum on me."

Lottie grips the back of my thighs, digging her blunt nails in, pulling me closer. I thrust into her hard, and she whimpers.

"Again."

So I do it again.

"Again."

I pick up speed until all I can hear is the sound of our skin slapping together. My knot threatens to slip inside her, her wetness inviting me in.

"Fuck it feels so good. I love it when your knot pounds against me. Oh, shit, I'm gonna come. Don't stop."

My balls tighten in anticipation, her walls clenching down hard on my shaft as her orgasm rips through her. Her screaming moans and shaking body, an instant aphrodisiac, causing my own orgasm to shoot up my spine, tighten my balls and shoot down my cock buried deep inside Lottie.

I press so close it wouldn't take more than a slight movement to thrust my knot inside her, but I don't. My shaft stiffens, and I roar out my release. Pumping my cum inside her tight pussy.

"That's it, take my cum."

Holding tight to her hips, I rock inside her, milking out every last drop of pleasure.

It takes a minute before my dick stops twitching inside her from every little movement we make. I slip my cock out of her and fall to the bed at her side, pulling her naked body against mine and find comfort in holding her until my racing heart calms.

Sing Sweet Nightingale

Lottie burrows her face into my chest and curls in. Wrapping my arms around her, my inner beast sighs in contentment. Our legs are tangled together, my grandmother's quilt crumpled beneath us. Needing to care for my mate, I'm unable to rest for long before standing and making my way to the bathroom.

Lottie makes a small, happy noise, nuzzling the blanket when I gently extricate myself from her. I return within moments, warm damp towel in hand to clean us both up. She lets me, and I tuck her under the blanket, joining her after depositing the towel in the hamper.

She easily finds a comfortable spot lying atop my chest and sighs blissfully. The sounds shoot straight to my heart and deeper. I never knew a person could burrow so deep inside my soul so quickly that my entire being wants to latch on to her and never let go.

Others have told stories of how it feels when you give in to the mate pull and connect with the other person on a level deeper than anything human could ever be. I just never expected to feel it for myself. Now that I have, I'll do everything in my power to keep her. Give her anything she asks of me and some that she doesn't.

My fingers move lazily over her bare shoulder and back, tracing the lines of her shoulder blades and spine, running up to play with the short strands of her hair. Her eyes are closed, and her breathing is deep and calm. I'm not sure if she's fallen asleep or not. When her hand begins to move on my chest in a similar pattern to mine on her back, I know she hasn't.

"How do you feel, my sweet Nightingale?" I whisper in a low voice.

"Well fucked and warm."

I chuckle and slip my hand down to squeeze her ass cheek. She giggles but remains languid on my chest, humming in pleasure as my grope turns into a caress.

"Ready for round two, or should I say three, already?"

"I am always ready for you, little bird. As many times as you want."

Lottie lifts her head and rests her chin on my chest, her ocean eyes glittering in the moonlight as she watches me.

"What's it like?"

"What's what like?"

She fiddles with my chest hair and gives me a playful scowl. "You know what I mean. Being a shifter. What's it like?"

I figured that's what she meant. She's so intrigued by non-humans and not at all afraid or freaked out. Wanting to know more, learn more. That's a good thing. If she were to react poorly to us, it would make all of this much more difficult.

"To me, it's normal. It's what I've always known. Having to hide it and deal with humans is time-consuming, and sometimes I wish it could go back to the way it was hundreds of years ago when we lived out in the open among each other."

Lottie is listening intently, tilting her head to the side. Her lips are kiss-swollen, and her hair is tangled, but she's never looked more beautiful to me.

"The shifting takes time to get used to. Bones breaking and rearranging and all that. It starts off painful but eventually lessens."

"And being a wolf? And your beast? Your true form. Does it feel different?"

"Sometimes. But it's part of me. Being in those forms can be freeing. There's less stress and worry about menial things like bills and work. Everything breaks down to a base level. Need, want, desire. I still have cognitive thinking and understand everything, but all I care about are things like running, hunting, eating . . . fucking."

Lottie laughs when I stroke down her backside and press my hips up, letting her feel my growing erection.

"I love your laugh. The sound of your voice is hypnotizing. Do you know that?" I ask, brushing the stray lock of golden hair back behind her ear that has fallen in her face.

She shrugs one shoulder as if shrugging off the compliment. "I've been told my voice is many things by many people. Not sure how much I believe anymore. It seemed like they were only saying it to butter me and get me to sing more songs to make more records and sales."

I stop her with a brush of my thumb across her lips, silencing her insecurities.

"I don't care what other people tell you. I'm not them. I don't care how many records you sell or how much money you have. Your voice is enchanting and beautiful, and if you were willing, I would listen to you sing, hum, or even grunt all day long."

The downturn to her lips eases and smooths out. Turning into a shy grin.

"Would you sing for me, my sweet Nightingale? Now that I'm in human form. Sing for me and not a stray wolf you didn't think could understand you?"

I try to coax the unease from her brow by smoothing my thumb over it and brushing along her cheekbone. After a moment's pause, she smiles and nods.

"Yeah. I'll sing for you."

Sitting up, the quilt falls away, revealing her tan skin and ample breasts tipped with hard, dusky pink nipples that divert my attention momentarily. Lottie stands from the bed, and I get a full view of her from every angle. My gaze lingers over every inch of her as she tip-toes over to her guitar perched on a stand in the corner. She grabs it and returns to the bed, sliding under the warmth of the covers next to me.

The blanket falls from around my waist, revealing my hardening cock as I prop myself up on an elbow and turn onto my side to watch her. She settles against the headboard and pillows, propping her guitar on her crossed legs.

"What would you like to hear?"

"Anything you're willing to sing."

Clearing her throat, Lottie adjusts the strings, confidently places her hand around the neck, and rests her arm on the base of the guitar, readying her fingers to play.

The majority of her nude body is shielded by the bulk of the guitar, but her nipples bob into view periodically as she moves and shifts to play. Seeing her bare before me in more ways than one has everything inside me sparking to life and paying attention.

The first few chords are unplanned and loose in their construction until she finds her stride, and a song emerges from her fingertips and then her lips.

The words are soft and smooth, flowing like cream over coffee. Rich and deep. I hear the words, but I don't process them with my mind. Instead, I feel their meaning, feel the emotions behind them—curious longing and tender affection. They're sincere and earnest, provoking the same emotions inside me through her song.

She bites her lip and looks up at me through her lashes when she's finished, bashful in a way that's so at odds with her personality.

"It's just something I've been working on. Something my mother and the studio didn't approve for my *aesthetic*."

Pushing myself into a sitting position, I gently grab the guitar and set it at the foot of the bed, taking care because I know how much she loves it. Gripping Lottie by the waist, I pull her to straddle my lap and press my lips to hers in a kiss that conveys the way her song made me feel.

She melts against me, and I wrap us both in the quilt to keep her warm and in the circle of my arms.

"When you're with me, you can sing whatever you want. Whatever pops into that beautifully talented head of yours. Because every word and note is you, and I want to experience all of you. Every happy pop song and corny love ballad. Every sad requiem and unhinged jam session. They are all you and I—"

I stop myself before admitting what I truly want to; that I love every part of her. Because admitting my affections are turning into love may scare her off, they almost scare me. But they can't because she's my mate, and I knew all along that it would lead to this. So, I tell her as much as possible without using the L word.

"I think you're amazing."

She smiles against my lips and wraps her arms around my shoulders, bringing our bodies flush and making me growl at the friction against my hardening cock.

"I think you're pretty amazing, too." She speaks the words so quietly directly into my lips before pressing a kiss to them. Then her expression shifts, and a devious little grin spreads across her lips. "I also think your knot is pretty amazing."

She emphasizes this with a roll of her hips pressing into my erection and swelling knot. And that's all it takes to ignite round three.

Chapter 30
Lottie

The morning starts with a large hand cupping my breast and a thick shaft nestled against my ass crack. There have been other mornings that I woke up after spending the night with a man or boyfriend, but none felt like this. None made my insides warm and gooey. They usually started with me calling Luna to escort my "guest" out the back door to avoid the paparazzi or me hurriedly scurrying out of bed and running out the door because I was late to something or another my mother deemed important.

Waking up happy and content without a scheduled event to run off to, being able to ignore the clock and stay right where I am, is something I've never had. Feeling sore and worn out in the best way, engulfed by a man I trust and only want more of, I've decided is the best way to start your day. Even better than a cup of Tobias's magical coffee.

I try not to move so as not to wake Hunter. I can tell he's still asleep by the slow, measured breaths tickling the hairs on my neck. His body is loose and comfortable behind me, even with his hand firmly in place around my right breast. We're both still naked from our escapades last night.

Just as I'm trying to figure out how I can get my hand around Hunter's cock without him waking up, my bladder takes the opportunity to demand I relieve it.

Peeling Hunter's slack fingers from my boob, I almost free myself when his big arm tightens and his hand repositions, not letting me escape.

"Where do you think you're going?" Hunter rasps in a deep voice made gravely from sleep.

I try to pry his hand away again, but this time, it doesn't free as easily as it did before now that he's awake and somewhat aware.

"I have to pee if you must know."

Hunter grunts but eventually releases me so I can scurry to the bathroom to relieve my full bladder. I snag my robe from the bathroom before returning to the bedroom, where Hunter hasn't moved an inch. It's cold in the cabin and I turn up the central heat on the control panel in the hall.

Crawling back into bed, I find Hunter is no longer even partially asleep because he instantly wraps both arms around my waist and pulls me under him.

His lips find mine, and I don't protest; he is an excellent kisser.

"Well, good morning to you, too," I giggle out between kisses to my lips, face, and neck.

"Yes, it is. Why are you wearing clothing? I distinctly remember you being naked when you got out of bed."

He tries to tug at the ties of my bathrobe, and I am unsuccessful in stopping him from opening it. As soon as my chest is exposed, his tongue flicks out to tease my nipple, hardening the peak.

I groan at the sensation that shoots straight to my core. How he manages to turn me on so quickly, and after thoroughly fucking me last night, I have no idea.

"What would you like to do today, Nightingale?" he asks between torturous licks of my nipple and feather-light kisses.

"Mmm, maybe start with coffee at the Ugly Mug. Then a late breakfast at Morning Star Café, after that . . ." my words trail off as his mouth trails south. "Stop trying to distract me."

"But it's so enjoyable."

"So is coffee and a hot shower."

Hunter perks up and grins at me. "I like showers. We get naked in a shower."

He moves so fast I can barely squeal as he jumps out of bed and throws me over his shoulder, carrying me to the shower. Where he thoroughly distracts me.

~

Walking down the sidewalk of town today feels different than other days. Just like how waking up naked in bed with Hunter felt different. It's a good different.

Hunter holds my hand, our fingers entwined as we stroll lazily down the street toward the *Ugly Mug* from where we parked. The last time I walked hand in hand with a boy and wasn't photographed by paparazzi, I think I was in the third grade and had declared Dillon McDermit was my forever boyfriend, and one day we were gonna get married and have ten children. That only lasted till second recess when he decided Jane would be a better wife, and I decided I didn't want to marry someone so fickle.

Before reaching the *Ugly Mug*, Hunter stops us in the middle of the sidewalk and turns me to face him, gripping at my lower back to hold me close. His other hand trails a path around my throat to grip the back of my neck, holding me possessively.

Leaning down, he places a scathing kiss on my lips, making my toes curl and my belly flutter. Public displays of affection have never been my thing, but I think they are now.

"What was that for?" I ask breathlessly when Hunter breaks the kiss.

"Because I can, and I want to," he answers right before he locks his lips to mine again, and I melt against him.

Click.

The sound filters in through the lust-filled haze Hunter has placed me in, but I don't register it until I hear it again.

Click. Click.

Shutter clicks from a high-speed digital camera. I'd know that sound anywhere; it haunts my nightmares.

Instantly, the warm and fuzzy feelings evaporate and are replaced with an ice-cold chill.

Please don't let it be cameras. Please let me be crazy and hearing things that aren't really there.

When I stop reciprocating Hunter's kiss, he frowns down at me, and immediately, concern washes over his handsome features.

"What's wrong, Lottie?"

Turning my head in the direction I thought I heard the clicking. I pray it's a local taking photos or Michael testing out a new lens. Hell, I'd even accept Ginger taking our photo to mock us with later.

No such luck.

There, standing on the corner right by the entrance to the *Ugly Mug*, stands the unmistakable figure of a classic paparazzi. More than one, there's at least three of them. Large digital cameras with wide lenses pressed up to their faces shift to a new position every other second to try to get the best angle. The shutter speed picks up when I turn to face them.

There's something different about these paparazzi than others I've seen before. Their skin is a sickly gray, but I can't seem to process anything else. I can't see any of their faces, as you normally can't with paps; all I can think is, *they found me.*

"No," the word is a whispered whimper on my lips, and I don't even think to explain to Hunter what's happening. I just run.

Turn and run back in the direction we came from. Run towards Hunter's truck, away from the cameras, the gossip columns, the limelight, and my mother, who will undoubtedly find me within days or even hours after they post those photos.

I need to pack. I need to leave.

But I don't want to leave. I like it here. I like the people. Ginger, Dottie, Becca, Tobias . . . Hunter.

I can't think about any of that. If I don't leave, they'll be exposed. Others will come; they always do. They'll turn this town into a circus or, worse, a science experiment.

My legs pump beneath me, strong and sturdy, carrying me far away and fast. Even with my long legs and speed, Hunter catches up to me quickly, hauling me to a stop just as I reach the passenger door of his pickup truck.

"What the hell, Lottie? I love a good chase, but what is going on?"

The tears are already streaming down my cheeks, and when Hunter sees them, he freezes but doesn't release his hold on me.

"Lottie. What's wrong? Why are you crying?"

His voice is stern but uneasy. I suppose I did literally just pull a one-eighty. Going from blissfully doe-eyed to running in terror.

Sucking in gasping breaths, I steady my racing pulse.

"They found me."

"Who found you?"

"The media. There were paparazzi back at the Ugly Mug. I don't know how they found me or knew where I was, but they were there. They took our picture. I have to leave." My words rush out in a panic.

I'm pulling on Hunter's sleeve, trying to get him to move, to go. He loosens his hold enough that I can break free and scramble into the passenger seat of his truck. Slamming the door, I don't bother with the seat. I slide down to the floor and huddle, making myself as small as I can so no one can see me from the outside. It's not the first time I've had to hide like this, but I had hoped I never would have to again.

So much for wishing; I should have known I could never escape them. They're vultures. They'll find me anywhere. As soon as I get an inkling of happiness or normalcy, BAM! They show up just in time to destroy it.

I hear Hunter get into the driver's seat and lock the doors. Thankfully, he doesn't comment on my current position on the floor. He just starts the truck and pulls out of the parking lot, hopefully heading somewhere with an underground bunker.

I don't look at him or speak to him while he drives. I just bury my face in my leggings-clad knees and thick sweater, hoping to disappear.

We must have arrived at our destination because Hunter opens the passenger door slowly. He doesn't try to force me out but coaxes me to unfurl and effortlessly lifts me from the truck floor, cradling me in his arms.

Tentatively, I raise my head enough to look around to see where he's brought us. There are many trees that look familiar, but the space is far too large and wide to be my little cabin. Swiveling my head around, I see a large two-story house that looks similar to a wood-planked lodge.

"Where are we?"

"This is my house. I wanted to bring you somewhere safe. Where I can protect you from any lurkers wishing to trespass."

The dread souring in my gut lessons, and I don't feel nearly as nauseous and panicked. Without me explaining or asking, he brought me somewhere safe without question or hesitation.

I manage a small smile up at him, and he quirks the side of his lips at me.

"You're not going to lock me in your sex dungeon, are you?"

His lip quirk turns into a full-blown grin, and he winks at me.

"Only if you want me to."

Maybe I do want him to.

The change in subject has the last embers of my anxiety fizzling out just as he opens his front door and enters his home.

The interior has the same style of décor as the cabin; it's instantly clear the two were decorated by the same person. Dark wooden floors and rich-colored upholstery and rugs.

Hunter doesn't set me down in the entryway as I expect him to. Instead, he walks through the open layout of a living room to set me down on one of the largest couches I've ever seen. It's plush and a deep navy blue. Behind us, I catch a glimpse of a kitchen with an island and dining table large enough for at least eight. There's also a large sliding glass door on the back wall that leads out to a wooden deck filled with outdoor seating, and, I think, a fire pit and bar-b-que.

Hunter sits down at my side and smooths my hair back from my face with a gentle hand you wouldn't expect from such a large guy.

"Tell me who you saw back in town, Lottie. I need to know so I can personally escort them back to the highway."

I love that he doesn't hesitate to take my side. He doesn't question my freak out or tell me to calm down and stop overreacting. He wants to make it better, not put the blame on me.

I explain to him the clicking sounds and then the men with the cameras, how their skin looked gray, but I had to have seen wrong.

"No, you didn't see wrong. Those were elves."

"Elves? You mean the bad elves like Vincent you told me about?"

He growls, and his entire body tenses.

"Yes. They may or may not work for Vincent, but I have a feeling they do. It's too much of a coincidence them showing up now after I've told him no, and he's already threatened to use you against me. He must have figured out who you were and sent them."

I frown and can feel the depth of my scowl scrunch on my forehead.

"So, they're not actual paparazzi, just guys he sent to freak me out?"

"No, they probably are paparazzi. Pretty much all are elves. They're well suited to be inconsiderate pricks."

The slight relief I just felt is already dissipating. I wasn't hallucinating, and they weren't just random guys sent to force Hunter to sell his land. They're legit paparazzi taking real photos that'll soon be posted on real gossip sites.

Panic starts to rise in me again, and Hunter notices. He takes my clenched hand in his and threads my fingers through his just like they were not ten minutes ago as we walked down the street without a care in the world. The action soothes me enough to focus on his face and not run away and hide in a closet.

"Don't worry, Lottie. I'll take care of it. We'll find the guys and get the photos before they have a chance to post them anywhere. And even if they do, Ginger will make sure they disappear within seconds. She doesn't let anything slip through the cracks."

"Ginger? What would Ginger do?"

He cocks his head at me in confusion. "Didn't she tell you what she does?"

"No."

"Ginger is our computer hacker. She monitors the internet and removes anything that mentions Snowberry or non-humans that may lead to people coming here and investigating," he explains.

I suppose that makes sense. How else could they manage to remain off maps and every online search engine? That's why Luna suggested I come here. Though I had no idea Ginger was so tech savvy.

"I need to call my brother. I need his help on this one. Are you okay here by yourself for a minute?"

I nod. I may be a puddle of a person right now, but I can handle sitting alone for a few minutes. It'd probably do me some good to pull myself together.

Chapter 31

Hunter

There are many reasons I've wanted Lottie in my house and in my bed; hiding out from elf paparazzi was not one of them. Leaving her in the care of my sister barely half an hour after the incident in front of the Ugly Mug was also not on my to-do list. But I have to. Ryder and I are going back into town to find Vincent and/or the photographers and beat a little—perhaps a lot—of sense into them.

Ginger did a quick cursory search online before I left, but none of the photos have appeared yet. Which means either they haven't had the chance to upload them, or Vincent has them. Either way we're going to find out who has them and repossess them.

The fact that strangers can follow people around taking their pictures without their permission and sell them to gossip sites is beyond baffling. Why haven't they outlawed this kind of crap yet? Isn't it an invasion of privacy?

Ryder is just sliding out of his truck when I pull up to Town

Hall. We don't know where Vincent is at this moment, so we planned to meet here to see if we could run down his location. Tap into the gossip network and check in with his deputies. Someone's always got an eye out in town.

I haven't seen my brother around much lately, though I suppose that could be my fault. Spending so much time with Lottie, I have been neglecting some—okay, probably all—of my other duties. A male with his mate in his sights and senses doesn't see much beyond until the bond is satisfied. I don't think I've been to my office in multiple days.

Nodding at my brother, we both stride up the steps and into the white brick building. We had intended to visit Ryder's office first to reach out over the radio but we both stop in the main entry that splits to either side. On the left is the mayor's office, and on the right is the sheriff's. Both offices have glass windows leading into them, allowing for an open and welcoming space. Through the windows to my office, I spot a gaggle of men sitting in the lobby chairs. Unfamiliar men, not locals. Most of them elves. Not to mention their stink wafting through the cracks, invading my senses and trying to wash away the lingering scent of Lottie.

Both Ryder and I growl simultaneously, redirecting our path straight to my office. When I enter, none of the men stand, but Levi does, quickly rounding his desk and intercepting us before I reach my office door.

"I was just about to call you. These *gentlemen* showed up without an appointment and wouldn't reschedule. They insisted on waiting. There's a few already in your office," he adds, his head hanging shamefully for letting people enter my office while I wasn't present.

I grip his shoulder and squeeze, offering him my best semblance of a smile while desperately trying to bite back my growing anger—not at him, but at the others.

I had plans to rearrange Vincent's face, which is best not done with witnesses. Not that I expect repercussions from my actions; no one but his men would care. But the possibility of a human seeing is far greater right in the middle of my office in Town Hall.

Not sparing a second glance at the thugs occupying my lobby, I burst through my office door to find Vincent and, no doubt, his second-in-command, lingering inside. Vincent leans in to closer inspect a family photo hanging on the wall as the other male sits stoically in one of the guest seats, staring straight ahead. I would think he were inept and incompetent were it not for the deer-like ears protruding from his ruddy brown hair, twitching and rotating towards the sound of my loud entrance. A nymph with animal attributes. Higher hearing and reflexes, good for surveillance.

"Is this your lovely sister?" Vincent inquires, pointing to the framed photo. "She is even more delectable than I remember."

Crossing the room to place myself on the opposite side of my desk, a sign of position and power, I stomp my feet to emphasize my displeasure with his unannounced presence. Even though it saves me the trouble of hunting him down, the hunt is the most satisfying part.

"Thank you for saving me the trouble of finding you, Vincent. You may not hear this very often, but you're just the man I wanted to see."

Vincent's smirk grows wicked as he turns from the photo and focuses on me. "I thought you may want to speak with me. Decided it best if I just came to you."

Stepping away from the wall, Vincent takes the vacant seat next to his nymph partner, not at all intimidated by his lower position than me. Comfortable with the power he thinks he holds over me.

Ryder steps to my side, bristling, his shoulders tensing, readying for a fight. I know exactly how he feels.

"All right, well, now that you're here, where are the photos? And the men who took them. I'd like to have a private conversation with them."

"They're of no consequence. They did their job. What really matters now is," the silent partner hands Vincent a cell phone and he leers at the screen, "what I'm going to do with these great candids of her and you canoodling on the sidewalk. I'm sure many people would love to see these and know exactly where and when they were taken. Since her relationship with that pretty boy second-class actor ended months ago, the press will be dying to know who the pop star Alexandria's new beau is."

So, he does know who she really is. I feared as much when she said there were paparazzi here taking her picture. He wouldn't have brought them in unless he knew they would spook Lottie or if they had a purpose. Vincent doesn't do anything without purpose.

"And I suppose you want me to sign over my land to you in exchange for those photos," I bite out in a terse, clipped tone.

What I wouldn't do to sink my jowls into his neck and rip him to shreds right here on the pristine marble floor of my office. Donna would kill me for staining the area rug she so tediously picked out, though. She'd get over it, considering the world would be rid of Vincent.

The pompous elf flashes me his fangs and runs a finger down his pointed ear, the many jeweled earrings glinting in the overhead light.

"And that is why I like you, Hunter. Why I need a man like you in my business. You cut the bullshit and get to the point.

You're smart, and you use it."

My hands ball into fists, and I can feel the skin stretch over my knuckles. Feel the shift squirming under my skin readying to fortify my bones and generate the claws needed to shred through flesh and muscle.

This fucker still thinks he can convince me to work for him. Can blackmail me into it. If I can't get those photos from him, he may have some leverage for about two seconds. I'm not concerned with those photos making it online. Ginger will have them removed and permanently deleted in less than five minutes.

My concern is not for our exposure or photos on gossip sites. My concern is for Lottie, for the stress and anxiety she's going through. She's had her life plastered all over the news and social media for years. Believing the old suspicion that once something is on the internet, it's there forever. Not with Ginger and her hacker tech heads. People like them are the only reason we've remained as concealed as we are today. Sure, snippets of things slip through the cracks, but they are usually grainy, blurred photos that can't be verified.

No, my purpose is to ease the suffering of my sweet Nightingale. And if ensuring those photos don't make it to the internet at all is what she needs, then that's what she shall get. I can deal with his demands for my land in other ways.

"Just hand over the photos, and we don't have to escalate this beyond a few unfriendly words."

I make the offer desperately hoping he refuses so I can escalate it beyond words to something involving fists, teeth, and claws.

"Now you know that's not how this works. If you want the photos, you give me what I want, and they disappear. Never to be seen."

He flitters his fingers like a bird flying away in the air. Leaning back in his chair, he believes he's still going to win.

"Not a chance. You stalked, photographed without permission, and threatened Lottie. That's means for vindication. You've crossed the line against one of mine and have no rights here. You're going to hand over the photos and walk away, leave town for good *without* my land, or I will take action as is my right."

Vincent's chuckle is dark and humorless but amused, not at all taking my threat seriously as one should. A person who's done all that he has should expect full repercussions. He's finally crossed the line, and I'm giving him one chance to leave before I lose control.

"She isn't one of yours. She's a human, not connected to any non-human here. She's not part of your pack and doesn't fall under your jurisdiction as alpha. Nothing I've done is against the human laws. I'm well within my rights to photograph anyone on public property and sell those photos to whomever I please."

My heart drops to the pit of my stomach and sticks in my throat simultaneously. To me, she is already pack. She's mine. I need to protect her; it's my duty as her mate to do so. But we still haven't solidified our bond or married in the human right. She isn't an official resident of Snowberry or a relative to anyone in town.

Fucking fuck.

I can see it the moment he sees my realization at my slip-up. He knows she's important to me, and he knows he is technically within his rights still.

"I tell you what. I'll still give you till next week after your full moon celebration. I'll come to your house with all the proper papers and all you'll have to do is sign. Photos will disappear, me and my guys will back off. You, of course, can remain in your quaint little log cabin out there in the woods, but the rest of the land is mine. And when I call on you for something, you'll answer. Understood?"

I don't answer. I can't. He thinks he's got me on a short leash. For now, I'll let him think that. I have until next Thursday to take action against him. Somewhere, not in the center of town. Somewhere where no one will question the howls and screams.

A thought occurs to me amidst my raging daydream of breaking Vincent's legs. Perhaps I won't have to. If I were to make her mine officially, he would have no rights, and I could take action against him without guilt for breaking our rules. Without fear of retribution from his "employees" and partners. I would be well within my rights.

Clenching my jaw, I allow him to rise and stand. He straightens his cuffs and fingers a strand of inky black hair out of his face like a goddamn runway model.

"Good. Now that we have that cleared up, I'll be seeing you soon. Maybe I'll see that sweet little human of yours even sooner."

My control snaps, and I bolt around my desk at a speed only a shifter possesses. Capturing Vincent in my hands before he has a chance to turn and leave. Shoving him against the wall, I hear a crack, no doubt the drywall behind him or a frame falling to the ground from the force of my strike. I press my forearm against his throat and grip one of his wrists with the other, holding him up just high enough he can only touch the floor with his toes.

I'm sure his partner is behind me attempting to assist. I trust my brother to take care of him, so I don't bother giving him a microsecond of my time.

Vincent laughs, and it pisses me the fuck off. I get closer, bringing my face within inches of his, making sure he hears every syllable.

"I don't care if she's a human and not technically part of my pack. If I see you or one of your men anywhere near her again, I will kill you despite the rules and laws. I will take pleasure in breaking every one of your bones and gnawing on them until they're blunt nubs. *Am I understood?*"

His dull gray face is starting to turn purple from the pressure on his neck, but his expression of arrogance and gleeful expectation doesn't waver. He also doesn't answer, and I don't release him until I feel Ryder's familiar hand on my shoulder.

Vincent slides down the wall, his knees buckling as he lands unsteadily on his feet. He rubs at his neck and glares at me with the wrath of an avenging god. He can go ahead and try me. I would revel in the opportunity to see which of us would come out victorious in a one-on-one.

No more words are spoken as Vincent and his lackeys leave my office. Making Donna practically clutch her invisible pearls at her chest as they sneer and mumble rude slurs under their breath. Levi uses his desk as a shield until they're gone.

"Good riddance," Donna mutters when they're gone.

"Everything okay, Boss?" Levi asks nervously.

"Yeah. Everything will be."

Chapter 32
Lottie

When Hunter returned from town, he looked pissed beyond belief. Strung tight as a bow. Coming to me the moment he returned, he pulled me close and held me tight. It seemed to ease him. Wrapping me in his arms and breathing in my scent. His deep inhales buried in my hair until they finally subsided into normal shallow breaths.

He told me about Vincent having the photos, that none were posted online, and that all the paparazzi were gone. Or so he believes. Just to be safe, we moved most of my stuff from the cabin to Hunter's place. I'll be staying here for the time being.

His house isn't as minimalistic as the cabin but it's still cozy. There's a large fireplace in the living room that he keeps lit. He puts my things in his bedroom, and I don't complain. His bed is large, and I look forward to cozying up under the covers with him.

We don't plan on leaving his house for a few days. Just in case there are other paparazzi in town who don't work for

Vincent waiting to take my picture. Our picture. If it were just me on my own in a town filled with nobodies I didn't care about, it wouldn't matter. I would just get in my car and leave. But I do care. I care about them more than I probably should after so short a time. The pull growing stronger between me and Hunter, and I don't hate it. I like it. It makes my insides all warm and tingly. Feels like home when I'm with him.

The rest of the day goes by in a blur, and the night is filled with bare skin, hot kisses, and talented tongues. Hunter shatters my mind, body, and soul into a million tiny shards over and over, distracting me so thoroughly from the paparazzi that I fall into a peaceful, deep sleep.

Today, we spend most of the time talking. I make us breakfast with my newly acquired cooking skills. Hunter shows me his workshop and wood carvings in progress. He's making a new pillar support for a broken one on his porch. I try to convince him to go for a run with me, and he almost gives in, but his paranoia and protectiveness win out, and we only take a leisurely stroll around the clearing behind his house.

Ryder decided to give us our space and went to stay at the cabin. Guess he doesn't like listening to his brother make me scream or the rhythmic knocking of the bed frame against the wall. We don't see him much, but Hunter did invite Ginger over for dinner.

Sitting out on the back porch after dinner around the fire pit is nice. We talk about simple things, like how we need to convince Dottie to add sushi to her menu and how cute Ginger was as a pup. We also talk about how she always forgot to remove her clothes before shifting as a kid and would run around in wolf form wearing pink princess underwear with her tail sticking out a rip in the back.

They tell me about the upcoming lunar eclipse which will

be a blood moon. How many shifters come to run in the forest on their land. Many of them locals, some visitors that they've befriended. In just three days, these woods will be teaming with shifters in their true forms running, hunting, and apparently fucking. I guess the moon does have an effect on them, even though they aren't actual werewolves. It doesn't control them but sparks a need and desire. I get a knowing gaze from Ginger after that revelation.

After Ginger leaves, Hunter wastes no time getting me naked and moaning beneath him. Tangled in his bed sheets and digging my fingers into the meaty muscle of his ass and through the soft strands of his short hair.

We lay in his bed, still naked, slightly sweaty, and blissfully sated. At least I know I am, my body soft and pliant draped over Hunter's strong but peaceful one. His hand mindlessly stroking through my hair down my back anywhere he can reach. Unable to stop touching me even though we were just touching quite a bit.

With every passing caress, I feel the touch deeper than skin only. I feel it steadily stoking the ember in my chest that feels more and more like love. A heated coal thar will turn into a raging inferno that once ignited will never deplete.

"There's something I've been thinking about that I wanted to ask you," Hunter begins, breaking the sex-induced silence we've been lying in.

Tilting my head, I look up to him but don't rise. I'm far too comfortable where I am, and Hunter's hand stops roaming and settles on my waist, holding tight. So, I take that as he doesn't want me to move either.

"What's that?" I ask, interested to know what's rolling around in his head that he wants to ask me.

"There are these rules that all non-humans abide by. Most

are about keeping our kind secret, protecting our anonymity, and staying out of the news. But a few have to do with dealing with other non-humans. How we treat each other and interact with other packs and groups.

"There's one that states if one or more non-humans were to make threats or attack any member of a pack, the alpha of that pack has the right to respond. To protect their pack by whatever means they see fit."

My brow pulls down in confusion. This is all very interesting, but what does it have to do with me? I don't interrupt and let Hunter continue, far too intrigued to see where this is going.

"As such I cannot act against Vincent for his actions against you since you aren't officially part of my pack."

I cock my head as best I can while still laying on Hunter's shoulder. An action I can't control with my inability to understand what he's trying to say.

"What do you mean? You are doing something to protect me," I argue.

Hunter's fingers curl into my side, and a small smile pulls at the corner of his mouth, but it doesn't quite reach his eyes.

"Thank you for thinking that, Lottie. But in the non-human world, what I'm doing wouldn't be considered taking action as I see fit. There are other things I could do to keep him away from you, to make him leave. Permanently. But I can't because, to them, you're only a human who isn't under my protection or part of my pack. An outsider who doesn't fall under the umbrella of my protection, officially."

I push up on my elbow to get a better look at him. To me, he's doing everything right. What more could he do?

Scooting up, he props his shoulders against the headboard, keeping me secure against his side.

"We deal with things differently than humans do," he

explains. "We're more hands-on, and if you were part of my pack, I could force Vincent to back off without repercussions."

"You said you wanted to ask me something. Does this have to do with that?" I ask.

"Yes. I want to make you part of my pack so I can make Vincent leave in the way I want."

Make me part of his pack? Would that mean staying in Snowberry? Staying with him? I wonder if becoming part of his pack means becoming part of his family or, I don't know, just paying an annual fee and getting a membership card. I'm unable to voice my questions or ask if what he's saying is that he wants me to stay. To become his. Would I agree to such a thing? I haven't even decided whether I want to return to music or not. Haven't even thought about where I want my future to go. Could my future be here with Hunter? Is that even possible? If Vincent figured out who I am, then someone else could. Events like the other day will happen again and again.

Then my thoughts take a different turn down a dark alley that makes my insides twist.

"Do you only want to make me a member of your pack so you can make a move against Vincent?" I ask a bit incredulously.

"What? No, that's not the only reason. And you wouldn't just be part of my pack. You would be my mate. My bonded mate," he says slowly, emphasizing his words carefully.

"Bonded mate. You want to bond with me?"

He gives me one sharp nod without hesitation. How can he know so soon that he wants to bond his life to mine? This isn't like a human marriage. There's no annulment or divorce. This would be permanent. For the rest of our extremely long lives. Because once we bond, I'll live as long as Hunter does. I would hate for Hunter to bond with me and regret it because he went on instinct instead of getting to know me first.

We've only been together for a few days, and I've only known him for maybe two weeks. Could it be that easy? That fast?

"Do you want to bond with ME? Or do you want to bond because your inner whatever says I'm your mate?"

"Both. The mate pull drew me to you, but it's because of you that I want it."

He pauses, seeing my reluctance as I shift out of his arms and pull the blanket up to cover my nudity. I like Hunter—a lot. I may even love him. But to tie our souls together in such a permanent way requires a little longer than a handful of days to decide. A better reason than the mystical pull told me to. Right?

"I know we've only known each other a short time, and you've just discovered this entire new world hidden within your own. I know you're concerned about the media finding you here and exposing us. I promise that won't happen; Ginger won't let it. But I don't need more time to know that if I were to bond with you, I would be the happiest male in the world. I know you are my perfect match because you wouldn't be my mate otherwise. We may disagree or even fight, but we'll work through it because no one else out there will understand and love you as deeply and fiercely as I will.

"I once heard the saying that good things come to those who wait, but great things happen all at once. People will wait and delay and put things off for fear they may not be the right choice and, in the end, kick themselves for wasting all that time when they could have had something great all along.

"I don't like wasting my time. I like schedules and being efficient. If I want something, I don't question it or worry that it might not be perfect. I grab on with both hands and take it."

He sits straight and turns to face me, reaching out to cup

my cheek and turn my face to his.

"I know I want you, Lottie. I know we'll be happy. I don't question that. Shifters live off instinct, and mine's telling me that you're it."

Leaning in, he brushes his lips against mine. The kiss is soft and loving, drawn out. The pull tightening in my chest—and my clit.

Hunter breaks the kiss and speaks into my lips, brushing his nose against mine.

"Think about Lottie. The full moon is in three days. You can tell me then. If your answer is no, that's okay, too. I'll be here either way; nothing will change. It'll just take me longer to convince you."

His words are what every girl wants to hear. The words of happily ever after's. But are they real? Everything in my life has been so fake for so long that it's hard to tell the difference anymore.

But this is Hunter. He has nothing to gain from lying to me. He doesn't want to become famous; he doesn't want my money. There's no reason for him to lie to me about such a thing. This has to be real.

His hand trails down my jaw and neck, over my shoulder, and down the swell of my breast, gently pulling the blanket away, revealing my tight nipples and aching breasts to him. He cups one in his large hand, rubs a thumb across the pebbled peak, and pinches it between two fingers. His lips trail in the path his hands just took, ending in the same position.

I grow wet between my thighs and squirm under his attention, needing more. He knows what I need and rolls us until I'm under him, his already thickening cock rubbing against my swollen clit and throbbing pussy as he wedges his hips between my legs. I widen for him and wrap my heels around his ass.

"Is this you trying to convince me?" I ask between kisses, our breaths mingling as our heart rates increase and our breathing becomes labored.

"Is it working?"

Kisses pepper my throat, chin, lips.

"Maybe. Perhaps you should try moving more than just your lips."

Hunter chuffs against my skin, his breath hot but creating goosebumps in its wake.

"You mean like this?"

He rocks his hips, the length of his erection sliding up and down my pussy. I groan at the friction against my sensitive core. We already went two rounds tonight, but my body is well and ready for a third.

"Yes. Just like that. Do it again."

And bless him, he does. He does more than just grind against me. Much more. With the first thrust inside, I'm lost to the pleasure, putty in his hands. My body is electrified and singing with every touch.

Hunter threads his arms under my knees, taking handfuls of my ass.

"Hold on to me, Nightingale," he commands in a soft whisper that I can't deny.

My arms wrap around his neck and hold on, rubbing my sensitive nipples against his hard chest. Hunter growls in approval. I like it when he growls; it makes me shiver.

With little effort, he lifts me, sitting back on his heels, and the new angle drives him deeper inside at an angle that has my eyes crossing.

"Fuck you feel fantastic," Hunter groans as he lifts and lowers me on his hard cock.

I use my well-toned legs to help the movement. Picking up the pace and pressing down hard on the swollen knot at the base of his cock. I really want to know what it feels like to have that inside me. I bet the stretch and fullness would be phenomenal. But he won't let me have it. Not until we fulfill the mate bond. One more thing to add in the pro column for mating.

Grinding down as far as he'll let me, I whimper into Hunter's mouth. Pressing hard demanding kisses against his willing and responsive lips.

"That's it, little bird, ride me. Use me. Make me yours. You want my knot, don't you?"

"Uh-huh," I moan, biting my lip and bouncing on his cock harder. That torturous knot rubbing my clit and backside with every slap of our bodies.

"When we bond, I'll give it to you. Push it inside that tight little pussy of yours. Seal myself inside you and come so hard, filling you to the brim. You'll shake like a leaf in a tornado with the force of the orgasm I'll give you."

My body shakes in response, the impending orgasm growing in my core, swirling tight and causing my inner walls to clench down on Hunter's shaft.

"You like that? Like hearing what I'm going to do to you? I want to hear you say it, little bird. Tell me what you want me to do."

Forming words isn't the easiest thing to accomplish at the moment, especially with his cock buried so deep inside. But I try as best I can.

"I want you to bend me over and fuck me until you can't stand it and thrust that fat knot inside me. I wanna feel it stretch me, and I want to make you fracture and break because of how good it feels."

Normally, my wordsmithing is more eloquent, but my brain can barely knock two cells together to form a coherent thought. I just open my mouth and let the words fall out of their own volition.

After that, there are no more words. Just heavy breathing, loud, unhindered moans, and the sound of our bodies sliding together. When I come, I nearly fall out of Hunter's arms, but he holds me tight. Riding out my orgasm with me as my body shakes and shivers, exploding with hot ecstasy. Hunter follows soon after, shoving his cock as far in as possible without allowing his massively swollen knot in.

When we've both allowed our releases to subside enough to move, Hunter carries me to the bathroom and gives me a long introduction to his large soaking tub.

Chapter 33
Lottie

Hunter is very good at distracting me for the next few days. We remain within the safe confines of his house and yard. Not straying into the forest for a run or walk like we used to. I hope that changes soon. Hunter promises it will. Which is good because although I enjoy all my time captive with Hunter, I would really like to regain my freedom to go where I want when I want. Being cooped up inside is vastly overrated at this point.

Thankfully, tonight is the full moon and eclipse. Hunter says many shifters like to gather at his place before and after the run; it's become an unofficial community gathering. Even though, from my observations, Hunter doesn't always participate in town events, this is one he's always present for.

I was worried about having people around and going out into the woods, but Hunter promised me there wouldn't be an elf or one of Vincent's men for miles. They're not stupid enough to risk being around so many shifters under a full moon. So,

I relax and instead worry about the decision I need to make before the moon rises tonight.

Will I bond with Hunter? A large part of me is screaming; yes, do it! Where the other small and still paranoid part of me questions if it's a good idea to commit to something so permanent so quickly.

I figure the best thing to do is let my gut and heart choose for me. When the time comes, I'll know if it's right or not. It won't be driven by lust, even though I have a lot of it for him. It won't be driven by someone else telling me I should be with him. With no outside interference, the decision will come from me. From my inner beast, my natural instinct.

I don't know what breed of non-human my ancestors were, but I don't think I have an inner beast. When I look inward, I see music. I hear the sounds of the world around me and the emotions they emit. It may sound stupid, but it's true. I don't know what non-human species would have such thoughts, internal feelings, or powers. I don't recall Ginger or Hunter mentioning any non-human that is connected to sound or music. They'd probably tell me to ask Fynn. I've come to learn he's the go-to with all the questions I have on, well, anything.

Trying not to freak out or have an anxiety attack while contemplating my possible decision tonight, I fill my time with Hunter until Ginger shows up with a rolling suitcase in hand and a mischievous smile on her face.

"Why do you have a suitcase with you, Ginger?" Hunter asks.

Glad to know I'm not the only one curious about it. I thought at first it might just be normal for her to bring it over on full moons with a change of clothes and whatnot for after her run.

"None of your business; it's girl stuff."

Hunter raises his hands in surrender, not caring to get into an argument over a suitcase. However, as a girl, I think I can ask.

"What kind of girl stuff?"

Ginger smiles at me, and for the first time, I see her canines poking out longer than normal. The sight is chilling but also makes me want to laugh because she looks far too pleased with herself.

"Oh, you'll see. It's for you."

"For me?" I ask, shocked.

I take a second long look at the bag as if I'll suddenly possess x-ray vision to see what's inside. It doesn't look too full. I narrow my eyes at the bag and then her.

"Yup. This is your first lunar eclipse, and possibly a very important one. So, you're going to celebrate in style. It's not mandatory, but I think you'll like it."

She looks at her brother over my shoulder, and I take a small peek back at him. He's sitting at the kitchen island, sipping on a cup of coffee, his expression unreadable.

Ginger grips me by my elbow and steers me away from Hunter and towards the stairs.

"Come on. I'll show you."

There's no room for protest with Ginger. She's kind of an imposing figure when she wants to be. I don't argue or resist; there's no harm in letting her decide my outfit. Truthfully, I was fretting over what to wear. Is it a casual event? Do they all walk around nude for easy shifting?

Hunter's been very casual about it, so I assumed whatever I wore would be sufficient. Although Ginger mentioned it being a more important night than just a standard lunar eclipse. Perhaps Hunter mentioned wanting to bond with me tonight? I haven't spoken with Ginger much over the last couple of days and haven't had a chance to discuss it with her more than the first night she explained everything to me. I now know she left out a few details.

We end up in Hunter's large bedroom, and Ginger shuts the door behind us, effectively blocking Hunter's curious gaze. Placing the suitcase on the bed, she opens it swiftly, revealing a small pile of clothing and beauty products.

The sight has me sighing regrettably. Picking out an outfit is one thing, doing the whole hair and makeup and couture gown is another. I'm burnt out from so many people putting designer pieces on me and teasing and curling my hair until every last strand is "perfect." I just want to be me for once.

"Ginger, I don't know about this. I'm really not in the mood to do the whole hair and makeup thing. I just want to be comfortable."

She turns to me, frowning, but quickly smooths it out when she sees my contrite expression. Dropping the curling iron back in the suitcase, she crosses the room to me. I perch against the dresser, crossing my arms over my chest, instinctually guarding myself.

"We don't have to do anything you don't want to. I just thought if you do end up solidifying your mate bond with Hunter, you might like to wear something that will not only be comfortable and cute but," she cringes and curls her lip in disgust. "Will allow for easy access. The last thing you'll want is to slink back to the house wearing a ripped shirt, trying to cover yourself because your pants are somewhere in shreds in the forest."

The image has my tight posture easing. Ginger rubs her hand up and down my arm, trying to soothe my tension. I give her a week smile, grateful she's willing to be so open with me. It's refreshing to have people just speak to me candidly.

Sing Sweet Nightingale

"So, Hunter told you about wanting to solidify the mate bond?" I ask.

She smirks and winks at me, her smile returning which only puts me more at ease. "Nope. I'm just really good at paying attention to things. I know about the mate pull, and from what I've seen, I kind of figured he might want to do it as soon as possible. Especially with the whole Vincent lurking around town and stalking you."

She waves her hand flippantly, sneering when she says Vincent's name.

"Personally, I would love for you two to bond. Having another girl in the family would be a blessing. Brothers are a pain in the ass, let me tell you."

Returning to her open suitcase, she digs through the neatly folded clothing, pulling out a bundle of white eyelet material.

"Now, I know you don't want to get all gussied up, *but* I think you might like this option. We can do whatever you like with your hair and makeup. Although I would highly suggest keeping your hair light and soft. No hairspray or perfume. Remember, shifters are very sensitive to smell, and mates have a very special and alluring scent. You don't want to cover it up."

"And what about the makeup?" I ask, watching her shake out the fabric, which looks like some sort of dress.

"We don't have to do much if you like. Keep it simple or none at all. Your choice. You're pretty enough without all that makeup you used to wear anyway."

I snort laugh because she has no idea how much I hated wearing so much makeup.

"Wasn't my idea. Stylists can be very pushy. I was basically their Barbie doll. My opinion had no place in the decision-making."

I hear Ginger growl for the first time ever, sounding more

like her brother than I could have imagined. He growls all the time, usually because he likes something I'm doing and is aroused. Kinda weird, actually, to hear it from Ginger. I hope it's an irritated growl and not a horny one. I like her and all, but that'd be really awkward with me being with her brother and all.

Seeing the scowl on her face, I conclude it's an angry growl.

"Did you really have no say in your own life? Like at all?"

"Nope." I pop the p in exasperated emphasis.

"Fucking assholes. I love your music, and not gonna lie, I did love some of those designer dresses and would kill to go to Paris fashion week or meet even a fraction of the celebrities you have."

Overhyped if you ask me.

"But now I really don't think you should return to work with them. They don't deserve you or your voice. You know, if you asked him to, Hunter would build you a recording studio. Building shit is kind of his thing," she concludes, obviously slipping in her vote for me bonding with Hunter.

My cheeks heat with a blush. I don't think Hunter would ever tell me no if I were to ask anything of him.

"Thanks. I'll keep that in mind."

The thought of building my own recording studio and making my own music has never been anything more than a fantasy. I've been part of a large studio for so long that it didn't even occur to me I could do it myself. There's always been someone or a team to do everything for me.

Now that I'm considering the possibility of making my own music, other ideas are forming. I could teach music to others, open a shop to bring music and instruments to town. There was an empty storefront right next to *Tall Tails* that would suffice.

My spiraling daydream is interrupted when Ginger leads

me over to the full-length mirror in the corner, spinning me to face it and standing behind me. She brings the white eyelet dress in front of me, draping it over my front and showing me how it would look. It's short, hitting mid-thigh with an empire waist and low scooping neckline that would probably show a bit of cleavage but not too much. The sleeves are soft but bubbly. The overall look is sweet but with just enough appeal to be sexy if worn right.

"I think my brother would bite his own tongue off if he saw you in this."

Reaching up, I brush my hand down the short, gathered skirt of the dress. It'll have a little volume but nothing too poofy. It's very cottage-core-meets-baby-doll.

"Where did you get this?"

"I may have had a friend in town whip it up for you. Fairies can be very good with fabric. I'll introduce you to Larken sometime. Whenever I have a craving for something I see on a runway, I go to her."

I have no idea why fairies would be better for the job, but I'm guessing this Larken is a seamstress of some sort. That would be useful way out here, where access to certain things can be limited.

Staring at my reflection, I take in the white dress and the soft smile on Ginger's lips. I may not want to wear any makeup, but that doesn't seem to apply to her. She's just as put together as ever, with pristine application of a smoky eye with winged liner and a deep crimson lip with her auburn hair in a stylish soft wave. My assumption is that when she shifts, it doesn't affect her human form. Must be nice.

Again, my mind snags on the *white* dress. White doesn't seem an appropriate color for being chased through the woods and then fucked under a full moon. It would seem to be the absolute worst color to choose since it would get dirty in about three seconds. But if bonding is like marriage to shifters, white would be appropriate.

My mind stutters at the thought. That is effectively what I'd be doing, marrying Hunter. I look at the white dress a little differently now. Realizing this could be my wedding dress, and that's why Ginger picked white.

Seems strange to possibly be getting married with so little pomp and circumstance. No invitations or registries. No bridal party or flower arrangements. No photographer or ring bearer. Hell, beyond Ginger, no one else even knows we might be bonding tonight. Am I taking away something special for Hunter and his family by keeping it secret? Will his parents hate not being there?

Ew, never mind, his parents should definitely not be there. That's something I don't want them to see; I would be eternally mortified. But would they want to know beforehand? Does it matter to them?

"Ginger," I start, quietly trying to mentally form the question I want to ask.

"Yeah?"

"If Hunter and I bond as mates tonight, am I ruining some sacred ceremony by doing it this way? Secretive and all."

She smiles, and the affection in her expression has me holding my breath.

"No. You're not ruining anything, and trust me, no one will be upset. We don't have big, rehearsed ceremonies for it. But if you want a human wedding or party later, I will gladly make it happen."

My shoulders drop, and my heart bursts with a sparking joy I never knew myself capable of.

"Thanks, Ginger."

Sing Sweet Nightingale

She nods and steps away, leaving me alone to stare at my reflection. Rosy-cheeked, smiling like a fool, and deciding that I think I am going to wear the white dress tonight.

Chapter 34

Hunter

The last couple of days have flown by in a haze. A wonderful haze filled with Lottie. We remained hidden in my house the entire time. No one bothered us that we didn't invite over. I never brought up the mate bond again. Just in case it would force her to withdraw from me when we've grown so close. When everything is going so perfectly between us.

Aside from Vincent and the paparazzi, everything is perfect. Once we bond, if we bond, that problem will cease as well. Then, we can properly start building our life together.

Tonight is the blood moon. Shifters have already begun showing up at my house, bringing food and drinks to share. It's become a bit of an unofficial potluck. Shifting and fucking takes a lot of energy, and all tend to get hungry after.

Some are not shifters, though, and just come for the community or to run with their shifter mates or spouses. There are also a few outsiders we've come to accept as friends who come for every lunar eclipse, especially the ones who don't live too far away. Most of them are already in town, staying with friends or at the motel.

Ginger showed up with a large bag in hand and pulled Lottie into our room, locking me out, claiming girl time or whatever. Lottie could use a little girl time. And I like that she's become so close with Ginger. I just hope my sister doesn't force her into anything too fancy. One, because I would hate ruining it in the chase, and two, because I know that's not what Lottie wants. Her old life may have been all glitter and sparkle, but after getting to know her it's obvious she likes the simple pleasures in life. High quality, yes, but simple. She's had her fill of rhinestones and sequins, and I don't want her to feel pressured to wear something she hates.

Puttering around the house I straighten things and set up tables for the evening, knowing they'll be overflowing with food and drinks in no time.

My parents are some of the first to arrive, with handfuls of Tupperware containers and bottles of wine. I didn't tell them about possibly bonding with Lottie tonight, but they appear to have done a little extra tonight. Maybe just knowing she'd be here, they wanted to show her what a life with me could be. Welcome her into the pack and our family even without knowing by tomorrow that may be all too true.

Parents can be like that sometimes. Knowing things without ever being told. It was obvious to anyone looking how much we're drawn to each other. Concluding we are mates isn't too far of a jump to make.

Dottie and her family appear soon after, bringing an entire buffet with them. They always bring more than others, but again it's like they knew tonight was special without being told.

I greet them with warm smiles and open arms. My pack, my

family. The people I care about most and would do anything to protect. They would do the same for me and anyone else in the pack. We're shifters, we can't help it. Because of that, we form close bonds with each other.

Not to mention seeing each other butt naked every eclipse means we know more about each other than we want to sometimes.

It isn't until the yard is half full with shifters, a few other non-humans like Evelyn and Becca, and even one or two humans, that Lottie and my sister appear.

Even across the yard, through dozens of horny shifters and mingling scents of food, I still catch her gardenia and clove scent. Maddeningly strong and alluring. Drawing my eye directly to her cutting off the conversation I was having with Luca. I expect he walks away when he realizes I'm no longer paying attention to him because I don't hear him anymore as my body moves toward Lottie.

She's wearing a white dress that sways in the light breeze. Its short hem brushes against her thighs, and I hope she's not too cold.

I know a way I could warm her. My extremely horny inner beast purrs.

The closer I get to her, the pinker her cheeks and neck become, but her eyes never break contact with mine, and I ignore anyone who tries to speak to me or gets in my way. I think I even push one chatty nymph out of my way. I think it was Kai, so I'm not too concerned.

Lottie stands perfectly still, patiently waiting for me to make my way across the yard to her. My sister wisely scurries away, leaving Lottie and me alone.

There's a pink glistening on her lips, and her hair has soft waves that I want to run my fingers through. When I'm within touching distance, and her mate scent hits me, along with a heaping helping of desire, a deep primal growl rumbles in my chest and throat.

If anyone questioned my intentions with Lottie upon hearing my possessive and claiming growl, they no longer do.

She stands just above me on the deck, only a few short steps away, and my feet stop just at the bottom.

"You look . . ." My words fail me trying to pick the perfect word to describe how my mate looks at this moment. "Divine. Flawless. Exquisite. Mouthwateringly luscious."

Each of my words is soft but certain, leaving no room for argument. I know she's heard many of these things before, but I want her to know I mean every single one. That my words aren't empty and hollow.

I slowly make my way up the few steps as I speak, ending when I reach her. Taking the opportunity our position offers, I run the back of a finger up her exposed knee and thigh, brushing just under the hem of her dress before retracting my hand. Her breath catches, and her scent spikes, making my cock throb and my knot swell painfully, knowing soon I may be sliding it into her heat and locking us together. Both experiencing it together for the first time. The sensations amplified when I bite her and send us both into the greatest pleasure we've ever experienced and tie our life forces together as one.

My anticipation has me quickly closing the remaining distance between us. Wrapping an arm around her waist, the other cupping the back of her neck, my thumb circling to press down on her pulse point ever so slightly in a way I discovered I like as much as she does.

"Thank you," she whispers breathily once I have her secure in my arms. "Ginger picked the dress out."

"Remind me to thank her later."

Sing Sweet Nightingale

Ignoring the dozens of people surrounding us, I take my time with Lottie. Leaning in to kiss her, tasting the flavored lip gloss staining her lips. Watermelon. The kiss is slow and unhurried as we both take what we want. Our tongues languidly tangling with one another. Lottie's hands come up to wrap around my shoulders, digging into the short hair at the back of my head, and pulling at the loose collar of my shirt.

I didn't want to wear something I wouldn't want to ruin, so I chose a plain black T-shirt that's been well-worn. I won't care if I tear it to shreds in my lustful hurry to shift and chase my mate. My Nightingale.

We pull away, breathing heavily once we've both taken our fill. Lottie's eyes are glazed and half-lidded, and I'm sure mine are a mirror of hers.

Her smile spreads slowly across her face as she inspects me, her eyes shifting from my lips to my nose and eyes, following the line of my jaw. I don't know why she's inspecting me so closely, but I stand motionless, letting her.

"Ginger told me there would be food," she says coyly nibbling on her bottom lip. "I'm starved. Help a girl out?"

My chuckle is low, and I feel the budding joy growing in my chest.

"For you, my mate, anything."

It's the first time I've directly called Lottie mate, the word slipping out of its own accord, but I don't stop it. She is my mate. Whether we form the bond tonight or not, she is. That won't change.

She doesn't flinch or pull away; she only smiles wider, letting me lead her to one of the overflowing tables of food.

Her appetite is big, and she tries to taste everything but grows too full. Claiming she'll come back later for more. Hopefully, I can help her burn off her first helping. If she runs and we mate, she will definitely be hungry again later.

Normally, I would run with the rest of the pack or a female I had planned to work out my sexual needs with, without knotting, of course. Occasionally, though, a member of our family likes to run alone or privately, a section of our land is reserved for us. None of the others ever run there, even if no one decides to use it. Ryder uses it occasionally but more often than not, he goes far out on the edges of our property line and even beyond. Liking to be on his own.

But tonight, I've made sure it's known I'll be using that area, just in case Lottie said yes. If she doesn't, I'll use it to hunt and burn off the strongest of the moon's afflictions.

I think I've spoken to everyone present tonight, but the one person I can't seem to find is my brother. He's a bit of a loner, but he always makes an appearance, if not for anything other than the food. Looking around, I try to spot him. I catch sight of him near the edge of the clearing where the tree line meets the neatly manicured lawn. He doesn't look happy, though he never does.

Leaning down, I press my mouth close to Lottie's ear.

"I'm going to go talk to Ryder. Will you be okay by yourself?"

She turns and smiles up at me. "I'll be fine. Besides, I'm not alone."

She gestures with her head towards the gaggle of females chatting animatedly nearby. Apparently, I was so enrapt with my mate that I completely missed them there.

I incline my head with a short nod and press a kiss to her cheek before stepping away to speak with my brother and find out what the hell crawled up his butt lately.

As I get closer, I can see his rigid posture and unhappy frown.

"Your face is looking more morose than usual."

"Good evening to you too, brother," he grunts back at me.

"What is it with you lately? I've barely seen you, and you always seem to be in a foul mood. Is it because of Lottie and the mate bond?"

Ryder rears his head back and looks at me with disbelief. Offended I would suggest such a thing. But I had to check to know if me finding my mate upset him for some reason. It's already bad enough that I'm his younger brother and became alpha when he didn't. Even if he's told me that he never wanted to be alpha, it's always bothered me.

I always felt insignificant and unworthy when he was such a great leader. Historically, an alpha has always been the eldest. I felt like I was stepping on his tail when I accepted my role as alpha. I never want him to feel that he isn't adequate just because something beyond our understanding decided I should be alpha and not him.

"Of course not. I'm happy for you and Lottie. She's a great girl, and Mom and Ginger already love her. Pretty sure everyone in town already does, too."

My shoulders relax a fraction, satisfied he isn't upset because of us, but I'm still worried about his demeanor lately.

"Then what is it? I know it's something."

He grinds his back teeth and clenches his jaw, letting out a long-controlled breath. It's not like my brother to keep things from me. If anything, in the past, he's been honest to a fault. Telling it to me straight and blunt. Lately, he's been quiet; running off the moment he is no longer needed, and I worry why.

"You remember that blogger I told you about? Tess."

"Yeah, I remember."

"Well, she's . . . been more to deal with than I expected."

I narrow my eyes at him, trying to read between the

lines, which is nearly impossible to do with him. But I try. His shoulders are tight, and he keeps flexing his hands. His eyes keep shifting rapidly all over the place but always seem to stray back to one area, expecting something or perhaps someone to appear.

"Are you waiting for someone?"

"What?"

His shifting eyes lock on to me and finally hold still for two seconds. In them, I read surprise and guilt? My brother has never felt guilty for anything in his life, including breaking my arm when he pushed me off the roof. Or so I believed, due to his indifferent and detached nature. Perhaps there's more to his emotions hidden under the surface that he doesn't share with anyone.

"You seem like you're waiting for someone. Expecting someone special?" I ask carefully.

He grunts and shifts on his heels, shoving his hands in his pockets.

"That's what I'm trying to tell you. That girl, Tess. Well, she sort of figured out what we are, and to keep her from exposing us, I promised she could come tonight. To see the shift and maybe prove to her we aren't as horrible as she thinks we are."

I've rarely been angry with my brother, but right now, I'm fucking furious. He was supposed to get her out of town and out of our hair. I don't need this shit tonight, not when it could turn into the best night of my life.

"What the fuck, Ryder? You were supposed to get her to leave town, not share all our secrets with her. What the hell is wrong with you?"

"I don't know, okay!" he barks back at me, growing angry right alongside me. The only emotion he rarely shows. "She's under my skin. She drives me fucking insane, but I also can't tell her no. I've tried; trust me, I've fucking tried. But I always end up giving in. I couldn't just dust her. Her obsession with shifters goes back too far, and it wouldn't work. I thought..."

He huffs out a reluctant breath, trying to gain control of his emotions. Something I've never seen happen before. He's always calm and controlled. To be frazzled and disoriented is uncharacteristic of him. I think about what he's said about this girl; maybe there's something special about her. Special like Lottie.

"I thought if I could show her shifters aren't the horrid beasts she thinks we are, that we're just normal people, she might give up her quest to expose us."

I watch my brother with quizzical and wary eyes. Depending on the circumstances, this could either end really well or very badly.

"So, you just thought you would bring her to a blood moon lunar eclipse with dozens of shifters and non-humans, and she wouldn't expose us after running a paranormal conspiracy theory website for years? Yeah, that makes sense." My tone drips with derision. I thought my brother was smarter than this.

"Look, I know it sounds crazy; I'm pretty sure I've lost all my marbles at this point. Just trust me, okay. I won't let anything happen to anyone or the town."

Gripping his shoulder and squeezing, I see the determination and need in his expression.

"I do trust you."

"How did you... how did you know Lottie was your mate?" Ryder asks sheepishly.

The question's surprising. Ryder never believed in love and all the sentimentality that comes along with it. Accepting a mate would be a big step for him. It's based on equal trust and exposing all your insides to the other. Something he's not very good at.

"I just did. I trusted my instinct to show me the right path, and it did. Once I learned it was possible for her to be my mate as a human, I stopped fighting it. Stopped fighting myself and gave in. That's all you can do. Allow it to consume you, and you never know, you might like it."

From his grim, sour look, he doesn't seem to like my answer, but it's the only one I have.

He huffs out a breath, and the tension in his shoulders slackens with . . . defeat? It instantly returns when his eyes catch on something and stick. I don't immediately turn to see what, instead inspecting my brother.

His flaring nostrils and dilating pupils, the tensing of his muscles, and the grinding of his jaw all indicate something more. His scent, although minimal compared to Lottie's, still lingers in my nostrils, it's sharp and musky. Desire, anticipation, anxiety, excitement, and anger linger together in a maelstrom of emotions. More than I've ever scented on my brother before.

Only after studying Ryder for a long moment do I turn to seek out what's drawn his attention. A tall, lean redhead is skirting around the yard's edges, avoiding contact with anyone, but watching curiously at everyone enjoying the food and drink. The moon hasn't fully risen in the night sky, and no one has shifted yet, except for one or two pups who are in wolf form, playing and running between legs.

She's dressed in all black, and I'm pretty sure I see the hilt of a knife in her boot. A rumble rolls in my chest, a small warning she can't hear, but Ryder can.

Turning back to my brother, I pin him with a sharp look. It takes everything in me to hold back the alpha command in my voice. I don't want to use it on him; I shouldn't have to.

"Keep her away from the others, especially the pups, and if she dares to try to use that knife in her boot, I will personally take care of her. *Understood?*"

A deep, agitated, and protective growl curls Ryder's lips. He dares to disrespect me and challenge my command?

I elongate my claws and prick them into the muscle of his shoulder before infusing my responding snarl with alpha power. It doesn't always have to be put into words. Just having intent and meaning infused into a growl or howl can be just as powerful.

His snarl quiets, his eyes flash, and his nostrils flare, but I can see him gaining control again, submitting to me as he drops his eyes to the ground.

"Yes, Alpha. I understand," he grits out.

It may not sound like he is submitting, but I know how hard it is to fight against your own instinct. He's trying. He doesn't yet realize what he's already involved in with this girl, but I think I'm starting to understand now.

"Good. Keep her away from the west woods. It's off-limits tonight. I'll be running there—with Lottie," I add, putting meaning behind my unspoken words.

Ryder's scowl softens, and his eyebrows lift a little in shock. His dark steely eyes look almost black in the dimming light, and understanding washes away his previous anger.

"Really? Tonight?"

"Maybe."

He nods, settling once again back into his normal stoic self—focused and diligent. His scent recedes back to the neutral, nondescript scent of bland coldness, lacking any sharp emotion of any kind.

"I will. And congratulations, brother. She will make a great mate."

"Thank you."

I scent the redhead Tess nearing us, and I decide it's probably best to leave Ryder to his own female while I get back to mine. Giving him one last reassuring squeeze, I release his shoulder and turn on my heel, heading for Lottie and her bright laughter.

Chapter 35
Lottie

This is it. The moon is full in the sky, and the eclipse is not far off, giving the moon a ruddy red coloring. The time has come, and people are peeling away from the crowd to enter the forest. Thankfully, before they strip naked.

Hunter eyes me with hungry anticipation, licking his lips and reaching for me. I let him pull me into his arms and kiss me. It's a deep, passionate kiss that I feel over my entire body. His touch is more electric than it has ever been. Because of the eclipse? The full moon? Who the fuck knows, but I love it.

"What is your decision, little bird? Will I be chasing you into the forest tonight? Or will I have to wait and ravage you when I return from my run?"

He doesn't try to guilt me into deciding or push me into choosing. Either way, he will return to me tonight, and I'll still be in his bed. There's no ultimatum or demand—just a question, the answer to which is completely up to me.

I give him my sweetest smile and step backward, slowly

slipping out of his hold. Trailing my fingers down his arms and biting my lip, I watch him practically grow bigger as he tamps down his shift, waiting for my decision.

I already know my answer. My decision was probably made the moment he asked me. I just had to come to terms with it.

Taking a few more steps away from him, I make sure he's out of arm's reach before stopping. He continues watching me, his cock straining against his zipper and his breaths heavy in his chest.

Slipping my hands under my skirt, I can see his eyes widen and dilate at the movement. His nostrils flare as he inhales my scent. I know that's what he's doing; he likes to smell me. A lot.

Hooking my thumbs on the sides of my panties, I slowly begin to pull them down my hips. I made sure to double-check that everyone else was already leaving or gone before starting my little seduction. That part of me that's still stuck in celebrity mode, ensuring there's no one around to witness or photograph our intimate moment.

The white cotton panties, which are damp with my arousal, slide down easily, and I step out of them. Bundling them in my hand, I toss them at Hunter, who catches them easily. Instantly, he brings them to his nose and inhales deeply. A rumbling purr growl emanates from his chest, and he doesn't dampen it, letting it roll out his throat.

"Your smell is heavenly, sweet Lottie."

"Then I'm sure you'll have no problem following it," I tease the moment before I turn on my heel and bolt.

I don't look back. I know I won't be able to outrun him, but I'll have at least a minute head start. Hopefully. He still has to remove his clothes and shift after all.

I don't pause or delay, wanting to get as much distance between us as I can to make the chase more exciting. Not bothering to pay attention to where I'm going, I run through the forest. I do make sure to keep the west, though. Ginger told me this area is off-limits to the others. It's just for us. So, I don't have to worry about other shifters chasing me or seeing my inevitable mating with Hunter. Because it is inevitable now. I've run, and he's chasing; there's no going back.

A high-pitched laugh escapes my throat and resonates through the trees whizzing by. My legs pump beneath me, years of forced fitness routines and running to try and escape my life but never getting anywhere, finally being put to good use. I make it far into the trees when I hear the howl. It sends a shiver through my body and collates in my pussy, making the slickness there grow.

Perhaps running through the forest without panties while extremely horny wasn't a good idea. It's only increasing the needy pulse between my thighs. The friction and pressure are a pleasurable torment.

In the near distance, I can hear breaking branches and howls growing in volume—closer than the far-off quiet ones, which I assume are the others. Above me, the moon continues to rise high in the sky and grow a deeper shade of red.

After what seems like forever, I stop to take a breath, holding myself steady on a large tree trunk. Looking around, I don't see anything—no movement of any kind. That doesn't assuage my racing heart, which grows more and more excited with every passing second. My blood heats in anticipation.

Then I hear it—a low growl and a quiet rustling of leaves to my left. I jerk to face the sound. I see nothing but a pair of glowing glacier-blue eyes in the darkness, washed in a red fog.

The sight should frighten me, but it only makes me smile. I crook my finger at Hunter, beckoning him.

"Come and get me, beast," I taunt in a low voice.

I know he can hear me, so I don't bother yelling. Again, I don't wait; I turn and run. My laughter rings out in the quiet night behind me. Twigs snap, and branches reach out to trying to grab me as I run. I'm glad I cut my hair; otherwise, it would have gotten snagged on a stray branch long ago.

I'm also grateful to Ginger for her choice of clothing. The dress is light and breathable, allowing a breeze to pass through as I run, keeping me cool as my temperature increases. I thought I would be cold, but it's exactly what I needed to help cool my heated flesh.

I can hear Hunter getting nearer, but he doesn't catch me—yet. Either he's enjoying the chase too much or he's waiting for something.

I sense more than see him on my left, so I turn right, banking hard between the trees, using my hold on a trunk to swing me without having to slow. The bark is smooth and worn so as not to scrape up my palms.

I realize as soon as I see the small clearing that Hunter was directing me here. He wanted me to turn right, so he ran to my left, forcing me in this direction.

It isn't until I step foot into the small blood moon-washed meadow that he pounces on me. All nine-plus feet of him and however many hundreds of pounds. He doesn't crash into me or knock me down; he wraps me in his large, furry arms and scoops me up off the ground.

My heart pounds in my chest, the chase having amplified that already burning desire and need inside. I can feel my nipples rub against the soft cotton of the dress since I opted out of a bra. Strangely, another of Ginger's suggestions.

Hunter's arms are secure around me but not tight enough to cause concern. His claws are retracted so as not to scratch me, and he pulls me against his chest, rubbing his face against me just like he did as a wolf before. Rubbing his scent on me, I now know.

His hot breath huffs from his snout. I reach up and wrap both arms around his jaw, not at all concerned or afraid of the razor-sharp teeth inside. At least not yet, soon he'll be biting me with those fangs. Hopefully, in a much smaller capacity, though. He's so much larger than me in his true form. If he were to try to bite me like this, he could easily remove an arm.

Walking a few steps deeper into the clearing, placing us directly under the moon's rays, he finally sets me down.

When I get my feet under me, I turn to face him. He's still in the same form, and I marvel at his body. Strong, feral, and all mine. That's also when I notice something else he didn't show me before.

His cock is out. And it's fucking huge. Like a small baseball bat. I suppose it had to be equivalent in size to his body. The larger the beast, the larger his cock. Makes sense.

The shaft is dark pink and thick, hard and stretching out towards me, leaking precum from the massive head. The knot at the base throbbing and swelling. Causing a corresponding throb to pulse in my pussy and clit.

I may have to take back what I said about women's bodies being able to handle a lot. I'm not entirely sure I could handle even half of him. For a moment, I'm bummed I'm not a shifter, so I could experience him in this form.

Before he can shift back to human form, or at least a smaller, more manageable size, I step forward and reach out. Slicking my fingers around the tip, spreading the precum around to moisten the head. He's large but not too large that I can't at least take a taste.

I may have been overexaggerating the baseball bat size. It's still immensely impressive, though the longer I consider it, the more I think with some prep, it might not be inconceivable to consider taking him like this. Thick enough I can't wrap my hand completely around it, and at least as long as my forearm. I don't think it's physically possible to fit that much length inside me. But oh, how I would enjoy trying.

Lowering my head, I lap at the tip, sliding the flat of my tongue up the underside of the crown, flicking the tip of my tongue in his slit.

Hunter groan-growls above me, his body shaking with barely restrained control. He wants to take me but doesn't want to hurt me. Gripping tight under the crown, I squeeze and seal my mouth over the entire head. Hollowing out my cheeks as I suck hard.

I can feel trickles of moisture leak onto my tongue, and I swallow greedily. His taste makes me wetter, and the slick between my thighs is embarrassingly growing as I suck on his giant cock. He's so tall that I don't even need to kneel and only have to barely bend over to reach him.

I try to take as much of him as I can into my mouth and throat, which isn't that much, but he seems to like it all the same. I feel his large hands reach down and slide up in between my legs from behind. His huge finger reaches the apex of my thighs, and my dripping pussy, and he doesn't hesitate, running the soft velvety pad of his finger through my slit. Rubbing the wetness into my clit with a gentle caress.

My body shakes with the force of the small touch, and I groan around his cock, which makes it pulse and thicken in my mouth and hand.

His fingers disappear from my pussy and grip my waist, pulling me away from him.

Without letting me go, he shifts so quickly it's barely a few seconds before he's more man than beast, standing in front of me, breathing heavily.

There's still fur up the sides of his neck and on his forearms, and from his knee down, he's still furry with large paws instead of feet. His teeth are still overly large and pointed, his ears poke through the dark tangles of his hair, surprisingly adorable fury points on top of his head. As if he couldn't concentrate enough to shift completely. A swishing movement behind him reveals his fluffy tail still protruding from his backside.

His mouth slams against mine with a snarl, and I can see the crazed lust fog glassing over his eyes.

"I need to fuck you now, Lottie, and I can't be gentle."

"I want you to. I want that knot of yours shoved so far inside me we may never separate."

His growl is a guttural groan, and I can feel the prick of claws on my waist. Forcefully, he spins me and presses down on my shoulders, bringing me to my knees. His body presses to mine and further forces me to my hands.

He nearly covers my entire body with his, hunching over me, larger than his normal human height.

I can feel the heat and hardness of his cock, now a more manageable size, slide against my back and bare exposed ass as he pushes the skirt of my dress up out of the way. One of his massive hands plants on the ground by my head, the lingering fur on his body tickling every inch of exposed skin it rubs against, sending pleasurable tingling shivers across my body.

"Yes, Hunter. Fuck, I need you," I moan, shamelessly trying to push my ass back against him.

He groans when I manage to grind his cock between us.

"Sit still, little bird, and I'll give you everything you want. You want this cock? You can have it. You want this knot? It's yours. You want my heart? You can keep it; it already belongs to you," Hunter purrs against my ear, promising me everything and more.

"Spread your knees for me, Nightingale."

I do as he commands, spreading my knees and arching my back to present myself to him.

"Perfect. Look at your dripping wet pussy ready for my cock."

Tauntingly he rubs the head of his cock through my wetness and teases my entrance without entering. I whimper in need, unable to do much else in my overly stimulated and mindless state.

"That's right, little mate. You want me to rut inside you and fill you with my cum. Seal myself inside you with my knot."

"Yes!" I scream. "Fuck me, fill me. I need it, need you. Now Hunter. Please."

I am not above begging at this point. My wetness practically drips down my inner thighs, and I can feel my pussy contracting around nothing because he's still not inside me. He's drawing this out and teasing me.

"As you wish, mate."

I can feel the head of his cock line up once again, but this time, he inches it inside, just the tip, and slowly rocks his hips.

"Oohh, yes," I moan. "More."

Since he's behind me, I can't see his expression, but I can see his one hand on the ground, his claws extended, and digging deep into the soft grassy ground below. The other hand is gripping tight low on my hip and ass. It shifts higher to cup my breast through the soft cotton material. My hardened nipples shamelessly poking through. The contact heightening my arousal.

A loud groan is my only warning before he slams his entire length inside me, knocking me forward onto my elbows. I shriek in pleasure and ecstasy at being filled so fully. The tight stretch is divine. My wetness makes his entrance easy and swift, only a tiny pinch as my body stretches and relaxes, adjusting to him. His size slightly bigger than normal. I realize I haven't even taken his knot yet. There's still more of him, and I whimper, wanting it all.

"Fuck you take me so good," he grunts, pumping his hips a few times in long hard thrusts. "Do you want more mate?"

"Yes," I answer immediately. "I want it all."

His chest vibrates with a growl against my back, and I feel him swell inside me, his cock growing. Not just getting harder but bigger.

"Oh fuck. Oh my god, Hunter. That feels..."

"I knew you could take more of me; you're my mate, after all. Your body is made to take mine. Don't worry, I won't give you my cock in its largest form, just enough to fill you to the brim and ring out every scream of pleasure."

His promise makes my pussy flutter around his hard length, responding to his words. He begins to move behind me in earnest now. Happy with how his cock fills and stretches me to the max. With every stroke and deep thrust, my body rocks forward, held in place by the hand on my breast and the arm at my shoulder.

The dulled tips of his claws prick at the swell of my breast, pulling the neckline down enough to expose my hard nipple. His dull claw scratches at the pebbled peak and circles the delicate flesh. The pain and pleasure mingling in a way I've never experienced before.

The sounds of his driving hips smacking into my ass fill the empty space around us, mingling with my broken moans and his feral growling. That swollen knot of his grinding against my clit with each pound into me.

I can feel every inch of him as he pulls out and slams back in alternating from long, hard thrusts to short, fast pumps. Those ones make my body shake with the force of the movement and coiling pressure at my clit. My orgasm builds, and I know it's going to shatter me when I climax.

"Not yet, Lottie. You don't come yet. You come when I tell you."

He punctuates his words with more punishing pumps, and his cock slides effortlessly inside me with the intense wetness of my arousal.

"Oh god, it feels too good, I can't. I need to come."

"You will baby all over me, but not until I knot you, understand."

It's not a question but a command, and it makes me quiver as he licks a path up the side of my neck and nibbles on the sensitive skin beneath my ear, his fingers pinching my bared nipple.

I whine, trying to not come, though I can feel it throbbing in my pussy. I won't be able to wait long.

Hunter's pace picks up, and his cock is hard and thick inside me, then he seeds himself to the root just above his knot, rubbing it against every part of me front and back, and I moan loudly into the grass, resting my temple against the soft blades.

With little resistance but just enough to cause a bolt of unimaginable pleasure, Hunter presses into me. His knot stretching and filling me in the most delicious way. It's tight and so fucking good.

"God damn it, you're so fucking tight on my knot. I've never felt anything like it. Fuck. Are you reading to come for me, Lottie?" he asks sweetly panting with his own excerssion.

I nod, so fucking ready. His hips cant and rock against me, unable to pull free now with his knot inside me, and the sensation is unbelievable. I've never felt so full and tight and connected to another, and not just physically. I feel him in my mind and heart. A warm presence I could find in the darkest of nights, even if I went blind. I would find him.

His movements become jerky and erratic.

"I need to bite you now. I promise it will only sting for a second. You ready, my sweet mate?"

"Yes," I whimper, the impending orgasm sitting on a knife's edge in my body, waiting desperately to crest and fall, crash with the force of a million hurricanes, and break me.

The graze of his sharp teeth runs along the column of my neck, and he doesn't have to say anything else. When the sharp points of his fangs break my skin, and his mouth locks onto my shoulder, my climax breaks. Crashes through me with a force so powerful my entire body quakes and shakes.

I scream, and my pussy clamps down on his cock just as I feel it pulse and throb and release his cum inside me. His orgasm wreaks its own havoc on his body as he spasms over me, pressing down, getting as close to me as possible. His hips press flush against my ass, his fangs and mouth suck at my neck, his slightly furry legs rub against the back of my thighs, his fingers pinch my nipple, and his massive cock spasms inside me, and every part of it intensifies my orgasm. It goes on for so long I fear I may pass out as I flutter and clench Hunter's twitching cock.

Gently, he retracts his teeth from my neck and licks at the wounds. My head is dizzy with the aftershocks of my orgasm. My body feels like goo, and I'm not sure how much longer I can remain in this position without falling over.

When I shift, trying to regain my balance, Hunter groans.

"Stay still, Lottie. I can't pull out yet. Not until my knot shrinks."

"Right, forgot. Just, my legs are like jelly. I don't know if I can hold myself up much longer."

Immediately, Hunter presses up off the ground. The movement causes another orgasm to ripple through me unexpectedly. Far smaller than the first but still a pulse of unimaginable bliss.

Hunter feels it too, and stills momentarily. His cock jerking inside me. Did he just come again, too?

"Easy Nightingale. Still sensitive and coming again only makes my knot swell further, and we'll never get it out," he chuckles, but it sounds like he might like that idea.

When he composes himself enough, he grips my hips and rolls to the ground, pulling me with him. Easing the strain on my legs and spooning me against his chest. Tossing my leg over the top of his, allowing for a more comfortable position with his cock still locked inside me.

"Much better," he mumbles into the back of my hair.

His arms wrap around me, and I notice they're no longer furry. When I sneak a glance at his legs, there are once again feet and not paws.

Hunter sighs in contentment, and as he relaxes, so do I.

I just mated a shifter, and I'm not mad about it. Because it was the most amazing thing I've ever experienced.

Chapter 36

Hunter

My mate is divine. Her scent washes over me, and mine over her, and as the bond solidifies, I can feel her there. Her presence a glittering shadow in my mind directing me to her—a blinding beacon.

I rumble a low satisfied purr against her back, and her light giggle is enough for me to feel it all the way to my cock. Which was softening but stiffens again at the small vibrations.

I don't fucking care if I'm connected to her for the rest of the night. There's no place I'd rather be.

Pressing up on my elbow, I lean up enough to see Lottie's face as she lies at my side. Her white dress crumpled up to her breasts with small grass stains and a leaf stuck to it. She looks perfect, like a wild animal. *My* wild animal.

Gently brushing back her tangled windswept hair, she looks up at me and gives me a smile that I'll remember for eternity. Whenever I'm overworked, stressed, agitated or angry, sad or contrite, I'll think of this smile, and every worry I've ever possessed will disappear. Because when a woman looks at you like this, you know you'll never love another, and you'll never want for anything more than her.

I hold myself over her and lean down to steal a kiss.

"I love you, Lottie Pickle," I whisper in the quiet stillness of the meadow. "With every fiber of my being I promise I will always protect you and love you. I would gladly give my life if it would ensure yours. You may think we haven't known each other long enough to claim such a thing, but we have the rest of our lives for me to prove you wrong."

I press another soft kiss to her lips, and Lottie loops her arm around my neck, holding me close.

"I love you too, Hunter Evans. I may not know everything about your world, and it may take me time to figure things out, but I do know that. Even if it scares me, somehow I just know everything will turn out okay."

Her words soothe the last aching fear inside. Melting away the lingering doubt and filling the space with euphoria.

"Good, because I plan on making you extremely happy for the rest of eternity," I proclaim with a nuzzle against her neck.

She giggles again, stoking my ever-present desire for her.

"You keep making that sound, Mate, and we'll be here all night."

"What sound? You mean my laugh?"

Her voice is laced with a purring seduction that goes straight to my balls, pulling them tight against the base of my knot. Which was coming loose from her pussy but now swells again with fresh arousal.

"Yes, that," I grind out between clenched teeth.

Then, my tempting Nightingale masterfully seduces me all over again, sending me into another rutting frenzy. This time I roll onto my back, shifting her to straddle me backwards, watching her perfect ass bounce on my cock until we both come again. Her hands firmly planted on my chest behind her, and her back arched like a goddamn contortionist, as trickles of my cum leak around my knot and down my thighs.

It takes at least another hour to satiate our hunger for one another and to get my knot to finally slip free. It didn't help that she kept tempting and seducing me every time it got close to releasing. Eventually, even my Nightingale tires from all the orgasms, and I carry her back to the house.

When we arrive at the edge of the clearing, I set her down and redress in the discarded clothing I tossed on the ground when I took off after her. My shirt is ripped as expected, but my jeans managed to survive my manic undressing. Her white panties are still tucked securely in my pocket. I don't give them back to her.

Lottie tries to straighten her dress and hair, but there's not much she can do about the grass stains. I rather like seeing them on her. I may have her frame this dress in remembrance of tonight. Stains and all.

Others have also returned to the house in just as disheveled a state, but most have shifted so often that they look just as put together now as they did when they first arrived, like Ginger. I don't see Ryder anywhere, though. Hopefully, he's keeping that blogger away. I'm not sure I trust her, even if she could be my brother's mate.

Ginger runs up to us, holding Lottie's Polaroid camera.

"Smile," she yells before snapping a picture of us. Barely allowing time for us to prepare.

She pulls the photo from the camera and waves it around, trying to get it to develop faster, even though we both know it does nothing.

"That is going to be a good one."

Ginger hands the camera and the photo to Lottie and catches sight of the healing bite mark on Lottie's neck. It will heal, leaving only minimal scars, just enough to be visible and remind us of our bonding.

"I see everything went well," she says with a joyous grin. "Y'all must be famished after such a vigorous night. There's still plenty of food; make sure to eat," she says, eyeing both of us.

"Yes, Mom," I chide in a sarcastic tone.

Ginger doesn't even scold me for mocking her. She's too happy for us both to care.

My parents meet us at the food table, all smiles and knowing glances. They make conversation but don't mention the bite marks or Lottie's state of dress, thankfully.

Every time a small breeze blows through the yard, Lottie has to hold down her skirt since she's not wearing any underwear. When I notice goosebumps on her skin as the night goes on, I bring a blanket from the living room and wrap it around her shoulders. It's long enough to cover her past her knees.

By the end of the night, it's only Ginger, Evelyn and her mate Abe, and Lottie and I sitting around a dying fire in the fire pit on the back porch. Lottie curled in my lap, wrapped in my arms and blanket, resting her head on my shoulder. Her fingers twine in mine, fiddling mindlessly. Her body has gone lax in my lap, and I can feel her drifting off.

"Come on, Lottie, let's get you to bed."

She mumbles something incoherent, nuzzling her face into the crook of my neck. Looping my arms around her back and under her knees, I cradle her close and stand.

"I think it's time we turn in. You're welcome to stay as long as you like, but my—" I pause, deciding if I should reveal our new mated status. Here, among my sister and two close friends

I trust, I feel comfortable enough that they'll respect Lottie and me. "My mate seems to be tuckered out after her first lunar eclipse celebration."

A chorus of quiet goodnights rings out, and even though I said they could stay, they all stand and gather their belongings to leave.

Carrying Lottie inside, I make my way up to our room and sit her on the bed, untangling the throw blanket from around her shoulders. It along with her white grass-stained dress end up on the floor, and I strip out of my own clothes before climbing into bed next to her.

Her warm, naked body curls against mine, and the moment we touch, I purr in contentment. I fall asleep with the scent of our mixed scents from our mating filling my nose. The feel of her soft golden hair tickling my neck and the heat of her body warming my own.

My *mate*.

My Nightingale.

My Lottie.

Chapter 37
Lottie

We sleep in after our long night yesterday, not getting out of bed until my stomach growls in protest of its emptiness.

"Sounds like my mate is hungry," Hunter mutters while pressing kisses to my bare collarbone. "It's a good thing I am an excellent cook, unlike my sweet Nightingale."

I laugh, his scruffy chin tickling my skin. Pushing him away, I try to escape his hold, which he only tightens at my meager attempts.

"Hey, I'm learning and getting better. A few more lessons with your mom, and I'll be a pro."

"But I like cooking for you. I like that there's something I can do for you."

He stops trying to kiss and tickle me and leans up to look down at me under him.

"I will never ask you to do anything you don't want to. We may be a partnership now, but I will honor all your decisions and never force you to make one unwillingly. I promise Lottie that you'll be happy here with me. If not, I will gladly move anywhere you wish. Even if that means going back to Los Angeles."

"I don't want to go back to LA," I state firmly, surprising myself with the declaration.

Until this moment, I hadn't even known I'd made that decision. But it feels right. That's not my home anymore. It hasn't been for a long time. I'll figure out how to get my personal belongings from the mansion, and something will have to be done about my royalties, records, and merchandise lines. Although I've never had anything to do with them before, why should I now? I don't even care about them.

"Does that mean you want to stay here?" Hunter asks quietly.

I smile, for once able to give him a definitive answer.

"Yes."

"Well, then, I guess I should get to making us breakfast."

With swift, easy strength, Hunter scoops me into his arms and carries me out of the room, both of us still completely naked. And that's how I end up watching him make breakfast in nothing but an apron.

~

It's been almost two days since the full moon, and Hunter has been restless all day. Not only that but there is an influx of people at the house today. Ginger and Ryder weren't surprises, but Fynn, Tobias and Kai are. I thought Hunter didn't like Kai? Whatever their presence means, I don't get the feeling it's a good thing.

I find Hunter standing out on the front porch, watching down the driveway expectantly.

"Hey," I call, rounding him to lean against the post to his

left. "What are you doing out here?"

"Nothing, just watching."

"Watching what?"

He doesn't immediately answer, his fingers twitching restlessly at his side. Watching him patiently, I wait to see if he's going to tell me what's going on or not. It irritates me when people keep me in the dark, thinking they know better for me than I do. I may trust Hunter with my life, but that doesn't mean he can keep secrets from me. I frown and he sees it, exhaling harshly before resignation settles in his gaze.

"I'm watching for Vincent. He said he would be coming here today to force me to sign my property over to him. I have no intentions to do so, and I'm trying to mentally prepare for his arrival and trying to decide what form I should take to make my final answer crystal clear to him. I'd like to rip him limb from limb in my true form, but I think I'll start with my bare human hands. A good beat down always sates my protective instinct."

My eyes widen in shock. I kind of wasn't expecting him to answer nor to divulge so much.

"I don't want to keep things from you, Lottie. I know that's how you used to be treated, and I don't want to do that. I won't lie to you, but I also won't sugarcoat it. I very much plan on fighting Vincent, and things will get bloody."

I cringe not just because of the prospect of blood but that he could get injured. I reach out and clasp his twitching hand in mine, and he squeezes.

"I appreciate that. But isn't there some other way we can convince him to just leave without reverting to violence? I don't want anyone to get hurt. Least of all you."

He cups my cheek and gives me what is supposed to be a reassuring smile, but I don't feel very reassured.

"I love that you're concerned for me, Lottie, but sometimes this is how things have to be handled. Elves are stubborn, selfish creatures and sometimes require more than words to persuade. Don't worry, everything will be fine. I'll be fine. Ginger and Ryder will be fine. We've done this before, and we'll most likely have to do it again in the future."

That doesn't make me feel any better.

Leaning into his touch, I attempt to be as calm and confident as he is. I'm not sure it's working.

Hunter's ears perk and his head cuts back to the gravel road leading to his property. I don't hear anything, but that doesn't mean there isn't anything there. His hearing is far superior to mine.

"They're here," he growls. "Inside Lottie. I don't want you getting caught in the middle of anything out here. I need you safe."

Guiding me quickly back to the front door, he motions me inside ahead of him. Ryder is there waiting to greet us. Most likely waiting the whole time for Hunter to announce Vincent's arrival.

"Ginger!" he barks out, and his sister immediately appears in the entryway. "Take Lottie upstairs. The rest of you, outside with me."

I'm handed off to Ginger, who gently but firmly grips my wrist, directing me away from the rest and the front door. Before I get too far, Hunter places a swift kiss on my lips that I barely have time to process.

And just like that, Hunter and the others are outside fanning out on the front drive, and I'm being led upstairs out of the line of fire.

We perch in a spare room with a window overlooking the front of the property. This allows us a view of the others below and the approaching black SUVs just breaking through the line of trees at the entrance to the property.

They circle and park, there are three, and all manner of non-humans spill from them. At least a dozen. Elves mostly, but there are also nymphs, one fairy, and others who must be shifters or meres because they look human even without a glamour. Which I can now see through, thanks to my fairy dusting.

The one I recognize without a shadow of a doubt is Vincent. His gray skin is dull in the hazy sunlight, but the adornments on his ears and fingers glint like crystal under a spotlight.

We're too far away to hear, and Ginger won't let me open the window or get any closer. But I can tell by their body language Hunter has just told him what he can do with his blackmail and demands.

The argument grows heated as we watch. Vincent's men pacing behind him. One of them slowly unbuttons his shirt; he must be a shifter. Another has grass green hair and skin the color of bark, and the trees around him grow and slither like living beings.

Although standing stock still, Ryder looks about ready to literally jump out of his skin and tear the face off the man opposite him. Tobias, the freaking fairy with gossamer wings and all, looks just as angry but like calm, focused anger that doesn't even scratch the surface of his unseen abilities.

Whereas Kai, the red-striped nymph, leans casually on the porch, his tail swaying lazily behind him, not a care in the world, rolling a tiny ball of fire in the palm of his hand. His red hair is the only part of him that looks similar to the man I met at karaoke. I may have stared for a whole minute at him when he arrived. He didn't seem to mind, but Hunter did.

I can't focus on any of the others right now for more than

a fleeting moment. Hunter and Vincent take up the bulk of my attention. They're mere feet apart, and I can see Hunter growing in size, readying for a swift shift. And in the blink of an eye, Vincent sparks the battle they were all waiting for with one sweeping arc of his fist.

Hunter's body rips through his clothing, and his beast emerges biting, jowls reaching for Vincent. I barely notice Ryder's shift and the others clashing together. A literal battle has broken out on the front lawn, and I'm stuck up here watching, unable to do a damn thing as those below slash, bite, and tear into one another.

A strange phantom pain begins to grow in my chest, and I clutch at it, breathing heavily. It's as if I can feel every swiping graze of Vincent's blade that catches Hunter's flesh. A pounding warning that my mate is in danger, his presence in my mind a blaring neon sign pointing me directly to him.

Ginger holds me by my shoulders, and it's then I realize I'm trying to break free. To what? Run out into the fight? I would be mincemeat in a matter of seconds.

I hate feeling so helpless and weak. I've felt this way for too long.

For too long, I let others walk all over me and control my fate and life. Years I've spent under the thumb of others. My decisions and choices taken from me, by people like Vincent. Like my mother. Others who believe themselves above me, better than me. As if their wants and desires outweigh my own.

A burning hatred grows in my stomach, igniting a fiery wrath that I want to unleash upon the world. I want to put people like Vincent in their place. To show him and others that we are not less than him just because he says so. We are not here to bend to his will and do his bidding simply because he says we should.

I am no longer afraid of self-centered, egotistical, narcissistic assholes like him. And I will not let him take my new family and life from me.

"Let me go," I growl out in command to Ginger, needing to follow that burning demand in my chest to go to my mate. Ginger, surprisingly, instantly releases me.

With my newfound freedom and burning ire, I run from the room, heading straight for the front door. Straight for my mate, my friends, and the new target of my anger. Vincent.

When I burst through the front door, none of the fighting non-humans notice. None except Hunter, who must have scented my arrival when I stepped out of the house. The momentary distraction allows Vincent an opening to attack, his shiny large dagger poised to slash down upon my mate, directed at his throat, wishing to slash and kill.

"STOP!"

My voice rings out loud and demanding, echoing in the open space. An angry command in a tone that I've never heard before. Much to my surprise and shock, every single one of them stops mid-movement. Freezing like statues. Claws about to rip into flesh, fire and water magic poised midair reaching for its target all come to a halt.

The ache in my chest that told me Hunter was in danger simmers out, only to be replaced with the hatred I have for Vincent.

With confidence I finally feel, I stride forward, weaving between shifters, nymphs, and fairies. Many drop their position of attack and watch me pass. Shocked perhaps that I would be ballsy enough to walk head lifted through the middle of a fight such as this.

When I reach Hunter and Vincent, I step directly between them, Hunter to my back, a hulking form that only fortifies my nerves, steeling my spine with his love and support.

Vincent stares at me disbelieving, a baffled frown on his face. His thin lips pinched tight in a straight line. He doesn't speak, and that suits me just fine.

"I have had enough of arrogant bullies like you thinking you have any right to control others."

I punctuate my words with a sharp finger poking into Vincent's chest. The action isn't strong by any means, but he still stumbles backward.

"I have had enough of being told what I can do and having people like you think they're better than me simply because they decided so. No more. No more sitting back and letting assholes like you walk all over me. From now on, I control my life, not you!"

I poke him again in the chest, and he takes another step back.

"You are no longer welcome here. You're going to leave, and I never want to see your ugly, smug face again. You're never going to try to buy, steal, blackmail, or force Hunter to give you his land ever again. As a matter of fact, how about you just forget you ever met us? Forget about Snowberry completely. Wipe it from your mind and never set foot here again. Any of you."

I glare at the non-humans Vincent brought with him, making sure they all hear my words.

I don't expect them to listen to me; why would they? But my patience has run out, and I don't give a damn anymore.

Vincent stares at me, his expression blank, his face going slack. Like a zombie, he sheathes his knife and turns around, heading for his vehicle without a word—all of them do. I stand there staring in disbelief.

That actually worked?

Holding my breath, I expect them to turn around and attack once again, but they never do. They all load up into the trucks silently and just drive off.

"Well, hot damn."

Kai's voice startles me so much in the eerie silence left in the wake of Vincent's departure, that I jump and turn to face him, not even realizing he'd approached me.

"Looks like we have a siren in our midst."

"A what?"

Kai doesn't answer; he just chuckles as he walks down the driveway.

"Let me know if you need any more help, Alpha. I am happy to assist whenever there's a good fight to be had."

He waves over his shoulder, meandering his way towards town completely calm as if he wasn't just part of a battle that very well could have killed him.

Hunter shifts beside me back to human form, uncaring of his nudity, and jerks me against his bare chest, slanting his mouth over mine in a punishing kiss.

When he finally pulls away, I look up at him, a little dazed and still very confused about how me yelling at Vincent made him leave.

"You were amazing, Lottie."

"I don't know how," I confess.

Hunter's eyes shift between mine, looking for something and finding it when he grins down at me.

"That explains a lot, actually," he says, but I'm still confused.

"What does?"

Fynn appears at our side, ignoring Hunter and his bare ass, to carefully inspect me. His studious gaze intense. So much so that I shrink under it awkwardly.

"I don't know how I didn't realize before," Fynn mutters to himself.

"Realize what? What did Kai mean?" I demand, tired of this wordplay.

"You're a siren. Or at least your ancestor was. Their greatest power is their voice. They possess the power to command and control any living being with just their voice."

My jaw drops in disbelief. *Is he saying I have power? Like magic power to control people like puppets?*

"It's minimal but still there," Fynn continues. "Apparently, growing stronger with your emotions. Perhaps that's why her singing sounded so mesmerizing to you, Hunter." Fynn inclines his head at Hunter, who only watches in amazement.

"I . . . you think I'm a . . . siren? Or at least part?" My gaze flits between Hunter and Fynn.

"Yes," Fynn answers smoothly. "I'll have to do more digging into your family history to confirm, but from what I've seen, that appears to be correct."

A siren, like a mythical mermaid in old sailor's tales. I smirk, liking the prospect. It makes me feel like I belong in their world and not just because of the mate bond with Hunter, but because of who I am.

Chapter 38
Lottie

When Fynn invited me over to learn more about being a siren and my ancestry, I immediately agreed. Ever since he and Kai made their proclamation about my heritage and potential abilities—that I'm still not sure about—I was eager to learn more.

My family wasn't exactly big on keeping records of lineage, and beyond my grandparents, I don't know anything about my extended family. I have no aunts, uncles, or cousins, at least not that I know of. Both of my parents were only children, as am I. Whatever family there is, we aren't close. And when I became famous, instead of trying to leach off me, they seemed to evaporate even more from existence.

Fynn lives in a large house that hangs over Blue Agate Lake on stilts. I hadn't seen the lake yet; it is just another part of Snowberry I want to explore. The sparkling blue waters ripple gently against the shore, the soft white sand beaches, and an island with green leafy trees sits in its center with a small golden beach that looks perfect for sunbathing.

Surrounding the lake are numerous houses abutting its shores or overhanging it like Fynn's, I realize. Fynn is a mere and likes to be close to the water. Hunter told me they need to shift into their true form regularly, just like the other shifters do. I haven't seen a mere in their true form yet since they have tails and only do so in water. Maybe I can ask Fynn to show me his.

Hunter dropped me off a short while ago, leaving me in the capable hands of Fynn and his books, muttering something about Donna and her badgering him about slacking on his mayoral duties lately.

Fynn showed me to his library, which I had assumed was just a term he used for his office, but I was sorely mistaken. He literally has an entire library in his house. Taking up most of the space are sturdy wooden shelves lining the walls filled with leather-bound books and tomes. Some of them look to be handwritten without titles on their spines, only golden embossed numbers.

We sit at a polished mahogany table with neatly stacked books filling one corner and thick parchment in another.

"Do you actually have all the non-humans history recorded here?" I ask, marveling at the sheer magnitude of books on the shelves.

"Not entirely. We only started recording it a few hundred years ago; before that, everything was by word of mouth. A lot was lost in translation and time. I collect as much as I can, trying to piece together gaps in time and history. But there's still much we don't know."

Fynn slowly paces by one meticulously organized shelf with golden numbered leather books, of which there are hundreds. Sliding his fingers along their spines, he straightens one that is a millimeter off from the others. I'm learning very quickly that Fynn is a bit of a neat freak.

His long golden chestnut hair sways behind him as he turns his eyes not focusing on me but on the books around us. The only time he's directly looked at me was back at Hunter's house two days ago when I forced Vincent and his men to leave with just my words and voice. No one has seen or heard from him since. Supposedly, returning to whatever large city he came from and completely forgetting all about Hunter's land and Snowberry, just as I had instructed.

"Like what?" I ask, curious what Fynn could possibly not know with so many records all around us.

"We know of family trees, all current species of non-humans, most abilities and traits, but we don't have any record of our origins. Unlike humans with their bibles, cave drawings, and evolutionary theories, all our ancient history remains in fables, fairytales, and myths. Each corresponding to the continent or culture it originated from, tainted with their own beliefs and folklore. None are written by non-humans from our perspective or recollection. Only what humans thought we were. We don't know our real origins, only that we've been here just as long as they have. But somewhere in history they began to outnumber us, and we sank into the shadows."

I watch in thinly veiled curiosity and intrigue as Fynn speaks, absorbing every ounce of knowledge he divulges about non-humans. Since I've just learned I am one, I want to know everything.

"So, you don't have special gods or goddesses you pray to or who you believe were your creators?"

"No, not particularly. Many believe in the same religions as humans, while others don't believe in anything at all. There are some who presume there are other higher beings and powers, but just like all religions and gods, none can be confirmed or refuted. It's become more widely spread to honor the earth itself. Something along the line of Wiccans," he explains, lost in his mind and world, pulling a book from the shelf and placing it in front of me.

"This one is all I know of Sirens. They are elusive beings, mostly remaining out in the ocean's depths, far from humans and other non-humans. We don't encounter many on the mainland. Even our records of them are more lore than verified facts."

I open the book to find a neatly curving script that I have a suspicion is Fynn's. Flipping through the pages quickly, I spot a few illustrations and diagrams. Stopping on one, I take a long look at the mermaid-esque creature. Its features are sharp and beautiful, yet upon closer inspection, deadly. With long claws and serrated teeth, a dorsal fin that looks like a saw blade, and long elegant necks. A note is written to the side explaining that the elongated feature is suspected to allow for their enhanced vocal chords.

"Thank you. Can I take this home with me to study better?"

I plan on being here for a while going over everything I can with Fynn, but I have a feeling this is going to take longer than an afternoon to go through.

"Of course. Just please don't write in the margins. If you like, I have empty journals you can use for your notes."

I accept his offer, and he crosses the library to a lower shelf and pulls out a small notebook, handing it to me. I was expecting a basic cardstock spiral notebook, but the one he hands me looks to be hand-bound in soft blue leather, the size of a standard-size novel. I try to give it back, insisting it's too much, but he ignores my refusal and pulls another book from the shelf, settling himself in the seat across from me.

We spend the rest of the afternoon talking of all things non-human past and present, including those who live in Snowberry and what I can expect of a life here.

"Why is it called Snowberry anyway?" I ask the question that I've been curious about ever since Luna told me all those months ago.

"Because of the snowberry flowers that grow wild in the woods. They basically owned this area before it was cleared for the town. They had always referred to it as the Snowberry Field and decided the name should stay. Thus, they named the town Snowberry. If you look at the town crest, it has snowberries on it as well," Fynn answers as if he were there when the decision was made, which he well could have been considering how long non-humans live.

His house does seem to be older in style and well settled into the lake and surrounding area's landscape.

"If you're going to be staying, we'll need to add you to the town census. I'll need a little more information from you if that's alright?"

It hadn't crossed my mind that I'd become a member of their town. In choosing Hunter and our mate bond, I instantly became one of them, and they expect me to live here now.

The thought is overwhelming but also thrilling. Starting a new life was what I was searching for, was it not? To become myself again and leave behind the *Alexandria* persona. I guess I just never expected to find it so quickly, so easily—well, sort of easily. Vincent posed a slight bump in our path, but thanks to my newfound ability, he won't be a problem ever again.

"Of course, I would love to be added to your records."

Chapter 39

Hunter

My sweet mate writhes beneath me, her throaty moans erotic music to my ears. She loves it when I press my knot inside her, as do I.

Her pussy tightens around me as her orgasm crests and breaks. The breathy scream she emits sends waves of ecstasy through me. Now that she's been practicing her siren abilities with Fynn, she unintentionally infuses it during sex. I don't mind since the emotions she's infusing tend to be ones I'm already feeling myself. Arousal, desire, pleasure, joy, love. It's particularly strong when she does it during her orgasm, though.

My knot swells and locks into place as her pleasure forces mine out of me, my balls tightening and my shaft pulsing out my release inside her. I can't get enough of my Nightingale mate.

I growl and press my face into the crook of her neck, Lottie's back arching off our bed and pressing us closer, sliding me deeper as she wiggles.

"You know what that does to me, Lottie."

She only giggles and does it again. My heart thumps with the love and affection and unhindered joy in the sound.

It's been six months since the blood moon and our bonding, and I still marvel at my mate and the love we've found in each other.

Lottie seems to be happy here. After choosing to stay in Snowberry, I was worried she wouldn't be. After a life lived in a large city like LA, a town like Snowberry is a big change. But it seems to be a change she likes.

I've already started work on her recording studio, a spacious shed in the backyard she helped design. Since I had no knowledge of what was needed for a recording studio, she was heavily involved in the decision-making process.

Lottie decided to leave the large studio and release herself from the responsibilities of Alexandria that her mother forced upon her. Something she said she was more than happy to do, the likes of which we aren't done dealing with yet. Which is why we leave tomorrow for California. Needing to settle legalities in person.

I knew the trip was stressing out my mate, and I was more than happy to assuage her anxiety. If she keeps gyrating her hips, I'll be doing it again very soon.

Laying cradled between her legs, I allow a bit of my weight to rest atop her. She likes feeling me close; I like feeling her close. But I keep the majority of my weight suspended on my elbows, my hips pressed flush to hers. However, my muscles shake with reignited passion, and I fear they may give out from beneath me. Rolling to my side, I pull Lottie with me, keeping her close so as not to hurt either of us, with my knot still keeping us together. She slings her leg over my hip and settles against my chest, sighing contently.

I let her do what she wishes, knowing my little Nightingale likes to tease. She doesn't, though. Instead, her body relaxes, and I can feel the unease and tension melt away as I cradle her close in my arms.

We lay naked with my cock still securely inside her in our bed, sated and deliriously content.

Lottie's hand rests next to her lips, pressing sleepy kisses to my chest, and I reach to twine her fingers with mine. The ring I gave her one month after our bonding on the second full moon we spent together, resting perfectly against her tanned skin. Lottie said she didn't need a big traditional human wedding or even a party, but I insisted on a ring. We may not be married in the traditional sense, but we are in our eyes. Nothing can be more permanent than a mate bond.

The ring is simple, with delicate engravings of blooming snowberry flowers encircling the band and, at its center, a nightingale. She told me she didn't want blingy diamonds and jewels but something simple and personal. So, I hand carved her ring from the wood of the trees in our forest. From one in the meadow where we first met. It's color, a deep brown polished to a shine, the engravings filled with yellow gold making them stand out against the wood.

Lottie had cried when I gave it to her, and I vowed she would only ever cry tears of joy from that day forward. So far, I've accomplished that, but we have many more years ahead of us that I plan on filling with happy memories.

My mate stirs in my arms and opens her eyes to look up at me, a tender smile on her lips.

"How do you feel, little Nightingale?" I ask.

"Perfect," she replies.

"Good. And how do you feel about tomorrow?" I ready myself for her tension to return, but it doesn't.

"I think I'm ready. It needs to be done. I need to settle everything so I can move on and not ever worry about it again. I also have a few choice words I'd like to speak to my mother."

A wicked grin spreads across my mate's lips, and I suspect that her hours of practice and training with her siren voice may have something to do with what she wants to say to her mother.

"Is everything set with the lawyer?" she asks. "Does he have everything he needs?"

"Yes. I checked in with him earlier. He'll be meeting us at the office we've secured for the meeting."

We figured it best to meet on neutral ground and not in one of the studios' offices, her mother's office, or even her old home. We will also be going to collect her personal belongings, including her father's guitar and record collection, which I know she is anxious to get her hands on.

The plan is to go over everything, sign new contracts, and settle all the royalty issues, rights to merchandise, and whatnot. Most of which Lottie doesn't want, which should make the label and her mother happy, enticing them to sign and agree to our terms. All she wants is her portion of the royalties for the music she created, nothing more. We hired a well-known non-human lawyer to assist with all the legalities, one referred by Luna who will also be there.

We invited Luna to visit whenever she wanted. It's the least I can do for the female who inadvertently found me my mate. She accepted our invitation and plans to visit soon once her current assignment ends guarding some dignitary's son from overseas.

"Well, then, there's nothing for me to worry about. I have you, I have my music, and soon, I'll have my father's guitar and my mother out of my hair for good. There's nothing more I could ever need."

"What about the music shop in town?" I ask sardonically.

"Okay, well, maybe that, too."

The music shop was an idea she threw out one night as we sat curled together outside by the fire, one that I grabbed onto and ran with. As mayor, I have a bit of pull in town, and getting a good deal on the empty storefront next to *Tall Tails* was easy since I technically own it. Well, the town owns it, but as Mayor, I have control over it. Not that any of the businesses in town pay much in rent anyway. Just enough to cover any costs the town might encounter, which thankfully isn't much.

Lottie has all kinds of plans for it, and with her substantial wealth, she can easily make it whatever she pleases. She wants to call it *Pickle-Lo Music* as a way of honoring her father. Offering music lessons, both singing and instrumental, selling instruments, and starting a lending program for those who want to learn but can't afford to purchase. She's even mentioned working at the school on their musicals.

I'm in full support of anything she wants to do. Whatever my Nightingale wants, I will strive to give her.

Right now, my Nightingale is rolling me over and straddling my hips, sinking back down on my cock and knot that had softened enough to slip free but is now hardening again.

"Enough talk of tomorrow," she scolds with a seductive little smirk. "Right now, all I want to hear is you cursing my tight pussy and the pounding of the bed frame against the wall."

I've discovered Lottie likes to be noisy, unfortunately for my brother, who has taken to staying at the cabin, especially now that he has a female of his own. He requires his own space and privacy. They have plans to build a larger house on another parcel of our land, but they're not in any hurry.

On the other hand, we will need that extra space sooner than expected since Lottie informed me last month that she is pregnant. What can I say? Knotting will do that, and my mate is insatiable.

She hasn't begun showing yet since she's not even three months along. Even so, everyone in town already knows. If there's one thing that spreads faster through the gossip tree than new people in town, it's a pregnancy.

Needless to say, we have been very busy and have no intentions of slowing down any time soon.

My hands span across Lottie's stomach as she rocks against me, my cock already fully erect again and my knot swelling.

Lottie takes her pleasure giving as much as she receives, and I try to focus on what she will look like when our baby grows large inside her belly to help slow my climax. It always comes faster the second time around, especially when she's on top.

It works to a degree, but I end up holding her by her hips and pounding up into her until she screams my name and squeezes my cock with her orgasm wringing mine from me with practiced expertise.

Lottie collapses on top of me, and I stroke down her back and short hair. Her skin is damp with sweat, and I love the smell of our sex lingering in the air. It's my new favorite scent, one that I'm glad I get to smell often.

"I love you," Lottie whispers before leaning up to press a kiss to my lips. "Thank you for being my mate."

I chuckle. "It wasn't my doing, but if I had to choose a mate, I couldn't have chosen better than you," I reply.

Lottie's body goes soft, and she finds her preferred spot tucked under my chin and splayed across my chest one leg flung over my hips. Falling asleep within minutes.

I press a soft kiss to her temple.

"Sleep well, my sweet Nightingale. I promise to be here when you wake. Always."

EPILOGUE

Lottie

"What do you two think you're doing?"

I stare across the living room at the twins, who have decided to begin undressing five minutes before dinner is ready.

"Nothing," they chime in unison. Savannah's—or Savvy as we call her—voice is higher pitched and less convincing than her brother Sawyer's.

We were shocked when the doctor told us we would be having fraternal twins, but we couldn't have been happier when we learned it would be a boy and a girl. Little did we know how much work it would be raising two babies simultaneously. But we love it, except right now, as I frown down at the two little hellions, narrowing my gaze at them.

I'd like to believe I've perfected the mom glare, but it doesn't seem to work most of the time. For example, now that they've been caught, they continue to remove articles of clothing faster.

"I told you, no shifting in the house. Especially right before dinner."

They ignore me, as children often do. They've managed to make it all the way down to their underwear before they stop and reconsider.

"Put your clothes back on right now," I command, pointing my finger at them in what I hope conveys my seriousness.

I don't have alpha power like my husband, but I do have my siren song. Over the years, I've worked on it enough to perfect it, and now I can use it at will, unlike before, when it would just appear during emotional moments. I try not to use it on the kids, though. Forcing them to behave doesn't teach them proper manners. They need to learn for themselves.

If I've learned anything from my mother, it's that you can't force your kids to behave the way you want. It only hurts them in the long run. For a while I considered not telling my mother about the twins. I may have also contemplated using fairy dust on her to make her forget about me, but Hunter explained it doesn't work like that, unfortunately.

In the end, he convinced me to introduce them to her. But I had stipulations. One of them was that my mother could never know about Snowberry and could never come here under any circumstances. I don't want her to know where I or they live ever. So, she's only seen them the handful of times we've traveled to her new mansion in Malibu.

My mother retained a good portion of the royalties from my merchandise, allowing her to continue living her life of luxury. I, of course, still receive a percentage of the royalties; I'm not completely inept. I use most of that money to pay for music lessons and instruments for kids in town who might not otherwise be able to. Donating to the music and theater program at the high school and some to the library as well.

It may have taken me a few years, but I've moved past my anger toward my mother for everything she's done to me. There's no way I can ever forgive her or forget, but I can move on. And that's what I'm doing—with my family, my music shop, and my self-produced music made in the custom recording studio Hunter built for me. I have everything I could ever want or need right here.

My mischievous twins look at each other, Savvy's black braid whipping around her little body with the sharp movement. Sawyer waiting for her to make the ultimate decision as usual. She's definitely the leader of their two-person pack, always the ringleader and head mischief maker.

When I see her sly little grin and hear her muffled giggle, I know they've decided not to abide by my rule.

In a flurry of fur, my not so little any more babies shift into their wolf forms. After their first shift at three years old, they haven't been able to do it enough. It's one of their favorite things to do, especially when they aren't supposed to. They're much faster at shifting than most at their age, being able to change in a handful of seconds with little pain. Probably because they do it so much. They and their father love to run in the forest behind our house nearly every other day.

Fynn was right when he told Hunter that us being mates, even though I'm mostly human, would allow for our children to be full shifters and not half-breeds. We're still not sure if a child of ours can be a siren, but if we have more, I suppose we'll find out then. I'm just happy the twins are shifters. They love it so much, and I would hate for them never to have experienced the joy they do every time they ignore me and shift whenever they want.

Their furry little bodies jump and bound, running in circles around the couch and coffee table, their fluffy tails wagging nonstop. Thankfully, I quickly learned not to place anything breakable at tail level.

Savvy's fur is jet black, just like her father's, but Sawyer has a lighter complexion. His fur a golden tan with a mixture of dark brown to match his golden blonde hair, just like mine.

They bark and chase each other, nipping and yipping, playing like any other wolf pups would. Their noises draw

Hunter into the house from his woodworking in the garage.

"What's going on in here?" he asks, grinning. "I didn't know we were having playtime. Why didn't anyone tell me?"

Of course, my husband instantly goes along with their antics. He loves playing with the twins in any form. He's a great father, and the kids adore him just as much as I do.

Hunter pulls his shirt off over his head and tosses it on the couch, giving me an eyeful of his broad chest. A spark of desire ignites at the sight. I can't help it; I find my mate extremely attractive, and no matter how many years it's been, the sight of him always stokes the fire of lust in me.

Hunter's gaze darts to mine, his nostrils flaring.

"*That playtime* will be later, Nightingale. Right now, it's wolf pup time."

Just as quickly as our daughter and son, Hunter shifts to his wolf form and is wrestling around with the twins on the living room floor. They bump into tables and jump over the back of the couch, yipping in delight at one another.

Laughing, I stride over to the threesome and try to grab Sawyer. He's always the easiest to catch first, succumbing to my hold easily. Sawyer lets me embrace him as we both stumble to the floor. He sits in my lap, snuggling his snout against my cheek. I love the soft sweetness of my son; I never want the harsh world to take it from him. Thankfully, he has his hardheaded, determined sister to protect him.

Twins among shifters is a special bond, not quite a mate bond, but close to it. Something invisible linking them together. They always seem to know where the other is and what they're thinking. Which comes in handy when they're trying to convince me of something.

"That's enough now. Dinner is almost ready, and I've been working all week to get the recipe right, and you three are not going to ruin it," I say, still laughing as Sawyer licks at my face.

I've continued my cooking lessons with Hunter's mom to improve my skills. I still can't manage certain things and, more often than not, let Hunter cook the dinners, but I do my part. Things that go in the oven are particularly pesky to me. Often, I forget they're in there and burn them. But not tonight. I will not let their insubordination burn my roast tonight.

Savvy whimpers in a way that I know means; *please, Mom, just five more minutes?*

"No. You all change back right now. You won't like dinner when it's cold." They all growl a grumble in protest, including Hunter. "Or burnt," I add.

They've eaten enough of my burnt food to know they don't like it. Even with the threat of burnt roast, they don't shift back immediately as I had hoped.

Hunter's massive wolf form joins our sons on my lap, followed quickly by Savannah, knocking me over till I'm flat on my back, with all three of their snouts tickling and licking at my face and neck.

My laughter becomes squeals as they bombard me from all sides. Hunter's wolf lays down above my head, trapping me from behind.

"Okay, okay, I get it. This isn't fair since I can't shift."

The twins finally release me from their attack and return to chasing each other around. Sawyer manages to get the jump on Savannah, pouncing on her head and rolling her to the ground.

I sigh, catching my breath as I sit up and lean against Hunter, who has shifted back to human form. He pulls a blanket from the couch to cover his lower half. Even if nudity is normal among shifters, he still tries to cover or conceal himself from the kids as much as possible.

His arms encircle me, and I relax back against him as we watch the twins play. Their sounds of joy engraved in my heart. Sounds I memorize and keep as my own personal soundtrack. Sounds I never thought I would hear before I found Snowberry, found Hunter all those years ago.

Another much more unwelcome sound cuts through the playful yipping of the twins: the sound of the smoke detector.

It blares out an ear-piercing shrill beep. The twins decide it isn't enough and want to join in, halting their play to sit and howl at the ceiling.

I clamber out of Hunter's laughing embrace to try and save dinner to the sounds of his boisterous laughter and my children's twin howls of protest. And when I pull out the slightly crispy roast, I wouldn't have it any other way.

Acknowledgements

To my amazing PA Rexy, for one, putting up with me and two, suffering through numerous calls and texts badgering her with questions regarding this story. Without her support and affirmation I may not have been brave enough to write it.

To my husband, who, as always, supports me no matter what I write and makes a good sounding board for ideas. Even if he doesn't really know what they're being used for.

Also by Rebecca Rennick

Snowberry Novels
Sing Sweet Nightingale
Pocket Full of Posies

Gummy Bear Orgy Series
Pinky Promise
Her Favorite Jack-O-Lantern
Just My Luck

About the Author

Rebecca spends her days daydreaming about love stories and witty banter, and how to avoid sweating in the Florida heat. When she's not writing, she's thinking about writing, visiting Florida's amusement parks, or watching horror movies and documentaries.

Born in California she's now a happy transplant in Florida, where she lives with her husband and dog.

www.RebeccaRennickAuthor.com
Instagram @RebeccaRennickAuthor
TikTok @RebeccaRennick.Author

www.ingramcontent.com/pod-product-compliance
Lightning Source LLC
LaVergne TN
LVHW092103060526
838201LV00047B/1560